SERENITY

TOM BLEAKLEY

Printed in the United States of America.

ISBN: 978-1-59571-798-6

Library of Congress Control Number: 2012945539

Designed and published by

Word Association Publishers
205 Fifth Avenue
Tarentum, Pennsylvania 15084

www.wordassociation.com

1.800.827.7903

Acknowledgment

Dedicated to the memory of Paul O'Reilly

Special thanks to Paul Lynch, Susan Pearce, William Moore, John Telford, Greg Nasto, Ron Reese, Tim Sullivan, Richard Williams and my loving wife, Mary Ellen Bleakley

Disclaimer

PREFACE

Let me tell you about myself. My name is Bob Riley. I need to say a few things so you can place the story that follows in the right perspective. I am dying. Quite likely, by the time you read this I will be dead. The diagnosis of my malady is malignant melanoma, a nasty form of cancer, as a result of excessive time in the sun playing golf without adequate protection, as apt a metaphor as one could describe as to how I have lived my life. A little more about me. I am a proud man--sometimes too proud. I love this country, what I do for a living, and--most of all--my family. Some people tell me that I'm the best damn trial lawyer they ever knew. Maybe you don't think that's saying much, but it means a lot to me.

The story that follows is mine, but there is an addendum. I represent people injured, in one way or other, by big business. In the course of my professional career, I have represented the interests of hundreds who were killed, maimed, or injured by the carelessness and neglect of large corporations who dismissed such damage as the price of doing business. What the public does not understand, however, is how big companies keep the public from knowing about their activities. As a rule, before--and sometimes during--a trial involving the revelation of secrets that would hurt the bottom line, huge settlement amounts are offered to hapless victims coupled with the requirement that information regarding the egregious conduct of the company that caused the harm remain undisclosed. The ethical restraints on practicing lawyers who represent such victims are such that they must disclose the requirements to their clients and have the clients make the decision; either accept the money being offered with the condition of secrecy or risk losing everything at trial. The injured, or their loved ones, always accept the money. They can't be blamed, but the net result in all cases is that business goes on as usual, and no one is the wiser.

What follows is pieced together from company records, depositions, court transcripts, documents, and interviews, plus a little creative speculation. I have put this story together the way I have without fear of retaliation because by the time you and others read it, I will be long gone.

PART I

SERENITY

If I should kill before I wake . . .

CHAPTER 1

Jay Slater looked at the pills in his hand, those remaining of the thirty that had been prescribed. He held them to his nose and inhaled deeply. They smelled of doctors' offices and hospitals. He glanced at the plastic container. The directions were specific--one tablet daily at bedtime. He grinned. If one tablet was good, two were better, and four would be perfect. He opened his hand and counted the pills again. He had done the math correctly. He threw four of the tablets to the back of his throat and swallowed them dry, putting the remainder back into the container and snapping the lid shut. He reached for the bottle of wine and took several large swallows. He sat back in the easy chair, closed his eyes, and let his mind drift. The effect was kicking in already, like heaven. He felt happy. He wanted to talk.

A sudden wave of loneliness broke over his reverie, pulling his thoughts in several directions. The room was spinning. He opened his eyes, blinked, and looked around. He felt and heard his heart beat. He slid his hand down inside the front of his pants and fondled himself. His penis stayed soft, but the touch of his hand felt good. Images started to flow, merging one into the next. He tried to sing and laughed at the strangeness of the sound of his voice. His lips felt numb. His tongue was thick and dry. He heard voices. Was someone talking to him? He closed his eyes tight. The images became unpleasant. He opened his eyes and tried to stand. He couldn't get out of the chair. So hard to move. Let me just rest, he thought. Just let me close my eyes for a minute and rest.

The voices changed. A deep male voice was calling his name. He opened his eyes. The room was still spinning--a different room, drab and gray. Where was he? He blinked several times.

"We're your lawyers."

He stared at the man who spoke. Said nothing. Why in the hell did he need a lawyer? He closed his eyes again. Something was wrong. Very wrong.

My impression of Adam Nowak? He looked like a bum, the kind of guy whose wife forgot to dress him, like he slept in his clothes. He reminded me of a fading hippie with his smoke- wrinkled skin and nose criss-crossed with little red veins competing for attention with his slicked-down, too-long graying hair. The only things missing were the gold chains, the pinky ring, and the flashing peace sign. Nowak's lime green suit, frayed at the cuffs and blackened at the elbows, completed the visual assault. He sure as hell didn't look like someone entrusted to conduct a homicide investigation for the City of Detroit.

The young prosecuting attorney, Lisa Candalero, asked a question of Nowak, who sat on the witness stand. Nowak, rheumy eyes, slight grin on his face, looked down at his file, then over at me and back to Candalero.

"What was the question, counselor?"

Candalero dropped her notes on the floor. Her face turned red as she bent over to retrieve them. I forced myself not to laugh and looked at the judge, who was losing patience. Nowak had been on the stand for nearly ten minutes, and nothing yet had happened. A seasoned prosecutor would have been finished by now. "And can you now tell us what happened next?"

Nowak looked at Candalero for a moment, and then checked his file. "On April 29, 2008, I received a call from a police officer at 12301 Weybridge, and he informed me that a homicide had occurred. My partner and I immediately went to that address and found the victim lying on her back in the garage area of the home. She had been beaten to death with a long-handled shovel that was found next to her body. I directed the crime lab people and the medical examiner to perform their duties in accordance to their usual practices, and they did so in my presence. The husband, the defendant, was present in the kitchen. He was incoherent and incapable of answering my questions. I was advised by the police officers who received the first call that they found him standing over the body of his wife, shovel in hand."

Candalero shuffled her papers. "What did you do next?" More shuffling. "I mean, how did you know it was the defendant?"

I jumped to my feet. This was getting out of hand. "Objection. Vague and misleading."

Judge Flick leaned forward and glowered at me. "Counselor, I've already explained this twice. This is a preliminary examination. In my courtroom, I conduct this procedure relatively informally. I know you are used to your fancy civil lawsuits where all the formal rules apply, but this is not the case here. We'll be here all day as it is. Let's not make it a week." The judge nodded toward Candalero. "Proceed, counselor. Please move this along."

Candalero looked toward Nowak. "Do you have the question in mind, Officer Nowak?"

"Lieutenant."

"Excuse me?"

Nowak glanced at me. Gave me a little grin. "It's Lieutenant Nowak." Candalero looked confused. This was a three-ring circus. Nowak continued, "If your question is 'how did I identify the defendant as the person who murdered his wife,' I thought I answered that." Candalero reddened again. Nowak's grin widened.

This old fart was having fun at the assistant prosecutor's expense. It really didn't matter. No matter what this young lawyer did or did not do, the judge was going to bind my client over on the murder charges. As Nowak droned on, I wondered for the hundredth time what I was doing here. I was a civil lawyer. I sued big corporations for failing to warn about the deadly effects of their products. I sued doctors for medical malfeasance. I was not a criminal lawyer. I had no business sitting in this courtroom. For the first time in nearly thirty years of law practice, I was defending a client being charged with a crime. Murder. A brutal, fiendish murder. And this man sitting beside me had done it.

An undisputed fact. No question about it. And I, superstar civil trial lawyer, had agreed to defend him. What the hell was I doing here?

I thought back to the meeting in my office yesterday with Ralph Musilli, the lawyer who brought me into this case.

I said to Ralph, "I do civil cases only. I don't do criminal work. You know that better than anybody. I don't have the slightest idea what to do in a criminal case."

Musilli smiled back, "But this guy did what he did because of this drug. This is right up your alley. This trial won't be about murder. It'll be about how this drug makes people commit murder."

Musilli was a law school classmate of mine who had referred civil cases to me since we started practicing law. He did not handle civil cases. Whenever he came across a potential civil case, he'd refer it to me. Musilli limited his practice to criminal law. His spectrum of clients encompassed the unwashed, unkempt undesirables who ran afoul of the law. He represented felons, pimps, prostitutes, drunk drivers, wife beaters and worse. More than half his clientele came to him by way of assignments from the various judges in Wayne County. Musilli was in good standing with all the judges because he'd never once refused to accept an assigned case.

Since the early 1960s, a person being charged with a felony was entitled to legal representation. If a person charged with a crime couldn't afford a lawyer, the state would appoint one at no charge by the judge handling the case. Most of these cases resulted in guilty pleas. Few resulted in trials. The system couldn't afford too many trials. Underpaid lawyers couldn't afford to handle too many trials, either. Musilli worked the system well. He knew what to do and how to do it. When he was assigned this case, Musilli took one look at the facts, saw that a drug was implicated in the murder, and thought of me.

"Where I come in," Musilli said, "is I'll do the leg work--the procedural stuff. I can't handle the sophisticated drug evidence. You can do that. We'll work as a team. You and your young doctor associate can handle this. It'll be fun. Just like old times." I wondered what old times he was talking about but said nothing because I didn't want to spoil any illusions he had about the nature of our relationship, such as it was.

I snapped back to attention as the testimony finished. The judge bound Slater over for trial on a first-degree murder charge.

Gary Newton and I went directly from the courtroom to the Wayne County jail and asked to see our client. Gary is my former son-in-law and is a doctor and a lawyer. He had been a practicing physician in his earlier life, and I'd been learning to rely more and more on his medical judgment in the five years since he'd been with my practice. His medical background is invaluable to me in my handling of cases involving complex medical issues. After a lengthy wait, we were directed to the second floor. Slater was waiting for us and looked pathetic in his orange jumpsuit. It was at least three sizes too large. He was unshaven, and a glazed look in his eyes caused me to wonder about the man's sanity, which was already under question, given what he had done to his wife. I had seen the look before in the eyes of the homeless persons grieving over the loss of loved ones, those injured in accidents. The small airless meeting room adjacent to the general lockup of the Wayne County jail was not the ideal place to conduct a meeting with a client. The background noise, a muffled roar of hundreds of men trapped like animals in steel cages, made it necessary to speak louder than one would wish.

I spoke to Slater, "I need you to tell me as much as you can remember about the death of your wife."

I sat and waited. He sat and stared at me. I continued, "Can you tell me what you remember before that day? What's the last thing you remember before you got here?" Another blank stare. "Can you tell me anything?"

"I don't remember anything," Slater said quietly. I had to lean forward to hear. I made a mental note to hire a psychiatrist to evaluate the man.

"Thinking back, you must remember something. For example, do you remember getting married?"

Slater looked at me blankly. No response.

I tried again, "Do you know who you are?"

A hesitant pause. "They tell me my name is Jay Slater."

This was frustrating. I glanced over at Gary Newton. "Any thoughts? Do you want to ask him anything?"

Gary shook his head, and I stood to signal the guard that the interview, such as it was, was over.

CHAPTER 2

Gary and I went to lunch. The Greek Town area of Detroit was two blocks away from the jail and, in my opinion, the best place in town to find good food. We had a choice of seven restaurants, and all of them served the real thing--authentic Greek food.

"Any thoughts?" I repeated my question after placing my order for my garlic-laden favorite dish. My breath would reek for the next couple of days, but it would be worth it. Gary thought for a moment. "I can't say the guy is lying, but it is strange that he claims no memory at all."

"What are you saying?"

Gary looked at me and shrugged his shoulders. "The type of amnesia one might expect in this situation is called anterograde. In other words, one would not expect a total global amnesia, but amnesia specific for the traumatic event. If this is truly drug- induced, he should remember events in his life prior to the onset of the amnesia. I can't tell you why he can't, and I think we need a shrink to help us understand."

The waiter arrived.

"I made a note on that already. I'll call Schneidermann. Now let's eat."

I called Ralph Schneidermann when I got back to the office. He was Michigan's answer to Dr. Phil. He had an answer for everything and, if the price was right, didn't mind sharing it with a jury. Not that he could be bought, but let's just say he was generous in seeing the side of the story of those who were paying him. He loved to testify and he had the credentials to impress a jury; board certified Harvard-trained psychiatrist.

"Ralph, I've got an interesting case I'd like you see."

"Tell me more."

I filled him in on the details and asked him to conduct a thorough psychiatric examination on Slater. We arranged it for the next day. I was anxious to hear what he had to say.

Two days later, he called me back. "Tell me what you know about this drug."

I pulled out my folder on Serenity. It was almost empty.

"There really isn't much to say. As you know, it's been on the market a few months. They've sold a lot and, according to one newspaper article, people use it for a lot of questionable reasons."

"Such as?"

I scanned the notes I'd taken. "Jet lag. I hear guys are slipping it into girls' drinks at the bar to get them to relax--that kind of thing. As soon as it hit the market, reports of violent acts started popping up all over the country. Alex Hartley dropped a bombshell on the company by going public."

Schneidermann responded, "I know Hartley. He's a good man."

I said, "He had a terrible experience in one of my cases early in my career. He'll be reluctant to get involved with me on this. I hope I can change his mind."

"Bob, can I be honest with you?"

I hesitated. "Sure. By all means."

"You're going to need all the help you can get."

"What are you trying to say?" Tell me something I don't know.

Schneidermann hesitated, and then said, "It is going to be difficult to prove that Serenity caused Slater to murder his wife."

That's why I came to you, I thought. I kept the thought to myself. "I understand that very well. I really need your help."

"You know I'm always willing to help. This one is pushing the envelope a bit. There's something fishy about this guy. I can't quite figure out why yet, but his claim of total amnesia is far-fetched. I'll need to spend some time on this--a lot of time. I need to know a lot more about this drug and about your guy."

I got it. Schneidermann was talking about money. "How much?"

Schneidermann didn't hesitate. "I'll need an initial retainer of twenty-five-thousand dollars."

I almost dropped the phone. Twenty-five-thousand dollars! My partners were going to go crazy if I spent that kind of money on Slater's case.

"I'll get back to you on that, Ralph. I understand what you're saying, but I didn't anticipate spending that much money."

"Times are changing, Bob. The days are long gone when I could walk into a courtroom and express an opinion based only on my education and training. No one knows that any better than you. Judges and juries are demanding a lot more today. It will take time and a lot of digging to develop a believable and reliable scientific opinion. No one is going to just take my word that this drug had an effect unless I have hard proof."

I knew that Schneidermann was right. This was a tough case-- maybe impossible. Michigan doesn't have the death penalty for murder cases, but unless I could convince a jury that Serenity caused Slater to kill his wife, he was going to spend the rest of his life in prison with no chance for parole. But twenty-five grand for one witness was a bit much.

Schneidermann interrupted my thoughts. "There's something else I should mention."

"What's that?"

"I received a called from an attorney representing Upright yesterday. He asked me if he could put me on retainer as a consultant on Serenity litigation. Apparently the company anticipates a lot of litigation, and they want a team of experts to be available as the need may arise. I might add that the amount of money he offered was substantially higher than I quoted you . . . just in case you think my price is too steep. From what I understood him to say, Upright is buying up the psychiatry community around the country to minimize the possibility of someone testifying against the drug. Gordon Nesbitt and Harvey Shattuck have already signed on."

I looked at the list of potential experts that I intended to contact. Shattuck and Nesbitt were on the list just beneath Schneidermann's name. I drew a line through the two names. It was an old drug industry trick. Identify which community of specialists could potentially harm sales when a problem appeared with a drug and then go out and buy up the big names by retaining them as consultants. These doctors would never be used in the litigation, but their retention by the company eliminated them as potential expert witnesses for the other side. I called it the New York Yankee approach to litigation. It was surprising here that it was happening so soon. There must be some big problems with this drug.

"Ralph, I really appreciate you mentioning this. The check is in the mail."

Schneidermann laughed. "One of the three great lies. I will do what I can for you, old friend, but keep in mind what I said. It's not going to be easy."

I cut the check the next day. In for a dime, in for a dollar, I thought as I signed the draft. The war against Serenity had begun in earnest.

CHAPTER 3

Richard Scruggs fancied himself a mean cuss. He prided himself on disagreeing with anyone simply for the sake of disagreement. His daily routine included reading the New York Times first thing in the morning. He read the online version of the newspaper because it was free, whereas the print version was--as he put it--a drain on his economic resources. He grumbled as he noticed on the screen that there was a rather prominent obituary section in the newspaper's index. He hadn't noticed that before. Why, he thought, did he happen to notice this for the first time this particular morning? He grumbled again. A lot of stuff like this was happening to him lately. His weekly golf game was curtailed by Joe Emerson's fatal heart attack while he was trimming bushes around his house two weeks ago. Some friend he was. The dollar bursting collapse of the housing market, followed by the free fall of the banks and financial sector, was another thing. He took these events personally.

"What time did you get up?" His wife, Susan, stood at the doorway of his mall cubicle, wearing an old bathrobe and sipping her coffee.

He stopped reading, turned, and rubbed his eyes. They were sore. "Did you know the goddamned Times has a section on obituaries?"

"All newspapers have an obituary section. Why are you so interested in that?"

"Online? Why would they waste time to put something like that online? Doesn't make any sense to me."

"People--especially important people--who die are part of the news." She rolled her eyes ceilingward, and then looked at him. "I asked you what time you got up."

Richard shrugged. "I don't know. Early. I don't look at the goddamned clock when I get out of bed."

"Don't get all huffy with me. I just asked a question."

"Everything's going to hell in a hand basket, and you expect me to keep a stop watch on what I do. What do you want from me?"

"I know you haven't been sleeping well. That's why I asked."

"What the fuck difference does it make what time I get out of bed?"

"I will not stand here and listen to that kind of language." She turned and walked away.

"Crazy old bitch," he mumbled as he turned back to the computer.

"Your wife says you're having trouble sleeping."

Doctor Edward Richter looked at Scruggs.

"That lady ought to mind her own damn business."

"How long has this been going on?"

"Doc, you're as bad as she is. Haven't you been reading the goddamned newspaper? The stock market is going all to hell, and it's taking every other goddamn thing in America with it. Let me ask you a question. Is there anyone with half a brain who can sleep with all this going on? Besides, I have to get up at night a couple of times to pee. If I stayed in bed, the wife would have me down at the Laundromat all day long washing piss out of the sheets. Instead she drags me here."

Scruggs forced a smile through clenched teeth. Got you, you bastard, he thought.

"Speaking of piss, the wife is just pissed at me for keeping her awake. Give her something for her goddamned snoring so I can get some sleep."

Richter looked at the old man. Dark circles framed his bloodshot eyes. His skin was pale, and beads of perspiration trickled down his forehead.

"Your wife says you're preoccupied with death."

Scruggs sneered. "Hell, when you get my age what else is there to think about? Guys my age are dropping like flies. Put them in the ground and, two weeks later, no one remembers their fucking names." He stopped to breathe. "They're the lucky ones. Don't have to worry about all the crap that's going on."

Richert studied the other man's face and waited. He looked into Scruggs's eyes.

"Have you had any thought about taking your own life?"

"Is that what this is about? You've been dying to ask me that question! Just beating around the bush until you could. Well, my answer is 'hell, no.' It would make the wife too happy if I did." He paused. "Can't say it wouldn't be a good idea."

Richert thought about the recent visit to his office from the Upright salesman.

"I've got just the drug to help you sleep for the next couple of weeks. You're right. A lot of people are having difficulty sleeping right now. I've had nothing but good results with this drug. Take one at night just before going to bed. Come back and see me in a month, and we'll see how you're doing."

He reached for his prescription pad and started writing.

Scruggs took the Serenity pill faithfully at eight o'clock each evening. He bitched about it, but he was pleased that he was sleeping better. The past few years had been brutal. As long as he could remember, he'd spent each night staring at the ceiling in a darkened room. He'd become accustomed to lying awake listening to the gentle snoring of his wife (if the truth were known, her deep breathing really wasn't snoring, but he would never let her know that). During these times, he'd think about things. All sorts of things popped into his mind--his children, middle-aged and married, who were too busy to bother with him much anymore. He thought that one through completely. Their neglect of him now was payback for his neglect of them during their formative years. He'd spent hours of sleeplessness ruminating about the Iraq War, his deteriorating golf game, the state of the economy, and the meal that his wife prepared for him, which caused a certain abdominal pressure and too much gas. But there was a downside to his newfound penchant for sleep. The fragility of the present--a sleep-filled night--took away cherished thinking time. Sleep was robbing him of time as the days went by faster than before. His world had sped up, and he found this threatening.

"I'm thinking of stopping that damn pill," he stated to his wife over breakfast.

She looked up between coffee sips and spoonfuls of strawberry-topped oatmeal.

"You weren't sleeping. The pill is helping you sleep. Why stop?"

He hated it when she gave this kind of response. For once, why couldn't she just agree with him?

"It makes me nauseated."

"You've been taking the drug for three weeks, and now you say it's making you nauseated. I know you well enough to know that you would have mentioned it before now if it really did."

Scruggs pushed his bowl of oatmeal away and stood. "You're a bitch. I'm sick, and you're telling me I'm a liar. I can't take anymore of this."

He strode into the bedroom and locked the door. He started rummaging through the closet. He kept his favorite things in an old box on the floor of his side of the closet. She was forever nagging about getting rid of the box, but he kept it--not only because it meant something to him, but also to spite her. If she wanted him to jump, he would sit. If she wanted him to sit, he would stand. Red was blue, and green was black. It was as simple as that. There was no getting along with the woman. He found what he was looking for--his treasured sidearm from the World War II. He hadn't fired the damn thing in fifty years, but he kept it as a memento of something in his life he had done for which he was proud. Probably the only damn thing in his entire life that he felt pride in doing. His whole life had been a waste--a real waste. And now that woman was pushing him. He jammed three of the cartridges into the weapon and chambered one. He walked into the other room, fired at her chest pointblank, and watched as his wife of sixty-seven years fell to the floor. He then turned the gun on himself.

CHAPTER 4

Jeremy Hall, the emergency room doctor at Detroit General Hospital on the afternoon shift placed the call to Doctor Alex Hartley.

"Alex, we've got two more. An attempted murder and a suicide. An old guy shot his wife at home and then turned the gun on himself. Taking Serenity for about three weeks."

Hartley looked at his watch. It was one o'clock in the morning. "Who made the connection?"

Hall said, "The pill bottle was on the kitchen table. He died at the scene, but it looks like she might make it. It happened yesterday morning, but their daughter didn't discover them until she went to their house just a while ago."

"I'll be right there."

The fourth one in two weeks, Hartley thought, as he drove to downtown Detroit from his modest apartment in St. Clair Shores. The drug hadn't been on the market that long. Four cases in such a short time was a red flag. Something serious was going on with this drug.

He'd been sound asleep when he got the call, but he looked forward to getting to the hospital. Something was always going on there on weekend nights. Friday nights in the emergency room at Detroit General Hospital resembled a combat zone for physicians. Staff doctors who'd worked on the battlefield said it was the same. Drugs and alcohol fueled weekly crises on the streets of Detroit. Shooting and stabbing victims were brought to the city hospital. Private hospitals avoided the mayhem whenever possible so there was a steady flow of patients here. It was a great place to work for anyone addicted to adrenalin, Hartley thought. During medical school and post-grad training, he worked there almost every weekend. Memories came surging back as he made the drive.

The waiting room was loaded with patients when he entered the building. He saw Jeremy Hall in a small cubicle tending to a patient and walked over to him. "Just look at the place. It's a zoo."

Hall sat up and stretched, popped his gloves off, rubbed his forehead and looked up at Hartley. "We've got a lot of people in here right now. I'll be another hour until we can talk. They just took the lady up to surgery. You can help out here while you're waiting."

Hall gestured around the room at the waiting patients. Most were strapped to stretchers, some moaning loudly. The key word was bedlam. Alex looked around. This was home. From his first days as a wide-eyed medical student, most of what he learned about people had been learned right here. See one, do one, teach one. The motto. He smiled. The hospital had a national reputation for training the finest trauma surgeons and emergency care physicians in the country. A medical student would treat more gunshot wounds here in a year than physicians trained elsewhere would see in a lifetime. By the third year of medical school, most students here could repair facial lacerations with the skill and savvy of a top Beverly Hills plastic surgeon.

"Are you just going to stand there, or are you going to help?"

Alex snapped back to the present and looked at Elizabeth Bentley, the head nurse, standing in front of him.

"I'm just taking a trip down memory lane."

"Keep that look in your eyes, honey, and I'll order up a straitjacket."

"Tell me what to do. I'm waiting for Dr. Hall."

Two hours later, Hall stopped by and watched Hartley finish the repair of a stab wound on the face of a young man who reeked of alcohol.

"I see you haven't lost your touch. Let's get some coffee and talk before the deluge begins."

Alex checked his watch. The bars closed two hours earlier and the real action would begin shortly. "Let me finish this." He placed the final suture joining the edges of a stab wound on the face of the grimly stoic black man. Hall peered over his shoulder.

"Nice work."

They retreated to the doctors' lounge and headed for the coffee pot. The room was the only place in the entire hospital where a private conversation was possible. Alex cradled a cup of coffee between his hands.

Hall looked at him. "They called down a few minutes ago. She's alive and doing as well as can be expected."

Here we go again, Hartley thought. Another drug and more deaths. Over the past few years, the problem was occurring more and more frequently. A drug company brings out a so-called new wonder drug, and people suffer all kinds of problems from the drug, which the drug company denies. He had developed the reputation of a lone wolf in bringing these kinds of problems to the attention of his peers. He needed to do it with this one. There was a meeting of the Wayne County Medical Society tomorrow, and that would be a good place to start. He would make a call in the morning and set it up. He also needed to go public, and he knew just the person to help him do that.

CHAPTER 5

Cassie Standard, the up-and-coming journalist for the Detroit Free Press, returned to Hartley's office with him after his presentation to the Society. She was the smartest newspaper journalist Hartley ever met. An added bonus was that she was attractive. He watched her sit down in the chair in front of his desk. He smiled at his adolescent reaction to her presence.

She looked at him, "This better be good. I am giving up a lunch at the DAC." "If you like, you can share my tuna sandwich. It's not the DAC, but I do use expensive mayonnaise."

She laughed. "I'll take a pass. Now let's get down to business."

Hartley answered her questions for the next forty-five minutes. He was amazed at her ability to grasp the essence of the situation. She snapped her notepad shut, stood, and straightened the short skirt that had risen well above her knees.

"Caught you looking." She grinned, as Hartley turned red. He had been looking.

"Busted."

"You men are all alike."

"So what do you think? You've heard enough to write something I hope. "

"I will write something. Obviously, I need to hear their side. Check out some facts with others."

"I would expect no less. I would like to hear what they say."

"I'll get back to you if I have more questions." After she left, Hartley sat back and closed his eyes. Her perfume filled the room, and he let his mind linger pleasantly on the meeting. Mixing business with pleasure was always fun.

CHAPTER 6

It was early when I awoke. I checked my watch. Hell, at least three hours until sunrise. The room was dark and cold. I walked in the dark from my bedroom into the bathroom and looked at my face in the mirror. I felt foolish at not turning on the bedroom light, still worrying about waking the woman who was no longer sleeping in the bed beside me. It'd been more than three years. I lived among the ruins of the home torn apart by the divorce. During the first year, I couldn't face going home--the emptiness, the silence, the echoes of my footsteps in each room. Initially, I felt detached--not only from other people and activities, but from myself. Eventually, the death of the marriage had made me realize the difference between sadness and depression. There wasn't much.

My initial response to the divorce was that nothing mattered. I was shattered--quashed by the force of the all-pervasive power of loneliness. It ate away at my soul, my energy, and my psyche. I rubbed my jaw, a gnawing dull ache, as I thought about the last painful years. I'd made a comeback of sorts, but I still felt old. Joyless, too. This joylessness was a tricky thing previously unknown to me. Bursts of sadness began when least expected. These moments appeared suddenly, without warning, leaving moistness in my eyes and a heightened sense of isolation--an intense longing for what had been. I'd come to understand--made peace, of sorts, with the chest pain which began shortly after my wife packed her things and left home, never to return. I knew what it was. A broken heart. It was real. It hurt like hell. The songwriters, the poets, the authors. They knew what they were writing about. If it wasn't for my work, I don't know what I would have done. My daily grind saved me, provided the opportunity to fill up aching lonely minutes and hours.

The solution was simple. I rubbed my jaw. Fill up time with work. Stay busy every available moment. The more work, the less despair. Hard work destroyed my marriage. Now, it was working to save me. I was working a lot harder now than I thought I would be at sixty-five years of age, but I needed the sense of purpose, the distraction, to fill the void. I rubbed my jaw again, took a last look in the mirror, and started getting dressed. I put on my overcoat and left the house. Winter weather was early this year. Michigan was like that. Last year at this time, I was still playing golf. Now the ground was covered with a foot of snow. I walked carefully from the house to my car. Last thing I needed was to fall and break a hip. I felt old enough already. Many of my friends spent their winters in Florida. On days like this, I understood the attraction. I nearly slipped as I approached the car. Ten minutes later, after clearing snow off the windows and warming up the interior of the car, I backed out of the driveway. The car was enveloped in the cloud of vapor that poured from the tailpipe as warm air met cold. I drove away slowly.

On the way to the office I thought about my work. Trying lawsuits was a bitch. It was about fighting. If you weren't fighting with the opposition, you fought with the judge, someone in your own office, or even the goddamned client. Someone was always getting in your face, telling you what to think, what you ought to be doing, how they would do it, what you should have done. Everyone watched TV, and that made them experts.

Traffic stopped. A complete standstill. My morning drive, usually ten minutes, had taken twenty-five. I looked at my watch. Still plenty of time. No worry about being late. Hell, it wouldn't be light for another hour. I checked my face in the rearview mirror, surprised by my dour expression. I grimaced. The student of the power of negative thinking. Hell, I don't need any enemies. I'm taking care of myself quite nicely.

I parked my car, negotiated the short walk, went into my office, and closed the door. When I was at work, I took on a new persona.

The rest of the world was non-existent. It happened every time. I could shut everything else out and focus on one thing--the item that I was dealing with at the moment. It was much like being married. My wife would say something, and if I were working on a case, I would mumble a response. The message from her never registered--was never stored or remembered in the processing center of my brain. It was a sore point in the marriage. She'd complain because I never listened. To her, my indifference was the defining point of the shattered marriage. That's what she told me. I was just doing what I thought I was supposed to be doing in order to be successful.

I grimaced as I thought back about the countless arguments. I missed my wife. I didn't miss the arguments. I would tell her that the law is a jealous mistress, and it would infuriate her. Our standard of living, the fancy cars, gourmet restaurants, the big house--all of it--required me to focus on the job at hand. It was as simple as that. Other men worked long hours with their hands. My work required long hours of thought. My brain was the instrument of my work. Without intense concentration, I'd be no good to anybody--not me or my wife. Especially not my wife. She couldn't have her cake and eat it too. She didn't understand. Never tried to understand.

My jaw ached. I rubbed it, took a deep breath, picked up the phone, and asked Mary to send in the new client.

I studied the young woman who sat across his desk from me, Janet Murley. Her father, Richard Scruggs, had shot her mother and then killed himself in a bizarre shooting two weeks ago. Janet looked like hell. Her hair and clothing were disheveled. She wore no makeup and had deep dark circles under her eyes. She spoke in a monotone.

"What? Could you repeat that?"

She stopped, and then continued. "I said that the day he started taking Serenity, he started acting different. He was never the same after that."

"What do you mean 'never the same'?"

"My father was a gentle soul. After he retired, he was so bored. He started complaining a lot. It was all good-natured complaining. He would say something, but always with a twinkle in his eye. He started having trouble sleeping, so he went to see his doctor, who prescribed Serenity to help him sleep better." She started to cry, blew her nose, took several slow breaths and continued. "Things seemed better. Then, out of the blue . . ."

"You mentioned Serenity."

"His doctor put him on Serenity. At first he said it helped him sleep. Then he changed. He would cry and then laugh, then cry again. Now he's dead, and my mother is an invalid." Her eyes filled with tears. "God, I miss him." She wiped her face and continued. "The doctor at Detroit Receiving Hospital said Serenity probably caused it. That's why I'm here. He said it was a really bad drug."

"Dr. Hartley?"

"I brought a newspaper article. It mentions a Doctor Hartley. He's the one I talked to. The one who told me about serenity."

She reached in her purse, drew out a folded piece of newspaper, and handed it to me.

Detroit Free Press - May 12 2008

Drug Causes Bizarre Behavior

By Cassie Standard

A prominent doctor has attributed a rash of violent acts across the country to the marketing of a new sleeping pill, Serenity, sold by the Ann Arbor-based Upright Pharmaceutical Corporation. Dr. Alex Hartley, a local physician who is recognized nationally as an expert in drug toxicity, described the potential connection between the drug and acts of violence, including murder and suicide, in a presentation to the Michigan Medical Society yesterday. Dr. Hartley emphasized the need for doctors and patients to be aware of the problem and vigilant about monitoring usage of the drug. He told the group of 150 doctors, "The reactions appear to be both time and dose-related. No one should take this drug for more than three weeks, and the Upright's current recommended daily dose of 1 mg may be too high for most people."

An Upright spokesperson commented that Dr. Hartley has a "track record of unfounded charges about the dangers of drugs which requires any statement he makes to be taken with a grain of salt. Serenity has been tested extensively by the FDA and has been determined to be safe."

Hartley reported that several unusual drug reactions have been seen at Detroit General Hospital in the past three months in patients who had been treated with Serenity. The bizarre reactions included two psychotic episodes, two successful suicides, four suicide attempts, and one alleged multiple murder. Serenity was approved by the Food and Drug Administration four months ago. Dr. Hartley stated that the reason he is reporting this information is to alert doctors and users of the drug to this potential problem. He urged patients currently taking Serenity to discuss this problem with their physicians. Hartley stated, "This cluster of unusual reactions in such a small geographic area should serve as an alert to potential problems with this new drug." He noted that many other countries throughout the world had banned use of the drug. The only country that currently permit its use is the United States.

"I'm going to have one of my colleagues take some detailed information from you." I dialed my secretary. "Mary, have Mr. Newton come in. Right now, please."

Gary Newton came in, and I made the introductions. I waited until the pair left for his office, read the news article again, and then dialed a number from memory.

"Alex Hartley? This is Bob Riley."

The line was silent for a moment.

"I knew this would happen. It's about Serenity, isn't it? You read the story in the Free Press."

"That's right. I just spoke with the daughter of a man who shot his wife and then committed suicide. She told me that you said there might be a problem with the drug. She brought the article with her."

"I'm not certain I want to talk with you."

Hartley and I went back a long time. Early in our respective careers, we became involved in a bizarre case that nearly cost Hartley his medical license when he was accused of scientific fraud. My obligations to my client at the time meant putting distance between my case and him. Although he was eventually vindicated, mutual colleagues had told me that he resented the fact that I abandoned him.

I proceeded cautiously. "I know that we've had a rocky relationship in the past, and I'm hoping that we can keep it in the past."

Hartley replied quickly. "You lawyers are all alike."

I did not want to get into the lawyer thing with Hartley. His animosity was palpable. I tried to think of something to lighten the moment, but failed. I decided an early exit was appropriate.

"Without any strings, at some point in time I'd like to speak with you about this drug. I can get back to you then."

"You do what you have to do, and I'll do what I have to do. I'm not promising you anything."

I said my goodbyes and hung up. My priority was to find a potential expert witness who knew something about Serenity, who would talk to me about it, and who was willing to testify as an expert witness. Hartley was perfect on the first point, but so far a dismal failure on the second and third.

CHAPTER 7

Two weeks later, Schneidermann called back. "I completed my evaluation of Slater. We should meet and discuss my findings before I put anything in writing."

I responded, "Good idea."

Schneidermann understood the game. We both knew that anything placed in writing could come back and haunt a witness or destroy a case if it hadn't been discussed with a lawyer. I drove out to his office that afternoon. He was located in Dearborn, a stone's throw from the corporate offices of the Ford Motor Company commonly known to the locals as the "Glass House." Schneidermann was waiting in his own version of the glass house. Two walls of windows extended from floor to ceiling, providing a fascinating view of adjacent buildings and the Southfield Freeway. I found it distracting and wondered if there was some deep Freudian implication in his selection. I kept my thoughts to myself.

Schneidermann watched me look around. "You're disturbed by the surroundings."

I said, "No. I'm not."

He persisted. "Go ahead. Tell me why."

I hesitated. "I'm thinking that a patient might be distracted. I gestured toward the windows."

Schneidermann smiled. "You are good. That is precisely the point of this setup. All of us create problems in our lives by reacting to outside stimuli. Part of my therapy is to teach my patients how to focus--to disregard the ever-present reality of outside distractions. One needs to learn how to focus on the within by ignoring the outside."

For just a moment I focused on my own inner reality. Here I was getting all this therapy plus an opinion on my case for only twenty-five grand. Once again, I kept my thoughts to myself.

Schneidermann handed me a folder containing a typewritten six-page report. "This doesn't exist until you tell me it does." He continued, "I've done a lot of work on this. I've read the available literature, which is pretty sparse, and I've talked to a couple of people. I sent my colleague, Dr. Ibrahim, out to test Slater. Ibrahim's a top-notch psychologist who is well versed in the latest testing techniques. Rather than sit here and watch you read my report, why don't I summarize it?"

I nodded. He continued. "There are three major subjects of concern. First is your client. The second is the drug, and the third is how the drug may have affected your client. Let me talk about the drug first. There is no doubt that Serenity can cause a user under the right circumstances to experience a dissociative state which can have two distinctive components--a violent act toward self or others which cannot be remembered. What I do not know at the present time is the frequency or the conditions that must exist in order that Serenity can cause this to happen. What are the triggering events? My guess is that studies conducted by Upright will have these answers. There should be some clues in their research they have chosen to ignore. Can you get them for me?"

I thought for a moment. "That might be a big problem in Slater's case. Technically, I can subpoena their records, but unless I can demonstrate some relevancy to Slater's case, Upright will move to block the subpoena on the basis of confidentiality and protection of property rights. Unless I have something specific to go on, the judge would undoubtedly agree with Upright and prevent me from getting the information. That's the reason the civil case may prove so helpful. In my civil case, I've got more liberal discovery options than in the criminal case. I can go right into Upright's headquarters and look at research--get copies of anything I want. The other problem is that the criminal case will move along faster than the civil case, so I'll have to move pretty quick to get what you think you need."

Schneidermann said, "I need animal studies and human studies in which different doses are used for varying periods of time. All of the reports so far suggest that it takes about three weeks on the drug to trigger the problem. I predict that the animal studies as well as human dosing studies will tell us that Serenity is capable of causing the kinds of problems we have here."

I started a list. "What next? What about Slater?"

"I was coming to that. Slater is a smart man. Remember how he appeared to suffer from total amnesia when he was first seen? During my recent interview, I suggested to him that the typical reactions seen with Serenity did not include total amnesia, but amnesia only for the time period surrounding the violent event. Fifteen minutes later in the interview, Slater's pre-event memory suddenly cleared, and he could remember his earlier life. Whether or not my coaching prompted this, I can't be certain, but it does raise a question. On the other hand, his total amnesia may have been brought about by a high dose of the drug that lasted only until the drug was totally eliminated from his system. After all, this episode occurred less than three weeks ago."

I asked, "So what does this mean?"

"Two possibilities. Either the man is faking, or he has experienced a horrible reaction to the drug resulting in his wife's death. I want to help you on this case, Bob, but until I get the information about the drug that we've discussed, any opinion I have is sheer speculation."

On the drive back to my office, I thought about Slater. If he was faking it, he was damn good. The first time I saw him, he was a mess. If he were as smart as Schneidermann says, why would he plan such a stupid murder? A smart person would have to know that the odds of beating the system in this way were remote. I felt a little better about taking Slater's case after meeting with Schneidermann. Maybe that window therapy stuff is the way to go after all.

When I arrived at my office, I looked at the two files on my desk. They were both thin--three or four pages of handwritten notes. In a few weeks, each file would be voluminous. Janet Murley for her parents and Jay Slater. What a combination. As far as their individual stories, the two cases were about as far apart as Mars from Earth. A civil case and a criminal case. An elderly couple and a socialite. An attempted murder/suicide and a hideous, grotesque murder. The commonality was the taking of Serenity before the commission of the acts. I whistled through my teeth. This was going to be tough. It was going to take time and money. A lot of time and money.

CHAPTER 8

Murder. The word itself made me shiver. Now here I was in a high profile, gruesome murder case with all of the issues that make lawyers so unpopular in America. How could anyone defend someone who murdered another human being? How could anyone fail to accept personal responsibility for murdering another and instead blame the act on some drug? Why is it always someone else's fault when someone committed a horrendous act? I heard the snide comments every day now. Most people didn't know any better, but what surprised me were the comments from other lawyers and judges. Didn't they understand that our system of justice was only as good as its weakest link? As to the Scruggs's civil suit against Upright, I was a realist. Quite simply, it was going to be tough to prove to a jury that Serenity caused Scruggs to kill himself after he tried to kill his wife. But the Slater case was something else again. It was a novel theory--that a prescription drug could cause someone to commit murder. I had my work cut out for me.

As both of these were tough cases, I kept my misgivings to myself. I didn't want my doubts to infect my staff. These cases were hard enough on their own. Besides, the advantage of taking these cases outweighed the disadvantages. I thought about the publicity. These cases were high profile. There was going to be publicity. It had already started. There already were four more Serenity suicide cases that had come into the office because of the publicity that both Slater and Scruggs had received. The publicity would generate a lot more new business for the firm. New business was the key to success in any business, but it had particular applications to the practice of personal injury law. The law firm that specialized in personal injury law did not have the benefit of longstanding clients who paid monthly retainers for legal advice. Personal injury clients remained as clients only during the pendency of their litigation. The average civil lawsuit took up to four years from beginning to end. Every current client of the office would be gone in four years or less, so new business had to be generated to assure the successful functioning of the firm into the future.

Over the years, I had cultivated my reputation as a fighter--as a champion of unpopular and difficult causes. People needed a lawyer who wanted to fight for them. They wanted blood and crushing victories. I tried to be that lawyer. Potential new clients came from one of two sources--referrals from other lawyers or from publicity generated by a case the firm was handling. The eight lawyers in my firm saw an average of seventy new potential clients each month and, after a vigorous pre-suit investigation and evaluation, we accepted only five of these cases for litigation.

Adding my former son-in-law, Gary Newton, to my staff had helped. How many small boutique firms had a doctor/lawyer on staff that knew more than most of the doctors encountered in the courtroom? Gary. I loved the kid. The thought of the pain Gary and my daughter felt as their marriage hit the rocks brought tears to my eyes. My daughter was raised as the princess in the family. Her reluctance to abandon the role doomed the marriage. I was responsible for that. Other than my ex-wife, I loved her more than anything in the world. I closed my eyes and thought about my ex-wife. My love for her right at this moment was as intense as the day we got married. That intensity never waned, and it killed me that it was no longer mutual.

My thoughts snapped back to the issue at hand. What was I going to do about these two cases? The specter of handling both multiple civil suits and the criminal case was daunting. How had I allowed myself to be dragged into the criminal case? In a civil case against a member of the pharmaceutical industry, my procedure for years had been to find out every scrap of detail and piece of information about a drug that could possibly be used at trial through the process of discovery. My team and I would examine hundreds of thousands of documents and take as many depositions of company employees and witnesses as time and money would permit. It wasn't just a simple matter of filing a lawsuit and waiting until the judge set a trial date. Hard work waited ahead. Nail-biting, gut-wrenching depositions of hostile witnesses protected by even more hostile lawyers.

Fending off countless barrages of technical motions that no one--except lawyers defending corporate America--would even dream up. Upright had a reputation in defending lawsuits with a vicious, take-no-prisoners approach. The name of the game was to gain a superior advantage when the case went to trial.

In the criminal case, there was to be no such luxury--no discovery remotely similar to a civil suit. A criminal trial was more like a cat and mouse game. In theory, the prosecutor was to turn over all the evidence that had been compiled in its investigation of the crime--even evidence that might help the defendant. That was in theory. In practice, human nature being what it is, the prosecutor would rarely turn over information that might hurt his case. It was the good guys versus the bad guys. Why do anything to help the bad guys win? It was tough enough to win a conviction without turning over evidence to the other side that might gain an acquittal. Musilli warned me that prosecutors couldn't be trusted.

The phone rang. I stared at it for a moment. I didn't feel like talking. I picked up the phone anyhow.

"Riley here."

"Mr. Riley. This is Judge Flick's office. The judge would like to see you in chambers. Now."

Flick was the judge on the criminal case. I looked at my watch. It is nearly six o'clock. What in the hell could be going on at this time of day?

"I have a pressing social engagement this evening." I spoke more sharply than I intended. The last thing I wanted was to start letting this judge push me around. Some judges were notorious for wearing you down--demanding instant obedience, like holding a dog on a short leash.

"Don't shoot the messenger. He's waiting in his chambers."

I sat another five minutes at my desk. I stood, switched off my office light, and headed to the courthouse.

Flick sat at his desk and informed the group of lawyers that because he was the trial judge on the Slater case, he was assigned the civil cases involving Serenity.

"I'm going to move these cases along on a fast track. We'll do the criminal case first, and then follow with the civil cases in order of their dates of filing. That means Scruggs will be second."

CHAPTER 9

Slater had thought about what Schneidermann told him about the effects of Serenity on memory. At my next visit he said, "My thinking is clearer than the last time we met."

"What do you mean?"

"Events before my wife's . . . death are clearer than they were before."

It wasn't what he said, but the way he said it. I felt like nitpicking. "What do you mean by 'clearer'? You told me earlier that you didn't remember anything at all."

My aggressive tone didn't bother him.

"What I mean is that I do remember certain things. They are clear in my mind. They weren't clear before. Like the rose bushes."

"Rose bushes?"

"Yes. My wife had some rose bushes planted in our backyard."

I raised an eyebrow. "When was that?"

I already knew the answer. It was the day before his wife's death. The men from the nursery who had delivered and planted the bushes had forgotten to bring a shovel. They used Slater's shovel for the job and left it standing next to the door leading from the garage into the house. Slater used the shovel to bludgeon his wife to death.

Slater shrugged his shoulders. "I'm not sure of the date. Maybe you could check with the nursery for the date. They should have a record."

I snapped at him. "I know the date. We're talking about what you know. Not me."

Slater thought for a moment. "I remember that I was leaving to go somewhere when they got there. They had to move their truck so I could get my car out of the garage. I remember being pissed at them because they didn't understand English. They were two wetback Mexicans. They kept jabbering and laughing. They thought it was funny because I had to wait because the goddamned truck was in the way."

"Why do you think you remember that?"

He shrugged his shoulders again. "Why? How would I know why? I just do. That's all."

I thought about my conversations with Newton and Schneidermann on the type of amnesia that Serenity causes. "Anything else that you remember that we haven't talked about? Do you remember where you were going? Do you remember why you were in such a big hurry?"

"Not really."

I snapped again. "Not really? What is that supposed to mean? Either you remember something or you don't."

I had the same feeling, as on previous talks with Slater, that he was toying with me. He looked at me with a little smile on his face.

He looked puzzled. "You know how it is when you're trying to remember someone's name? It's just there on the tip of your tongue, but you just can't bring it out. That's the way I feel. Something is there, but I just can't bring it out."

Usually I'm a good judge of people. I can't read their minds, but I'm pretty good at assessing their character. What I heard from Slater and what I felt were two different things. He made my angry. He was my client, and I knew that I wasn't supposed to be judgmental, but it was hard for me to get past the fact of what he had done to his wife.

I took a deep breath.

"Have you mentioned this to anyone else?"

Ralph Musilli had warned me about cellmates turning into snitches. I wouldn't put it past the authorities, given the high profile of this case, to put someone in Slater's cell to attempt to get him talking.

"Do you think I'm stupid?"

"I didn't say you were stupid. I don't want you talking to anybody. Period."

"I haven't . . . and I won't."

I spent the rest of our session filling him in on the progress of the case. To be honest, the rest of that interview remains a blur. It dawned on me that I'd reached a crossroad in Slater's representation. Part of me, the good person part, wanted to believe that my client was not guilty in the eyes of the law. Sure, he had killed his wife, but a dangerous and powerful drug made him do it. The drug was doing the same thing to hundreds of people around the country, causing them to kill loved ones or take their own lives. The other part of me, the cynical lawyer part, had difficulty believing anything Slater said.

As I walked away from the jail, I wondered which part would prove to be correct.

PART II

THE DEVELOPMENT AND MARKETING OF SERENITY

"A corporation, essentially, is a pile of money to which a number of persons have sold their moral allegiance."

-Wendell Berry

CHAPTER 10

Upright Laboratories in Ann Arbor, Michigan. Three years earlier.

Cyrus Messner sat back and smiled. He closed his eyes and went through the plan again. He savored the intensity of the pleasure his thoughts brought. Almost as good as sex, he thought.

The project was moving toward completion, and everything had gone much smoother than he'd anticipated. To be sure, there were some problems, but nothing that he couldn't handle. He opened his eyes and sat straight in his chair. He looked at the files spread out on his desk and smiled again. There was nothing to do now but wait. Once the Food and Drug Administration approved this drug, he would catapult up the corporate ladder to a position more in keeping with his own frank assessment of his abilities and talent.

He thought back to his recent meeting with Theodore Cooper, the president and CEO of Upright. Cooper told him, "Cy, the Upright Corporation needs men like you running the show. It needs leaders with an entrepreneurial spirit. We need to be bold and fearless in areas where few dare to venture."

In his seventeen years at Upright, a number of good drugs had been abandoned midstream in development simply due to the fear that something might go wrong. Lesser men than he had dropped promising new drugs under the rubric of science when one or two studies revealed a hypothetical potential for harm. Messner, in his position as the Director of New Drug Development, was not going to be shackled by fear. He was not going to allow the theoretical possibility of harm doom this project. He smiled. Fear was not going to stand in the way of either his pet project or his future at Upright. No way.

From the night at the hotel bar in Philadelphia to this day, Messner's plan had gone well. Not perfect, but well. He smiled again as he thought back to that evening.

"Get my friend another drink." Messner signaled to the bartender and gestured toward the small man sitting next to him at the bar. He marveled at the man's ability to hold his alcohol, and he didn't want him to stop talking. "You were talking about dosage."

Professor Adam Sotheby looked at Messner, picked up the fresh drink, took a large swallow, and wiped his mouth with the sleeve of his jacket. "Are you hungry? You want to get something to eat?"

This was Sotheby's fourth drink since the two of them came to the bar after Sotheby finished his lecture late this afternoon to several hundred drug company executives. The man still appeared to be sober, Messner thought.

"Yeah, why not? Why don't you finish telling me about your findings on dosage before we do?"

"Like I said at my lecture, dosage is the key to the likely success of my new drug."

Messner had the feeling that Sotheby was just toying with him. "You did say that, but I'd like to hear the details."

"The details? The details are here in my head." Sotheby pointed to his head. He continued. "They are also in the patent application in my hotel room."

"Your room?"

"Yes, my room. I wasn't scheduled to speak at this conference. They called me at the last minute and asked me. I have a few small details left on the patent application that summarizes my findings on dosage, so I brought it along and finished it early this morning. I'm going to drop it in the mail when I leave tomorrow morning after I review it one more time for possible errors."

Sotheby was a distinguished pharmacologist who worked for the Olafson Drug Company, a major competitor to Upright. He was held in the highest regard throughout the pharmaceutical industry for his brilliance and ingenuity. Messner was intrigued by the possibility that he might find out something of importance. He had taken careful notes during Sotheby's lecture and went out of his way to isolate him after it ended. Sotheby accepted his invitation to come to the bar and drink on Messner's tab.

"Tell me more. I really would like to hear the details."

Sotheby grinned. "My lips are sealed." He put his hand to his mouth and turned an imagined key. "I can tell you that the procedure I discovered is going to change the face of the pharmaceutical industry. Every single drug on the market can be modified to be used as a single daily dose. Think about what that would mean for the elderly and the very young."

This sounded like drunken talk now, Messner thought, but the idea was fascinating.

Sotheby continued, "Just like we heard this morning. What was that speaker's point? That the drug industry must become more responsive to people's needs? Well, our company is way out front on that one. We're going to reformulate all of our drugs so that people only have to take them once a day."

Messner sat up straighter. Olafson had a reputation for excellence that the rest of the drug industry found hard to match, so he had to take what Sotheby was saying seriously. Drunk talk or not, he'd better listen. "How can you do that?"

Sotheby looked down at the empty glass. Messner raised a finger to the bartender, who nodded and poured again.

Sotheby lifted the drink, took a sip. "Let me give you a hypothetical. Suppose you have a drug that needs to be taken three times a day to achieve a therapeutic level. What do you think happens to the half life of that drug when a methyl radical is attached to the molecule?"

"I don't know." Messner shrugged his shoulders.

Sotheby took another sip of his drink. "I shouldn't be telling you this." He looked around, leaned closer to Messner, and whispered, "It takes longer to metabolize a drug with a methyl radical added than it does the parent compound."

This was basic pharmacology. This was nothing but drunk talk.

Messner sat back. "That doesn't sound new and exciting. Every first year pharmacology student knows that." Messner stood. This was a waste of time.

Sotheby put a hand on his shoulder. "Wait. I'm not through. What we do is add a methyl radical to a drug that has a short half life, and the drug takes longer to metabolize." The man leaned toward Messner and lowered his voice again. "It all depends on where you attach the methyl radical. That's what I want to ask you about. I don't think my company appreciates what I've done. I like Upright. You can hire me and I could bring this process along with me."

Messner sat down. The possibility of a major coup flashed through his mind. He'd give Sotheby another five minutes. Maybe he would offer Sotheby a job. Messner envisioned all kinds of problems if Sotheby jumped ship from Olafson with a major new drug development project in hand. There would be lawsuits. Maybe he could pump the guy for some important piece of information instead.

He watched while Sotheby removed a pen from his shirt pocket and made a short sketch of a chemical compound on the cocktail napkin in front of him. Sotheby wiped his mouth with his hand again and gestured at his drawing.

"We don't attach the methyl radical to the primary site, but to a secondary site. It prolongs the time it takes to metabolize the drug. The human liver has an enzyme system that selectively removes the methyl radical first before the remaining part of the molecule is metabolized. This increases the half life of the drug about three to five times."

Sotheby sat back, looking smug. Messner was no chemist, but he knew enough to know that the drawn chemical structure was different in two major respects. The location of the methyl radical was placed at a secondary site, but it was also attached to the parent molecule via a sulfide bond.

Messner pointed at the crude drawing. "This is not a methyl radical. It has a sulfa component."

"Exactly. That's the secret you see. It is just not simple methylation, but a union of sulfide with a methyl radical attached to a site that takes the body time to degrade to the parent molecule. That's the secret." He sat back, looking proud of himself. "That's the good news. If I stay at Olafson, the bad news for you and the rest of the industry will be that I'm the patent holder of the only chemical process that can do this cheaply enough to make it profitable. The problem is that I haven't been able to convince my own company of its value . . . or my value. Two or three years from now, every drug company in America should be using this." He gestured at the napkin. "And they should be paying me or my company to do it for them. That company could be yours."

Messner smiled to himself. Held up another finger toward the bartender. "You sound pretty sure of yourself."

"Got the patent application in my room right now, putting on the finishing touches. I send it out tomorrow morning, and the rest will be history."

Messner's wheels were turning. This made sense, drunken talk or not. He looked down at his watch, and then scanned the room. No one was paying any attention to them. This guy was a respected chemist. It wouldn't hurt to check this out. "I've got to call my wife. Don't go away. Have another drink. I'll be right back."

Messner rode the elevator up to the seventh floor and quickly walked to his suite. He spent thirty minutes arranging the details, and then went back to the lobby bar. Sotheby was still there, drinking. Ten minutes later an attractive blonde entered the bar, looked around, and selected the barstool next to Sotheby. Messner exchanged a nod with her, and she flashed a smile.

She touched Sotheby on the arm. "Buy me a drink?"

Two hours later, she tapped softly on Messner's door as he sat and waited.

"Here it is."

She handed Messner the bulky folder, and he gave her the envelope containing the cash. She opened it, counted the money, and smiled at him sweetly.

By the time Sotheby awoke from his drunken stupor and discovered that the package was missing, the application had been delivered to Upright's patent lawyers who were hard at work modifying the application on behalf of Upright.

Messner smiled now as he thought about that night. Perfect. Just perfect. He didn't need to hire Sotheby. Sotheby was in no position to object to Upright about the loss. He didn't know that Upright had used his materials to submit its own application, but even if he found out, he could hardly object given the way that Sotheby had 'lost' his package of materials. It took Sotheby several days after his return to his company to redo his work and, by then it was too late. Upright's application was filed first and, as such, took precedence over Sotheby's work.

The anticipated drug, codenamed RU237, was the product that would make this happen, and it was Messner's brainchild--the key to his good fortune. He was on top of the world, high on triumph. He was the pilot--the driving force, the sole reason for the movement of the project that had been looked at skeptically by others. He had taken the idea and moved it through the company pipeline in record time--had developed and marketed a drug with a billion-dollar potential. It was his baby. The fact that he had stolen Sotheby's work didn't bother him at all. His ingenuity in getting his hands on the other man's work was just another example to him of how smart he was.

Even before receiving approval for the patent, Messner formed a small group of scientists to implement his plan after presenting his project to upper management. He smiled when he thought about the group. Spare no expense, he had been told. Do whatever it takes, but get these men together and finish this project and do it quickly.

First, he selected Eric Hagstrom, the chief of scientific research at Upright. Others called Hagstrom 'the Whale' because he was big, bald and fat. Messner thought Hagstrom looked like a stuffed lizard instead. Hagstrom was included in the group because he had a reputation of never letting the truth stand in the way of a successful project. The other five men were respected scientists in their fields. Larsen the microbiologist, Smythe the pharmacologist, and the chemists Putnam, Downes and Georgiou. The chemists synthesized the compound and developed a manufacturing procedure following the patented procedure set forth in the stolen documents. The animal testing being done by Ken Smythe was nearing completion.

Human testing was about to begin, and Messner was excited. The protocol in front of him for the human study was a detailed plan for the observations to be made by the doctor who would supervise the project. From Messner's perspective, the human studies were only a formality to satisfy the Food and Drug Administration. The only obstacles now were time and paperwork. Messner wasn't interested in how humans tolerated the drug. He didn't care. His bottom line was to get FDA approval of the drug so that Upright could sell it. He would get it done because he understood the labyrinth of FDA approval better than anyone else in the company.

His good friend, Mort Levitt at the FDA, was in charge of the department that would evaluate the application to be submitted by Upright when the human study was completed. Messner knew he had a winner here. He knew what would cause the FDA to reject the drug and also what the agency would find acceptable. Levitt would help gain approval. Messner would make certain he did.

He returned his attention to the human study protocol. The study itself was simple. The drug would be administered to twenty prison inmates. Another twenty prisoners would serve as controls and would receive no drug. Instead, this group would receive a placebo--a look-a-like pill containing inert ingredients. All forty men would be housed in the facility inside the prison provided by the company for drug research. Neither the prisoners nor the persons conducting the study would know what group each prisoner was in. Daily blood samples would be drawn, and at the end of each week, a social worker would sit down with each inmate and ask a series of questions about sleeping patterns and possible side effects from the drug. Each response would be carefully noted. The prisoners would take the drug for twelve weeks. Absent some unforeseen problem, Messner's situation was as good as it got. Millions of people suffered from insomnia. This product was a gold mine. Who cared whether it worked or not? As long as people thought it would work, it would sell. It was going to be a huge success.

Messner had chosen his scientists on the team carefully. He had worked with them all before, except for Smythe. Smythe's reputation as a scientist was important to the success of the project. Messner made sure that his role was limited to the animal research. He didn't want Smythe to be involved in the human research. He trusted the rest. The others knew what to do and how to do it. He laughed aloud. The FDA actually believed that a drug company would voluntarily report something wrong with one of its products. Yeah, and the tooth fairy was now leaving gold under kids' pillows. Messner laughed aloud again.

Messner imposed security restrictions on the project well beyond the usual precautions. He was worried that somehow Olafson might get wind of the project and try to sabotage it in some way. He couldn't take that chance. Nothing in writing left Messner's office without his approval. Memos left trails. Anything in writing could come back to haunt them. Any potential negative information posed an unacceptable risk to the project. When the drug obtained FDA approval and reached the marketplace, if problems surfaced with the drug, the blame would fall on the FDA, not on the company. The situation was perfect. He was positioned to take full credit for anything good that happened. If something went wrong, Messner could blame the FDA. Simple as that. He looked out the window. Rain again. The sixth or seventh day in a row. Michigan was a cloud factory, and he hadn't seen the sun since he'd gotten back from New York.

CHAPTER 11

"The little bastards are sleeping?" Eric Hagstrom, the director of research for Upright Pharmaceuticals, Inc., walked back and forth in front of the steel-meshed cages which lined the room.

Scores of rats filled the cages, the subjects of various drug studies. More than twenty different drugs were being tested at present, although Smythe's primary focus had been on the new drug for the past six months. This was the first time in four months, Smythe thought, that his boss had come into his laboratory, and the timing couldn't be worse. Smythe was still reeling from the disclosure just made to him by his lab assistant, Lisa Bernsdorf, a few moments before. Hagstrom looked at him through his hooded eyes, and Smythe cringed. He needed to maintain his composure. Hagstrom's size and demeanor were intimidating. The guy scared him, particularly in light of what he might do about this new information.

"Yes. They were dosed six hours ago." Smythe gestured to a row of cages. "The effect should last another four hours. Four different doses to twenty-four animals each day for three weeks. Six days left."

"Anything else you should tell me? They look pretty ragged to me." Hagstrom stopped pacing and looked at Smythe, who struggled to maintain eye contact with the big man.

He hesitated. "Not really. The high dose animals are sleeping longer than the others. That is to be expected."

He knew that he should mention the new findings, but he shouldn't say anything until he had the opportunity to check out the problem more thoroughly.

Hagstrom broke eye contact. Looked around. "What about the other studies?"

Smythe nodded toward his research assistant, Lisa Bernsdorf, who was weighing an animal at the instrument table in the middle of the room. She acted as though she wasn't paying attention, but Smythe knew she was listening to every word.

"We're right on schedule."

"Good. Keep it that way."

Hagstrom stared at him again, and Smythe felt the hair on his arms rise. The Whale walked away from the lab, and Smythe took a deep breath. He looked at Bernsdorf. Her dark hair stood in sharp contrast to the rest of the room. Everything else was white--cages, floor, walls, ceiling, lab coats, scrubs, shoes--everything except for the color of her hair.

She said, "You missed your chance."

"I know."

"You're pale as a ghost," Bernsdorf said. "I'm glad I'm not the one to have to tell him. He frightens me."

He scares me too, Smythe thought. He was afraid. What if this information killed the drug? He didn't want to be the pariah whose research ended the promise of a blockbuster drug. Messner had made the point loud and clear. Upright needed this drug. The problem was that the drug did have problems. If Bernsdorf was correct, the drug was in trouble. The problem was how to break the news.

Smythe looked at her and said, "Any further thoughts?"

She shrugged her shoulders. "My guess is that it's dose-related. It only happens at the highest dose, and I can't think of any other reason."

Smythe nodded, "Let's go take another look."

They walked to the back of the lab and entered a small room where more cages were stored. Smythe turned on the light.

"Look at him go." Smythe gestured toward one of the cages where a large rat scurried on the wheel inside the cage.

Bernsdorf replied, "At lower doses we don't see this."

Smythe watched the rat scurry for a few moments, "How long has this one been going?"

"Four hours. Last dose was yesterday at noon. It slept for sixteen hours. When it woke up, it started running." Bernsdorf paused to chew on a cuticle. "Hasn't stopped since. It'll run until it dies."

Smythe shivered. "We haven't seen this with the other animals. Tell me again how you came up with this."

She looked at her feet. "I made a mistake. I missed sacrificing one of the animals in an earlier group. The next day, I found it running like this one." She nodded toward the animal in the cage. "It's my fault. I feel terrible, but it's good we found it now." She looked up at him with a hopeful expression. "The research protocol didn't call for observations after dosing was stopped. I sacrificed the rest of the animals on the day dosing ended. There was no way we could have known this if I hadn't made the mistake."

"What's done is done." Smythe forced a smile. Hagstrom was going to be angry. There was going to be hell to pay. "Better to know now before the drug is given to humans. Maybe it's unrelated to the drug."

Bernsdorf replied, "That's what I thought at first. I repeated the test with three more animals before bringing it to your attention. The four animals, including this one, have all done the same thing on the highest dose. It doesn't happen at lower doses."

Smythe grimaced. "We'll have to report our findings. There really is no choice."

Smythe shivered. Why did this have to happen now? Next week the drug was to be given for the first time to human beings--the inmates at Jackson Prison. He couldn't tell Bernsdorf because that project was shrouded in secrecy. He needed to tell Hagstrom or Messner about this new development right away, but he needed to be careful.

He looked over at Bernsdorf. "Have you kept accurate records?"

"Of course. I keep records on everything I do. You know that." She looked offended. He said, "Let me see your notebook."

Smythe spent the rest of the day poring over the results. Everything was just as she described. Totally unexpected. There must be some explanation. He surfed the Internet for research on other drugs in the same category. He found nothing. This was always a problem with research conducted in-house by the drug industry. No company ever published their failures. No company ever published the results of research that might show a problem. Only the good results got published. There was no way of knowing whether anyone else had seen these results in this class of drugs.

He stood and stretched, walked over to the window, and stared out for a long time. He feared that the worst was about to happen. He would be the jerk in research that pulled the plug on a promising new drug intended to bring a pharmaceutical giant back from the brink of bankruptcy. How could a drug that was supposed to cause sleep drive these animals into a sleepless frenzy? It didn't make sense. More importantly, what would happen if the same thing happened when this drug is marketed and used by thousands of human beings? It would be marketed if he didn't say something--if he didn't tell the Whale and Messner about these findings.

He thought back to the meeting and remembered how proud he'd been being taken into the inner circle of distinguished scientists involved in the drug's development. He looked at the results again and thought about the dying animals. There must be an explanation. There was no getting around the fact that something was wrong. No sense in putting it off any longer. He picked up the phone and dialed.

"Hagstrom." The rough voice on the other end of the line startled him.

"Can you come back down to the lab for a minute? We need to talk."

Hagstrom barked, "Why don't you come to my office?"

"It's better we speak here. There are some things you need to see."

While he waited for Hagstrom, Smythe located the cages of the most recent animals and watched for a minute. They looked haggard and had neglected their grooming. Their agitation was palpable.

"What happened to those animals?"

Smythe hadn't heard Hagstrom approach. He jumped. "That's what we need to talk about."

It took fifteen minutes for him to tell the story. Hagstrom looked at him the whole time through those hooded eyes. He smiled when Smythe finished. "This is easy. It's a paradoxical effect. Like cats receiving morphine. Makes them agitated. Just the opposite effect as on humans."

Smythe was startled by Hagstrom's response. The Whale didn't appear to be surprised by this new information, nor was he upset. Hagstrom's answer was a good one. It was true that a dose of morphine that would put a grown man to sleep would cause a cat to climb the walls. He nodded, "I hadn't thought about that. You may be right."

The Whale looked at him. Smythe felt like the man was staring right through him.

Hagstrom spoke, "We certainly don't want to do anything that would hurt this project."

Smythe thought Hagstrom's suggestion of paradoxical reaction was a reasonable explanation for what they were seeing in these animals. There were certainly many examples of animals reacting differently to a drug than humans. Still, he was concerned that these findings needed to be considered when determining whether or not the drug would be safe in humans.

He nodded. "I agree, but I think I should do some more work so we can understand the problem."

"No time. My suggestion," Hagstrom said, "is to just forget about these studies. No conclusions. No summaries. Just put the raw data in the new drug submission to the FDA and see if they're smart enough to figure it out."

He looked at Smythe again and continued. "If we make too much of this paradoxical effect, some mid-level bureaucrat at the FDA who never spent a day in the real world and wants to be a hero will kill this drug. Can't let that happen, can we?"

Smythe looked at the large man and said nothing.

Hagstrom watched him closely. "Have a problem with that approach? Let me know right now, and we'll deal with it. If not, let's move on to something important."

Smythe swallowed and blinked. "The remaining studies should be finished next week."

The Whale and Messner met that evening after work at the Blue Goose, a bar across town from headquarters. They could sit and drink with little fear they would be spotted by other Upright personnel. The Whale related the conversation with Smythe to Messner, who sat quietly until the big man finished.

"Paradoxical effect. That's good. You're good." Messner smiled. "Actually we already saw something like this in humans."

Hagstrom looked surprised. "What's the story?"

"Total global amnesia. We saw it in the South American trials."

"Never heard of it. What is it?"

"Read my lips. It is what is says it is. Figure it out. What don't you understand about the word total?"

"You mean the person can't remember anything?"

"You sure are smart."

Hagstrom thought for a moment. "Smythe's animals killed other animals. Anything like that."

Messner shrugged his shoulders, "A few scattered reports. A couple of suicides."

Hagstrom asked, "Why such goofy behavior?"

"I don't know. Probably releases some inhibitions--some deep-seat feelings normally kept under control."

Hagstrom shrugged. "If this gets out, it'll kill this drug."

"If this gets out, it'll do more than kill the drug. Our fucking jobs will go down the drain."

"So what are we going to do?" The Whale's facial expression never changed

Messner smiled. "A man does what he has to do."

The Whale looked down at his empty glass, and Messner nodded.

"Ready?"

Hagstrom gave a rare smile, "If the company's buying, I'm drinking."

Messner waved the waitress over. The Whale had downed three drinks in the past hour. Messner was still sipping on his first glass of wine.

Hagstrom looked at him.

"So what are we going to do about Smythe and his study? Paradoxical effect or not, it could mean trouble if Smythe talks about it."

Messner laid out his plan. "We need to deal with him. This is how." He would put Smythe in charge of the submission of the new drug application to the Food and Drug Administration. In that position, Smythe would be forced to put a positive spin on all of the studies, including his own. Making him the point man for the drug would neutralize him and any potential concerns about danger. When Messner finished, he looked at the Whale. "You think it'll work?"

"It's risky. What are you going to do if Smythe doesn't go along?"

Messner smiled again, "The answer to that is simple. You don't need to know."

Hagstrom sipped his drink. "You can be a pain in the ass."

Messner laughed. "I may be a pain in the ass, but I'm your pain in the ass."

"What is that supposed to mean?"

"You get surly when you drink too much."

"You're my boss, not my babysitter." He glared at Messner and tossed back the rest of his drink. "If you stop ragging me about drinking, I'll keep my mouth shut about all the broads in your life."

Messner returned the glare. The Whale repulsed him. He did look like a big fat lizard basking on a rock in the sun. "You can really be an asshole," he said.

"Don't screw with me, and I won't screw with you."

"What's that supposed to mean?"

"It means what it means."

He's drunk, Messner thought. He stood. "I've got to go." He started to walk away. Hagstrom mumbled something under his breath.

Messner stopped. "What did you say?"

The Whale gestured with his empty glass. "I said give my regards to Linda."

"I don't know what you're talking about."

"Right. And I'm Santa Claus."

Messner turned and walked out of the bar. He was pissed. How did he find out about Linda? No one knew. They'd been careful. He hated the thought that employees might be spying on him. He hated the thought that others were talking about him behind his back. He took a deep breath and resisted the temptation to storm back into the bar and fire the asshole. He couldn't do it. The Whale knew too much. He was too valuable.

CHAPTER 12

Messner called Smythe and asked him to come to his office. Smythe walked in and sat down. "Ken, I am really impressed with your work on Serenity."

Smythe smiled. "Thanks. I assume you have spoken with Mr. Hagstrom about some of the difficulties we have seen?"

"I have, and I am satisfied with Hagstrom's explanation. Are you familiar with the studies of the effects of morphine on cats?"

"Yes sir, I am. They are classics."

"Call me Cy."

"Yes, sir--I mean, Cy."

"I didn't call you here to talk about your studies, however. I have given the project a lot of thought. I want you to be the point man for us with the FDA. You would be the officially designated representative of Upright to deal with the FDA regarding the approval of Serenity. Are you interested?"

Smythe was surprised. When he received the call from Messner, he assumed he was going to be chastised for making a big deal with Hagstrom about the problem with his animal studies on Serenity.

"Are you sure that I would be the best person? I don't know much about the drug besides my animal work."

Messner gave him a friendly smile. "You could familiarize yourself with the clinical work. I think you're the best man for the job."

"What would it involve?"

"First, you should know that it would mean a substantial raise. You would sign off as the company representative on the new drug application. You would meet with FDA officials in Washington to discuss the drug and address any safety concerns they might have. Most of all, it would involve significant advancement for you in Upright's management structure. You would report directly to me."

Smythe waited a moment, "Can I think about it?"

"What's there to think about?"

Smythe shrugged his shoulders, "This is all so new to me. I am a scientist and just never envisioned moving into management. I love doing research. That's who I am. I want to talk this over with my wife."

"I can give you a day. Please tell your lovely wife that this offer would double your current salary." Messner grinned and winked. "Also, we would have to throw in some stock options if the two of you drive a really hard bargain. This task will not take you from your research. If anything, it will expand your responsibilities in our research and development arena."

Smythe left the office walking on a cloud. He called his wife as soon as he got back to his office.

"Annie, I've been offered a promotion. And a big raise. Double my present salary." He told her about the new job.

"Kenny, I'm so proud of you. When do you start?"

"I haven't agreed to it yet. I told Mr. Messner that I needed to talk to you first."

"What's there to talk about? Why wouldn't you take it?"

"I thought you might say that. I just need a little time to gather my thoughts. To make sure that I'm doing the right thing."

"The right thing? Twice as much money as you're making now? How could it be anything but the right thing?"

"Money's not the most important thing in the world. I just want to sit on this for a day or two."

"Well talk about it tonight, but I can tell you what my vote will be right now. You should take it before they change their minds."

That evening, Smythe expressed his concerns and reservations while they were getting ready for bed.

"Honey, I've got to tell you what troubles me about this offer."

"And just what is that, Mister Big Time Drug Company Executive?" Anne Smythe stood in front of her husband wearing a sheer negligee. She stretched and held the pose.

"You're making it difficult to concentrate."

She turned to the side and stretched again. "I wouldn't do that." She smiled.

He couldn't take his eyes off her. Since they met he'd thought she was the most beautiful girl he'd ever seen. The sexiest. Better than any Playbook magazine model. In truth, he didn't want to talk right now. He just wanted her. She turned again and walked over to him. She whispered in his ear. "Is Mister Big Time Drug Company Executive ready for a special treat?"

Over breakfast the next morning, Smythe smiled. "I'm going to accept the offer."

Anne bent over him and kissed him on the lips. "I thought you might . . . after my special gift. Do you have time for a repeat?"

He looked at his watch.

"Rain check tonight?"

Messner was delighted when Smythe walked into his office and told him the news.

CHAPTER 13

"I'll kill that mother fucker if I get my hands on his white ass." Cedric spat in the dirt as the burly guard walked toward him, swinging his baton and glaring at him. There was no love lost between the two men. A year ago, Cedric had spent four days in solitary confinement simply because he was black. The guard, Ed McMasters, had selected him out of a small group of prison inmates as being the one responsible for an altercation. Cedric had the misfortune to be the only black guy in the area when two of the others threw a couple of punches.

"Mother fucker," Cedric repeated under his breath as McMasters came close, tamping the wooden baton against the palm of the other hand.

"The warden wants to see your black ass, pal. Right now."

"What he want with me?"

"How in the fuck do I know? What the fuck do you think I am? Your fucking babysitter? Just get your black ass over there."

Cedric didn't move. "You a big man hiding behind that stick and uniform. When I get out, we meet someplace and see jus' how big you is then."

McMasters snorted. "If I had my way, a scum like you would never get out of here. Now get your black ass moving." He pointed the baton at the direction of the administration building.

Cedric stood motionless for a moment, and then shuffled off toward the building, never losing eye contact with the guard. He waited outside the warden's office for nearly twenty minutes, sitting on one of the wooden benches positioned across from the reception desk, where the trustee behind the desk had wordlessly directed him with an abbreviated motion of his right index finger.

Cedric didn't mind waiting. He had nothing better to do. He'd be waiting for the next ten years while he served out his sentence for armed robbery. The warden stuck his head out of the office and, without looking at Cedric, spoke to the trustee.

"Send him in."

The trustee pointed at Cedric, then at the open door, and resumed his typing.

Cedric shuffled through the door.

"Sit down, Mr. Duffield." The warden nodded toward one of the two chairs in front of his desk. "Smoke?"

Cedric sat down and nodded. The warden proffered a cigarette and pack of matches. He watched while Cedric lit up and pocketed the matches.

"A while back, you indicated you would be willing to volunteer for drug research." He gestured toward a document on the desk. "A new drug project is starting here next week, and the company sponsoring the research has indicated a desire to have you participate. Is that acceptable to you?"

Cedric smiled to himself deep inside. He'd heard about these drug projects. He could sit around all day, watch TV, and play cards or basketball--whatever he wanted to do. He'd heard that a guy had even fucked one of the nurses running the program. Sure as hell he was interested. That was why he'd put his name on the list. He nodded soberly at the warden and suppressed the grin that threatened to break out on his face. He didn't want to appear too eager.

"Good. You'll be transferred to the Drug Center Sunday evening, and you'll stay there for three months. Unless . . ." he paused momentarily, " you have a drug reaction or violate one of our rules. If you break a rule, I'll send you back to solitary for a long time."

No way was Cedric ever going to let on that he had a drug reaction. He was going to stay there for the whole three months. That was a sure thing.

The warden nodded toward the door. Cedric stood, mashed his cigarette out in the ashtray on the warden's desk, and shuffled back out of the room.

After the prisoner left the room, the warden picked up the phone and dialed.

"Got another one. Thirty nine down and one to go."

He listened for a moment. "Yes. I told you already. Armed robbery. No history of violence. He'll do just fine."

Cedric looked around at his room. His own private room. He couldn't remember a time in his life when he hadn't shared a room with someone else. As a youngster he and his four brothers had shared the two double beds crammed into the tiny room in the bungalow on the east side of Detroit. When most guys in their late teens went off to college or the army, he'd come to this place--to a cold, damp cell shared with two other inmates. He'd been here for four years now. Except for that stretch in solitary. That didn't count. Even now, as he thought about it, Cedric shivered at the strange disorientation that had overcome him during that period of isolation. He sat on the bed, bounced easily, and forced himself not to think about that. The room was clean--one of forty identical rooms in the Drug Center. The rooms created a perimeter enclosing the recreation area on the first floor, and the medical clinic and dining room were on the second floor. Each room had a lock-free door, which could be closed if the drug study participant wanted it that way. The recreation area had a large TV at one end of the room with easy chairs and couches gathered in a semi-circle. The center of the space contained ping-pong tables, a pool table, and an area for weights. Cedric liked this place. The remainder of the recreation area was half a basketball court. Showers and toilets were located at the end of the basketball court.

The three months had just started, and Cedric already knew he didn't want it to end. The routine was going to be easy. His only obligation each day was to report to the medical clinic at seven o'clock in the evening where he would take one tablet of medicine dispensed by the nurse. She would check his blood pressure and other vital signs, and he would provide a urine sample. Other than that, his time was his own. He knew that half of the group of forty was going to get the real thing and the other half was getting a sugar pill. No one was supposed to know who was getting the real thing, but Cedric knew within a half hour of receiving his first dose. By the third day, he couldn't wait for the drug because he was high. Man, did he get high. Never felt better in his whole life. He'd snorted some coke, shot a little smack, but none of that shit made him feel as good as what he was getting here. Life was great.

He confided in Robert, another study participant. "Man, this shit's good."

"Wha' you talkin' about?"

"Shit, man. This stuff's better than coke, reefer, or smack combined." Cedric sat back in a lounge chair, closed his eyes, and smiled. He chuckled. "Better than fucking reefer." He felt his heart beating--not an unpleasant feeling. A sense of numbness enveloped his body. With his eyes closed, he was floating through the air. He opened his eyes and grinned at Robert. "Only thing better than this would be to get some of that white pussy what passes this shit out."

"You be right about that, bro. She sure be a fine looking woman." Robert rolled his eyes and laughed. "I must be getting that sugar pill 'cause I sure ain't feeling nothing like you. Don't feel nothing at all."

"I be seeing the way she looks at me. She be wanting this fine nigger to fuck her." Cedric laughed and closed his eyes again. The thought of fucking that little white bitch nearly made him moan aloud. He kept his eyes closed and felt himself drift away.

He awoke with a start. Robert stood over him, jabbing at his arm. "Get your black ass up and go to bed. Can't sleep out here."

Cedric shook his head to clear his mind. "Don't be fucking with me." He stood, felt dizzy, and grabbed the chair to steady himself.

"What time is it?" It was difficult to focus. Robert appeared blurry. The dizziness ended, and Robert was looking at him with a funny expression on his face.

"Man, you look like shit. It's three o'clock, and you been sleeping in that chair like a baby. 'Cept I never heard a baby snore so fucking loud."

At this, he laughed and went back to his room.

Cedric started walking toward his room, stumbled, and nearly fell. Still feel high, but it don't feel so good. He made it to his room, flopped across the bed fully dressed, and went right back to sleep.

Shirley Crenshaw checked Cedric's wristband just to make sure she hadn't made a mistake. She checked his blood pressure a second time, this time more slowly and carefully. It was still high. Forty points higher than the past two days.

"Mr. Duffield, are you feeling all right?"

The man stiffened in response. He looked at her, blinked a couple of times, and spoke slowly. "Yes, ma'am. I be all right. I feels just fine."

Crenshaw started to say something. Thought better about it. She nodded. They both understood the ground rules of this project. Everybody was looking over her shoulder--the doctor, the drug company. As Dr. Sipple had said, "No news is good news." If she reported the elevation in Duffield's blood pressure, Duffield would be removed from the trial. They needed to keep as many men in the trial as possible.

"Did you do anything different today?"

"Played a little ball." He gestured toward the basketball court.

That's probably why, she thought. Physical exercise is known to raise blood pressure. She looked at the sheet and carefully recorded Cedric's blood pressure as normal, just a couple of points higher than yesterday's.

"Been sleeping really good. Best I ever did."

"That's good." She felt a sense of relief. She was doing the right thing. "I know the drug company would be happy to hear that. It is a sleeping pill we're studying. Did you know that?"

It was still dark. Cedric crept away from his room and left the building. The general population was asleep, and a solitary light illuminated the guard station across the darkened prison yard, creating dark shadows in the rest of the space. Cedric headed for the southeast corridor and pressed back against the wall when he saw McMasters approaching. As the man walked by, Cedric stepped out of the shadow and struck him from behind. McMasters fell face forward and, before he could react, Cedric kicked him. McMasters went limp. Cedric continued to kick until the man's facial features were obliterated. Cedric stopped, took a few deep breaths, kicked the man again, and walked back to the Drug Center.

"What happened to your hand, bro?"

Cedric looked at his hand and was surprised to see that it was swollen. "Damn. I don't know. Just woke up this morning, and it was hurting something awful. Maybe somethin' bit me during the night."

"Looks to me like you tried to put your fist through a cement wall." Robert guffawed. "Ain't no bug do that."

Cedric sat still, looking at his hand. He opened and closed it several times. It hurt.

"Tell the nurse about it. Maybe she fix you up. Maybe she feel sorry for you and fuck yo' black ass." Robert laughed again.

Cedric looked at his hand. "That's a good idea. It hurts." He stood and walked upstairs to the small office where Crenshaw was sitting at the desk.

"Come in, Mr. Duffield." Her eyes dropped to his hand. "What happened? How did you hurt your hand?"

Cedric held the hand out. Turned it back and forth. "I don't know. It be hurting. Bad."

Crenshaw stood. "Have a seat. I'll be right back." She patted the back of the plastic chair alongside her desk and edged past Cedric on her way out the door. She went into the next office, turned the light on, closed the door, and locked it. She reached for the phone and dialed. "Doctor. There's a problem. Cedric Duffield is in my office with a badly swollen hand. His shoes are covered with blood."

She hung up the phone, sat down on the chair, and waited. A couple of minutes later, she heard loud voices and scuffling, followed by a soft knock on her door. Dr. Sipple looked at her soberly when she unlocked and opened the door.

"It's safe to come out now. You did the right thing. Duffield killed a guard. Ambushed him early this morning."

Crenshaw shivered. Her family and friends warned her about working here at the prison. She should have listened to them. They were right. Duffield could have just as easily killed her. She half-listened as Sipple spoke.

"Obviously, Duffield is out of the study. Upright won't be happy about this. Stay here while I call Mister Messner. He may have some questions for you." Crenshaw nodded numbly and sat down.

Sipple placed the call and put Messner on the speakerphone. "We've had a little problem up here."

"And?"

"One of the inmates in the study attacked a guard early this morning and killed him."

There was a long pause at the other end of the line. "Who was it?"

"Duffield. Cedric Duffield. He's being held in solitary confinement. Had blood all over him and a busted hand. Claims he doesn't remember anything."

"Hold on just a minute." Papers were shuffled. "I just looked at the study protocol. Duffield was getting the placebo. Say nothing about this to anybody. Prepare your report, and send it to me at once. Send me everything you have. I'll handle it at this end."

CHAPTER 14

At the weekly meeting of the Upright Research Committee, the group spent less than thirty minutes discussing the ongoing research projects, including Serenity. At the end of the meeting, Messner signaled to The Whale that he should stay after the others left.

Smythe saw the gesture. "Do you want me to stay too?"

"It's not necessary, Ken." Messner nodded toward the door. Smythe gave him a quizzical glance, turned, and left the room.

"Do you think he knows what's going on?" The Whale nodded toward the closed door.

"I don't know how he could. We're the only ones outside of the prison doctor who has a clue."

"Have you decided what to do?"

Messner looked at The Whale for a moment.

"It's not about trust. It's just that I think you're better off not knowing. If this ever comes out . . ."

Hagstrom said, "Give me a break. I already know enough to cause trouble if I wanted. It's better if I know everything."

Messner looked at the big man. "You may be right, but let me think about it."

Hagstrom spoke quietly, "I've got some information that will help you change your mind. I questioned the nurse rather extensively. At first she told one story, but I could see she was hiding something. When I pressed her, she admitted that the man's blood pressure had been sky high for about three days before the incident . . . Before he went off the deep end. The best part was that she failed to record it properly, and she admitted it."

Messner asked, "How does that help?"

"Don't you see? It helps because, if this ever does come out, we blame it on her--sloppy bookwork and record keeping. We can't be held responsible for mistakes like that."

Messner laughed. "Blame it on the nurse. Clever, but I've got a better idea. I told Sipple that I broke the code, and Duffield and the other two who committed suicide were in the control group. He's clueless. Turn negatives into positives and positives into negatives. Then, if it ever comes out, blame it on the nurse."

The two men laughed aloud.

The Whale stood and moved ponderously toward the door. With his hand on the doorknob he turned at looked at Messner.

"You are one devious son of a bitch."

They both laughed again. Messner smiled. "I take that as a compliment."

CHAPTER 15

Ken Smythe and Janice Emrich, the Food and Drug Administration monitor for Serenity, stood side-by-side at the main entrance of Building H, the administrative office building on the campus of the Food and Drug Administration's rambling complex.

Emrich swept her arm and pointed over the vista of gray non-descript buildings that occupied several square miles of prime real estate in the Washington, D. C. suburb of Rockville, Maryland. She smiled at Ken Smythe. "I don't think anybody lives around here. There's nothing here other than a bunch of government buildings and a few small stores in the area we all call downtown. But there are a lot of apartment buildings being built."

He locked eyes with her, and then looked away. He felt his face redden. She was striking; clear blue eyes and china-doll face framed by fashionably cut brunette hair. Not at all what he'd expected. When Messner had made the arrangements, he thought that the J. Emrich he was going to meet would be some stuffy middle-aged male bureaucrat. The petite brunette with the stunning figure standing beside him hardly fit his image of an employee of the Food and Drug Administration. It certainly made the prospect of spending his day at FDA headquarters much brighter.

Smythe had spent an extra twenty minutes in the cab that brought him from National Airport while the driver searched for the building. There was no rhyme or reason to the lettering sequence of the various buildings. The cab driver, who spoke no discernible English, stumbled across the building by accident.

"Who is the genius who came up with the labeling of these buildings?" He tried to keep his tone light.

"We hear stories about people getting lost on their first day of work and not showing up until they retire." She looked at Smythe again. She smiled. A weary smile. "Seriously," she continued, "somebody came up with the idea a few years back that it was in the Agency's best interests to label the buildings randomly. Keeps away those who have no business here."

Smythe wondered if she was trying to be funny, but he kept his mouth shut. They turned and entered the building. Once inside, he sniffed the air. He wondered what kind of perfume she was wearing. He smiled to himself.

"What's so funny?"

"Nothing. Have you had the opportunity to review the summary of our submission?"

"Let's wait until we get to the conference room." Another smile. He followed her down one long corridor, and then another past a dozen identical doors. He kept a step behind her. She stopped at the last door in the corridor and tapped gently. A rotund bald man wearing jeans, blue Oxford cloth shirt, and a wrinkled sports coat opened the door and extended his hand. His blue eyes struck Smythe.

"You must be Ken Smythe. I'm Mort Levitt."

He smirked at Emrich. "I assume the delay was for the usual reason." He turned and looked at Smythe. "No one can find this damn building on the first try."

Smythe didn't like the way Levitt looked at Emrich. He felt instant dislike. He stepped into the room and looked around. It was small and cloying, the effect enhanced by the scent of stale tobacco. The few pieces of furniture in the small room were battleship gray.

Levitt put his hand on Smythe's shoulder and laughed.

"Everyone's reaction is the same. Obviously, we're not throwing away your tax dollars." He laughed again. Too loud.

Levitt continued, "We're going to work down in the conference room. Not enough room in here for the three of us."

He picked up a large folder on the desk and ushered them back out the door to a larger room down at the end of the hallway. When they were seated at the conference table, Levitt spoke, "I talked with Messner this morning. He assures me everything is in order with the application. Said you'd be the man to answer any questions we might have."

Levitt reminded Smythe of an old country-western singer whose name he couldn't remember

Smythe nodded at Levitt, "He sends his regrets. He wanted to be here."

Levitt nodded back. "We've known each other for a long time. A good man."

Messner had told Smythe about Levitt and his preferences-- beautiful young women, plenty of liquor, and expensive dinners. Levitt would be keen on viewing things from Upright's point of view as long as these basic wants were satisfied. Judging from the way the man looked at Emrich, Smythe thought, his appetites extended to the workplace.

"Shall we get down to business?" Levitt gestured toward Emrich and continued, "Dr. Emrich has a few specific questions for you. It won't take long. I've got some telephone calls to make. Stop by my office when you finish."

He pushed the file toward Emrich, stood, and left the room.

"You're a doctor?"

She nodded, "I have a doctorate in pharmacology."

"That's impressive. Is Levitt a doctor?"

She shook her head. "He isn't. I'm part of the new breed here at the Agency. We're trying to catch up with the twenty first century. We take heat from time to time about our decisions. We're doing our best to remove politics from science. Sometimes it doesn't work real well."

She gestured at the folder Levitt had placed in front of her.

"I have my questions for you right here."

They spent the next two hours discussing Serenity. She made careful notes of his responses. Smythe was surprised by the questions--a series of superficial inquiries. If she had a degree in pharmacology, Emrich had to be aware of the problems with the animal studies, he thought. She was too sophisticated not to be. She danced around the subject like a ballerina, never getting specific enough to challenge the implications of the damaging research. Instead, the questions dealt with how Upright conducted studies to document the safety of the drug-- not on results. Finally, she slapped the folder shut. "That's it."

"That's it?"

"Yes. I'll type this up for Levitt. Let's go back to his office."

"You'll type it? No secretary?"

"I wish. Funding for secretarial assistance disappears each year from the budget."

She stood, and he followed her back to Levitt's office. Levitt gestured for him to sit. Emrich excused herself and left the room.

"That wasn't too bad, was it?"

Smythe knew better than to voice his concerns. "No. As a matter of fact, it was pleasant."

"Most people feel that way after spending a couple of hours alone with Emrich." Levitt laughed.

Smythe said, "She's a remarkable person."

Levitt guffawed. "A remarkable person? That's a good one." He studied Smythe for a moment. "Are you staying tonight? Do we have dinner plans?"

"Messner has everything arranged. He said that you should call him, and he'll tell you the details. I'm not staying over. My daughter is in a play this evening at school, and I can't miss it."

Levitt smiled, sat back, and smiled. "It's nice to have friends. Here's what I am going to do. Emrich will take you back to the airport." He picked up the phone before Smythe could respond, dialed a number, barked a command, and hung up. Several moments later, Emrich appeared at the door.

"Take Dr. Smythe someplace nice for lunch and then to the airport."

"Aren't you coming?"

"No. I'll be working late tonight. I'll probably be here all night." Levitt winked at Smythe. Smythe looked at Emrich. She hadn't missed the gesture, and her face reddened. Her fixed smile disappeared.

Emrich and Smythe drove in near silence to an upscale restaurant in Georgetown. When they were seated at the table, Smythe pretended to study the menu, but his curiosity got the best of him. "He's an interesting guy."

"Who?"

"Levitt." He studied her reaction.

Her facial muscles tightened. "I suppose." She avoided looking at Smythe. "He knows how to play the game."

"The game?"

"Yes, the game. The dinner you planned for him tonight. He'll show up at work about noon tomorrow reeking of alcohol."

Smythe kept quiet. He didn't know what to say. How did she know about tonight? That was supposed to be between Levitt and Messner.

She put her menu down and looked at Smythe. "How many girls have you lined up for him tonight? And don't tell me you don't know what I'm talking about."

Smythe studied the tablecloth. "I know what you're talking about, but I had nothing to do with it. And I don't know the details."

Emrich stared at him. She started to say something. The approach of the waiter brought a short reprieve. They placed their orders. The waiter scurried away. She muttered something to herself. He stayed silent. He didn't know what to say. She searched through her purse for a handkerchief and blew her nose.

She looked at him. "I'm sorry. I don't do politically correct very well."

The waiter arrived with coffee. Another reprieve. She held her cup up in a mock toast. "To Serenity." Smythe did likewise.

Smythe took a sip. It was good. "How long have you been at the FDA?"

"Five years. Do you like the coffee?" She sipped from the cup in front of her.

Smythe nodded.

"You want to know about Levitt? He has this control thing. Do things the way he wants, or you don't do them at all. Resistance is not good for job security. It's as simple as that."

"Are you saying you don't have a choice?"

She eyed him warily. "You really don't know anything about Washington, do you?"

"I guess I don't."

"Washington is about power. People with power do whatever they want. Rules don't apply. If someone in a position of power wants to screw you over, you let it happen. Roll with the punches. If you don't, you may not lose your job, but you sure as hell are never going to get the next promotion."

"I find that hard to believe."

"Believe it. Do you think Upright would get Serenity approved without taking care of Levitt?"

Before Smythe could respond, the waiter arrived with the coffee pot and refilled their cups. Emrich took another sip, wiped her mouth with the back of her hand, and looked at Smythe.

"As I said earlier, I don't do politically correct very well. Did you know that we have to accept your scientific data without questioning its authenticity or accuracy? If you say it happened, it happened. We don't go beyond that."

Smythe grimaced. "I didn't know that."

"I call it the ostrich approach. We keep our heads buried in the sand. Unless a drug company is accused of scientific fraud, everything that is claimed about a drug must be accepted as accurate. Both you and I know that Serenity has some problems."

Smythe squirmed.

"Come on. Don't act dumb. It's obvious from your face that you know what I'm talking about." She took another sip of coffee. "You're recommending that the drug be used for an indefinite period of time, yet you don't have results from a study longer than two weeks in animals. I'd bet that if you had studies covering a longer period of time, you would see some problems in the animals. How's that for starters?" She half-smiled and continued. "Don't worry. Your precious drug is going to be approved. Levitt will see to that. I'll be good the rest of our lunch. We can change the subject and talk about something else."

Smythe pursed his lips and thought for a minute. "Let me ask you one simple question. If you know all this, why do you go along with it?"

She licked the tip of her index finger and drew an imaginary line in the air. "Score one for the good guys. You finally got it." She looked serious now. "When I first came to Washington, I was naive as hell and ready to change the world. That lasted about a month." She finished her coffee, wiped her mouth again, and leaned forward. "I'm just biding my time. If I'm a good little girl, my time will come. I can't change the system if I'm on the outside looking in. Ready for a refill?" She looked around for the waiter, caught his attention. and gestured again.

"Let me get this straight. You're suggesting that, no matter what we did, Serenity would still be approved?"

"We see shoddy research all the time masquerading as legitimate. Companies like yours do what they want to do . . . and we rubber stamp it. We sure as hell aren't going to accuse a company of doing something wrong when we've accepted the same conduct for years from the entire industry."

Smythe looked at her. She was definitely not just another pretty face. She was a knowledgeable scientist mired in a system that was hopeless. "How can you put up with this?"

She looked back at him. "Where else can you get a job where you can spend the afternoon with a nice looking guy?" She grinned. "Seriously, I don't expect to spend a lifetime at the FDA. Like everybody else here, I suspect that some day I'll get a nice comfortable job in the industry someplace. That's about all you can do when you have a doctorate in pharmacology. You know that. That's what you do. If you bite the hand that feeds you, you better make the bite a good one 'cause a second chance is never going to come along. So it appears to me that you should be asking yourself the same question."

"It sounds like the whole system is really screwed up."

She grinned again. "You've got it. Welcome to Washington. Let's eat. I'm starved."

In the plane on the way home, Smythe went over the day in his mind. Nothing had happened quite the way he'd expected. Everything had gone so smoothly. As a scientist dealing with other scientists at the FDA, Smythe had expected a barrage of technical questions. He'd expected a challenge to the findings of the animal research. He'd expected the give and take of a good scientific debate. He had not expected the cavalier attitude that Levitt had demonstrated. He had not expected that most of the day would have been spent having lunch and overdosing with coffee. If this was what Washington was all about, he was glad not to be part of it.

He felt disappointed. He was struck by a lack of respect for the drug approval process. As the flight attendant handed him a soft drink and peanuts, he wondered if the system of drug regulation in the U.S. was a sham. If it was, P.T. Barnum was right. A sucker was born every minute. In this case, there were in excess of two hundred million suckers, the citizens of America, paying high taxes to fund a bureaucracy to regulate drugs so that they could pay top dollar for drugs that may or may not work--that may or may not kill them. It was scary.

He thought back to his meeting with Messner in preparation for this trip. He'd been surprised by Messner's candid disclosures about Levitt. It turned out that Messner had understated the situation. Not only did it involve Levitt, but Emrich, as well. At the time, he'd felt privy to the secret that obtaining FDA approval to market a drug was a process of knowing the right people and taking good care of them. It had apparently nothing at all to do with good science. It was a matter of form over substance. It was good form to take care of your friends.

The more Smythe thought about it, the more anxious he became. He fidgeted and fussed on the plane. His seat felt confining. He couldn't wait until he could talk this over with his wife--sort out these ideas in his mind. The dosage, he knew, was a problem. It was a problem because the drug didn't work. It didn't do what it was supposed to do. When the dosages were adjusted to a level that did work, all the animal tests showed this strange toxicity. The hyperirritability and strange behavior that Lisa Bernsdorf had seen and described. As the plane touched down, Smythe asked himself the question he'd avoided over the past several months. Would he want his wife or kids to take this drug? Would he recommend it to his mother or father or a friend? It disturbed him that he knew the answer to these questions, and it was not the answer you would expect coming from a member of the dream team. It troubled him that he and Upright hadn't told the FDA about the animals who died--hadn't even mentioned the results of that research in its new drug application. While Emrich had studied Smythe's research data sufficiently to suggest that she knew about the problems, she ignored them. As he walked out of the plane and across the tarmac to his waiting wife, a sense of hopelessness overcame him. What could he do to offset the dread that he was directly responsible for placing the lives of others at risk?

He was a significant part of the process that was ongoing, and he felt helpless.

"Honey, what's wrong?"

"Nothing. I'm just thinking."

Smythe was lying in bed. It was three o'clock in the morning, and he still hadn't been able to fall asleep. He wondered if it was the coffee, but he didn't think so.

CHAPTER 16

Timing was everything. Messner convinced the corporate hierarchy that the Serenity research team needed a timely show of support--a sign from the company that their individual efforts were being recognized. The meeting with the FDA had gone very well, and Messner anticipated approval of Serenity within months. So far, he'd managed to compartmentalize the information available to each member of the team, except for The Whale. The human trials had proceeded independently of the animal studies and vice versa. Same with the basic pharmacology research. It wouldn't do right now to have these guys sit down, compare notes, and start asking questions. Not without some show of good faith. Particularly from Ken Smythe.

His secretary reserved a private dining room adjacent to the lobby in the Grand Plaza Hotel at the elegant Lafayette restaurant. It was a black tie affair limited to the small group and the president of the company, Theodore Cooper--and all their wives. Including the wives was smart, Messner thought. Once these women found out what was in store for them, there was no fucking way there'd be any problem. No fucking way.

"This is very nice, sir." Messner smiled at Cooper. Cooper smiled back and clinked his drink glass against Messner's.

"Cyrus. You've done a great job. This is an exciting evening, and I'm proud to be part of it."

Messner felt intimidated by the man who loomed large in front of him. He was tall--nearly six feet four inches tall and impeccably groomed. A lustrous head full of dark hair with a sprinkle of gray crowned a face with deep blue eyes and perfect teeth. Movie star good looks.

"Thanks. This is a wonderful group of scientists who have worked hard and accomplished a lot."

The maitre d' came over and whispered in Cooper's ear. Cooper whispered back, and the maitre d' nodded. The bartender and waitress attending the small group followed him out the door.

Cooper looked at the small group and tapped a soupspoon on his drinking glass. The chatter in the room stopped.

"It's time to eat. Before we sit down, I wanted to say just a few things in private. I've asked the help," he nodded toward the closed door, "to leave us alone for a minute."

He sipped his drink. "First of all, I want to tell you how proud I am of this group. I say this not only as an individual, but also as the president of the best pharmaceutical corporation in the country. Your efforts are greatly appreciated, and Cyrus advises me that these efforts will result in the approval and marketing of what will become one of the best-selling drugs of all time. In recognition of your fine efforts, each of the five of you will find an envelope under your place setting. In each envelope is a ten-thousand-dollar bonus check, plus a certificate for five hundred shares of Upright stock. At today's closing price, the value of the stock is more than seventeen thousand dollars.

"Before I came over here with these envelopes, I asked our chief financial officer what Serenity's approval would mean. If our projections are correct, the additional value of this stock will exceed a hundred thousand dollars within the next two years."

Cooper looked around the room. He was beaming. Messner took a deep breath. Looked around. Everyone was in shock at this news. The room stayed silent. Messner set his drink on the bar and started clapping. Within seconds, the entire group was applauding the good news. The group surrounded Cooper, thanking him and shaking his hand.

"Let's eat now," he yelled above the din.

Messner walked to the door, opened it, and gestured for the wait staff to begin service. He turned and looked at The Whale. Nodded. "This ought to keep everybody in line."

Anne Smythe gave her husband a repeat performance when they returned home.

CHAPTER 17

A telegram arrived addressed to Kenneth Smythe, but Messner got to it first. He ripped the message from its envelope. It was from Morton Levitt in his official capacity at the FDA. "We are pleased to inform you that this agency has approved your new drug application for permission to market Serenity as requested. Please submit twelve (12) copies of your promotional information, together with your proposed package insert for the drug, for our approval before you begin marketing the drug."

He picked up his phone and spoke to his secretary. "Gather the Serenity group in the conference room right now."

Ten minutes later he walked into the room with a big smile on his face.

"Serenity has been approved for use. I've ordered up some champagne, and it should be here shortly. I want to congratulate you all on a fine job. Those options we got from our company are going to change all of our lives."

Everybody stood, and there were handshakes and back pats all around. The group spent the rest of the afternoon working seriously on the generous supply of champagne.

CHAPTER 18

David Wilder, the late night TV host with the largest audience in the country, needed no introduction. When he strode from the back of the room to the stage and flashed his silly grin, he received a standing ovation. He raised his arms and threw his head back.

"Give me a U."

The audience roared back, "U."

"Give me a P."

"P."

Wilder finished the spelling of Upright's name and waited for the applause to stop. He then continued, "When I got to my hotel room last night I needed a workout, so I changed into my gym clothes and headed to the athletic center. There was this very attractive girl working out on the treadmill, so I asked the trainer what machine I could go on to impress her. He studied my physique for a moment and said, 'Try the ATM in the lobby.'" The audience burst out laughing, and Wilder settled down into a forty-five minute monologue that kept everyone in the room smiling and laughing. He was good.

Messner stood against the wall at the side of the room and watched as Wilder went through his routine in the ballroom of the Grand Hyatt Hotel in downtown Chicago. Upright was paying the celebrated comedian fifty thousand dollars for his forty-five minute appearance. It would be money well spent if everything went as planned. The sight of four hundred Upright Pharmaceutical representatives in their characteristic green blazers and charcoal slacks gathered together to celebrate the launch of Serenity warmed his heart. He basked in the glow of his achievement.

On time and under budget, he'd accomplished what most of the others thought was impossible. The drug had passed FDA scrutiny in record time, and the moment had arrived. At nine o'clock tomorrow morning, the drug would be formally released for sale throughout the United States. Ample stock packages had been sent to every licensed pharmacy in the country. Wholesalers had been given enough of the product to meet the expected deluge of prescriptions that would result from the two-month high-intensity promotional campaign set to begin tomorrow. The national sales staff was here to find out about Serenity-- to find out what to say to doctors and how to sell the drug.

Messner had sat in on the marketing meeting yesterday. First-year sales were projected to be one billion dollars. He'd been stunned by the amount. He'd known the stakes were large, but a billion dollars was something else again.

He turned his attention back to the meeting. The cheering was over. Wilder finished his warm-up routine, and everyone was smiling. The emcee introduced the director of sales, Whitmore Jensen, a good-looking George Clooney clone, who clamored to the stage and held up his arms to quiet the standing ovation his introduction had caused.

Messner looked to his side. The Whale stood beside him. "Nothing like planned adulation, is there?"

Messner couldn't bring himself to join the applause. The Whale didn't either. "Guys like him have no problem stepping forward to take all the credit." The Whale nodded toward the front of the room.

Messner grunted. "My thoughts exactly. If it translates into increased sales, then it will be worth it."

Messner felt uncomfortable about public speaking. Still, he knew exactly what the sales staff needed to know about the drug in order to convince doctors to prescribe it. He'd met with corporate counsel, doctors from the medical department, and copywriters from marketing whose function was to turn the information known about the drug into a winning sales presentation.

Now here they were. He had the script in front of him. More than half of the sales force were pharmacists, highly-trained professionals who had grown weary of counting pills and had opted for the big money in pharmaceutical sales. The remainder of the sales force had college degrees in the fields of biology or chemistry. This was a sophisticated group, he thought, as Jensen finished introducing him. He stepped onto the stage and approached the podium. Another canned standing ovation.

He tapped the microphone. Waited for the room to become still. He jabbed an index finger in the air. "I has a dream." He laughed and waited for the group.

The audience slowly caught on, and a few initial chuckles soon became a chorus of hearty laughs. Messner looked out at the only black member of Upright's entire sales force, easily spotted in the back of the room. The man stared down unsmilingly at the table in front of him.

Messner looked down at his script. "My dream is that every doctor in America knows about a new and exciting drug for their patients within the next month. My dream is that doctors prescribe this new drug for their patients. My dream is that this exciting new drug becomes the number one best-selling drug in America by the end of this year."

The entire room rose as if on cue, and the applause was deafening.

The crowd settled back into their chairs. Messner continued. "By the end of the day, each of you will know all you need to know to make this dream happen. For the next three months, each of you is going to participate in the biggest and most dramatic promotion of a new drug in the history of medicine. Each of you is going to participate in making our new drug, Serenity, the best-selling drug in America."

The group again rose in unison and started applauding. I do have a dream, Messner chuckled to himself. My dream is to be a fucking millionaire by the end of the year. Messner raised his hands in the air to signal for quiet. He had more to tell them. A lot more.

CHAPTER 19

The first three months of Serenity sales exceeded all expectations. Messner threw the latest sales report on his desk, sat back, and laughed aloud. Not only had the number of prescriptions doubled the initial projections, but also physicians were prescribing the drug for longer periods of time than anticipated. Sales were almost three times higher than the early estimate. His star was shining brightly. Upright's stock was up sixty percent from the day Serenity was marketed. He was on top of the world. He intended to stay there. He glanced over at another stack of documents piled neatly on a corner of his desk.

It was easy to ignore those documents. Since the day of initial marketing, the company had received a number of reports from doctors reporting side effects of the drug. Many were instances of suicide or attempted murders by users. Each of the documents on his desk was a letter from a doctor reporting a suspected side effect or adverse reaction to Serenity. By law, Upright had to respond to the doctors, as well as report these reported reactions to the Food and Drug Administration. It was Messner's responsibility to do so.

The stack was two inches thick and growing daily. He flipped through the edge of the stack with his index finger. So far, he'd done nothing. Can't put it off any longer, he thought. He reached for the Dictaphone and sat back in his chair.

"Dear Doctor Blank: Thank you for your interest in Serenity and your recent letter describing what you think may be a potential side effect of the drug. Upright Pharmaceuticals is very concerned about the health of your patients and the safety of our drug. It may be reassuring to you that the kind of incident you described in your letter has never been reported in other users of Serenity, either in pre-marketing clinical studies or in post-marketing experience.

"Because we appreciate your interest, I have enclosed two stock packages of Serenity which you may use to distribute to your patients as you may determine in your clinical judgment.

"Sincerely yours, Cyrus Messner, Director of Research, Upright Laboratories, Inc."

He removed the tape from his machine and placed it on the stack of documents. He stood and carried the materials to his secretary's cubicle.

"One letter for all. Just fill in the names where the blanks are. Use my signature stamp."

He sat back in his chair and thought. He'd send the FDA this information next week. No use rushing things.

CHAPTER 20

Ken Smythe sat at his desk and reviewed the monthly summary. As the FDA liaison for Serenity, he was getting the same information as Messner. Serenity had been on the market for three months, and reports of bizarre reactions were springing up all over the country. People were shooting themselves or killing others, jumping from windows, and doing all sorts of equally crazy stuff. The increasing volume of similar reports and the similarities of the reported experiences increased his suspicion that the drug was responsible. He had a sickening sensation in the pit of his stomach as he thought about the animal research. He never should have allowed himself to be pushed into minimizing the significance of his work. He had allowed his ego and greed to get in the way of common sense and reason.

Lisa Bernsdorf, his lab assistant, had been giving him a hard time and she was now becoming relentless. She too had read the summary sitting on his desk.

"How can you do this? You see what's happening to people all over the country? Have you forgotten the animal results?"

Smythe sat back and looked at her. "Back off. Don't use that tone of voice with me. You've got no right to judge me. Neither of us has the information necessary to make an informed decision about this drug. There's a lot that goes into a drug well beyond animal studies insofar as evaluating safety."

"You should listen to yourself. I know all I need to know." Her dark eyes flashed, "And you do, too."

He looked at the young woman. She was fanning the same fire that he and his wife debated last night. He was exhausted. He hadn't slept. He could think of nothing other than the problems the drug was causing. Lisa was single and had no kids. Her family was scattered around the country, and she never mentioned them. She had no ties to this community. It was easy for her to be critical. There was nothing at stake for her. If Serenity went down because of something he did, his wife and kids would suffer. He might lose his job. He would lose any opportunities for advancement. Whistleblowers in corporate America bought a one-way ticket to nowhere.

He looked down at his hands as he spoke. "I can play an important role in seeing that the drug is used safely. No matter what I say or do, the company will continue selling the drug anyway. One person can only do so much."

Lisa's eyes narrowed. "That's pretty lame, Ken. If you really mean what you just said, why don't you start now?"

"You're out of line."

"It's your ass that is on the line. Not mine."

"That's precisely my point. It is my ass that is on the line. I have a family to think about. Did that ever occur to you?"

She eyed him sharply. "What does occur to me is that a lot more people will die if you do nothing."

She left his office without looking back. He sat there, feeling numb.

When Messner had placed him in charge of the drug, the net effect was to buy him off. It was a set up, and he knew it at the time. Now he felt trapped by his own stupidity. Greed, he reflected, was exactly what it was. He had been seized by greed. Greed and fear. He was a small fish in a big pond, and Upright would throw him to the sharks without hesitation if he didn't go along with the program. What the hell was he going to do? Sweat trickled down his back, and he noted a slight tremor in his hands. His career and reputation were at stake. Why had he allowed himself to be used? He didn't need Bernsdorf's reminder to feel responsible for what was happening.

He wrote out a draft letter. He would suggest that Messner send it to doctors and the FDA. After he finished, he read it over and made a few changes. Because of the sensitive nature of the topic of his letter, he didn't give it to his secretary. Instead, he typed his own draft with his hunt-and-peck technique on his computer. As he did, he thought about Emrich and how she typed all of her own reports. When he finished, he read his handiwork.

"Dear Doctor:

I am writing to bring you up-to-date on emerging information about Serenity that has now been on the market for three months. A disturbing trend of suicides and violent acts, including murder, by some users of Serenity has been reported since its introduction. Most of the incidents appear to have occurred after three weeks of use of the drug. While premarketing data indicated no potential for these types of occurrences, the marketing experience to date is considered to be important information for physicians and the FDA to properly evaluate the safety of the drug. Until these incidents can be fully investigated, it is suggested that the drug be used for two weeks or less. Use beyond two weeks should be with extreme caution only in patients with documented sleep disorders. Such patients should be carefully monitored."

He re-read the document and sat for a few minutes, thinking. He reached for the phone and dialed Messner's extension. "I need to speak with you and show you something."

"Right now?"

"Yes. Right now."

CHAPTER 21

Smythe stood across the desk and watched Messner's face as he read the draft letter. He looked like he was going to explode, Smythe thought. When Messner finished, he looked up.

"Explain it to me," Messner said, "Where in the hell do you get off being Mister High and Mighty?"

Smythe blanched and felt his knees buckle. He looked down at the desk and avoided eye contact with Messner. There was no reason to keep his concerns to himself any longer. Nothing to be gained from it. Nothing to be lost. He was not the only one in the company who knew what was going on.

Smythe spoke after a moment's reflection. "It's only a matter of time before everybody will know the drug is dangerous. It's not about me. It's about doing what is right . . ."

"Don't give me this Pollyanna crap," Messner exploded. "You knew right from the start what you were getting into." He paused for a second and looked out the window. He turned back and looked at Smythe. "What have you done? Who have you talked to about this? Don't lie to me. I know more than you think I know."

Smythe forced himself to focus at a spot on Messner's desk, thinking what he was going to say. He stayed silent.

Messner glared at him. "I asked you a fucking question."

Smythe flinched. "I haven't talked to anybody." He felt Messner's eyes boring through him, as though he could read his mind, as though Messner knew he was lying.

Messner gestured at the letter. "Do you know what it would cost us if we sent this piece of garbage out? You've got a big fucking decision to make. There's no middle ground here. You're either for us or against us. You've got it pretty goddamned good here. This company feeds and clothes your children and pays you a goddamned generous salary. The people that work with you deserve better than your pious, self-righteous fucking attitude." Messner paused, "Go home and tell your wife that you're going to throw your life away--that you're going to commit professional suicide."

Smythe felt numb. He'd turned the need to do something over and over in his mind the last few days and had not been able to resolve the terrible conflict that burned in his gut.

Messner continued. "I don't know what you have in mind, but let me tell you something. If you send anything like this to anybody outside the company." He gestured at the draft. "You won't be able to get a fucking job as a dishwasher at Burger King after I get through with you. Don't test me on this. You'll be sorry for the rest of your fucking life. Go home now and talk it over with your wife. Think hard about it. I'll call you at home tomorrow morning. Now get the fuck out of here. I've got work to do."

Smythe stood still for a moment and watched as Messner turned his attention to the materials on his desk. He felt so alone. He turned and left the room. After the door was closed, Messner picked up the phone and dialed.

The next morning, Messner stretched and looked out at the pond in his backyard through the large window of his bedroom, the sun leaving his cheeks red and hot. He had slept less than an hour, but the cause of his sleeplessness had passed. In his mind, he played out the scenario. Having made his decision, he felt at peace, and the warmth of the sun comforted him.

Meanwhile, Ken Smythe shaved in the kids' bathroom in his home several miles away. He had also spent a sleepless night. He did not want to wake his wife. She was still sleeping, and he wanted to keep her that way.

She woke up, anyway, and he saw her reflection in the mirror behind him, leaning against the door, hands in her robe pockets.

"Have you decided?"

He turned and looked at her. She was so beautiful. He finished shaving and wiped the shaving cream from his face with a towel.

"It's a tough decision. It would be a lot easier if it didn't affect you and the kids so much."

She stepped closer and put her arms around him. "I know it's a tough decision, but you have to be practical. Your career—your whole life's work—is at stake. I don't see that there's much choice."

He held her and stared numbly at the wall. "You're probably right."

She backed away and folded her arms across her chest. "There's no probably about it. You've worked too hard. I've worked too hard. We can't throw our lives away just because of this. We have to keep our priorities in order, and this family comes first."

"You're right." He wished he felt her sense of conviction. A range of emotions swept over him. Fear, frustration, love, and sadness. The cauldron of mixed feeling overwhelmed him. He wanted to talk it over with her, work it out, but he was numb. He looked at her and nodded.

"I know that you'll do the right thing." She patted his shoulder. It felt condescending. He was dismayed at her willingness to compromise his integrity and sense of worth in return for material comfort. He felt used, helpless. He turned away. Why was this so difficult? He checked his watch. It was time for the call.

Messner reached for the phone and dialed. Smythe answered the phone before the second ring.

"Any decision yet?" No hello or greeting. Just get right to it. This was potentially very messy. Best get it over quickly.

There was a long pause. Smythe finally spoke. "I need more time to think."

"What's there to think about? There are only two choices. You're either for us or against us. It's as simple as that. No middle ground."

Smythe hesitated. "It's not as simple as that."

"Listen to me carefully, Ken." Messner sounded like a stranger. "We've worked together on this project. You've done some great things for the company, and the company has done some wonderful things for you. Don't throw it all away."

"That's exactly the problem I'm having. What about right and wrong? What about ethics, my scientific integrity, Upright's scientific integrity? Why is my career being threatened just because I happen to believe in doing what is honest--what is right?"

Messner paused, then spoke slowly, "You've worked in a corporate structure long enough to know that, at our level, those kinds of thoughts don't count. Right and wrong? That decision making is done in the upper echelons."

"That's why I need time to think." Smythe looked up at his wife standing in front of him, arms folded across her chest. She was pissed. "Can I have another day or two to think?"

Messner said, "I will give you twenty four more hours to come to your senses. Stay home today. Talk with your wife some more. Tell her it's my opinion you are committing professional suicide."

Smythe hung up the phone and looked at his wife. Her expression had not changed.

"He's given me another twenty four hours too think about what I should do."

"You know how I feel. I am not going to change my mind to make you feel better. You've got a family that needs you. The kids need a father and I need a husband. Do you have any idea what they'll do to you if your raise a ruckus about this damn drug?"

CHAPTER 22

Messner's phone started ringing when he walked into his office. He answered the call on the second ring.

"Trouble." Hagstrom was on the other end of the phone.

"Trouble? What's that supposed to mean?" Messner hated it when the Whale forced him into his cat and mouse game.

"Two more case reports with Serenity. One on each coast. Two deaths. Both high profile cases. Both prescribing doctors think Serenity was the cause. One's a lead dancer in a Broadway musical and the other a Hollywood star."

"Damn." Messner broke his pencil in half as he was writing. Put out one fire and another one starts. First Smythe, now this.

"It's not taking long, is it?"

Messner didn't appreciate what passed for humor from the other man--not about something like this. He knew it was just a matter of time before some problems with the drug started popping up, but he didn't expect it so soon and so frequently. He couldn't let it get out of hand. He had to put a lid on it.

"Let's get on it. We can't let this go public. I want you to meet with the East Coast doctor right away. I'll take the other. We've got to stop this before it starts."

Messner left for Los Angeles at noon. On the plane, he reviewed the newspaper accounts of the death of Candace Rivers--one of the leading movie stars in Hollywood. She had committed suicide after leaving a specific note apologizing to her fans for her actions. Five hours later he was sitting in the Rodeo Drive office of her physician, Dr. Herold Merilott, a prominent Hollywood psychiatrist.

"Candace has been a patient of mine for a number of years. Did you see her in Seasons of Surprise?"

This self-important asshole needed a good kick in the ass, Messner thought. Who in the fuck had time to sit around and watch movies? He shook his head. "No, I missed it. I am sure it was a great movie."

Merilott continued, "Too bad you missed it. Candace was wonderful in it. It was her second Oscar nomination. I was with her every afternoon throughout the shooting. She said she could not have done it without me. But, you're here to talk about what this horrible drug did to her." He picked up a chart from his desk and read briefly. "I put her on Serenity and three weeks later she drove off the road at the canyon near her home. She left this note. She intended to kill herself." He shoved a note in Messner's direction. "Never, in the years I've known her, has she ever talked about ending her life. How could it be anything but Serenity?"

Messner waited until the guy stopped talking. He ignored the note. "I don't need to defend the drug. Our research and the positive feedback we've received from all over the country supports our position that Serenity, when used properly, is both safe and effective." Messner watched the other man closely as he spoke. Obviously, Merilott hadn't heard one word of what he said. He decided to push the envelope. "Our information is that your patient was an alcoholic. Alcohol, as I'm sure you know, is absolutely contraindicated with the use of Serenity. Let me state it this way to you, doctor. It would be most unfortunate if the National Enquirer, or another sleazy tabloid, tried to put the blame on you for prescribing Serenity to her."

"You wouldn't."

"This is not about me and what I would or would not do, doctor. It is about what the press might do with it when it's called to their attention."

"I can't believe you would threaten me." Merilott fidgeted behind his desk. He would make a terrible poker player, Messner thought.

"I have no interest in doing or saying anything that could harm you professionally. Nothing. What happened is a tragedy. Alcoholics commit suicide all the time. As wonderful a person as she was, she was no different than any other drunk. Serenity had nothing to do with her death. But there's something else I'd like to talk with you about. We are looking for a psychiatrist on the West Coast who is willing to consult with us regularly on issues pertaining to Serenity. On my the way out here, it occurred to me that you would be the perfect man for this. We'd pay a large annual stipend if you're interested."

A sly grin broke out on Merilott's face.

Three hours later, Messner was on a flight heading home. In his briefcase was a letter signed by Merilott attesting that Serenity had nothing to do with the movie star's untimely death. The greedy bastard snapped at the opportunity to be a consultant. A job well done. He ordered his second martini from the flight attendant and sat back. He needed to sleep. It had been a rough few days. Before he nodded off, he remembered he'd given Smythe twenty-four hours. The time would be up by the time he got back to Michigan.

CHAPTER 23

Alex Hartley scratched his head and read the letter from Upright again. He compared the language with the two letters he had received yesterday from Upright. The language in all three letters was identical. So far, Hartley had seen seven patients manifesting aggressive behavior on Serenity and he had reported the seven cases to Upright in three different letters. Upright was treating each of his letters as if it was the first one Upright received. No one was even reading his reports, he thought. Upright probably had a pool typist sending out these standardized letters.

This angered him. Upright's new drug was going to make millions of dollars. Why pretend it was absolutely safe? All drugs had side effects. He'd gone through this before with other drugs and other drug companies. They were all alike. They all tried to get away with murder. Hell, he thought. If this drug was doing what he thought it was doing, Upright was literally trying to get away with murder.

He picked up the phone and called Cassie Standard, the Free Press reporter. "I've got some more good stuff for you on Serenity."

Two hours later, she was sitting at his desk, notepad in hand.

After showing Upright's responses to her, he summarized his concerns.

"A doctor has to ask himself why these case reports are pouring into the company if the drug is safe. These reactions are being seen across the country. When I talked to you the last time, I mentioned that the early reports acted like a red flag indicating some potential for harm. Given the huge increase in the problems reported, coupled with Upright's pretense that there is nothing going on, creates an even greater sense of urgency. Something's got to be done about this drug right away."

"Mind if I write that down?" She asked. He nodded.

"That's why I called you. Just don't spell my name wrong." He smiled.

"Upright says that you have a track record of crying wolf when it comes to drugs. Why should people listen to you now?" She flashed him a pretty smile.

"Good question. It deserves a good answer. How much time do you have?"

"All the time you need." She looked at her watch. "I've got all afternoon."

"Let's start right at the beginning. Serenity is a benzodiazepine. There are a number of benzodiazepines that have been on the market for several years. All of these drugs have been shown to cause people to do crazy things, such as killing themselves or others. The only difference between these older drugs and Serenity is that Serenity causes it about one hundred times more often."

Standeart shifted in her chair. "Why couldn't this greater number be just because of increased news coverage?"

"Good question. Each one of these drugs has had their time in the spotlight, so to speak. If increased public awareness was a factor, one would assume that it would be the same for all these drugs. Not just Serenity."

"You mentioned amnesia. Can you tell me about that?"

Hartley studied Standeart for a moment. She looked good. He picked up a scent of perfume. She smelled good too. He shook off the distraction. "The amnesia that is seen is called anterograde amnesia. What this means is the person cannot remember anything from the time of taking the last dose before a violent act takes place until the body eliminates the drug. People committing aggressive acts cannot remember anything about what they have done. Of course, if they commit suicide, the point is moot."

"Isn't this amnesia just a convenient way for these people to avoid taking responsibility for the harm they cause?"

"No, not at all. Upright and law enforcement people look at it that way, but I can some fine and respectable people have done some pretty crazy things while taking Serenity without the slightest idea of what they were doing and without the slightest memory of what they had done."

Hartley waited while she caught up with her note taking, then continued, "One of my colleagues right here in the department took Serenity just before he was getting on a plane to New York. He woke up four days later in a bowery hotel without the slightest idea how he had gotten there. His clothes, wallet, and valuables were all missing. The last thing he remembered was taking a sip of water to swallow the tablet."

"What's the explanation for that? How does that happen?"

Hartley rubbed his chin. "There's a great deal about brain chemistry that we don't know about. I would say right now this phenomenon falls into the unknown category. My educated guess is the amnesia is part of a toxic syndrome associated with use of the drug. I say that because people can remember in detail what happened to them before the drug effect kicks in and their memory returns after the drug is eliminated from their body."

Standard looked at him. "I should mention to you that I've been contacted by the Weissman family and I've got a story appearing in tomorrow's paper on the tragedy.

"Is he the kid that killed nine people and then himself?"

"That's the one. What you've given me this afternoon will be a big help. I can go back and modify my story to include it. Do you want me to quote you?"

Hartley nodded. "You can quote me if you like. I don't know anything about the case other than what I read in the paper. Was he taking Serenity?"

"The family gave me a copy of the prescription label. The original was given to the police."

Hartley shrugged his shoulders. "I suppose we'll see some more lawsuits."

Standard nodded. "I understand that some of the families have already gone to see Bob Riley."

"Riley . . ." he smiled, "gives me a strong case of indigestion."

They both laughed.

CHAPTER 24

The Detroit Free Press

Family Wonders if Serenity Prompted School Shootings

By Cassie Standard

In their sleepless search for answers, the suburban Detroit family of Sam Weissman, the teenager who killed nine people and then himself, says they are left wondering about the drug he was prescribed for his sleeplessness, which his doctor had attributed to a state of depression.

On Friday, as Tammy Weissman prepared to bury Mr. Weissman, who was her nephew, and her father, who was among those killed, she found herself looking back over the last month when Mr. Weissman began taking the sleep medication Serenity.

"They kept upping the dose for him," she said, "and by the end, he was taking three tablets each day. I can't help but think it was too much--that it must have set him off." Leo Koch, another relative, agreed Weissman's medication had increased a week before the shootings last Monday. "I do wonder," Mr. Koch said, "whether on top of everything else he had going on in his life--on top of all the other problems--the drug could have been the final straw."

Morris Smilevitz, a spokesman for Upright Laboratories, Inc., which sells Serenity stated, "Without knowing Mr. Weissman's medical history or precise diagnosis, it is virtually impossible to speculate on what factors may have affected him--the drugs, his underlying depression, a gloomy childhood wrapped in tragedy, or something else entirely. What I can say is that his physician appears to have prescribed the appropriate dosage of Serenity based on his clinical findings." The dosage range of Serenity, Mr. Smilevitz said, runs from 20 milligrams to 80 milligrams a day, so Mr. Weissman's 60-milligram dose fell in that bracket. Mr. Weissman, though just 16, was taller than 6 feet and weighed 250 pounds.

On Monday, in the hours before the shooting, Mr. Weissman had seemed cheerful and normal, Ms. Weissman said. His teacher, who was spending an hour a day at his house as part of a "homebound" study program, arrived to give him his homework assignments as usual. At 12:30 p.m., less than three hours before the shootings, another aunt, Sondra Weissman, stopped in. "He was watching a movie on TV," Sondra Weissman said. "There was nothing out of the ordinary. People keep saying he was depressed, but if you saw him, he didn't seem depressed. All we can think of is, what about the drug?"

Though Upright says that research has apparently not linked Serenity to acts of violence in others, several incidents have gained wide publicity. Last month, Joseph Weidenbach walked into a printing plant in Louisville, Kentucky, with a bag of guns and killed eight co-workers and himself. He was taking Serenity, which had been approved two months earlier. According to a prominent local physician, Doctor Alex Hartley, there have been a number of similar instances of murders or suicides in users of Serenity since the initial marketing of the drug. Doctor Hartley thinks that the recommended dosage of Serenity is too high, and that its use should be limited to two weeks.

Messner read the article by Standard. *Goddamn Hartley! Goddamn reporters!* Every time there was an article like this about Serenity, people would run to lawyers, claiming that Serenity had caused everything in their goddamned lives. Now, four months since launch day, the pile of negative reports on his desk was getting larger by the day. He slid the stack toward him and flipped through the files. His secretary had prepared a list. Of the eighty-two reports received so far, fifty-seven people committed suicide, and each one of them had a doctor who attributed the death to the drug. Seventeen other reports described murders committed by takers of Serenity. While these numbers were no big surprise to him, it was upsetting to see the pattern emerging so quickly after the drug was put on the market. No doubt, he scowled, the goddamned article in last month's Detroit Free Press instigated these new reports. Standard's latest article now attempted to place this multiple murder incident on Serenity. He made a mental note to discuss this with the Whale. He'd have some ideas how to deal with this increasing flow of negative crap.

Since the appearance of Standard's first article, he'd received numerous phone calls and letters seeking reassurance about the safety of the drug. He felt his blood boil. If it hadn't been for that damn reporter, none of this crap would be happening. This new article would ramp up attention to Serenity. If Smythe read this article, it would set him off again. He would tell Hagstrom to keep an eye on him. He looked at the stack of reports again and then at the newspaper article. Damage control was the first order of business.

CHAPTER 25

Smythe waited until the laboratory cleared for lunch. This morning, he'd read the article by Cassie Standard in the Free Press. He'd made up his mind. He had to do something. He went into his office, picked up the phone and dialed. She answered on the first ring.

"Dr. Emrich, this is Ken Smythe. Smythe from Upright Laboratories."

"I remember. What can I do for you?" She sounded cold.

He whispered into the phone. "I can't really talk on this phone, but there are some very important issues that I need to discuss with you."

She hesitated. "Hold on. Let me make some notes."

"No notes. I need to talk to you confidentially."

"There is no such thing as an 'off the record' discussion. Any contact I have with anybody in the pharmaceutical industry must be reduced to writing."

Smythe thought back to her comments during lunch. "You're joking."

"No joke.

Smythe looked at his telephone receiver. "You and I just can't have a chat about certain things without you putting it in writing and reporting it to your superiors? What about our lunch? You certainly didn't put that in writing."

Emrich paused. "I'll tell you what. Let's just have a conversation."

"I can't let anybody know I'm involved. Can you give me that guarantee?"

"Absolutely. Without question."

"It sounds like you're writing."

"Just doodling." She drew a line under Smythe's name, which was written at the top of a report form--a single straight line.

Smythe whispered into the phone, "Can we do this in person? Meet face to face?"

"Who in the hell are you talking to?"

Smythe jumped and turned around. Hagstrom was standing there with a scowl on his face. How long had he been standing there? What had he heard?

"My wife. One of my kids is home sick."

Smythe looked at Hagstrom and then said into the phone, "Can I call you back? My boss is here."

Hagstrom glared at him under his heavy eyelids.

"Ken, I think you're lying. I want to know who you were talking to."

"I am not lying. I was talking to my wife. I have to go home and see about my daughter." Smythe hands were shaking. He put them under his desk to keep Hagstrom from noticing.

"Why all the whispering then?"

"I . . . My wife was crying. I was just speaking softly to her."

"Messner has filled me in on your little talk with him. I think you were talking to someone about that."

"I was talking to my wife."

"Tell you what. I don't believe you. Get her on the phone, and we'll find out one way or the other."

"I can't. She just left for the doctor with my child."

"I thought you had to go home."

"I do. She left the other kid home alone, and I need to go take care of him."

"The more you stick to that story, the more you sound like you're lying."

"I don't know what I can say to make you believe me. I am not lying."

"You can start with telling me the truth. Who were you talking to? What is going on that you had to ask your wife--if it was your wife--that she couldn't put your conversation in writing or talk to her superiors about? That didn't sound like a man talking to his wife. It sounded like a man trying to keep secrets."

Smythe felt his face redden. Hagstrom knew he was lying. The two men stood there and looked at each other for several moments.

Hagstrom spoke. "Tell you what. I want you to go home. Right now. Call me tomorrow morning to see if it is okay for you to return to work. Leave. Right now."

He stood and waited as Smythe left the laboratory.

After the phone call from Smythe, Emrich tried to assimilate what she heard. Trust. The whole system of drug regulation is built on trust. The law is written, Emrich thought, in such a way that the FDA is obligated to trust the information presented to them by drug companies. Trust when principles of science are involved is one thing. Pure science had several built-in systems--peer review, replication, and independent validation, which required validation of observed results by other researchers before a new piece of information could be said to fit into the gigantic puzzle of what was known with scientific certainty. Research conducted within the drug industry skewed that process. There was no peer review and no guarantee that research was done accurately or honestly. Unlike the process in pure scientific research, work conducted within the industry was carefully guarded and shielded in secrecy. All there was left was trust. The countering force was the potential for making millions of dollars, if not billions, of profit if trust and scientific integrity were ignored.

Emrich looked at her notes. If Smythe did have information that could hurt Serenity, she understood why he was afraid. He was concerned about the potential loss of his job and becoming an outcast in the industry. If he did have information of value, she was in the same boat. They would sink or swim together.

CHAPTER 26

Ann Arbor, a city of 110,000 people, is the sixth largest city in Michigan. During the 1960s and 1970s, the city gained a reputation as an important center for liberal politics. Ann Arbor also became a focal point for left-wing activism and served as a hub for both the civil-rights and anti-Vietnam War movements. The internationally acclaimed University of Michigan is the dominant force in the community and a substantial number of technology firms are located nearby to take advantage of the university's research and development money as well as the steady supply of its graduates. By the mid-nineteen nineties, the political winds had started to shift and the core of the city, aside from university students and professors, became solidly conservative largely as a result of financial backing for local politicians from the core of corporations whose physical plants surround the university like parasites clinging to a host.

No one had played the game of supporting local politicians and judges any better than Upright Pharmaceuticals Inc. and no one inside Upright had played it any better than Cyrus Messner. The making of large financial contributions, with a wink and nod, were his stock in trade for local elected officials. The contributions bought favors. Mr. Smith from our corporate offices was arrested for drunk driving. It's his third offense. Can you help? We have a zoning problem. Two of our neighbors won't sell us their houses. Can you help? One of our board members is going through a nasty divorce. Just because his wife caught him in bed with a twenty-year-old prostitute, she wants to take everything he has. Can you help? Favoritism, the name of the game. Year after year the chits built up in addition to a dossier on each recipient of money kept under lock and key by Messner. He called it his 'good, bad and ugly book.' The 'good' part was the record of money paid out. The 'bad and ugly' component was a compilation of various sordid activities on the part of the recipients of the money. Almost everyone had a career-destroying secret or two if the information became public. Messner scanned through the book until he found the name he wanted. He needed a favor, a big favor.

He picked up his phone and dialed the number of Judge Alfred Heckmann who owed his judgeship to Messner. During his recent campaign for election, Messner had arranged to make it appear that more than three hundred Upright employees donated one thousands dollars each to the judge's campaign. The money enabled Heckmann to easily defeat his rival. The fact that these employees didn't know they had made these contributions was irrelevant. Messner's theory was that whatever they didn't know would hurt them. So he simply didn't mention that corporate money in excess of legal contribution limits had been used to help the judge get elected. When Messner finished telling Heckmann what he needed, the judge balked.

"I don't think I can do that."

"Sure you can. All you have to do is listen to some testimony and sign the papers. It's only three days."

"What if some newspaper reporter walks in and hears what's going on? I don't like it."

"You don't have to like it. You just have to do it. Besides, you can hear the testimony in chambers, or just lock the door of your courtroom. Don't forget that you have three hundred thousand good reasons to help me out on this."

"Do you have any idea of what would happen to me if this becomes public?"

"Just keep it a private hearing." Messner looked at a photograph on his desk. I do know what will happen if this photograph was made public, he thought. In the photograph, the good judge was enjoying a lap dance from a dancer in a Detroit topless bar. Messner had the photo because he had arranged for it to happen. Messner wasn't going to use it unless it was necessary to convince the judge to honor his request.

"Besides, I can document the threat to our employees. I have a doctor who will testify to his mental state. Everything is in place. I just need your signature on the commitment papers. It's for only three days."

Later that afternoon Doctor Elmer Garrity sat on the witness stand and talked to Judge Heckmann. Garrity described an event at Upright headquarters that never occurred. He was telling the story Hagstrom had provided.

"This," he said, holding up Smythe's bench book, "is an example of what I just described. This collection of thoughts demonstrates a pattern of paranoid thinking which contains half content and half delusion. Doctor Smythe has taken great pains to document his perception- I repeat, his perception, of the truth that is actually nothing more than a series of half- truths colored by his delusional perception that the company is doing something wrong. Everyone in the company is wrong but him."

Garrity paused long enough to make sure that the point had registered with the judge. "The paranoid personality is always concerned about whether he will be believed by others. Doctor Smythe makes a substantial effort to search for facts that will support him and can, as indicated in his bench book, marshal an effective and sometimes convincing argument, but only if you accept his paranoid pattern of thinking." He smiled at the judge. He knew that the image he projected was that of a kind professional--a grandfatherly type who would do nothing to harm anyone.

The judge leaned toward him. "Doctor, let me ask you this question. My task here is to determine whether Kenneth Smythe presents a danger to himself or others sufficient to justify placing him into protective custody. With respect, I've heard nothing yet that would come close to meeting those requirements."

Perfect, Messner thought, sitting in the back of the courtroom. This guy was following the script exactly.

Garrity cleared his throat. "Judge, please forgive me. I wanted you to hear some of my preliminary observations before I get to the topic at hand. I do understand why we're here, and I do have an opinion that Doctor Smythe represents a potential danger to both himself and others. The basis for my opinion is that, in the past two days, he has verbalized threatening behavior."

Garrity opened his briefcase, shuffled through some documents and checked his notes. "For example, yesterday Mr. Hagstrom, his immediate superior, walked into Doctor Smythe's office, and Smythe started yelling at him. He indicated that it was his intention to 'go public' with his charges unless the company would halt all marketing and selling of a drug that it has spent millions of dollars and untold thousands of man hours in research in developing for the betterment of mankind. Smythe himself did a lot of this work. Smythe also represented Upright in its dealing with the Food and Drug Administration. In his own research and his efforts with the FDA, he never mentioned any potential dangers of the drug. However, in the past couple of days, Smythe has started making accusations and charges that are totally unfounded. Mr. Hagstrom, fearing for his own safety and the safety of others, called security to forcibly remove Doctor Smythe from the premises."

The judge peered at Garrity over the top of his bifocals. "Are you trying to tell me that anyone who has a disagreement with his employer should be locked up?"

"Certainly not, Your Honor. This situation is different. It goes far beyond a mere disagreement. After Doctor Smythe was removed from his office, the computer at his workstation was found to be wiped clean of all information. Nearly three years of research wiped out. Of course, the company has all this information stored on other computers, but it was his intent to destroy this information that is the issue." Garrity fumbled around his briefcase. "This note was found at his desk. Let me read it to you. 'Messner: You will be sorry for what you are doing. If you continue to go ahead with this project, I shall personally destroy you.'

"Let me see that." The judge reached over and Garrity handed him the note. The judge read it several times. He slammed the gavel on his desk out of force of habit, even though there was but a handful of people sitting quietly in the courtroom.

"I've seen and heard enough. I'll sign an order of detention allowing Kenneth Smythe to be held for three days for complete psychiatric evaluation. It is my finding that detention is justified on the basis that Doctor Smythe presents a risk to others in his current state. He should be taken into custody immediately and, by signing this order of detention, I am directing the county sheriff to do so. Unless there is anything else, court is adjourned."

He looked around the courtroom, nodded at Messner, slammed the gavel again, stood, and left the room.

Messner sat in the back of the room and chuckled to himself. The judge knew which side of the bread the butter was on. The good old American way.

CHAPTER 27

Smythe didn't tell his wife about the incident at the laboratory. He knew it would upset her. Instead, he went home with some flowers. "Just decided to come home and see you and the kids."

Anne was surprised he came home so early. "Is everything all right?"

"Everything's fine. Just need a little extra time with you." He looked at her. "I don't know what I'd do without you. I'm crazy about you." He put his arms around her hugged her tightly. "Think we could sneak upstairs before the kids come home from the sitter?"

"I've got to pick them up. Let's wait. I'll make it special for you tonight if we wait." She gave him that look--the look that made it difficult for him to refuse anything she asked. He went into his den and called Emrich after his wife left the house.

"Dr. Emrich? Ken Smythe calling back. My boss overheard the end of our last phone conversation and sent me home. If we're going to do something about this, we've got to move fast."

"It sounded like there was a problem. I'm glad you called back." Emrich flashed back to the lunch. He was a good-looking guy, devoted husband and family man. She remembered being surprised that he hadn't made a move on her.

"We need to talk. I'd rather not do it by phone. Can I meet you someplace in Washington? I can be there any time. Or can you come here?"

"You're talking about Serenity, aren't you?" Emrich had read the newspaper articles about the deaths. "Tell me what's on your mind."

Smythe's reluctance was obvious. "Let me stay hypothetical. At our lunch, you made reference to changing the system."

Emrich thought back. She really didn't remember what she said. She remembered being pissed at Levitt for playing her like a pawn. "And?"

"You made it pretty clear that the FDA wouldn't do much if it found out that a company had cheated on a drug submission."

"Did I say that?"

"Yes, you did. What I need to know is whether or not that is true. I need to know what would happen if you did find out that a company had done something wrong."

Pieces of their lunchtime conversation floated back into her mind now. She hesitated before responding. "How seriously we would take something would depend on the situation."

"I have some serious concerns about Serenity."

"Can you be a little more specific? Give me more information? Tell me enough to convince me?"

She could hear him take a deep breath. "First, I know you can help me. This is an emerging situation that requires action from the FDA. If something is not done, thousands of lives may be lost."

She did not doubt Smythe's sincerity. This could be a ticket away from Levitt--a way to shed her past. If what Smythe said was true, and she planned it right, who knew? Levitt might be working for her. Or, better yet, she would get his ass kicked right out of the agency. "I'll tell you what. Fax me what you have. Let me see something. I'll think about it and then get back to you."

"I'd rather not give you anything in writing. Not just yet."

She nearly groaned aloud. "I'm afraid I can't do anything on your word alone. Give me something to go on here."

Another long pause. "Let me think for a moment." He spoke slowly. "If I were able to show you that we withheld data in our new drug application, would that get your attention?"

He had her attention. "It would have to be based on something other than your word." She was already thinking about how she might go about this without Levitt finding out.

"I can fax one page. Hopefully it will whet your appetite for more. Read it and get back to me."

She smiled again. "Send it on." She already had a game plan in mind.

"Let me think about this. Give me a number where I can reach you."

"I have a private line right to my desk in the laboratory. That would probably be the best way to reach me."

CHAPTER 28

Anne came home with the children a few minutes later. Ken spent the evening playing with them. It was a nice evening. The kids took a bath and went to bed. Smythe read a book to them for the first time in a long time. Then, the couple watched television for a while and went to bed. Smythe thought about his phone call with Emrich and the fax he'd sent. He had finally done something. For the first time since all this crap started, he felt at peace. He moved over and put his arms around his wife. She sat up and looked at him. "You seem different tonight."

"How so?"

"You've been so sweet."

"Aren't I sweet all the time?"

"Honey, you sure are. But tonight, you seem happy sweet."

"Happy sweet? What does that mean?"

"I don't know, but you're just different." She leaned toward him and kissed him. "I told you I'd be extra nice if you waited."

They began to make love, gently at first. He heard a loud banging on the front door. They stopped moving.

"What was that?"

"Somebody's at the front door. Let's ignore it. They'll go away." His wife giggled, and they resumed their movement slowly, in unison.

Then the pounding again. They stopped.

"What if something is wrong?"

"The kids are asleep. If it was your mother, she'd call first." He kissed her. "Let's get back to what we were doing." He started moving, but she froze.

"I can't do this. Go see who it is."

Smythe reluctantly complied. He stood and put on his bathrobe. Leaned over his wife and kissed her again. "I'll be right back."

He strode into the living room.

"Daddy. What's that noise?" Smythe was startled as he nearly tripped over his youngest child in the dark. He bent down and scooped the him into his arms.

"I'm going to see right now, big guy. You can come with me."

"Daddy, I'm scared."

"No reason to be scared." He carried the child to the front hallway, flipped on the outside light, and opened the door.

The powerful beam of a flashlight blinded him, and he stepped back.

"Who are you and what do you want?"

"Are you Kenneth Smythe?" Two good-sized police officers were standing on the porch.

"That's me. Is something wrong?"

"Put the kid down and stand still. Don't make any trouble." One of the men grabbed the outside door handle and flung the door open, stepping quickly inside, backing Smythe against the wall.

"What's this all about?" Smythe clutched the child tighter.

His wife came to his side. "Honey. What's going on?"

"Stand back, ma'am." The second man stepped between Smythe and his wife and placed his hand on his holstered weapon. "I said put the kid down."

The first man forcibly removed the little boy from Smythe's grasp and placed him on the floor. He then grabbed Smythe in a bear hug that pinned his arms to his side. He couldn't move.

"What the hell's going on? Honey, go call the police."

The second man grabbed his arms and handcuffed him from behind. Threw him face down on the floor. His wife stepped forward, and the other man grabbed her and wrestled her to the ground. Their older child came into the room, rubbing her eyes. Both children now stood in the middle of the room, wide-eyed with fear, crying loudly.

The cop holding Smythe down held out a piece of paper. "I have a court order to take you into custody. Stand up, and don't give me any more trouble." Both cops stared at Smythe's wife. Her robe had fallen open, revealing her nakedness. She struggled to cover herself, but was prevented from doing so by the grasp of the man.

She squirmed. "Let me go!"

"You shut your mouth, or you'll be going with us too."

Smythe could taste his fear. His voice cracked. "Can I make a phone call? Can I get dressed? Let her go. Let her cover herself, for God's sake."

The kids' wailing nearly drowned out the sound of his words. The first cop pulled him to his feet, spun him around, and propelled him out the front door. Both men walked him down the sidewalk and shoved him into the back seat of the squad car. They drove away as Anne stood on the sidewalk and cried. She didn't know what to do. What good would it do to call the police? They were the police. The police had come into their house and dragged her husband away. She slumped to the ground in the darkness, held her two children close, and cried until there were no more tears.

In the back seat of the squad car, Smythe squirmed. The more he moved, the greater the pain and discomfort from the tightness of the cuffs. He gathered his thoughts. What the hell was going on? It didn't make any sense. He leaned forward. "Can I ask a question? What the hell is going on?"

The cop in the passenger seat turned around. "Your wife has nice tits. You're a lucky guy. Maybe someday you'll get a chance to see them again." Both of the men in the front seat laughed.

"What is going on here? This is America. I've got rights."

Both men laughed again. The driver looked back. "No, sir. Not with this commitment order, you don't. No, sir. No rights at all."

The phone rang. Messner answered and listened silently for a minute. Then he placed the receiver on its cradle. The deed was done. A big obstacle out of the way. After that smart-ass lawyer Dockery would get Smythe released, Smythe's credibility would be zero. No one would believe one word he said. Nothing. Nada. He placed a call to Dockery and gave him his marching orders.

CHAPTER 29

In Washington, Jan Emrich's looks didn't mean much since the town was filled with good-looking women. Good-looking and educated. They were a dime a dozen, she thought. When she first came to the nation's capitol from Binghamton, New York, she'd been surprised by the sheer numbers of available men-hungry women, and it took awhile for her to get used to the rough and tumble life of the single woman in the city. What made it unique was the number of predatory married men who viewed access to these women as the spoils of power.

The rules were simple, Emrich thought. Morality was defined by the status of the individuals involved in the game. It was acceptable to sleep with a married man, as long he possessed power. No power? No thanks. Get lost. Have a nice day. Power? My place or yours? The city's bars, every night of the week, were filled with attractive women waiting, looking vainly for that power connection.

To Emrich's great chagrin, she had become part of the process. She'd become accustomed to men, particularly married men, trying to proposition her that when they didn't, she was puzzled. Sometimes she felt rejected. She had also learned that there was no such thing as a free lunch. In her five years in Washington, she had slept with four married men. The list included one congressman, one Army general, and two FDA officials, including her boss, Mort Levitt.

Levitt, she mused, was the biggest mistake of her life. He now thought of her as his own piece of personal property. He kept her on a short leash, and his possessive attitude, coupled with the power he held over her, combined to make her feel she was stuck in a black hole. Sex on demand was not her thing, but it was sure as hell his. Nothing in her life, she thought, had prepared her for getting out from such a situation. He played her like a violin and reminded her daily just how much any further advancement for her at the FDA was tied in with their relationship.

At first, she'd thought he cared about her. Now she realized how wrong she was. That was just part of his scam. He regularly demanded sex with her in his assertion of control. She had thought about recourse--even thought about bringing a lawsuit. The horror stories about what happened to women who claimed sexual harassment in situations similar to hers kept her immobile. Her career was important to her. It was a catch-22. If she spoke out, her career was over. That much was true. How could a woman claim sexual harassment when she slept with her boss when they were both consenting adults? She found herself ruminating about the situation more and more.

The ringing of the telephone interrupted her rambling thoughts. She checked the caller ID. It was the fax coming from Smythe.

CHAPTER 30

The fax got Emrich's attention. She compared the information from the fax with the materials in the new drug application for Serenity. There was a substantial difference. Smythe was right. Even though the information on the fax dealt only with animals, it was obvious that Upright's animal research indicated that the drug was going to cause problems and they hadn't given the information to the FDA.

With reports of deaths caused by Serenity coming into the FDA since the drug was marketed, it was obvious that the animal research should not have been ignored. The fact that it was watered down made it clear that Upright knew there was going to be problems, but tried to hide it. Something needed to be done--and fast. She needed to act because she would be blamed for missing the obvious even though Upright had withheld it from her. This was the way Levitt did business at the FDA. He always had someone else set up to take the fall for what he should be doing. What Smythe had given her was blockbuster information. Serenity would join the ranks of spectacular failures. Upright would become the pariah of the drug industry. She felt nervous. This was big. Who in the hell at the agency could she go to with this?

She thought about her co-employees. Who could she trust? One of her biggest surprises since she'd joined the agency was the number of back-stabbers, an abundance of mid-level employees who would screw her over in a heartbeat. Most of the rest went through the motions just to collect a paycheck. She sure as hell couldn't count on anybody in these two groups. She thought about Levitt. She should take this information to him, but she knew what he would do. Either laugh at her, or report Smythe to that asshole Messner. Either way, Levitt would see that she was demoted to some obscure part of the agency where she'd be stuck reviewing labels for cat food or other demeaning tasks.

She was between a rock and a hard place. She decided to wait on this information until she could come up with a plan that wouldn't mean professional suicide. She needed time to think. She locked her notes away in the top drawer of her desk, away from prying eyes.

She spent the better part of the next day trying to reach Smythe by phone. He'd told her the private number rang only at his bench. It went unanswered. She was reluctant to call through the switchboard. Smythe had asked her not to. She Googled Smythe's home number. No luck. She called directory assistance. The number was unlisted.

CHAPTER 31

Jumbo Dockery made a comfortable living as a lawyer. In a city like Ann Arbor, where Upright Pharmaceutical Co was the largest employer after the university, turnover was great among the army of professionals, students and graduates who passed through the University of Michigan and the high-tech companies in the area. For Dockery, it meant a continuous influx of fees for real estate closings, often for the same properties time and again. Hell, he must have closed on some of the same houses five or more times in his twenty-four years of practice. The real estate contacts led to a considerable amount of additional legal work from divorces, drunk driving arrests, and the writing of wills to court appearances for traffic tickets. From the time he started his law practice, he'd cultivated the director of personnel and the heads of other departments at Upright because these key people were in a position to recommend the services of a lawyer. A substantial part of his law practice came from Upright through such referrals. Which is how he'd come to represent Anne Smythe when she'd been arrested three years ago for drunk driving.

One of his principles in his legal work for Upright personnel was to not bite the hand that fed him. On demand, he'd provide information to key Upright supervisors about Upright employees as a show of gratitude for his services being recommended. The background on Anne Smythe's arrest was just the kind of situation that met the criteria for sharing. As Anne told the story to Dockery, she'd gone out for an evening with a couple of girl friends and the trio went to a bar. They danced to the jukebox and drank. Alcohol flowed freely and soon the dancing women became the entertainment for the rest of the bar patrons. Shortly before last call, Smythe and her friends removed their tops and danced suggestively at the request of a group of guys who sat at an adjoining table. When the bar closed, Smythe drove her friends home and was stopped by a police officer three blocks from her home when she ran a stop sign. She begged Dockery not to tell her husband about what happened at the bar. The drunk driving charge was bad enough because she had agreed to stop drinking at her husband's request as a result of previous embarrassing episodes triggered by her drinking. Dockery never mentioned it to Ken Smythe, but did report the details of the incident to Messner. Dockery got the drunk driving charge reduced to a lesser offense with the judge's admonition to Mrs. Smythe to do something about her drinking problem.

When Anne called him late last night to tell him what had happened to her husband, he listened patiently to the story. He promised to come over in the morning after making some inquiries so she could know what'd happened and what he could do about it. When the phone call ended, Dockery called Messner.

"I'm sorry to bother you so late, but I've just heard from Anne Smythe that her husband has been taken into custody and I'm wondering if you know anything about it."

Messner replied, "I knew you might be calling. Let me fill you in on what's going on."

Messner spent the next few minutes describing what had happened to Smythe. "I need you to see that he stays in the hospital for the full seventy-two hours. Any problem with that?"

Dockery didn't hesitate. "No. Not at all." Not at all, he thought again. The three days might give him an opportunity to spend some time with his client.

He told Anne that he'd be at her house by nine o'clock, but decided to show up earlier. It was seven o'clock and, as he'd expected, she hadn't dressed yet. She sat opposite him in the tiny kitchen wearing a robe that did a poor job of concealing her figure. Jeez, he loved his work.

She repeated the entire story and he sat and listened.

"Could I have a little more coffee, please?"

She stood and got the coffee pot from the kitchen counter and refilled his cup. As she did, he enjoyed the view.

He took a sip of coffee and the heat scorched the back of his throat. He felt the liquid burn its way down to his stomach.

"You all right?"

Dockery coughed. The searing heat dissipated inside him. "I'm all right. Coffee's hot. Should have been more careful."

"Let me get you a glass of water."

More movement around the kitchen. Man, this lady is hot. He looked at her as she returned to her seat. "Has your husband had a lot on his mind recently?"

Dockery felt his heart beating. A warm layer of perspiration coated his body.

"The coffee is making you sweat."

He dabbed at his brow with one of the paper napkins she'd placed on the table.

He smiled at her. "Actually, I'm sweating because I'm not used to being in the company of such a pretty lady."

He looked directly at her. Right in her eyes. Neither of them spoke for a moment. His mouth felt dry, and he licked his lips. His eyes wandered down to her cleavage. She stood abruptly.

"I'll be back in a minute. Have some more coffee if you like."

He watched as she turned and left the room. He sat and waited. Five minutes later, she came back into the room, fully dressed--slacks, heavy sweater hiding her figure.

"You asked me if my husband had a lot on his mind." She hesitated. "Upright is pulling some pretty shady stuff with some of the studies done on a new drug that my husband has been working on. He's been pretty vocal about why they shouldn't go ahead."

She'd brushed her hair and put on some makeup. She smelled nice. Man, she was hot.

"Do you have to know what Kenny told me?"

"If I'm going to help you, I have to know what you know. I'm your lawyer. What you say to me doesn't go outside these four walls." He made a sweeping gesture around the room.

Anne stood and began to pace. "I don't want to get Ken in worse trouble than he already is." She sat down. She started to cry. She looked up at him, and her mascara had streaked--two dark splotches below both eyes. "Why is this happening to us? What is going to happen to Kenny?"

He leaned forward and patted her arm.

She dabbed her eyes with a Kleenex. "I must be a mess."

"Take a lot more than smudges to hurt your pretty looks." He leaned forward and took hold of her hand. "Now, why don't you just tell me what it is that you know about your husband's work?"

She paused again. "Kenny is a pharmacologist. He studies the effects of drugs on animals--sometimes on people. He's been involved with a drug called Serenity for the last two years. Just after I met you the last time."

Dockery remembered that time very well. She'd come into his office in a tank top and a pair of shorts that made him hard when he thought about it. He thought about the information in his file--a little problem handling alcohol. More than a little problem. She couldn't keep her clothes on when she drank heavily. Knowing that about her was what pushed his buttons last night when she called.

She continued. "A few months ago, there were some problems with the drug at Jackson Prison. Apparently, a couple of guys went crazy and at least one of them tried to kill someone." She pulled her hand away from his. He realized he'd been holding it tightly. "Let me get you some more coffee." She stood and refilled his cup. God, she was sexy.

"If your husband works with animals, why does this involve him?"

"A while back, he was called to a meeting and was told that Upright was going ahead with the plans for the drug and that they would be asking the Food and Drug Administration for approval. Kenny was given the responsibility of dealing with the FDA. The drug was approved and there have been some big problems with the drug since it started to be sold.

She started to cry again. "A couple of days ago, Kenny went directly to his boss and demanded that the company do the right thing or else he would call the FDA himself. For all I know, he did. Now he's been arrested and locked up some place--being treated like a criminal for trying to do the right thing."

Dockery sensed that this was a good time.

"From what I found out before I came here this morning, your husband said some things to his boss that put the man in fear for his life. Upright management was concerned enough about the incident to seek some protection so Ken has been hospitalized by court order."

She began crying harder. He stood and walked over to where she was standing. Put his arms around her. She buried her face in his chest and sobbed. He held her tighter and enjoyed the feel of her body against him.

"Mama, where's Daddy?" Dockery jumped as the little boy walked into the room, rubbing his eyes with his hands.

She bent down and hugged. "Daddy's not home yet, honey. This is Mr. Dockery. He's come to help us. Say hello to him."

"Why are you crying, Mommy?"

Anne ran her hand through the child's hair. "Everything is all right. Mommy cries some time because she is so happy."

Dockery had forgotten about the damned kids. He looked at his watch. "I'm going to head for my office, and I'll be in touch with you when I find something out more. Don't worry. I'll get him out and back to you real soon"

CHAPTER 32

It was a quarter past five. Messner was sitting at his desk when the secretary from Smythe's laboratory knocked on the door, entered meekly and placed a sheet of paper in front of him.

"There were twelve calls today. All from Dr. Emrich."

Messner picked up the paper and studied it. His directions had been followed explicitly. "Did anybody answer the phone?"

"No, sir. Just like you said. I followed your instructions exactly. I just let it ring."

"How do you know it was Emrich calling?"

"When I saw the same number time and time again, I dialed the number, and she answered the phone and identified herself. I just hung up."

Messner studied her. She was attractive and sexy in a quiet way.

"Please sit down, dear." He gestured to one of the chairs fronting his desk. "How long have you been with us?"

Three days after Smythe was hauled away from his home in the middle of the night, he was released. Dockery had obtained an order from the court authorizing the release on the morning of the second day of Smythe's confinement, but Dockery kept the information from Anne Smythe at Messner's request. He called Messner and told him.

Messner told him, "Hold on. I need another day to put things into place."

"I can do that." Dockery nodded. He thought about what he could do in the next twenty-four hours. He would drop by the Smythe residence when he knew that the children were gone. They spent the day in school. He would use the information about Anne Smythe's past to his advantage. All's fair in love and war, he thought, and lusting after her body was close to his definition of love.

He smiled into the phone. "Yes, I can do that."

Dockery waited in his car down the street from the Smythe home until he saw Anne return home after dropping the kids off at school. He waited ten minutes, parked in the Smythe driveway. and knocked on the front door. He carried his briefcase, which held the bottle of magic that would seal the deal, he thought.

"I want to report to you about some progress I've made. I thought it would be best to do it in person."

"Come in." She was wearing a t-shirt and shorts. The outfit left little to the imagination.

They sat down at the kitchen table. "Would you like something to drink? I can put on coffee."

"I've got a better idea. I've brought something to celebrate some good news." He reached into his briefcase and brought out a bottle of Jack Daniels. "Why don't you get a couple of glasses, and I can bring you up to date."

"I haven't had anything to drink in a long time."

"No problem. You can have just one to celebrate."

"What's the good news?" Is Kenny coming home today?"

"First the drink, then the news."

"I really don't think I should. You can if you like."

"Just a small one. I don't like to drink alone."

"He's coming home, isn't he?"

He nodded.

"When?"

"Tomorrow."

She stood and walked past him to the sink. Took two glasses down from the cupboard and put them on the table. "Just one."

Dockery removed the cap from the bottle and poured a generous amount into each glass. He handed her one and lifted his glass. "To good news."

Anne hesitated, and then picked up the drink, touching her glass to Dockery's. "Good news." She repeated.

Dockery drained his glass in one swallow. Anne hesitated, and then did the same.

"So tell me the details."

"Let me refill our glasses first." Dockery felt the warmth from the drink in his stomach. He removed the cap from the bottle and filled the glasses again. He looked at Anne and stared at her chest.

"I spent the entire morning in court arguing on Ken's behalf. I asked the judge to release him immediately, but he wants one more day so your husband's evaluation can be completed. I will be bringing him back to you tomorrow."

"That's wonderful. Really wonderful. I can't thank you enough." Anne took a sip of her drink. "This is really nice." She slurred the words.

Dockery leaned across the table and put his hands on hers. "I agree. This is nice."

She took another swallow of her drink. "Can I have a refill?" She nodded toward the bottle.

This was better than he imagined, Dockery thought. He poured a generous amount in her glass. Much better. "I am so happy for you that I can be of service."

"I can't tell you how much I appreciate it." She took another swallow. She stretched her arms over her head. "I am getting drunk. This is going to my head fast."

Dockery thought for a moment. "You really look nice in that outfit."

"This? It's just an old t-shirt and shorts I wear around the house."

"You have such a terrific figure."

"Thank you."

"You should plan on wearing something special for your husband when he comes home."

"I've got just the outfit in mind. You should see it."

"I'd like that. Why don't you go put it on?"

"I'll show it to you as soon as I finish this drink." She drained the glass. "You can pour me another while I get it."

When she came back, she held a nightgown in front of her. "Do you like this? It's one of Kenny's favorites." It was a black and sheer.

"Put it on."

She stood in front of him and removed her top. He'd been right. She wore no bra. Her breasts were beautiful. She slipped the nightgown over her head.

"Do you like this?"

"It looks fantastic. You have such a perfect body."

She spun slowly around. "Thank you."

"You forgot the bottoms."

"I'll leave my shorts on. If I take them off, who knows what might happen? You know why I don't drink. I go a little crazy. I can't help myself. That's why I don't drink much. My clothes just fall off, and I want to fuck." She giggled. "Oops, shouldn't say the f word. Sorry."

"I could look at you all day."

"That's why I stopped drinking. I love having men look at me." She turned around again. "I took my top off in a bar once."

"I remember. That's when I represented you for that traffic stop.

"Oh, that's right. I nearly forgot." She giggled.

She was driving Dockery crazy. He was hard as a rock. "You should see what you're doing to me."

She smiled. "I'm sorry. I'll put my t-shirt back on." She slipped the nightgown off and stood in front of him. "You're such a gentleman. Some guys would be putting their hands all over me."

She put the t-shirt over her head and tucked it into her shorts. "That's better. Safer for both of us."

He thought he was going to explode.

She sat down at the table. "Let's have one more drink. I enjoyed showing off for you. I feel safe doing it. Kenny wouldn't approve. But, he doesn't have to know, does he?"

Dockery shook his head.

She continued, "Kenny would be really mad if he knew I was drinking. He knows how I am."

"I won't tell him."

She giggled. "You're my lawyer. You'll keep my secrets."

Dockery smiled at her. "I'd like to see the secrets again."

"Oh, you." She stood and removed her top. "You like?"

"Very much." He couldn't stand this.

"Do you want to touch me?" She moved closer.

He reached out and fondled her breasts, pinched her nipples gently. She gasped.

"That feels so nice. You have a nice touch."

"You are so beautiful."

She closed her eyes. "You know what I think? I think I should do something special since you've done such a great job for Kenny."

She went to her knees and reached for Dockery's belt buckle.

Dockery left the house a half hour later a happy man.

CHAPTER 33

After Dockery left, Anne experienced a feeling of panic. What had she done? That part of her past was over, she thought. She should know better than to drink, particularly with another man. Now her craving was back. She loved the feeling that alcohol gave her. She loved the attention from other men. She thought about the afternoon with Dockery and the good news that Kenny was coming home tomorrow. The children would be home in two hours, and she didn't want them to detect the odor of alcohol. Dockery left the bottle of Jack Daniels for her, and she wanted another drink. She picked up the phone and called her mother.

"Mom, Good news. Kenny is coming home tomorrow. Could you pick the kids up at school and let them spend the night with you so I can get the house ready?"

"Sure, honey. No problem."

Now she had the house to herself. She sat at the kitchen table and looked at the bottle on the sink. She thought about how thrilling it was for Dockery to see her in the nightgown. She poured a large amount from the bottle into her glass. Took a deep swallow. Sex with Kenny was good, but the afternoon with Dockery was great. What she wouldn't give right now for a repeat. She loved it when men admired her body. She knew she had a great body, and she had to suppress the urge to show it off. Alcohol released that inhibition. It had been a long time since she had gone out to the bars to drink and pick up men. She did that a lot before she got married. There was that one time just after they moved here. Kenny was away on business. She'd worked hard in AA and with counselors to forget the excitement and this afternoon made her realize just how much she missed it. She took her drink and the bottle upstairs and stood in front of the bedroom mirror and undressed. She studied her body. She thought about phoning Dockery and asking him to come back. She finished her drink and poured another generous amount into the glass. She lay down on the bed and closed her eyes.

When she awoke, it was dark. She was cold. Her mouth was dry and tasted terrible. She moved her tongue with difficulty. What the hell was she doing on top of the unopened bed? Why was she nude? No wonder she was cold. She stood and nearly fell over. She was still drunk, she thought. She turned the light on next to the bed and stumbled into the bathroom. She examined her face in the mirror and was horrified by her appearance. Dark circles rimmed her bloodshot eyes. She remembered. Kenny was coming home. What had Dockery said about when he would be released? How much time did she have to get herself together? She tried to reconstruct yesterday's events, but failed. She remembered drinking with Dockery and telling him about her nightgown. Nothing after that.

Kenny would be furious if he found out that she'd been drinking.

She spent the next hours getting herself together. She made a pot of coffee and drank as much as she could. She emptied the remainder of the Jack Daniels in the sink and threw the bottle in the garbage. She picked her nightgown off the kitchen floor and wondered how it got there. She took it upstairs and placed it in her lingerie drawer. The ringing of the front doorbell startled her. She looked at herself in the mirror again. Makeup had done its job, but she still felt terrible.

Dockery and Kenny were standing at the front door. Her husband looked gaunt and tired. She rushed to him and hugged him.

She looked at Dockery out of the corner of her eye. He had a slight grin on his face. She knew the look. She looked at Kenny.

"I've missed you so much."

Ken stared vacantly at her. "I've missed you too."

She looked at Dockery. "He's on something. Did the doctor say anything?"

"He's on a prescription of some kind. Needs to stay on it for a couple more weeks. The doctor wants to see him every day for the next week." Dockery took a prescription bottle from his coat pocket and handed it to her. She read the label and didn't recognize the name of the drug.

She led her husband by his hand into the living room. "Honey, are you all right?"

He looked straight ahead. Not at her, but through her. "I'm fine," he said.

"What did they do to you?"

"Don't remember."

She looked at Dockery. "Do you have the doctor's number? I need to speak with him."

"I don't have his number, but I do have his name and address. Ken has an appointment at one o'clock. You can talk to the doctor then."

Dockery grinned again at her. What the hell happened yesterday, she thought, that makes him look at me that way?

"Mr. Dockery, I can't thank you enough for bringing Kenny home. Please send the bill, and we'll pay it promptly."

The grin stayed on his face. "The bill is paid. The pleasure was all mine."

She glanced at her husband to see if he detected the innuendo. He stared off into space. She looked back at Dockery. "Again, many thanks. I'd like to be alone with my husband now. You've been very kind."

She ushered him back to the front door. As he went through the door he stopped. "I'll see you again. Soon, I hope."

Damn. What had she done?

CHAPTER 34

Getting ready for a criminal trial was different from preparing for a civil trial, I thought. Civil cases encompassed depositions of witnesses, examination of thousands of documents, and preparation of expert witnesses and clients. Because of huge backlogs of civil cases pending in courts around the country, discovery in civil cases took time--a lot of time. It was unusual for a case to be called for trial less than two years from the date of filing a lawsuit, and it could take up to four years in some jurisdictions. Criminal cases, on the other hand, came up for trial fast.

The Criminal Speedy Justice Act required that a trial be scheduled within 180 days from the time that the defendant is charged. The purpose was to allow individuals being charged with a crime to avoid having to spend extra time in jail waiting for a trial date when such persons were considered innocent until proven guilty. So I had to move faster on Slater's case than in my usual civil cases. That meant I had less time to get to know him personally, but knowing him was imperative if I was going to conduct the kind of trial he needed. I needed to spend time with him. I scheduled a time with the jail administration for me to see him on a regular basis to accomplish that purpose.

This was my third visit and Slater was looking better. The haunting look in his eyes was gone.

"You're looking a hell of a lot better than the last time I saw you. Sleeping all right?"

"Yeah. It's a fucking resort."

So much for the power of positive thinking. On the other hand, Wayne County jail was not the kind of place I'd want to spend one night in.

"I meet with the judge this afternoon to set a trial date. Probably about three months from now."

"Three months? I've got to stay in this hell hole another three months?"

Knowing what he'd done to his wife made it difficult for me to be sympathetic about a little jail time for him. Even if the drug Serenity obliterated his role in the death of his wife, the guy had screwed around on his wife so much while she was alive that he deserved some time. Wait a second, I thought, I am the one with the attitude. I better be careful.

When this case came to trial, a jury would be certain to detect my concerns about Slater, despite what I was saying, if I didn't get myself together. I shouldn't be representing him if I was feeling this way. Juries could tell. They had a sixth sense when it came to a lawyer's demeanor in the courtroom regarding the merits of a case, particularly if he didn't like or believe his own client. I'd better get it together.

"The problem is, Jay, that there is no bail on a charge of first degree murder."

"I know that. You told me that already."

I bit my tongue and looked down at my notes.

"I want to ask a few questions. Last time you mentioned that your memory was 'clearer.' Is there anything new on that point?"

"Not really. I remember the days leading up to what happened more clearly, but nothing after what I mentioned previously--that incident with those two Mexican assholes."

"Incident? You didn't describe it as an incident last time."

"I told you that they laughed because I got mad about having to wait while they moved their truck. We exchanged a few words, although they didn't know what I was talking about, and I sure as hell didn't know what they were saying."

What day was this?"

He looked at me for a long time before he answered. "I'm not sure. From what I understand, it was a couple of days before my wife died."

"How do you know that?"

"Didn't you tell me? I thought you did. Somebody did. I don't remember. I just know that it was a couple of days before."

I wrote out his response in my notebook. When I finished, I looked at him.

He blinked and said, "Why? Is that important?"

"Is what important?"

"Is it important that I know the date when I had the argument with those spics?"

I decided to change the subject. "How are they treating you?"

For the first time since I'd met him, Slater looked me in the eyes. "You ask like you almost care. I asked you a question. Is it important for me to know the exact fucking time and date those wetbacks tried to fuck me over? The bitch was egging them on."

"Your wife was present when you had this disagreement with the two gardeners?"

Slater chuckled. "You lawyers crack me up with your fancy language. Disagreement? I suppose you could say the Civil War was a fucking disagreement. Hell, yes. We had a disagreement. And, yes. My wife was present."

I made a note in my book. I did my best to stifle the anger building inside me. I took a deep breath and looked at Slater. "You gave me the impression last time that it didn't amount to much. Just a request for them to move their vehicle so you could get your car out of the garage. You said you had the impression they thought it was funny about your having to wait. You never mentioned that your wife was present."

"I got in late the night before. I asked her nicely if she could ask those guys to move their truck. She wouldn't do it. I asked her again, and she refused. I had some plans. I had to be somewhere. She knew it. I was late. I had to take matters into my own hands."

"And?" I arched an eyebrow at him.

"And nothing. I told the fucking wetbacks to move their fucking truck. End of story."

"And?"

"They wouldn't do it, so I did. The keys were in the truck, so I moved it for them."

"You moved the truck? You didn't mention that before."

He glared at me. "You didn't ask me before."

We were getting nowhere fast. One thing, however, was certain. Slater remembered more than he was willing to talk about. That realization bothered the hell out of me. I ended the meeting with the admonition to him not to talk to anyone and left the jail with more questions than when I arrived.

CHAPTER 35

We received a firm trial date on Slater. I had put off contacting Alex Hartley as long as I could. Now, I had no choice but to take a chance on talking him into testifying. He was an ideal potential expert witness. Given his earlier reaction, I had looked elsewhere without having too much success. I still hadn't found the person who fit the bill quite as well as he did. I called for an appointment and went to his office at the designated time.

"This is a bad drug." Hartley shrugged his shoulders. "A bad drug."

I studied the man's face. It'd been a long time since I'd seen him. Not since the DES cases ended nearly twenty years ago. We had worked well together in that litigation, but it had ended badly between the two of us. Hartley's career had been placed in jeopardy when he was accused of fraud in the conduct of a study that served as the scientific basis for my case. He and a co-worker demonstrated a strong relationship between pregnant mothers taking a potent synthetic female hormone and the occurrence of damaged immune systems and homosexuality in the male offspring of those pregnancies. The cases ended abruptly when several witnesses came forward at the end of the trial and exposed the perpetrators of the false claim of scientific fraud. I made a lot of money for my clients and for myself. The massive settlement was subject to a protective order, so Hartley was prevented from going public with his vindication--with the information about what the drug company had tried to do to him.

I knew that Hartley blamed me for the situation--that he held me personally responsible for the dilemma of not being able to go public. What I didn't realize over the years since was that many of his colleagues in the medical community didn't realize that he'd been clearedof the charges against him. He'd gone on and developed a national reputation in pharmacology, the study of drugs, but I now understood that a taint from the fraud charges still lingered. From time to time since the DES fiasco, I had tried speaking with Hartley about potential cases involving serious drug reactions, but he always declined to speak with me.

So I was surprised, but pleased, when he agreed to talk and meet with me about Serenity. Hartley had seen both Slater and Mrs. Scruggs as patients.

"What makes it so bad?"

"I don't know the answer to that yet. I suspect it's a dose-related problem. Did you know the drug has been banned in every country in the world except Australia and the United States?"

"Why did the other countries ban the drug?" I knew the answer. I wanted to hear what Hartley had to say.

He sat back in his chair. Thought for a moment. Not much had changed in his physical appearance in the past twenty years. He had the same slender build. Obviously he'd taken good care of himself. A tint a gray coursed through his thick, dark brown hair. He looked like a distinguished kid, I thought.

He said, "The better question is why only two countries in the world would permit its use."

"The company has friends in high places. Did you know that the previous chief of the new drug section at the FDA recently became the president of Upright?"

"I knew that. A revolving door in the chicken coop so the fox can come and go." Hartley did not smile at his own quip.

I hesitated. Finally, I took the plunge. Here goes nothing. "Are you willing to work with me on these cases? I really need your help."

Hartley mulled over the question. "You being here stirs up terrible memories. I've done a good job trying to forget what happened. I don't want to go through anything like that again. The answer is no."

It was quiet in the small room. Hartley's office was tucked away at the end of the corridor on the second floor of Detroit General Hospital. Through the closed door, I could hear the muffled sounds of the loudspeaker paging various hospital personnel. I looked down at my shoes. They needed a shine.

"From what I've heard, you're the most knowledgeable scientist in the country about this drug." I stopped. Hartley was staring at me.

His face turned crimson. "I said forget it. Go try your bullshit flattery on someone else. You see that door behind you?"

I looked over my shoulder and nodded. "Don't let in hit you in the ass on the way out."

Hartley waved dismissively and turned his attention to the papers on his desk. I sat motionless for a moment. Then I stood and left the office.

CHAPTER 36

Hartley's rejection made me seek other potential expert witnesses. I couldn't help but think that, without his participation, the Slater case would be significantly compromised because I wouldn't have the advocate that I needed in front of a jury. In Slater's case, it seemed to me that Hartley would be even more important because he also had treated Slater. Of course, I had the option of issuing a subpoena to him to compel his appearance, but that was hardly a guarantee he would say something in front of a jury that needed to be said in favor of Slater.

Because of Hartley's rejection, I needed to find someone who knew what was going on and would be willing to testify--someone who would be a credible witness. I had Schneidermann, but he was a shrink, not a scientist. I needed a scientist in the courtroom to explain things to the jury. Schneidermann would be good in his own arena of psychiatry, but not in the scientific realm.

I made an appointment and flew to Buffalo, New York, to meet with a man who was highly regarded by a couple of my lawyer friends who did the same kind of trial work I did. Professor Arthur Cartwright was the prototype college professor. Rotund and balding, bifocals perched on the end of his nose, he was dressed in jeans, white shirt, a narrow tie that was loosened at the neck, and a corduroy sports coat with leather patches on the sleeves. He looked at me over the top of his glasses and gestured at the materials on his desk that I'd sent him.

"The pattern of these adverse reactions is amazingly consistent. Each one of these people experiences a period of amnesia after taking the drug for fifteen to twenty days. During the period of amnesia, some have gone on to commit bizarre acts, including suicide, murder, and other acts of violence." He paused to check if I was listening. "It's the amnesia that makes this drug so unique and interesting."

This guy was certainly no Alex Hartley, I thought. A little too smug. Cartwright leaned forward. "You stopped listening a few moments ago, Mr. Riley. Is this subject matter too difficult for you to understand? Am I going too fast?"

My attention snapped back to the present. "I'm sorry. I wandered a bit. I was trying to relate this amnesia information to my clients' cases."

I sat up straighter and looked him right in the eye. Prick. His pompous attitude was exceeded only by his rudeness. He was one of the leading neurobiologists in the world, but the guy had a short fuse coupled with an ego that needed constant attention. This might cause some problems in the courtroom. Jurors hated arrogant know-it-all witnesses. I had a bad feeling where this was all going. There was nothing I could do about it without Hartley on my team.

"Is there a logical explanation for how this happens?"

"Yes, there is." Cartwright gloated, obviously pleased with my discomfort. "The time period from the beginning of therapy with Serenity until the onset of amnesia, as I said, is in the range of fifteen to twenty days. This suggests to me a toxic buildup of the drug. Not everyone reacts in this manner, of course, but perhaps a few unfortunate individuals are unable to metabolize the drug properly either via the liver or the kidneys, with the net result that high levels of the drug remain in the body. Probably because these users are missing some enzyme that most people have, they cannot remove the drug as efficiently, and each successive dose causes a greater and greater toxic level in the body."

Now, we're getting someplace, I thought. "Is there a test for this? Can these people be identified?"

Cartwright smirked. "No. As I said, this is theoretical. Of course, it is based on my own sound theoretical analysis, but it is as yet scientifically unproven."

We sat in silence, looking at each other. I had something to tell him, but I didn't know quite how to say it. If Cartwright's opinion was based on theory alone, no judge would ever permit him to venture an opinion in a courtroom. Any such opinion would be rejected as conjecture--speculation. Cartwright might be able to regale his students or fellow scientists with his brilliance and his theories, but the common courtroom required something more concrete. How to tell this guy this was my problem.

"Doctor, let me ask you. Have you ever testified before?" I sat back, picked at a loose thread on my coat jacket, and waited for his answer.

Cartwright sipped his coffee, brushed his hand through his hair, and picked at the sleeves of his starched lab coat. "No. As you know, I have reviewed some matters for several of your colleagues. I've been asked to testify several times, but it's not something I've ever wanted to do--until this drug came along. It bothers me a great deal that so many innocent people are being hurt."

I was touched by his vulnerability. It came as a surprise. I didn't expect it. His heart is in the right place, I thought. I risked alienating him if I told him that his opinion would be rejected unless there was some scientific basis to back it up. Maybe I could devise a game plan that would limit the scope of his testimony and still permit him to render an opinion. His credentials were outstanding, and the jury would be impressed. "If you were going to test your theory, what would you do?"

"I know exactly what I'd do. I would conduct a series of animal experiments and see if I could replicate this pattern that is being seen."

I rubbed my chin. "What would that cost?" Somehow the idea of a trial lawyer paying for basic research that should have been done by a goddamned drug company just didn't feel right.

"Twenty-five grand." No hesitation. Cartwright had thought about this in advance.

"Upright has already done animal studies. I sent copies of their research to you. What would be the purpose of repeating them?" Twenty-five thousand dollars was a lot of money. I thought back to my partners' objections to getting involved in these damned cases.

They would blow their stacks if they knew that I was having this conversation.

"Mr. Riley, you surprise me. Do you really think that the company's studies would show any problems? You should be a minister rather than a lawyer." He grinned, showing fang-like, tobacco-stained teeth. "Upright did studies, but none of them were run long enough to detect problems. Testing animals for one to three months would measure the impact of this drug on the central nervous system of the animals. The old adage fits here. 'If you don't look for something, you're not going to find it.' Well, Upright wasn't looking. They sure as hell weren't looking. I read somewhere that Kenneth Smythe signed off on the studies that were submitted. I know of Smythe, and he has an excellent reputation. Quite frankly, I'm surprised that a respectable scientist like him would sign off on these studies."

"Smythe?"

"Yes. Kenneth Smythe. Dr. Kenneth Smythe. His signature is on the letter of transmittal to the FDA with respect to these studies."

Other than Cartwright, I had few others I could rely on to present a compelling case to a jury. Schneidermann would be good, but what I was lacking at the moment was good information about what this drug was doing to people. What I really needed to know about the drug was what Upright knew. Based on my past experiences with Upright, I would be certain that the company was hiding problems. What I really needed was an insider from the company who knew about Serenity and would be willing to talk to me about it. True, I could always take depositions of company employees, but lawyers who had spent hours preparing them for their testimony would surround them.

But for now I had to go with Cartwright. The two of us agreed to give the animal research possibility more thought. As I flew back to Detroit I realized the meeting with Cartwright had raised more questions than answers.

CHAPTER 37

Levitt glared at Emrich. "You're pissing off some pretty important people."

She hesitated. "I'm not sure what you're talking about."

"Don't play dumb with me. It doesn't suit you. Tell me what's going on."

"Why don't you tell me what you're talking about?" She already knew, but wanted to hear what he had to say.

He smirked "Talked to your buddy Ken Smythe lately?"

"I don't know what you are talking about."

"It's been reported to me that you made twelve phone calls to Smythe's laboratory office yesterday. What do you have to say about that?"

"I didn't talk to Ken Smythe yesterday. You better check your source of information."

"I didn't say you talked to him. I said you called his office twelve times. You couldn't have talked to him because he was hospitalized in a nuthouse two days ago. You have to be careful about the company you keep."

She hesitated again. "I know nothing about that."

Levitt glared at her for a long moment. "Don't speak to me in that tone of voice, and don't lie to me. Just sit there and listen. There are two points you need to keep in mind. First, you are the chief investigator for the FDA on this drug. If you do what I think you are planning to do, the big question will be how you missed it in the first place. You will be blamed. Second, there are over forty employees in this agency who will be leaving in the next two years. The only place these people can go is to the drug industry. Someday, you'll want to get out of here too, and the same limitations will still be there. However, you step on the wrong toes, and the only job you'll ever find is slinging hash in some diner."

He stopped and then continued, "Let me put it another way, Jan. Have you ever heard the saying 'don't bite the hand that feeds you?'"

She had to be careful about what she said.

"I'm really disappointed to hear you say these things, Mort."

He sat there soberly. "Don't get sanctimonious with me."

Emrich stood. She didn't know what to say or do. She just knew that she had to get out of Levitt's presence. She walked to the door.

"I'm not through. This is a warning to you. Smythe is in a nuthouse because he's been making some outrageous claims about the safety of Serenity. If you listen to his bullshit or try to do something about it, you will regret it."

She stood there. She didn't know what to say. The look in Levitt's eyes chilled her to the bone.

Levitt flicked his hand like he was swatting a fly. "Get the hell out of my sight."

As she left the office, she was frightened. What in the hell was she going to do?

CHAPTER 38

Two weeks from the day he was seized and taken to the psychiatric hospital, Smythe was cleared by the doctor to return to work. He had sat around since his release doing nothing. He was glad to get out of the house. He walked into his lab and looked around. He nodded at several of his co-workers. It was good to be back, but felt strange.

"Welcome back."

He mumbled his thanks. His legs felt leaden, and he moved slowly to his office. He sat behind his desk.

Lisa Bernsdorf walked into the office and looked at him.

"Ken, you look like crap."

"I feel like crap."

"What did they do to you?"

"I'm not sure. I don't remember much."

"You look like you're stoned."

"That's how I feel."

"You think they did this to you because of Serenity?"

"I know they did."

"What drugs do they have you on? How much medication are you taking? Whatever it is, you've got to stop. You're a zombie."

"They let me come back to work because I agreed to continue the medication. Messner said, if I didn't take it, he'd remove me from any responsibilities for Serenity."

"Those bastards. They want to shut you up."

"They're doing a good job of it. I have a hard time remembering my name."

Lisa looked around and then spoke softly, "You've got them worried as hell. You've got to do something. You've got to let the FDA know what's going on."

"I don't know if I'm up to it. I have a hard time just getting out of bed and dressed."

Lisa was alarmed. This was not the Ken Smythe she knew. "Ken, you have to stop taking whatever it is they have you on."

He looked at her dully. "I told you. I need to take the medication to keep my job."

She wanted to cry. Serenity was killing people, and the company she worked for was deliberately eliminating the one guy who could do something about it.

CHAPTER 39

Dockery was pestering Anne Smythe. He kept on calling. "Can we meet? Can I come over?" He always called when Ken was at work and the children were at school.

She knew what he wanted, but she avoided the situation by putting him off. "Not now" or "Not today" were her usual excuses. She thought she'd rebuffed him successfully until he appeared on her doorstep with a bottle of Jack Daniels inside his briefcase in the middle of the day. She didn't want him standing out on the porch where the neighbors could see him, so she let him in.

"I wish you would have called first. I am really busy today."

"I have called a lot, and you always turn me down."

He went directly to the kitchen, took out two water glasses, and filled each halfway with the liquor. He walked back into the living room and handed one of the drinks to Anne.

"I can't do this." She stood wringing her hands.

"You should do this. Let me tell you why. You owe me. I haven't asked for much. I never submitted a bill for my services. Is it asking too much to have the pleasure of your company for a few minutes?"

"If I start drinking, I can't stop. That's why I can't get started. Ken will be home in a couple of hours. My children will be home in an hour."

"You know that I know all about you. I know all about your escapades of picking men up in bars and going to bed with them."

"I told you that stuff in confidence." She cringed at the thought of what he knew of her past. "I need you to leave."

"I'm not leaving until I get what I came for."

She picked up the glass of liquor and threw it in his face. "I said leave. Right now, or I'm calling the police."

His face reddened. He slowly wiped his face with the sleeve of his sports jacket.

"And just what will you tell the police when they get here? That you undressed for me last time and gave me a blow job, but you don't want to do it anymore?"

"You're lying. You're making that up."

"Who do you think they'll believe? Better yet, who do you think your husband will believe?"

"You're lying."

"And you were too drunk to know better. I'm sure your husband will love that excuse."

"Just leave me alone."

"I can't. I want you."

"Please leave."

"No. Not until I get what I came for."

Anne felt helpless. She felt dirty, debased. Sad. This is never going to end.

"I'm not proud of my past, but it's different now. I made the mistake of drinking with you. I'm not going to do it again. You say we had sex, but I don't remember. If we did, I can tell you that it's not going to happen again. I will call the police if you don't leave. I'll tell them you tried to rape me. That should really boost your law practice. A reputation for raping clients' wives."

"I like this. It makes me hard when you get mad."

"You've got two minutes to get your sorry ass out of here."

She dug into her purse and brought out her cell phone, held it in front of her, ready to dial. "I'm counting."

He stood and walked towards the front door. "Take your bottle with you."

He turned. The look on his face froze her heart. "Lady, I'm leaving that as a reminder that this is not over. Sooner or later, you are going to regret this."

After he walked out, she locked and bolted the door. Her hands shook. She was afraid. She was angry. She busied herself by emptying the whiskey bottle in the sink and throwing the empty bottle in the trash. She washed the two glasses and put them in the cupboard. Why would Upright hire a sleazy lawyer like Dockery? What kind of company did Kenny work for? She sat in the living room and cried.

What a mess. She cried until it was time to pick the kids up from school. When she got back to the house with the children, the phone was ringing. She answered, hoping it wasn't Dockery.

"Mrs. Smythe?" It was a pleasant female voice.

"Yes. Who's calling?"

"My name is Lisa Bernsdorf. I work with your husband."

"Is he all right? Did something happen?"

"No. He's right at work here. Busy in the lab. I'm calling from my cell phone on my break because I need to talk with you about him."

"Why? What about?"

"Mrs. Smythe, I realize I'm taking a big chance on calling. Your husband is acting strange. Since he got back to work, he's different. I think the medication he's taking is too strong. He's like a zombie."

"I know. The doctor said he needs to continue it for awhile until he starts feeling better."

"That's what I wanted to talk to you about. I don't think it's the doctor who's making that decision. I think it's his boss who wants to keep him quiet."

"Quiet about what?"

"The drug he did so much work on. Serenity."

Anne already knew the answer to the question she was going to ask next. She wanted to hear what Bernsdorf's would say.

"Why would they want to keep him quiet about Serenity?"

"I . . . I don't know how to answer that question, Mrs. Smythe. I don't know how much you know about the drug or how much Doctor Smythe told you about his concerns."

"I probably know more than you think." A lot more, she thought.

"Let me say this first. I work with your husband, right alongside him in his lab. I cannot think of a scientist here at Upright who I respect more for integrity than your husband. Before he went into the hospital, he was upset about reports coming in that showed that the drug was doing terrible things to people. He talked to his bosses, and they didn't want to hear it."

"I'm not sure why you're telling me this." After her experience with Dockery, she didn't know if she could trust anybody associated with Upright.

"I think he should stop taking whatever he's on."

Anne thought about it. Since coming home from the hospital, Kenny had acted strange. She had no reason to question his medication. The doctor has seemed sincere in his reasons. "And why do you think that?"

"Your husband told me that Mr. Messner, the big boss, told him he had to stay on the drug or else he couldn't come back to work."

Anne wondered why Kenny hadn't mentioned that to her. "I didn't know that."

Bernsdorf hesitated. "I hope you don't think I am trying to cause trouble. I'm just really concerned about your husband."

Anne thought for a moment. She wondered if Kenny had something going with this girl. She remembered that Kenny had remarked how cute Bernsdorf was. Was this the reason for the girl's concern? On the other hand, who was she to judge when she thought about what happened between her and Dockery?

166

"I'll talk to my husband tonight. I won't tell him you called me."

"I don't mind if you do tell him. I'm concerned about him--his safety."

After Bernsdorf's call, Anne sat down and thought. She went back through the events as she recalled them. She felt a flash of shame when she remembered the hard time she gave Kenny when he wanted to do something about Serenity. Lisa is right, she thought. He's got to get off that drug. She wanted her husband back--the loving, caring and concerned husband. Screw Serenity.

After the children were in bed, she and Ken sat down at the kitchen table. "We need to talk."

"About?" Ken looked at her dully. "I'm tired. Can this wait?"

"No. It can't wait. Kenny, I love you. I want you to stop taking the drug. You're not yourself. I don't think it's helping you. I think it's hurting you."

"I need to take it."

"Why? She wanted to hear if what Bernsdorf had said was true.

"They let me come back to work on the condition I take the drug."

"They? Who is 'they?'"

"Messner. Hagstrom."

"You're telling me that it's Messner and Hagstrom--not your doctor--who want you to stay on the drug?"

"The doctor will do whatever Upright tells him to do."

"Why do you say that?"

"He works for Upright."

"You're telling me that the doctor who placed you in a mental institution and still treats you works for Upright?"

Ken nodded. "He told me."

"Kenny, why didn't you tell me this? Do you realize why they are doing this to you?"

"I suppose."

"You suppose? What kind of answer is that? There is no 'suppose' about it. They did this to shut you up about Serenity."

"I'm tired. I'm going to bed." Ken stood slowly and left the room. Anne sat for a moment. She knew what she had to do. She followed Ken upstairs, went into the bathroom and locked the door behind her. She removed the prescription bottle from the cabinet, emptied all the tablets in the toilet, and flushed them. She filled the empty bottle with aspirin.

Ken knocked at the door. "I need to take my medication before I go to bed."

"I'll get it for you." She opened the medicine cabinet. He watched while she took a tablet from the prescription bottle. She handed it to him with a glass of water.

"I feel a lot better this morning." Ken smiled at his wife across the kitchen table.

"You look a lot better."

"I feel like a new person."

He smiled again. She returned the smile. Welcome back, she thought.

CHAPTER 40

"Hello."

"Who's this?" I shrugged my shoulders and scowled. I was busy. The female voice on the phone was vaguely familiar, but I couldn't place it. I was in no mood for guessing games

"You don't remember? You ought to be ashamed of yourself." A little giggle.

Jesus Christ. What was this? Fucking twenty questions?

"Just tell me who you are. What can I do for you?"

Another giggle. "You sure know how to hurt a poor girl's feelings. You used to know exactly what you could do for me."

I searched my memory and came up blank.

"Look, whoever you are. I've got a busy day going here, and I really don't have time to play this silly game. Tell me who you are and what you want, and I'll listen. If not, this conversation is over."

"My, my, aren't we the somber one? I'll give you a hint." Another giggle. "Remember a big couch in the living room of your apartment at college?"

"Linda?" My God! It was Linda Easterbrook. I felt my face redden

"Bobby. I'm disappointed it took you so long."

"It's been a long time." I shuffled the phone on my shoulder and checked my watch. I was running late.

Linda said, "Could we get together for old time's sake?"

I hesitated. Since my divorce, I'd given no time and less thought to a male-female relationship of any sort. None. Nada.

"Can I take your number and get back to you?"

"Jesus, Bobby. I'm not in a butcher shop waiting to have you call my number. I am a friend. If you want me to get lost, just say so. Just don't give me the 'I'll get back to you' crap."

"Linda, I'm sorry. I'm not trying to be rude. It's just that . . . I haven't had much of a social life lately. Lots of trials. That sort of stuff."

"I heard about you and Peg. I'm sorry."

I felt a visceral reaction at the mention of my ex-wife.

"I've got to get to court. I'm already late. Do you know where Dunleavy's is? We could meet at Dunleavy's about five for a drink? How does that sound?"

"That would be wonderful, Bobby, I'll be there."

I hung up the phone and sat motionless for a few minutes. The divorce had been an abject lesson in controlling my feelings. In order to survive the pain of separation, I taught myself how to shut down, forget the past, and deal only in the present--one moment at a time. All the joy of living was gone--torn apart at the seams. My friends told me that I'd stopped smiling. They missed my stories--the twinkle in my eye as I wove fact and fiction together, just to make them laugh. I shuddered. I avoided my feelings by keeping myself busy. I hated having time on my hands. Free time led to thinking, and thinking led to feeling sorry for myself. Twenty years ago, a call from Linda Easterbrook would have sent a surge of testosterone right through me and made it damn near impossible to think about anything else. Instead, the planned meeting was just another item on an already crowded calendar.

I stood, checked my watch again, and packed my briefcase for the motion in Judge Flick's courtroom.

Linda looked as good as I'd remembered. She was sitting at the bar. As I approached, she swirled on the bar stool toward me.

I walked up and pecked her on the cheek.

"You look great. Haven't changed a bit." And I meant it.'

She looked brightly at me, her face was slightly flushed. She looked pretty hot.

"Thank you. You have changed. You were always a hunk, but now you're so . . . handsome."

I squared my shoulders and tightened my abdominal muscles.

"I see that your taste in men hasn't improved." I smiled, and she laughed aloud, reached over, and patted the seat of the bar stool next to hers.

"Sit. Saved this just for you."

I gestured toward the back of the room. "Why don't we sit at one of the tables?"

Wordlessly, she slid gracefully off the bar stool and walked in front of me to a booth at the back of the room. I noticed that most of the men in the bar watched until she sat down.

Her skirt was short. She wore a lacy powder blue sheer blouse covering a white shell, which nicely accentuated both her trim figure and pale blue eyes. I flashed back to the times when she would sit naked next to me on the couch in the living room of my college apartment. Not much had changed. She looked as good today as she did then. Better. I felt a bead of perspiration form on my upper lip. Before I could react, she leaned across the table and touched it with her index finger. She slowly withdrew her hand.

"Do I make you nervous?" Impish little grin.

"I feel a little awkward. The way we ended things, and all that." In fact, I felt like a heel. I'd ended the torrid romance abruptly. The best sex of my life for six months. Then no phone calls, no further contact, no apology, no explanation. Over. Just as quickly as that. Nothing. Period. Until her phone call earlier today.

She smiled at me. "I don't know that 'we' is the right word. I must admit that, at first, I was hurt. Then I heard about you and Peg. I've never been one to make trouble--get in the way. So I just let it go. I've learned a lot since then. Let bygones be bygones." She lifted her glass and offered a toast. "To good friends."

"That's very kind of you." I fumbled for something else to say. "Would you like another drink?"

"Sure." She smiled again, slid her empty glass toward me, her fingers lightly touching mine. "Chardonnay, please."

I stood. Too fast. Almost upended the table into her lap.

"Sorry. A little clumsy. I'll go get it from the bartender. If we wait for the waitress, it'll take forever with this crowd."

I avoided looking back at the booth while I waited for the bartender to fill the drink order. One glass of wine for her, scotch on the rocks for me. That ought to smooth out my discomfort. I felt her eyes on me as I returned.

"Watch out. Clumsy oaf closing in."

"I can't wait, Mr. Oaf." Her eyes sparkled.

I sat down, raised my glass, and she did likewise.

"Now, a proper toast. To old--No, Forget old. To friends."

She gently tapped her glass against mine.

I took a sip and waited for the warming sensation in the pit of my stomach.

I looked at her. "Did I tell you how good you look?"

"It's only been twenty years. I'm not ready for the nursing home yet."

It's been twenty-seven years, but who's counting? I thought. "Forget the nursing home. Try the Miss America pageant."

She flashed a brilliant smile. "Flattery will get you everywhere." She leaned forward again, patted my hand, and looked directly into my eyes. The touch jolted me like an electrical current. I sat back, picked up my glass and emptied it.

"Ready?" She nodded, and I edged my way out of the booth.

"Be right back." I ordered another scotch for me and another wine for her. As I carried the drinks back to where we were sitting, I nearly laughed aloud.

"Why the big grin? What's the secret?"

I slid back into place after placing the drinks on the table. "I was just thinking about one of the laws of thermodynamics." I smiled.

"And what would that be?"

I held my glass up in a mock toast. "Not saying." I grinned. Took a big swallow. The closer a guy gets to a good-looking woman, I thought, the hotter the temperature. I looked at her. She looked good--real good. The alcohol was definitely having an effect.

"That's not fair." She pouted.

"So tell me. What possessed you to call me after all these years?" Change the subject. Turn the heat down a bit.

She looked down at her empty glass. "I was wondering when you were going to ask. I have a big favor to ask."

Here it comes. I knew there must have been a reason other than just her wanting to see me after all these years. I raised my glass again. "Ask, and ye shall receive."

She fidgeted with the glass. "Bobby, I've heard through the grapevine that you are looking for a paralegal. I need a job. I've worked as a legal assistant and kept my skills up, but I need a job. Real bad." She bit her lower lip, and I thought she was going to start crying.

"Is that all? I can help. You're right. We are looking for someone."

She paused. "I'd like to work for you. I know I could be a big help." She leaned forward and placed her hand on top of mine.

I thought back to a conversation with Gary Newton. The timing was good. Gary was looking for somebody to organize the Serenity file. I could assign her to Gary. I ran the potential ramifications through my mind. Forget about what Peg might think. That didn't matter anymore. As far as Peg knew, we were just old friends anyway. I smiled to myself.

Maybe I ought to find out more about her qualifications before I made the leap.

"I know what you're thinking." She smiled. "You're wondering about whether or not I've got what it takes. The answer is yes. I've been with Forbush and Jampolski in Ann Arbor for the past five years . . . as a litigation specialist."

I was impressed, but puzzled. Forbush and Jampolski was a silk stocking corporate law firm--a take no prisoners, spare no expense firm. They started first-year lawyers at an annual salary higher than most Michigan lawyers would ever dream of making, and they were well-known for taking real good care of their personnel. Something didn't fit. A couple of questions popped into my mind. "Why did you leave? I know what they pay their employees. How can I afford you?"

"One of the senior partners tried to hit on me a couple of months ago. Cornered me in an elevator. Touched my breast. I rejected him. Made the big mistake of not reporting him immediately. Since then, he's made my life a living hell. I quit two weeks ago. Couldn't take it anymore." She started sniffling, dug a Kleenex out of her purse, and blew her nose. "As for the money, I know now that I'd rather do something I can believe in. Money is secondary."

I studied her face. I tried to focus, but my thinking was a little fuzzy around the edges from the scotch. I saw no downside. If she worked for Forbush and Jampolski, she certainly knew what the hell she was doing. I was going to hire somebody. Why not an old friend? No apparent negatives.

I grinned. "When can you start?"

"You mean you'll hire me?"

"You're hired."

"I can start right away. Tomorrow." She slid out of the booth, leaned over, and kissed me on the mouth.

"Let me get the next round. A celebration drink."

I watched as she strode to the bar. Everyone else in the place did, too. I looked forward to working with her. Old friend, good friend, Linda. I felt like smiling for the first time in a long time.

By the end of her first day at the office, Linda had shown me enough to dispel all doubts. She was all business, and she knew what she was doing. Upright had already inundated us with documents, and the prosecutor in Slater's case was sending us half a box of written materials every day. Before Linda arrived, we all stood around and just looked at the boxes, scratched our heads, and wondered what the hell we were going to do with them.

Not so with Linda. By four o'clock her first day, she'd set up a system for reviewing and analyzing the materials that was simple and easy. I felt stupid for not thinking of it first.

And so it went. Day after day. Linda demonstrated her skills and acumen in matters large and small, making my job--our job--much easier.

And she was nice. Within two weeks, she had everybody in the firm, including the secretaries, eating out of her hand. The secretaries, usually the toughest nuts to crack--particularly with a new attractive employee--became her biggest advocates. She helped them. They helped her. Honest to God, she was good.

CHAPTER 41

"Lisa, can you come in here for a minute?" Smythe sat at his desk. Bernsdorf walked into his office and sat down. Smythe stood and shut the door.

"I'm missing some files. Files on Serenity."

"While you were gone, Mr. Messner asked me to pull your Serenity file and send it to him."

"I was afraid that might happen."

"Ken, I made a copy before I took it over."

"You did?"

"Yes. We both know why he wanted it. He wanted to shut you down. I took my copy home. I'll bring it over to your house. I don't think he should know you have it."

"I agree. Bring it over Saturday. Come for dinner."

"I'll just drop it by. I have other plans for Saturday night, but thanks.

On Saturday morning, Lisa rang the Smythe doorbell. Anne answered the door wearing shorts and a t-shirt. Lisa had on the same.

"Mrs. Smythe. I'm Lisa Bernsdorf. I told your husband I would drop a package off for him today." She handed Anne a bulky manila folder.

"Can you come in for a minute? Ken is not home, but I'd like to talk."

They sat at the kitchen table.

Anne smiled at the young woman, "I can't thank you enough for bringing the drug information to my attention."

"It's obvious that you acted on it right away."

"I've got to confess something. It's important that you know."

Bernsdorf raised an eyebrow. "What is it?"

"Ken thinks he's still taking the medication. I tossed it out and put aspirin in the prescription bottle."

"You didn't tell him?"

"No. This way I figured that if they ask him if he was still taking the drug he wouldn't have to lie about it. He's not a very good liar."

Lisa laughed. Anne joined in. She walked Lisa to the door and they shared a hug before Lisa left. Anne thought about her as she drove away. She had made a good friend in Lisa.

CHAPTER 42

I had a sleepless night thinking about what needed to be done for Slater's trial. I left early for the office and by the time others arrived, I was ready to dole out assignments. As soon as Linda settled at her desk, I called her into my office.

"Linda, can you check and see if we have a file on an Upright employee named Ken Smythe?"

She looked up, "I will check. Where does he fit in?"

"His name appears on the animal studies. I've read these studies. He also signed the new drug application submission to the FDA. A couple of things don't fit. I need to take his deposition."

She returned after a few minutes later, "Mary sent a letter to defense counsel asking for his deposition and they responded saying that Smythe had left the company. They said his address and whereabouts are unknown."

"Try the telephone directory. Maybe he left on bad terms. A disgruntled former employee can be a treasure trove of information. If he's no longer with the company, I can talk to him without their lawyers hanging around."

"I will do that."

"Also send defense counsel a letter. Ask for Smythe's last known address. Ask for his personnel file. Let's try to get this stuff quickly. I have a feeling about this guy."

"I'll try."

A week later, Linda came into my office and placed a letter on my desk.

"What's this?"

"We heard back about our request for information on Mr. Smythe."

"And?"

"They've changed their position. They now claim that he is still an employee, but he's unavailable for health reasons. They won't provide his home address because they say he's still an employee."

I read the letter. This was strange. Why would they do this? It kept me from speaking to the guy without an Upright lawyer present. I thought for a moment. I wondered if I could speak to him in Slater's case because we were not suing Upright in that case. This was another difference between criminal and civil cases again. In a criminal case, you didn't have to notify the other side that you were going to talk to a witness.

I made a note to have the law clerks research the right of a lawyer to interview a potential witness in a criminal case when that witness is an employee of a company in litigation with the lawyer on another matter. I didn't know the answer but I suspected that I'd have to take the question to Judge Flick by way of a motion. I wanted to avoid that route if I could, because Upright's lawyers would then know about my intentions.

"Did you find his home phone number?"

"No. It's unlisted. But you can't call him anyway, can you?"

"No, I can't. But, if he's married, I could speak with his wife if we had the number. Hell, if the guy's got health problems, she'll probably be pleased to think someone is interested. Get me the number somehow." Upright's waffling on Smythe's status raised my index of suspicion that they were trying to keep him away from me.

I didn't ask how she did it, but an hour later Linda came back with the Smythe phone number. I picked up my phone and dialed the number.

"Hello. Smythe residence."

"Hello. Is this the home of Mr. Kenneth Smythe?"

"Dr. Kenneth Smythe? Yes, it is. Who's calling?" The pleasant female voice was wary.

"Is this Mrs. Smythe?"

"Yes. Who's calling?"

"Mrs. Smythe, my name is Bob Riley, and I'm an attorney representing a couple of people who took a drug made by the company your husband works for."

"This is about Serenity, isn't it?"

I hesitated. "Yes, it is. I need to ask . . ."

"Not over the phone. Can we meet? Some place in person?" She was whispering.

"Of course." I whispered my response.

She continued to whisper, "How soon can we meet? I can be anywhere you want within the hour."

I checked my schedule. "I'm completely jammed today. Is this evening good? Tomorrow morning?" Why were we whispering, I wondered?

"Can you be at Angela's Café, Bistro and Seventh, in Ann Arbor at seven o'clock tonight?"

I didn't have the slightest idea where Angela's Café was, but I'd find out. "I'll be there."

I walked over to Linda's cubicle. "Good job on getting that number. I think we have our first big break in the case."

The day passed slowly. My afternoon meetings dragged, and I guarded against checking my watch every minute. My last appointment of the day ended earlier than planned. It was nearly four o'clock. Three hours until the meeting. I couldn't remember the last time I'd been this excited about meeting a potential witness. I'd thought about the meeting with Smythe's wife in my mind constantly during the day. She had some vital piece of information that was going to blow this case wide open. I could tell by the urgency of her voice on the phone call.

My phone rang. I answered.

"Bob. This is Lester Hempstead. We've scheduled an emergency motion with Flick at five o'clock in his chambers."

I looked at my watch. "That's less than an hour from now. What's the rush? Can't it wait?"

"I'm afraid not."

"What's it about?"

"You'll have to wait to find out when you get there."

"What's going on? I'm entitled to some notice."

"Just be there. You'll find out."

Forty minutes later, Hempstead and I were seated in the two chairs across the desk from Judge Flick in his chambers. Two of Hempstead's minions sat on the backless bench placed against the wall. The judge nodded at Hempstead to begin.

"Judge. I appreciate your agreeing to hear us on such short notice."

Flick smiled. "Lester, you know me well enough to know that I'm available to the parties anytime." The judge's patronizing attitude almost made me gag.

Hempstead began, "Judge, we have an emergency situation that requires your immediate attention. As you are well aware, it is improper for a lawyer to directly contact an employee of a defendant who is represented by counsel without notifying that counsel."

I sat up straight. By no means was the law as settled as that.

The judge nodded. "I know that."

Hempstead continued. "We've been advised that, this afternoon, Mr. Riley spoke with the wife of one of our key employees and has scheduled a meeting with her at seven o'clock this evening. I am here seeking to prevent this meeting from taking place."

I felt my face redden. What the hell is going on? Why would this woman sound so desperate to meet with me, but then report my contact with her to the lawyers? It didn't make sense.

The smile disappeared from the judge's face when he looked at me. "I am assuming that Mr. Hempstead is telling me the truth. How could you do such a thing? You know the law as well as I do."

I took a deep breath. "Your Honor, it is true that I spoke with the wife. Counsel here," I nodded toward Hempstead, " . . . answered my request to take her husband's deposition with a letter to me telling me that the man left the company. If he left the company, I can talk to him."

Hempstead interrupted. "Judge, as usual, Mr. Riley tells you half of the story. We sent a follow-up letter to him stating that the employee was still employed by my client, but was on a medical leave of absence. That means he can't talk to him . . . or his wife, either."

Flick stared coolly at me. "I've heard quite enough. Quite frankly, I'm a little disappointed in you, Mr. Riley."

"Judge--," I started to respond.

Flick held up his hand. "I said I've heard enough. Your planned meeting is not going forward." He stared hard at me. "You are to have no further contact with this woman, her husband, or anybody else affiliated with the defendant unless Mr. Hempstead is notified. Do I make myself clear?"

I glared back. Bit my lip. "Yes."

Anne Smythe waited in the Angel's Café until eight o'clock before she decided that the lawyer was not going to show. She checked her watch, shrugged her shoulders, stuffed the thick manila envelope back in her purse, paid her tab at the counter, and left for home. It was strange, she thought, that the lawyer was so eager to meet when they spoke on the phone, yet he failed to show.

CHAPTER 43

Smythe called Emrich from home.

Emrich was more than eager to hear from him. "Where have you been? I've been trying to reach you."

Smythe paused, "It's a long story. I've got a lot of documents. I've got some things to tell you as well."

Emrich spoke softly. "You should know this. I got caught trying to reach you. Upright monitored the calls coming into your lab and told my boss about them. He raised hell with me. If he finds out I'm talking to you, he'll try to get me fired."

Smythe thought. That's why Messner took the files from his office. He looked at the materials Bernsdorf had brought to the house. Before the call, he'd organized the packet into several stacks according to topic and placed them on the table in front of him.

"I'm sitting here looking at documents that I don't think you have seen. Do you have time now to talk about what I have?"

So much for small talk, she thought. "I'd like to hear what you have to say provided you can back it up with documentation."

"I have photographs of animals exposed to Serenity that clearly demonstrate the toxic effect of the drug. These are animals that should be sound asleep given their dosage levels they were given. Instead, they're running around, tearing their own fur out, attacking everything in sight. If two of the animals are placed together in the same cage, they fight to the death. These are reactions we would not expect given the pharmacology of Serenity. "

"I don't remember seeing anything like that in the Serenity new drug application."

Smythe hesitated, "They weren't included. My assistant made a mistake when the studies were being done. The study protocol called for killing the animals after two weeks and conducting autopsies on the dead animals. She forgot about a group of animals that were housed in a different section of our lab that got the drug for three weeks by mistake. The photographs I am talking about are of those animals."

"Why weren't they sent to us anyway?"

This was the same question that Smythe had asked himself many times since the discussion with Hagstrom. Smythe knew these results should have been sent to the FDA. It was time for him to own up to his role in this nasty business. A pang of guilt swept over him, nearly overwhelming him.

"These animals were outside the protocol. We discussed what happened to them and concluded that what we were seeing was a paradoxical reaction, similar to what happens when cats are administered morphine. The results should have been reported anyway. I knew better, but I allowed myself to be convinced by my boss not to include them when I knew better."

"Will you send them to me?" Emrich stopped herself from criticizing him. Smythe was being cooperative. She didn't want him to stop.

"Yes. As we talk, I'll make notes of everything you want to see. I'll make copies for you and send them right after we finish today."

"You do understand that I need to know everything?"

"I worked only on the animals, but there are other things of importance."

She said, "Let's go on. You faxed me the page about irregularities in the Jackson Prison testing. Let's talk about that."

Smythe breathed a sigh of relief. The discussion of the animal research was over. "All right," Smythe said. "There were some problems there. The death of a prison guard, two suicides."

Emrich nodded to herself, "I got your fax. It was vague. Can you be more specific?"

"I've pieced it together. The three deaths, one murder and the two suicides, occurred after the prisoners received the drug for three weeks. It wasn't reported that way to the FDA. The three death cases were moved into the control group and three controls were included in the exposed group although they were never given the drug."

She whistled through her teeth. "Do you have documents to support that?"

He hesitated, "I'm working on that. There's been some talk about that happening, but noting in writing that I've seen yet. But I spent some time just going over what I have and it couldn't have happened the way it was reported."

"Why do you say that?"

"In the report submitted to the FDA, they say that the occurrence of one murder and two suicides in a control group of twenty person is quote 'what one would expect in a normal prison population' end of quotes. I'm reading from the submitted document now. The plain and simple math of the statement defies belief. Combined reports of murders and suicides in prison settings nationally show an incidence of substantially less than one percent. The percentage of this study as reported is fifteen percent."

"I see your point. I'll have to think about it. Anything else?"

"Next is the marketing experience. We're receiving reports from doctors all over the country about deaths--murders and suicides. The FDA is supposed to be given weekly summaries of adverse reaction reported during the first six months of marketing. We're four months from initial marketing and I know for a fact that nothing has been submitted to you yet. I have documents that tabulate what we have received from doctors and what we have told you about them. They simply don't match. There's a whole lot going on that you don't know about."

Emrich shuffled some papers. "Let me summarize where we are so far. You question the details about the Jackson Prison study but you have no documents to support your contention, and you describe some major problems with the animal studies. You say that adverse reactions reports are being withheld. Anything else?"

"Remember that none of this came from me."

Emrich almost laughed aloud. Could he really be that naive to think that she could protect him? Keep his identity secret? She didn't respond.

Smythe continued, "The doctor who supervised the prison study is an old family practitioner in Jackson. Maybe you can talk to him."

CHAPTER 44

Emrich sat at her desk, thinking about what she learned from Smythe. True to his word, he'd sent her the materials they discussed over the phone. She agreed with Smythe's conclusion. She had no choice but to pursue this and she knew she needed to know more about the prison study. She had to have hard proof. The problem now was how to avoid Levitt and his certain interference. She thought about his warning.

She reflected on the documents in front of her. She spent the day drafting and redrafting a summary of what she knew. By evening she was satisfied that she had it right. She knew what was in store for her if she took this to Levitt. The blame game would start. He would say that she was in charge of Serenity from the start and any problems that came up were due to her incompetence. She had to make an end run around him. It was going to be tough to keep him out of the loop. He knew everything that was going on inside the Agency.

She looked at the summary:

1. The human study conducted at the prison resulted in serious adverse actions--thirty percent of which were not reported to the FDA. Two subjects administered Serenity committed suicide while on the drug, and a third subject taking Serenity murdered a prison guard. All three subjects were reported in the study submitted to the FDA by Upright as being in the control group. All three subjects took Serenity for longer than fourteen days. Upright's report of this study to the FDA contains the following language; "This study supports the safety of the use of Serenity in human beings. There were no reports of adverse reactions in the twenty prison inmates who were given Serenity, while there were three serious events noted in inmates in the control group." The report of this study in this manner by Upright was in violation of the provisions of the Food, Drug, and Cosmetic Act.

2. Animal studies conducted by Upright revealed serious adverse effects of the drug appearing after fourteen days of exposure to the drug. Dosages administered to the animals were equivalent to Upright's currently recommended dosage in humans. These adverse effects in animals would have served as a warning of the potential for harm when the drug was administered to human beings. Instead, this scientific data was never presented to the FDA in Upright's new drug application. The animal data that Upright did report to the FDA misrepresented what was known by Upright and made it appear that the drug was safe when, in fact, it was not safe. The report of the animal studies in this manner was in violation of the provisions of the Food, Drug, and Cosmetic Act.

3. Upright sought, and received, approval of Serenity for long-term use, even though the scientific evidence available to them in their own research indicated that use for longer than fourteen days was potentially dangerous. This potential danger was not reported to the FDA by Upright in its new drug application, and such failure to do so was in violation of the Food Drug and Cosmetic Act.

Emrich was satisfied with her conclusions. She smiled. Hell, she should have been a lawyer. She took a long, hot bath and went to bed. She slept soundly the entire night. She awoke early--refreshed and anxious to get going on this mission. She had to find someone who would listen to her story. She stored her findings on her computer, went in to work early, and made three hard copies on the Xerox machine.

She stood at the machine, thought for a moment, and then made an additional hard copy. She placed the extra hard copy in a plain envelope and tucked it in her briefcase. She locked the other three copies in her desk. This was emotional, she thought. She was proud of what she was doing. Now it was time to start the process of getting around Levitt.

She had met a young lawyer, Sean Harris, in the agency's legal department in a bar a month ago. They exchanged cards and promises to call each other for lunch. She'd turned him down several times since. She rummaged through the drawer in her desk, but she couldn't find his card. She called the legal department's main number and asked to speak to him. He sounded excited when he answered and realized it was her calling.

"Sean, can we meet somewhere for lunch?"

"Sure." He sounded eager.

Emrich needed to clarify the situation. "This is not personal. I have some company business to discuss, but I think it is best to do it in private."

Harris sounded enthusiastic. "When would you like to meet? Today? Tomorrow?"

"I was hoping today."

"That's good for me. Where should we meet?"

"How about Five Guys? I'm buying." Emrich tried to keep it light.

Harris hesitated, and then laughed, "I love it. The girl remembers that a guy's basic food group is hamburger. When?"

They met at noon. To make sure she had his attention, she'd unbuttoned an extra button of her blouse. She dabbed extra perfume behind her ear. Harris sat and listened. Took several glances at her cleavage. He read the summary of the conclusions that Emrich reached. He looked across the table at her.

"I love the language. You should have been a lawyer. This is dynamite, but I can't imagine the agency doing anything that might hurt Upright."

"What about Electra? What about Sansome?" She knew that Harris had been involved with criminal prosecutions involving two small drug companies who sold contaminated vitamin products.

The lawyer laughed. "Small fish in a big pond. Sacrificial lambs. Much ado about nothing. Pick your cliché."

"What do you mean?"

"You know what I mean. It's common knowledge that the FDA leaves the big boys alone. You do know that Ted Cooper left us to become CEO of Upright?"

"Cooper wouldn't stand in the way of this." She gestured toward her report.

He snorted. "You are naïve."

"That's not true."

Harris smiled. "I tell you what. I'll bet you a steak dinner that nothing results from your report."

"That's why I've come to you. To make sure that something is done."

She looked him directly in the eye. She leaned slightly forward, making sure he'd get an eyeful. Borderline seduction, she thought, but what else was she going to do?

Harris took another glance at her cleavage. "Why don't you go to your boss?"

"He's really tight with the Upright big shots. I don't think he'd do anything about it. He's in bed with them."

"Levitt's not only in bed with Upright, but with a lot of gals in the FDA, from what I hear."

"I've heard those rumors, too." Her face felt hot. "But, I need to do something. We need to do something. There are people dying from taking this drug. Levitt has orchestrated the whole approval process, so if the drug turns out to be a disaster, I'm the one who will take the fall. Do you have any ideas?"

"I do have a couple of ideas. Can I take this with me?" He held up the copy of her summary. Took another quick glance at her chest. "Let me think about it and talk to a couple of people. I can tell you what I come up with when we have dinner tomorrow night." He smiled.

She couldn't back down now. She was the one who brought seduction into the equation. "Good idea. I can't wait."

She went back to her office and caught up with paperwork on her desk. It helped to stay busy with mundane matters. She stayed away from Levitt. At the end of the day, she waited until her co-workers were gone and Xeroxed portions of the Serenity new drug application. It was against regulations to make personal copies, but there was no way she could do this unless she had her own copy. She brought a big purse in the next day and stuffed the copies into it. She took it to dinner with Harris.

Harris leaned toward her over the small table and checked out the cleavage. He wasn't disappointed. She'd dressed to make sure he'd get an eyeful. He stammered as he spoke.

"My boss has a contact in the upper echelons of the Justice Department. We spoke with him, and he thinks there is enough to warrant an investigation. His major interest was in the prison study. If the prison study result was changed deliberately, and we could prove it, we could get a felony conviction. It is important to have some confirmatory evidence. Smythe's words alone won't do it. There must be some way to document the changes. Can you can talk to the doctor who did the study? We need to be certain that the report was deliberately altered and is not just an innocent mistake by the doctor. If Upright lawyers have the chance to blame it on the doctor, they will-- just like Levitt would place the blame on you."

Emrich sat and thought. "I'll go and see the doctor. I'll tell him that I need to verify the details of the study. I won't tell Levitt that I'm going, and I won't notify the doctor or Upright in advance."

"That's great," Harris smiled. "Nice dress, by the way."

She had to admit it. The sex with Harris was pretty good that night.

CHAPTER 45

Doctor Paul Sipple liked what he saw. Jan Emrich was a looker--a seriously attractive grown-up woman. She was going to spend the day with him. He estimated she was about thirty years old. She was trim but well built. Her dark hair was short and framed a face that he would enjoy staring at all day. Hell, she could ask him anything she wanted about the study as long as she took her time.

Emrich interrupted his reverie. "Do you know why I'm here?"

"Sure." Her controlled demeanor added to her beauty, he thought.

She slid a document across his desk. "Is that your signature at the bottom of the first page?" It was the signature page of the prison study.

He glanced down and nodded.

"Yes. Is there any reason to doubt that it is?" He smiled.

She ignored his question and the smile. He studied her face as she looked down at her notes. All business. He liked that.

"I have reasons to believe this is not your signature." She looked at him, unsmiling. "That's why I'm here," she continued. "To find out why your signature was forged."

He started to speak, swallowed. "Do you mind if I smoke?"

"It's your office." She continued to look at him.

His hands shook as he removed a cigarette from its pack and lit it. How was he going to handle this?

"That is my signature." He exhaled

She looked at him coldly. Waited until the smoke cleared.

"If this is all you have to say, I suggest you get a lawyer. I think you're lying."

He bit his lip. "What is it that you want to know?" His mouth was dry. He tried to moisten his lips with a parched tongue. He was losing control of the situation--knew that there would be hell to pay if he screwed up.

"What I want is very simple. I want to know why your signature has been forged on this document. You claim to have done the research. If it is your research, federal law requires your signature on the research summary."

He responded too quickly. "Probably my secretary signed my name for me."

The look on her face chilled him.

"I want you to understand something, Dr. Sipple. I may look young and naive. You may think you can just say anything and I'll go away. That's not going to happen. This research you did for Upright is a piece of garbage." She gestured toward the report on the desk. "You know its garbage. I know its garbage. I'm here to find out who forged your signature . . . and why."

Messner had told him not to speak with anybody about the study. He remembered the gist of that meeting. It seemed so long ago. Messner's orders were specific. If someone approached him to talk about the study, he was to notify Messner. This lady sitting in front of him, busting his balls, just showed up without an appointment. He should have called Messner right then--before he started talking with her. He stubbed his cigarette out in the ashtray. Trouble is, he thought, I can't think right now. His mind was a blank. He wished she would stop looking at him with that cold stare. He broke eye contact and looked down at his hands. They were shaking.

Emrich pressed forward, "I need to have you tell me about patient C.D. in the study. I know his name--Cedric Duffield. I need more information about him."

Sipple nodded dumbly. This wasn't going the way he expected. Not at all.

"What kind of information?" He should excuse himself and call Messner right now. Tell him what was going on. "Can you excuse me for a minute while I make a call?"

Emrich shook her head. "I'm not leaving this office, and I'm not leaving you alone so that you can call Upright. I want answers from you . . . now."

He sat and looked at her. She didn't look so attractive at the moment.

She continued. "Listen to me. Upright falsified your research findings. When this comes out, they will blame you. They'll say you did it on your own. You will be the fall guy. You could lose your medical license. When this hits the newspapers, and it will, you'll be the laughing stock of Jackson, Michigan. You may wind up in Jackson Prison on the inside looking out. I suggest you come clean and start telling me what happened."

Sipple felt trapped. He didn't know what to do.

"I should get a lawyer."

Emrich sat back and glared at him.

"Fine," she snapped. "If you didn't do anything wrong, you wouldn't need a lawyer. That tells me a lot. That's what Upright has been telling me. It was you. They're hanging you out to dry. You're going to let them do this to you. You're not only dishonest, you're stupid."

She stood and walked to the door. She turned and looked at him. "If I walk out of here now, your troubles are not over. They're just starting." She opened the door and took a step out.

Sipple stood quickly. "Stop. Close the door. Sit down."

She closed the door and returned to the chair in front of his desk. She continued to glare at him.

This woman is a ball-crusher, he thought. He shuddered involuntarily.

"What is it that you want to know about Mr. Duffield?"

"Do you have a copy of your research in the office?"

Sipple hesitated.

"What is it?" Emrich asked.

"I'm not supposed to have a copy. But, I kept a copy for my records."

"Let me see it."

Sipple rolled his chair back and turned to the file cabinet behind him.

"It's right here." He searched for a minute, retrieved a file and handed it to her.

Emrich removed the official copy, the FDA copy, from her briefcase and set it beside Sipple's. "Give me a minute," she said. She compared the copies paragraph-by-paragraph. The two documents were identical until she reached the bottom of the second page. There was a chart in both documents, but the FDA chart was different from Sipple's. The twenty men who received Serenity were listed in tabular form by their initials. In Sipple's copy, C.D. was listed as having taken Serenity. In the FDA document, C.D. was listed in the control column as not having taken Serenity. She found that the two men who committed suicide were similarly listed as being given Serenity in Sipple's copy, but in the FDA document, they were included in the control group. Smythe was right, she thought. The math didn't add up because they had been altered.

The other difference between the two documents was found in the summaries. In Sipple's summary, the conclusions were simple.

"This study clearly demonstrates a toxic effect of Serenity when taken in the dosages used for two or more weeks. It is recommended that the study be repeated at lower dosages and/or for a limited period of time not to exceed two weeks in duration."

Emrich smiled for the first time since she'd arrived at Sipple's office. The FDA version gave Serenity a complete whitewash on the safety issue.

She looked at Sipple, "I'd like to keep this. Please make a copy for me."

When he returned with the copy, Emrich put it in her briefcase.

"Keep this original safe. Do not show it to anybody. I think it goes without saying that you don't tell Upright about my visit. Do you understand?"

Sipple nodded. "I understand."

As she left the office, she had a hard time to keeping from smiling. She couldn't wait to show this to Harris.

CHAPTER 46

Emrich headed back to Washington feeling very pleased with herself. What else could she do now to bolster this effort? There were a couple of Upright employees she could interview. How much would Upright try to interfere with that approach? There was the issue of what was happening in other countries around the world. A number of foreign medical journal articles had been published depicting problems with Serenity. One Dutch scientist had presented convincing data on a connection between Serenity use and suicides in his country. The publication of his research led to a public outcry and a total ban of the drug in that country. Other studies confirmed the Dutch scientist's results and banned the drug as well. In European countries, the reporting of suspected adverse drug reactions was mandatory. In the United States, reporting was voluntary. The net result was Serenity appeared to be safer in the U.S. experience, whereas European countries provided a more realistic view of the dangers.

Emrich looked at her watch and did the calculation. Western Europe was five hours ahead of Washington. It was four o'clock in the afternoon there. She placed a call to the Dutch scientist whose research had triggered the European interest in Serenity's dangers.

He answered the phone.

"Ja? This is Paul Vogelgang."

"Doctor, my name is Doctor Jan Emrich. I am with the Food and Drug Administration in Washington. I am in charge of evaluating the safety of Serenity, and I've read your paper in the British Journal of Medicine. Do you have some time so we can talk about your research?"

"Ja. Right now would be fine. I might say that it is high time that your agency is addressing an issue that the rest of the world has known for months."

"I agree with you. I have a question about the dosages of Serenity used in your study."

"My study revealed a clear risk of suicide no matter what level of Serenity is used. That is the reason my government banned the drug after my research was published. Now, what is your question?"

"You have answered the question before I asked it. May I ask a favor?"

"What is it?"

"In the course of an investigation, I have discovered there are two versions of a study conducted by Upright at a prison. The purpose of the research was to evaluate the safety of Serenity. Would you be willing to examine these two versions and provide me a written report of your conclusions?"

"I would be pleased to do that. You can mail me the two reports. Better yet, fax them to me, and I will evaluate them immediately. You should also know that Upright has filed charges against me here in my country, accusing me of slander. I mention that to you because any unfavorable conclusion that I may draw in my evaluation may also result in a similar response. There are doctors in my country with longstanding financial ties to Upright who have a vendetta against me because of my research. I should add that the majority of physicians and scientists throughout Europe support me and my work."

Emrich hung up, concerned. Upright's tentacles were wide and far. Nothing about this was going to be easy. She faxed the two versions of the prison study and then mulled the question of whether she should try to interview the two Upright employees she had in mind. There was no choice but to go ahead and try.

CHAPTER 47

Emrich received Dr. Vogelgang's reply two days later. He called her. "This is outrageous. I find it difficult to believe that a reputable drug company would do such a thing. How may I help you in bring this information to the medical community of your country? "

Emrich thought about his question. "Let me think about it for a couple of days. I'll talk to several people to see what might be most effective. Let me get back to you."

"I will do whatever I can to help."

Vogelgang's reply was exciting. If she was able to rally foreign scientists around her cause, the FDA would have to take her seriously. This issue would become a lot larger than Levitt. She glanced through her notes and made a call to Upright headquarters to arrange for appointments with Cyrus Messner and Myra Huggins.

"Get this. This bitch Emrich calls me and wants to set up an interview to talk about Serenity."

"What did you say?"

Messner smiled at Hagstrom. "I told her I'd be happy to speak with her. She's going to meet me in our headquarters in New York. She almost choked when I asked if she was going to bring my good friend Mort Levitt. It was funny as hell."

"Why do you think she wants to meet with you?"

"I called Levitt right away. He told me she's on a fishing expedition about some of the work we've done on Serenity. He said he told her to back off. We agreed that she was going to have to learn the hard way not to mess with the big boys."

Emrich arrived fifteen minutes before the scheduled time at Upright corporate headquarters in midtown Manhattan, far away from the clinical and scientific laboratories in Ann Arbor. She cooled her heels in the waiting room for forty-five minutes past the scheduled time. Everything in the reception area was mahogany--the reception desk, the chairs and couches topped with overstuffed cushions, the end tables and the paneled walls. The effect was to create a dark and somber, but elegant, atmosphere. Emrich thought it was depressing. She was finally ushered into a conference room, where the mahogany theme continued. The corporate offices were on the 46th floor and looked out over Central Park. Emrich chuckled to herself. Maybe all the trees in the park were mahogany. Who knows?

Messner walked into the room and was flanked by an army of six lawyers--dark-suited, non-smiling New York types, none of whom bothered to introduce themselves. The group positioned themselves on one side of the long mahogany conference table, and the apparent leader--the oldest of the group--gestured for Emrich to take the other side. He spoke first.

"Let's set a few ground rules. First, we are voluntarily producing Dr. Messner for this interview. Second, a copy of any notes you make during this interview must be provided to us before you leave the building. Third, if, in my judgment, any question is considered improper, Dr. Messner will be instructed not to answer. If these terms are not agreeable to you, there will be no interview. Any questions?"

Emrich stared the man down, "I think you mean Mr. Messner. From my understanding, he is not a doctor." Might as well start this off on something she knew Messner was sensitive about. He had flunked out of medical school. Messner's face reddened, and he glared at her. She pondered the ground rules. She had no problem with the notes request. She wasn't planning on taking notes, anyway. She was just there to listen to what Messner had to say. She nodded. "Let's proceed."

The lawyers exchanged glances. Eldest spoke, "Go ahead."

"Mister Messner. I do have that right, don't I? You are not a doctor, isn't that right?"

"Hold on, Ms. Emrich. You are not going to use that tone of voice in this room."

She ignored him. "Mister Messner, what are your areas of responsibility with respect to Serenity?"

Messner turned and looked at the lawyer sitting closest to him. The lawyer stopped writing and put his pen on the table. "That's a vague question and probably would require three hours for Mister Messner to answer. Why don't you ask a more specific question?" A directive. Not a question.

Emrich was tempted to argue, but knew it would be futile. These guys were just looking for an excuse to abort this meeting. "Let me see if I can ask it simple enough for you to understand. What is your current position with the company?"

Messner looked at the lawyer again. The lawyer fumbled inside his brief case and handed Emrich a piece of paper. "All of his Messner's professional qualifications, including his current position at Upright, are on this resume. There's no need for you to waste time on his background."

Emrich sat back and took her time reviewing Messner's resume. Messner had yet to open his mouth, except to yawn. "Can you tell me when you first personally became involved with Serenity?"

Messner looked at the lawyer again, who nodded. Emrich breathed a sigh of relief.

"All of my work with Serenity has been of a professional nature. I have never been personally involved with Serenity."

What an asshole! Emrich felt like slapping the silly smirk off Messner's face. "Tell me, then, when did you first become professionally involved with Serenity?"

Messner again looked at the lawyer.

"Ms. Emrich. Mister Messner is here to voluntarily answer your questions. Do not use that tone of voice. This is the second time I've

202

warned you. If you persist in being disrespectful, this interview will be terminated."

"Doctor."

"Excuse me?"

"Unlike Mister Messner, I am a doctor. You can call me Doctor Emrich." Emrich glanced around the room. The whole group had smirks on their faces. This was going nowhere fast. She questioned the wisdom of being here. She clenched her jaw muscles and tried to remain calm. She reminded herself, Take a deep breath. Speak slowly. "Also, I don't need you to tell me how to conduct myself. I have asked him a question, and I'd like an answer to that question."

"Ask the question again."

She looked at Messner. "When did you first become professionally involved with Serenity?"

Messner looked again at the lawyer. "Do I answer that?"

The lawyer nodded. "If you can."

Messner smiled at Emrich. "I don't know what you mean by 'professionally involved.'"

This was a complete waste of time, she thought. "What is it that you do not understand about the phrase 'professionally involved'?

The lawyer spoke sharply. "Ms. Emrich. I warned you about the tone of your voice once. You continue being disrespectful to a person who has agreed to meet with you. We are terminating this interview and will report your conduct to your superiors at the FDA."

Emrich sat and thought. She was dumbfounded. She had not expected this, but she kept her thoughts to herself.

"I'd like to speak with Miss Huggins now."

The lawyer shook his head. "You're not going to talk to anyone in this company without a court order. One of my associates will show you out."

CHAPTER 48

Linda was already in her cubicle when I arrived earlier than usual.

"Morning, Bobby." She was always a sight for sore eyes.

"Good morning, Linda. I've been thinking. I want you in court with me on these trials. I can't possibly handle all these documents and witnesses by myself."

Linda was flustered. "I'll be more valuable to you right here in the office. I've never worked in a courtroom before." The smile disappeared from her face. "I just don't think that's a good idea."

I studied her face. This was puzzling. "What's the big deal? We work great together as a team." I laughed. "All you've got to do is wind me up and point me in the right direction."

She looked at me with a somber expression.

I continued, "You'll love it. Nothing like it. The tension. The drama." I paused. Maybe she didn't feel appreciated. "Besides, without you being there, I'd be a fish without water. I need you. You're the only one who really knows what's going on."

"That's not true. You know this case like the back of your hand. You don't need me. You'll do great."

"I don't think so." I hesitated and thought carefully before speaking. "Let me put it as politely as I can to you. I need you in that courtroom with me." My way or the highway, is what I really wanted to say. No point, yet, in being too confrontational.

Her reaction had surprised me. Hell, she was better than any two lawyers. I was perplexed. Never in my lifetime, I thought, would I ever be able to understand the female mind.

The rest of the day, she avoided contact with me. She was always in and out of my office any number of times during an ordinary business day, but today was different. She made herself scarce. That she might quit her job if I forced the issue entered my mind. What would I do without her? How could I try these document-driven cases without her at my elbow, feeding me the appropriate materials? In her four months with the firm, she had made herself indispensable. No one knew more than she did about these cases. No one. Including me, I thought. It was that thought that concerned me most. What would happen if she did quit? It was my responsibility to be prepared. I had given her the responsibility of seeing that I met that obligation.

CHAPTER 49

Gary Newton walked into my office holding a newspaper. "Read this." He set the newspaper on the desk in front of me and pointed to an article he'd circled in red.

Upright Pharmaceuticals, the maker of Serenity, the hot-selling sensational new sleeping pill, announced today that it would provide assistance to prosecutors throughout the country when allegations of violent behavior due to Serenity as a defense are made in criminal proceedings. A substantial number of criminal cases have surfaced blaming Serenity for causing defendants' violent behaviors. Within legal circles, this type of defense is being called 'the Serenity defense.' Cyrus Messner, Upright's Vice-President of Scientific Research, issued a statement today saying, "These bizarre accusations are totally unfounded. It is unfair for someone who murders another to blame Serenity for their actions." According to Messner, there are twenty-four criminal cases pending throughout the country that are being offered this assistance. Messner also indicated that Upright would continue to support any additional cases that may be filed.

"Holy shit."

"I thought you'd say something like that." Gary laughed.

"This company not only makes a bad drug, but then it figures out a way to cover its ass."

"I thought you'd say that, too."

I looked up. "What are you? A broken record?" I mustered a grin.

"This may be a blessing in disguise. We ought to be able to exploit this. Point out to the jury that this is a fabricated position bought and paid for by the company that makes the drug."

"A good point, Gary. Have a law clerk prepare a brief on this issue. It's sure to come up during trial."

I didn't realize, at the time, that I would soon be faced with this issue in a manner that would rock me to my core.

CHAPTER 50

As the trial date on Slater's case grew closer, my working hours increased. It was my practice to be in the office by six o'clock in the morning. I generally stayed late--past eight o'clock in the evening. Gary Newton, Linda, and Mary, my secretary, dealt with the procedural issues that constantly arose in the civil cases while I focused on Slater. In addition to Scruggs, we now had six more civil cases in the office involving Serenity in deaths of users. The morning hours were precious. I could sit at my desk with my Egg McMuffin and coffee and concentrate on Slater without interruptions. Once the business day began, the interruptions were endless. Phone calls and questions from office staff made it impossible to concentrate properly, so I took advantage of quiet time before and after the business day.

I was irritated when Gary interrupted me shortly after I arrived this morning. Gary looked at the food wrapper on my desk and grinned. "Breakfast of champions?"

"You didn't come in here to mock my breakfast choice. What's on your mind?" I wasn't in the mood for small talk.

"Upright's filed an unusual motion in both Slater and Scruggs."

"Slater? They're not a party in Slater. How can they file a motion if they're not a party?"

"That's why I came in. To ask you the very same question. Look at this." Gary held up the papers he held in his hand. "This was hand-delivered after hours last night. I got here a little before you did today, so I looked at it before bothering you. It's a motion for a protective order to prevent you from using any information or documents we've obtained in the Scruggs case in Slater."

"That's crazy. How can they do that?" Even before I asked the question, I knew the answer. Upright would do anything possible to prevent the Serenity story from becoming public.

"Gary, have the law clerks research the issue of standing. The question is 'does a non-party to a criminal case have standing to prevent use of evidence in the criminal case?' When is the motion scheduled?"

"That's why I interrupted you. I know you like quiet time in the morning. Upright has scheduled the motion for this afternoon."

"You're kidding?"

"No, I'm not. No law clerks are scheduled for today."

I winced. "Leave the papers with me. I'll drop what I was going to do and work on this. Let Linda and Mary know what's going on, and that I'm not to be disturbed."

Linda delivered a Big Mac and coke at noon, but other than that, I worked uninterrupted until it was time to leave for court.

Lester Hempstead was seated beside the assistant prosecutor, Alison Feeney, when I walked into the courtroom.

Judge Flick took the bench. Hempstead stood. "Your Honor. This is a motion for a protective order. As the Court is aware, Mr. Riley has a civil lawsuit against the Upright Corporation for alleged injuries sustained by his client in that case that is attributed to the alleged use of Serenity. In that litigation, Mr. Riley has conducted discovery and received documents from my client, the Upright Corporation, under a protective order issued by you. The terms of the protective order limit Mr. Riley's use of the documents he has received to that specific litigation. Our realistic concern is that Mr. Riley may intend to use the information he has obtained in the civil case in defending his client in this case. This motion is brought to prevent him from doing that."

The judge looked at me. "Mr. Riley, what do you have to say?"

I stood and checked my notes. "First of all is the issue of standing. Upright, through Mr. Hempstead, has no standing to come before this court on a criminal matter in which they are not a a party. No standing whatsoever. Second, in my defense of Mr. Slater, I do intend to use my knowledge that the drug Serenity temporarily destroyed his ability to act as a reasonable person. Information to that effect can be found in the documents provided in the civil litigation, but I do not intend to use the documents."

"Are you saying you read the document and use the information on the document, but don't intend to admit the document into evidence?"

"Yes. That's correct, but only partially correct. Information regarding the harmful effects of Serenity, Upright's drug, is a matter of common knowledge disseminated throughout the world wide medical community. There is nothing in Upright's documents that is not well known."

"Okay. I understand your respective positions. I'll issue a written opinion in less than a week."

The next two weeks went by quickly. I had plenty of things on my agenda without sitting and waiting for Flick's opinion. Mary walked in and put the mail in front of me. The judge's opinion was on top of the stack. I felt my blood pressure go higher with every sentence I read. Upright's motion was granted. Not only did the judge's ruling say that I couldn't use the documents in the criminal case, he ordered me off the case as Slater's lawyer unless I agreed not to do so. Flick never even addressed the issue of standing, whether or not Upright had the right to come into the criminal case with this motion.

I felt like I'd been slapped in the face. How could a third party like Upright come into a criminal proceeding and complain about the evidence that might be presented by the defense? How could a judge order me off the case unless I waived the only defense Slater had? It didn't make sense.

CHAPTER 51

I had to do something quickly or I was out of the Slater case, and he would have to find himself a new lawyer. Agreeing to drop the Serenity defense was not a consideration. To drop the defense was to condemn Slater to life in prison. Other than the Serenity defense, he had no defense. That was all he had. I woke up the next morning with a thought burning in my brain. There was a possible way out of this dilemma. I arrived at the office early, but I waited until eight-thirty to place the call.

"Mr. Hempstead, please."

"May I tell him who's calling?"

"Bob Riley."

"One moment please."

"Bob. What can I do for you?" Hempstead had a deep booming voice.

"We need to talk about Flick's order. You and I have disagreed about a lot of things over the years, but I think we both agree that Flick is dead wrong on this one." I waited for a comment. All he did was grunt. I continued, "I have to appeal his decision, and there is no question the court of appeals will reverse it. My problem is that Slater has to sit in jail until the appeal is over. That's not fair to him, and Upright will take a negative hit from the publicity that will follow from this ruling. And I will guarantee that I will take this effort to every damn newspaper in the country. I propose a compromise. We stipulate to set aside the judge's order, and I agree not to use any documents you produced to me in Slater. Simple as that. What do you say?"

Hempstead paused for a moment. "Let me think about it for a couple of days."

His reaction told me all I needed to know. He agreed with my analysis. He called back two days later.

"Bob, I have a proposal. Your terms are agreeable, except I have one additional item. You must agree to allow me into Slater as co-counsel for the prosecution."

"You're kidding."

"No, I'm not. Feeney's supervisor tells me that Feeney is lost. Hell, she can't even pronounce anterograde amnesia, much less understand what the hell it is."

I hated to agree to anything Hempstead suggested. I particularly hated to lose Feeney as the prosecutor on the case because she was a terrible lawyer. If Hempstead came into the case, it would be a new ballgame. On the other hand, if I didn't agree, I was out. I didn't see I had much choice. "I agree."

"I thought you'd see it my way." Hempstead chuckled.

I thought for a moment. "How will we handle Flick in telling him that his decision was so stupid that both parties want to set it aside?"

Hempstead grunted. "Don't worry about Flick. I'll handle him. All I have to do is withdraw the motion and his order will be null and void."

The next day it was a done deal. Order was restored in the Slater case. I was back in the case, but so was Hempstead.

CHAPTER 52

Alex Hartley was concerned about the dangers of Serenity. He kept a Serenity file on his desk, and it was getting thicker by the day. What really pissed him off were the form letters he received from Upright, signed by Cyrus Messner. "We never heard of this, we never heard of that, no one has ever reported this before." All bull shit, Hartley thought. And he was mad as hell about it. He looked up the number and placed a call to the FDA in Washington. He asked to speak with the drug monitor for Serenity. He wrote the name down in his phone book. Janice Emrich, PhD. She was not in, and he left a message for her to call back.

She returned the call late in the afternoon. "Doctor Hartley, this is Jan Emrich. You left a message for me to call?"

"Yes, I did. I wanted to speak with you about my concerns about Serenity."

"Okay."

"I'm an internist with a special interest in pharmacology. I work out of Detroit Receiving and treat most of the adverse drug reactions that are seen in the hospital. I am seeing an alarming number of serious reactions to Serenity--particularly suicides and murders. I have sent nine case reports to Upright. Upright tells me that have no information about this and keep sending me form letters suggesting that I'm the only doc in the country seeing this. I suspect that what they're telling me is wrong. Can you give me any more information?"

Emrich responded "I have a stack of reports on my desk. There must be over two hundred case reports of either suicide or murder right now."

"If you know this, why isn't something being done? Is the agency going to act on these reports?"

She hesitated. "We're in the process of evaluating these case reports."

"If you pardon my saying so, it sounds like a runaround."

"I have given you the official response. If I had my way, the response would be different."

"Different how? Meanwhile people are dying." Hartley felt himself getting angry.

She hesitated again, and then spoke softly. "Can I call you later? I'd like to talk some more about this. After business hours?"

"Sure." He gave her his home number. She sounded nice. He liked her voice. He had a picture in his mind of what she might look like.

It was after nine o'clock when she called that night. They spent two hours going over the Serenity situation. Alex was surprised to find that the problem was more serious than he thought. Emrich told him about the altered animal and human studies that created an illusion of safety.

After talking with Emrich, Hartley knew he had to contact Riley.

Linda and I were sitting in my office discussing our plan for the day when the phone rang. I raised an eyebrow when Mary told me who was calling. She put the call through.

"Good morning, Doctor Hartley. This is a surprise," I said.

Hartley wasted no time. "There are some things you need to know."

"What's going on?"

"I found out some things about Serenity. We should talk."

"Should we meet or can we do this now over the phone?"

Hartley responded quickly. "We can do it by phone. There's quite a bit of information. "

"Do you mind if my assistant listens? I'd like to have her take notes, if you don't mind."

"Its okay with me. There's a lot of detail."

I gestured for Linda to pick up the other phone at my conference table.

"Go ahead."

Hartley began his recitation. He sounded like he was reading from something.

"There's a source inside Upright who has gone to Doctor Janice Emrich at the FDA about Serenity with proof of scientific fraud. She's the monitor of the drug for the FDA. She thinks an investigation should be started, but as soon as her superior got wind of it, he ordered her to stop. Emrich went to the Justice Department instead."

"This is good stuff." I looked over at Linda. She was busy writing.

For the next forty-five minutes, Hartley filled me in on the details. Everything he'd learned from Emrich. Names and more names. What to look for and how to find it.

"Hold on for just a minute. Are you getting all this, Linda?"

She gave me a look, said nothing. She kept on writing.

Hartley concluded, "The bottom line is that both Emrich and I are on the same page. This is a dangerous drug. People are dying. Your cases can be an important way to highlight attention to the problem. I'll help you in any way I can."

I was excited to hear this.

"Doctor Hartley, I can't thank you enough for calling. Do you think Emrich will talk to me?"

Hartley hesitated. "I don't know if she will or not. She's taking some heat from her bosses. She's young and ambitious, and I don't think she wants to jeopardize her job by getting involved with lawyers. We both know all about that, don't we, Bob?"

It was my turn to hesitate. I tried to think of an artful response that would avoid turning this conversation into a pissing contest between the lawyer and the doctor.

"Alex, we have had our differences of opinion in the past. When all was said and done, however, we both did the right thing. You wound up suffering a great deal from your involvement, but please remember that that was not of my doing. You stepped on some pretty big toes and they reacted by trying to discredit you. By helping me, I have no guarantees that Upright won't try to do the same thing to you here. The same goes with Emrich. Her going to the Justice department tells me that she's a pretty tough cookie."

Hartley digested my little speech for a moment. "You're right. Sorry I brought it up. You can call her and ask her if you want, but I got the general impression she doesn't like lawyers."

After Hartley's phone call, I thought about the best way to approach the FDA investigator, Jan Emrich. I had a number of past experiences--all negative--in dealing with the FDA. The agency, most simply put, didn't want its employees talking to lawyers and wouldn't allow its employees to become involved in litigation. I had an idea. I would approach Emrich indirectly--through another doctor. I picked up the phone and called Ralph Schneidermann.

"Ralph, I've got a big favor to ask."

"Tell me."

I filled him in on the details, and he agreed to contact Emrich. He suggested the best way to do so was in writing.

CHAPTER 53

Emrich read the letter a second time.

Dear Dr. Emrich:

It is my understanding that you are the FDA monitor for the drug Serenity. I am writing to determine if there are any reported incidents similar to a matter I have recently observed.

The patient murdered his wife in a particularly brutal fashion after being placed on Serenity by his family doctor nearly one month earlier. The patient suffers amnesia for the event.

There are various newspaper accounts of similar events but, as you know, these types of reports hardly qualify as scientific proof. If you have any information that would allow me to properly evaluate the safety of this drug or the role of Serenity in this man's current dilemma (he is being charged with the murder of his wife) I would appreciate hearing from you.

Sincerely yours,

Ralph Schneidermann, M.D., F.A.C.P.

She set the letter back on her desk and put her head in her hands. She closed her eyes and gathered her thoughts. There was a definite problem with this drug. And the problem was getting bigger every day. She'd given Sean Harris the prison study documents she got from Sipple and Harris had promised he'd push the Justice Department contact to take some action. Two weeks had gone by and he hadn't returned her calls. She had to push Harris harder, but if he continued to avoid her what could she do? She thought about her conversations with Hartley, with Vogelgang. People were dying. It was frustrating to just sit and wait for others without knowing whether or not they'd do anything about the situation. She read the letter again. She placed a call to Schneidermann.

"Bob. This is Doctor Schneidermann. I heard back from Doctor Emrich at the FDA this morning. I think you're going to enjoy hearing the news."

"I can use some good news today. Go ahead."

Schneidermann replied. "Emrich said that she had important information about the drug, but she didn't want to talk over the phone. She wants to meet me in person."

This was good news. We needed all the help we could get on the Serenity cases.

"Will she meet with us?" I asked him.

"She said she would meet with me. I didn't ask about you. She was upset about Serenity, so I acted on this right away. I booked a flight for her into Detroit tomorrow afternoon. My travel agency will bill you. Emrich will meet me in the lobby of the Renaissance Hotel at six o'clock. I think you should be there too."

The next day, as the time approached, I was excited about the meeting. I spent an hour going over the notes Linda made for me from the Hartley conversation. My office was a five-minute walk from the hotel. At a quarter of six, Schneidermann called to say he couldn't make it. Something about a psychiatric emergency, but from the noise in the background, I suspected that it was something else. I walked over to meet Emrich by myself. She was sitting in the lobby when I got there.

I introduced myself.

She was polite but cold. "I thought Dr. Schneidermann was going to be here."

He would be here if he'd known what a knockout she was. I kept this thought to myself. "An emergency came up. He sends his regrets."

She looked at me. "What do you have to do with this?"

"I assume that Dr. Schneidermann told you about his involvement with me in matters involving Serenity?"

She shook her head. "He didn't say anything about you."

"I'm sorry about any misunderstanding. Rather than standing here, could I sit down?"

"I'd rather have you tell me why you're here in place of Dr. Schneidermann."

There was no sense in avoiding her question. I took the direct approach. "I'm a lawyer who represents a couple of clients who had serious problems with Serenity. I hired Dr. Schneidermann to evaluate these cases. Particularly, he is helping me in defending a man charged with the murder of his wife."

"Schneidermann's involved in litigation?" She made the word sound like a four-letter word. I nodded.

She was upset. "I wouldn't have come if I knew it involved litigation."

"I understand you're upset. Dr. Schneidermann should have told you. My client's going to spend the rest of his life in prison unless I can help him. I also represent several others who have killed themselves or murdered their loved ones while taking the drug."

I looked directly into her eyes. "I'm desperate, but I can't force you to talk to me." I left the statement hanging. It was her turn to respond. Neither of us broke eye contact.

Finally, she spoke. "Anything I tell you has to be strictly off the record. We have special rules at the FDA for dealing with lawyers. I'd be fired if they find out I talked to you."

I thought fast. I thought back to my conversation with Hartley.

"I understand we also have Alex Hartley as a mutual acquaintance."

"You know Doctor Hartley?" Her eyes brightened at the mention of his name.

"Yes, I do. I've know Alex for a long time. He's a wonderful doctor and I do know that he is concerned about the safety of Serenity." I felt like a namedropper. "You do know that he's in the city here? He works out of a major hospital just a few blocks from here."

"I knew that he was from Detroit."

I looked around the lobby. Most of the chairs were filled and the area was unsuitable for a serious discussion about Serenity.

"Would you like a drink or dinner?" I nodded toward the lounge.

"A drink would be nice." As we walked into the lounge, Emrich drew admiring glances from others in the bar. I couldn't help but notice that she was very attractive. It was going to be a pleasure to sit and talk with her.

We found a table in the corner of the lounge and ordered our drinks. She looked around the room. "I can't tell you how nervous I am."

"I don't bite." I thought about a couple of other comments I could make. I left it at that.

Our drinks arrived. She took a sip and set her glass down. "I thought I'd feel comfortable talking to a psychiatrist."

"Rather than a lawyer?" I smiled. "I already told you I don't bite."

"Mr. Riley. That's your name?"

"Yes, but please call me Bob."

"And you can call me Jan."

For two hours, we sat and talked. Actually, she did most of the talking. I took notes, and asked few questions. She knew what she was talking about. I nearly filled a legal pad with my scribbled notes. I wrote so much my hand cramped, but she still kept talking. The sum total of what she said was everything that Hartley had already told me. It was refreshing to hear it firsthand from the FDA monitor of the drug. Finally, she stopped and looked at me.

"That's it. That's the story as far as I know."

I asked, "How can you remember all this stuff?" I gestured at my note pad.

She smiled. "It's what I do for a living. I also spent the afternoon reviewing the documents."

"Documents? There are documents that support what you're saying?" This was the first time in two hours that she mentioned documents.

"I have documents in support of everything I've mentioned. I've brought them with me."

"Would it be possible for me to see them?"

She smiled again. "Sure, but then I'd have to kill you." She laughed. "Just kidding."

She stood. "I'll be right back."

She returned fifteen minutes later with a large, bulky package.

"You didn't get this from me." She handed me the package.

"I don't know how to thank you. Would you like dinner?"

"I'm tired. I think I'll just go back to my room and order something through room service."

We said our good-byes and I took her documents back to my office. Emrich was a bright, articulate and knowledgeable woman. And she was as attractive as she was smart.

The next morning I closed my door and opened the bulky package as if it was a Christmas present. Inside the envelope was a detailed summary by Emrich. Every "i" was dotted, and every "t" was crossed. A number of documents were appended to her report. It was all good stuff. Really good stuff.

As I finished reading the material, I remembered to call Hartley and tell him that Emrich was in town. He told me he'd give her a call.

He called me later in the day. "Bob, this is Alex."

"Did you talk to Emrich?" I asked.

"I certainly did."

"Do you think she might be willing to testify?"

"We really didn't talk about that. I can ask when I visit her this weekend."

"You're going to Washington?"

He sounded like he was grinning. "Yes."

I smiled to myself. I felt like a matchmaker.

CHAPTER 54

Time went fast, and I was getting closer to trial on Slater. Things were also moving along on Scruggs and the other civil cases as well. The good news from Hartley's trip to Washington was that Emrich was willing to testify in the Slater case. Hartley also made it clear to me that his commitment was as strong as ever. There must be something in the water in Washington. I needed to add both of their names to the witness lists in both Slater and Scruggs. The deadline for the listing of witnesses in the Scruggs case had passed two months ago, but I felt that Flick would be reasonable in letting me add both their names. It would be necessary for me to explain to Judge Flick why additional witnesses should be permitted and why this information was unknown to me until now. I knew the judge would be angry when I asked for these late changes. To my surprise, Flick granted my request and denied Hempstead's motion for an adjournment. Apparently, the judge was as eager to go to trial as I was. We were headed for trial.

PART III:

THE TRIAL

"Ladies and gentlemen, let me tell you again what you are to presume. I am the judge. I am telling you that. Presume he is innocent. When you sit there, I want you to look and say to yourself, There sits an innocent man."

- Scott L. Turow

CHAPTER 55

Dimitrios Loukas, the grocery store clerk, would tell people that, if they wanted to sit on a jury, they better be prepared to sit and do nothing over long periods of time. It was the most boring thing he'd ever done. More boring than standing behind a cash register all day and ringing up purchases of a loaf of bread or pack of cigarettes or a head of lettuce (Fresh in today. Yes, ma'am). He'd done the latter for years, but this jury stuff was worse. The waiting was interminable.

Loukas looked at his fellow juror, Hector Gonzales, who sat in the seat next to him in the courtroom. Loukas couldn't decide if the guy understood him. Maybe he didn't speak English. Whenever Loukas spoke to him, Gonzales just looked at him, eyes glazed over like he'd been smoking dope or peyote or whatever the spics did to get high. He never said anything in response.

"That lady lawyer is driving me nuts. That constant whining." He nodded toward Alistair Feeney, the assistant prosecutor handling the case against Slater, along with that big fat guy with the silly red bow tie, Lester Hempstead.

Later, during a break Loukas and Gonzales stood there, both leaning against the handrail in the stairwell adjacent to the courtroom, smoking. The building was smoke-free, but the bailiff suggested with a wink that the jurors who smoked could use the stairwell. With all the delays, Loukas was spending more time here than in the fucking courtroom.

"Didya ever hear anyone whine so much?"

Gonzales looked at him. Said nothing. Maybe he really couldn't understand English. Only in America, Loukas thought, would they select a juror who didn't understand the language. For four days, he'd put up with this crap. Two days ago, jury selection was finished, but they still hadn't heard a word of testimony. Every time it looked like something was going to get started, the bitch would stand up and complain about something else. The lawyers would huddle in front of the judge and speak in whispered tones, and the judge would then send the jury out of the room while "things were worked out." Loukas hadn't felt so helpless since before he figured out in high school that no one cared whether or not he showed up for school. That was years ago. He toyed with the idea of just not showing up, but he knew the judge would care then. The jurors were told that the police would come looking for them if they decided not to show up. Four days. It felt like forever. Fifteen bucks a day. What a joke. It was costing him more than that for his smokes. Civic duty. Bullshit.

The bailiff opened the door leading from the hallway to the stairwell. "Time."

Loukas tossed his cigarette on the floor, ground it out with his foot, and followed Gonzales back into the courtroom. He'd been hopeful this morning that things would get underway. He was mistaken.

"Ladies and gentlemen. I'm sorry about the delay. The lawyers and I still have some unfinished business, so I am going to excuse you until two o'clock this afternoon. That gives you two hours for lunch. Walk around and enjoy downtown Detroit. Do some shopping. I'll see you back here at two, and we'll start with opening statements at that time."

The judge stood and left the courtroom. Loukas made eye contact with Gonzales. Shit. Walk around downtown Detroit? Target practice for some junkie trying to pay for his next fix. This was aggravating. Fifteen fucking dollars a day. Where in the hell in downtown Detroit could he find lunch for less than fifteen dollars? Loukas checked his watch. Not enough time to go back to the store. Too much time to kill here. What a waste. When he received his notice of jury duty, he'd thought this was going to be a vacation--a day or two off from the store, a brief respite from the rigid daily routine. So far the time spent here felt as long as the entire sixteen years he'd been at the store. That was bad enough. Sixteen years as a grocery clerk at his father-in-law's store. Twelve hours a day; six days a week. Now this. Then there was last week.

Last week. His eyes stung when he thought about it. The casual announcement by his father-in-law that, after careful consideration, he was going to give the store to Loukas's wife and her brother when he retired next year. The half-wit brother who hadn't even been inside the store for as long as Loukas could remember. It wasn't fair. For the past sixteen years, the old man treated him like scum, and he'd put up with it, only to have this thrown in his face. His wife's asshole brother never worked an honest day in his life. Since his father-in-law's edict, he had not been able to sleep. Last week, his wife coaxed him into seeing the doctor who prescribed some medicine for him to sleep. So far, it hadn't helped much.

When the jury was in the courtroom, Loukas tried everything he could to divert his attention away from the need to close his eyes. It was so warm in the room that it made him sleepy. When he complained, the bailiff told him that the court reporter needed warmth because she always got cold. Loukas kept his mouth shut, but he felt like telling her to put on a sweater. He brought a newspaper to read, but the bailiff told him he couldn't read it in the courtroom. The only thing that kept him going was the attractive assistant that came to court every day with lawyer Riley. Occasionally, she'd look up and reward him with a smile. He started fantasizing about her. He mentally undressed her, his imagination filling in the missing details about what was underneath her dark business outfit with the short skirt. And her legs. She had a fine pair of legs.

Everyone in the courtroom stood whenever the judge entered the courtroom, and Loukas was able to catch a glimpse of the paralegal's legs as she smoothed over her skirt. His face flushed when he thought about it. Yesterday, he figured out how to improve his view. He would just change seats in the jury box. Yesterday afternoon after lunch he sat in a chair he knew would improve his view, but was ordered back to his original seating assignment by the bailiff. A fat, gum-chewing, middle-aged woman who spent her time crocheting sat in that assigned seat. What a waste.

Loukas checked his watch. Two hours until he had to be back to court. He wolfed down a tasteless sandwich in the basement cafeteria of the courthouse and then went outside to the front door of the courthouse to wait and smoke. He stood where he could watch the stream of humanity pass through the metal detectors and was fascinated by how many people went in and out of the courthouse each day. In his entire life, he couldn't remember wasting this much time each day just standing around doing nothing. When he returned to the courtroom after lunch, the judge announced that the lawyers were ready to begin. It's about time, Loukas thought.

"Good afternoon, members of the jury. We are about to go ahead with the trial. The first thing you will hear will be the opening statements of the lawyers. Flick looked at Feeney and Hempstead. "Proceed."

To my surprise, Feeney stood. I thought Hempstead was taking over the case, that he would be giving the opening statement.

Feeney walked to the lectern. "Ladies and Gentlemen of the jury. This is my opportunity to tell you what this case is all about. The state of Michigan has brought first-degree murder charges against the defendant, Jay Slater, for the murder of his wife on April 29, 2008. We will show that Mr. Slater bludgeoned his wife to death with a long-handled shovel from the couples' garage. We will prove to your satisfaction . . ."

I jumped to my feet. "Your Honor, this is not closing argument. The innuendo contained in Ms. Feeney's statement is totally inappropriate in the context of an opening statement."

"I agree, counsel. Ms. Feeney, confine your remarks to what you think your proofs will show."

I could tell by the look on her face that Feeney didn't have the slightest idea why I objected or why the judge sustained my objection. She stood there, dumbfounded.

"Please proceed, Ms. Feeney." Flick gave her an irritated look. He was probably wondering the same thing I was--why Hempstead wasn't giving the opening statement.

She stammered. "As I said, the proofs will show that Mister Slater led a fancy life, which was paid for by his wife. She received a substantial income each year from a trust established for her by her parents. Mister Slater had many affairs with other women, and his wife began divorce proceedings. If the divorce became final, his money supply would be cut off because there was a pre-nuptial agreement between him and his wife that stated, in the event of a divorce, he would take nothing.

"If, on the other hand, she should die during the course of the marriage, he would inherit all of the substantial assets of the trust fund. You will hear testimony from one of Mr. Slater's many girlfriends about how he told her he found out that a drug named Serenity was reported in the newspapers as causing users of the drug to commit murders. He told her what an ideal murder weapon the drug could be. Shortly after that conversation, Mr. Slater visited his family doctor and obtained a prescription for the drug. He took that drug for twenty-one days, according to the prescription, and then he murdered his wife. The state will present expert testimony to the fact that the drug didn't have anything to do with Mrs. Slater's death. This case is as simple as that. At the end of the trial, you will be asked to return a verdict of guilty against Mr. Slater. Let me thank you in advance for your time and attention."

Feeney's opening statement was short and concise. I was actually impressed. She had done a good job. Now it was my turn. I had the option of waiting until the prosecution rested its case before I gave my opening statement. Flick looked at me. I stood and looked at the jury. One of the rules of trial practice it to get your licks in early, so the jury just doesn't hear just the other side's version of the case. But there were always exceptions to the general rule. I thought long and hard about the right approach. Now or later? I was convinced that it was better strategically for me to wait until the prosecution was over before I tipped my hand on Slater's defense.

"Mr. Slater reserves his opening statement until the completion of the prosecutor's case."

CHAPTER 56

Feeney began the presentation of the case against Slater. Loukas and the other jurors listened for two days about the forensic details of Mrs. Slater's death buttressed by Feeney's constant whining. Her first witness was the pathologist who conducted the autopsy, and he described in minute detail the havoc that Slater had wrought on his wife. Even though it had been agreed by the parties that it was Slater who had committed the murder, Feeney apparently thought it important to burden the jury with minutiae. The testimony then shifted over to the finer points of pinning the death on him, including fingerprint analysis and the details of the scene of death vividly described by two different police officers.

Loukas didn't like Feeney at all. She lectured to the jury like she was the schoolteacher, and they were a bunch of morons. Her presentation was slow and boring, and this bitch's trial technique was overkill. Her voice sounded like the scraping of fingernails across a chalkboard. If a point could be made in one complete sentence, it would take her an hour. Loukas stopped listening. Instead, he fought the urge to sleep. It was difficult for him to keep his eyes open.

On the third day of trial, things started to get more interesting. Feeney's first witness of the day was Doctor Ralph Greene. He was a fit-looking guy about Slater's age. After he was sworn in, Feeney began her questions.

"Doctor Greene, what is the nature of your occupation?"

"I am a physician with a specialty in family practice."

"Where is your office located?"

"I practice with a group of five other family practice specialists in a clinical setting on Ten Mile and Hoover in Warren, Michigan."

"How long have you been in practice?"

"Ten years."

"Do you know the defendant in this case, Jay Slater?"

"Yes, I do. He and his wife were social friends with my wife and me. He was also a patient of mine."

"Prior to 2008, how long had Mr. Slater been a patient?"

"If I may look at my records. Here it is. I saw Mr. Slater for the first and only time in my office on April 8, 2008."

"What was the purpose of his visit?"

"It says here he was complaining about not being able to sleep."

"Do you remember any of the conversation?"

"Not really. Not without checking my notes."

"Can you tell the jury what your notes say about Mr. Slater's visit to your office?"

"As I said, he was complaining about not sleeping. We talked about the possible reasons for his difficulty. He said that there were some marital difficulties that he really didn't want to go into. I told him about Serenity and suggested that he give it a try. I wrote a prescription for a month's supply with three refills and told him to come back if there were any problems or if the drug wasn't helping."

"You made reference to his marital difficulties. Did he say why he didn't want to discuss them with you?"

"No. As I said, we were friends, and I just assumed that he didn't want to talk about it for that reason."

Feeney checked her notes. "That's all the questions I have. Thanks, Doctor Greene."

As I stood to question him, I wondered why Feeney had put him on the stand. She didn't need him in her case, and the time interval of taking the drug by Slater exactly fit what was known about its problems. His testimony was helpful to Slater. I decided to take a pass. "I have no questions for this witness."

Feeney called her next witness. "The State calls Alison McKechnie."

Slater sat up as the woman approached the witness stand to be sworn. She was a tall attractive blonde--a real knockout. He whispered to me, "I know this girl. That's not her name."

Feeney started, "Could you state your name, please?"

"Alison McKechnie."

"What kind of work do you do?"

"I work various jobs. Mainly, I work as a personal consultant."

"In your work as a . . . personal consultant, have you ever met Jay Slater?"

"I don't know who that is."

Feeney looked at the judge. "Your Honor, may I request that the court direct Mr. Slater to stand so that the witness can see him clearly?"

"Of course. Stand up, Mr. Slater."

Feeney continued, "The record should reflect that Mr. Slater is standing. Ms. McKechnie, do you know the gentleman standing?"

"Yes, I do. His name is Walter something. I forget his last name."

"In your work as a personal consultant, did you ever perform . . . services for him?"

"Yes. On several occasions. About six or seven times, I think."

"When was this?"

"From February through April, 2008."

"How can you be so certain about the dates?"

"I keep track of my . . . contacts in a notebook."

"And Walter's name appears in there?"

"Yes. That's him standing there."

I stood. "Your Honor, may my client sit down?"

Flick nodded, and Slater sat down.

Feeney checked her notes. "Can you tell me about your work as a personal consultant? What is it that you do?"

"I provide stress relief."

I heard a suppressed laugh coming from the jury box. I looked over. It was Dimitrios Loukas, the guy who constantly ogled Linda. He covered his mouth with his hand.

"Stress relief? What's that?"

"It's a personal service. A lot of people are under stress. I teach them ways to reduce the stress. I provide comfort for them."

"Comfort how?"

"Just listening to a person can provide a lot of comfort."

"So that's what you do? Listen to people?"

"I make people feel comfortable. I help reduce their stress."

"So you listened to what Walter had to say. Do you remember anything he might have said while you were trying to relieve his stress?"

"I remember he was not happy at home. He said his wife was going to divorce him. He wasn't happy about it. He also told me that he started taking a sleeping pill, and it helped. He made a weird kind of comment about it."

"What did he say about the sleeping pill?"

"He said he read in the newspaper that someone killed his wife while taking the drug, and he hoped it didn't happen to him."

"Did he say anything else about his wife or his marriage that you remember?"

"No. That's all I remember. My clients usually focus on other things to reduce their stress. I get them to try and not dwell on the stress that has brought them to me." She smiled coyly.

I looked over at Loukas again. He was still hiding a smile with his hand. He knew what was going on, and I wondered if the rest of the jurors did.

"That's all the questions I have."

Flick said, "Your witness, Mr. Riley."

I thought for a moment. She hadn't said much that would hurt my client. She obviously wanted to avoid the fact that she was an escort who sold sex for money. I had no interest whatsoever in making this unstated fact more obvious than it already was. Maybe there was someone on the jury who didn't make the connection. That would help Slater. I stood.

"Ms. McKechnie, when the man you know as Walter mentioned the sleeping pill, did he say he was taking it so he could kill his wife?"

"No. He said he hoped he wouldn't kill his wife."

"I have no more questions for this witness."

When I sat down, Slater learned over and whispered, "Why didn't you ask her why she was lying about her name?"

"Not now. I'll tell you later."

As the witness left the stand, Feeney once more went to her notes. "The State calls Deborah Anton."

This time, a good-looking brunette walked to the stand and was sworn in. "Would you state your name?"

"Deborah Anton."

"What do you do for a living, Ms. Anton?"

"I work as a barmaid at the Shelby Inn in Mount Clemens."

"How long have you worked there?"

"On and off for the past eight years."

"Do you know Jay Slater?"

"Yes."

"Is he in the courtroom?"

"Yes."

"Would you point Mr. Slater out for me?" Anton pointed at Slater. Feeney continued, "Let the record reflect that the witness has pointed out Mr. Slater. Now let me ask you how you know Mr. Slater."

"He is—was--a regular customer at the Shelby Inn. I waited on him many times."

"Other than Mr. Slater being a customer at the Shelby Inn, have you had anything else to do with him?"

"Yes. Mr. Slater and I have been friends for a number of years."

"Friends? What kind of friends?"

"Good friends."

Loukas tittered again. Covered his mouth. He is finding this funny. I wonder what he's thinking. What impact is this having on him?

"Can you be more specific? What kinds of things would you and Mr. Slater do?"

"I didn't say we did anything together. We are good friends."

Anton sat up straighter in the witness chair. She obviously didn't like Feeney, and the questions were making her uncomfortable.

"Did you and Mr. Slater go out on dates?"

"What do you mean by dates?"

"Like dinner or a show?"

"No. We never went out to dinner or a show."

"Well, what activities did you do together with Mr. Slater?"

"On occasion he would drive me home from work. That's it."

"That's it?"

"Yes. That's it."

Feeney couldn't help herself. "Have you ever been physically intimate with Mr. Slater?"

"You mean did he ever touch me?"

"Yes."

"Well, I suppose if you call a quick hug or a peck on the cheek being physically intimate, then I would say yes. But it sure wouldn't fit my definition of physically intimate. If what you're really asking me is if we had sex, no we didn't."

"Did Mr. Slater ever talk to you about his problems?"

"What problems?"

Feeney looked down at her notes. She was stuck. She apparently didn't know what to ask as a follow-up, so she stopped. "I have no more questions."

I stood. "I have no questions." Let sleeping dogs lie, I thought.

Flick dismissed us for the day.

CHAPTER 57

The next morning, Feeney called Professor John Olmstead to the witness stand. He was an asshole, Loukas thought. Just the way Olmstead strutted to the stand you could tell he thought he knew everything. Loukas found it difficult to follow the man's reasoning.

In response to a question, Olmstead gave a long speech. It was obvious to Loukas that he thought Slater was as guilty as hell.

"A common defense in murder cases is 'focal retrograde amnesia.' The defendant claims to have simply forgotten what occurred around the time of the crime, perhaps due to having consumed too much alcohol or other drugs. In fact, 'amnesia' is claimed in as many as 45 percent of murders. Psychologists know that this sort of amnesia is actually quite rare, so it's very likely that most, if not all, of these defendants are faking amnesia. It is my opinion that Mr. Slater is one of those who are faking amnesia to attempt to excuse his actions in murdering his wife. I have confirmed that many of these cases are faked. When defendants are given multiple-choice questions about the crime, they get the answers wrong too often.

"Think about it this way: If you are given a ten-item true/false test, and you know none of the answers, you should get five of the answers right just by guessing. But if you actually know the answers and are just pretending not to know, you might get every single answer wrong. Unfortunately, this sort of test can't tell us who's faking and who's not because some honest respondents might legitimately have an especially 'bad' performance, purely based on chance. On a large scale, we know there's a lot of cheating going on, but there's no way to reliably pick out the cheaters. But, in testing for faking amnesia, a secondary phenomenon seemed to be appearing. Several studies found that people who were asked to pretend to have amnesia were later unable to recall as much as people who told the truth from the start."

Loukas struggled to keep his eyes open. He glanced over at the paralegal every once in a while.

Feeney interrupted. "Did you test Mr. Slater?"

Olmstead looked at her with an icy stare. "I haven't completed my explanation. Would you like me to stop now, or do you want to know about my research?" Feeney looked perplexed. "I'm sorry for interrupting. Please continue."

Loukas sat there trying to decide who was a bigger asshole, Feeney or Olmstead. Olmstead continued, "The studies worked like this: Volunteers were told a story--or actually acted out a story--where they were the primary character: 'You' robbed someone, or beat a man to death with a pool cue, or killed a girl in a car accident. Then half these participants were told to pretend not to remember the key details of the crime in an effort to avoid punishment, while the other half was told to remember as many of the details as possible. They were tested on their memory, or their false reconstruction, immediately after the story, and then they returned to the laboratory a week later. This time, everyone was asked to try to recall the details of the crime accurately. The volunteers who told the truth the first time around did better on the second test. So I designed a study to address these problems. We divided the student volunteers into three groups: fake amnesiacs, truth-tellers, and untested. Students heard one of two stories while they read along with a script. Here's an excerpt from one of the stories."

Olmstead read from a sheet of paper, "You are a student at a party, and there is a dog named Ollie in the house. When you walk into the kitchen, you find it empty except for Ollie, who is curled up and sleeping in a little ball on his blue shag rug in the corner. Hearing you, he wakes up and leaps toward you, trying to play. You pick him up, and he licks your face. When you put him down, he keeps jumping up, trying to reach the counter. You realize he's trying to get at the pile of chicken bones that have been left on an aluminum platter next to the sink. Thinking, 'Dogs like bones,' you pick the biggest one and give it to him, saying, 'Here you go, Ollie. You'd better not tell Sam I gave this to you!' You turn around and realize that Ollie is choking. You realize that it could be that he's choking on the bone you just fed him, which is now nowhere in sight. Ollie dies."

Olmstead put the paper down and continued, "The students in the fake amnesic and truth-telling groups were asked to imagine confronting the owner the next day and explaining what happened. They wrote out a description of the key events and also answered a multiple-choice test. Then, a week later, everyone returned to write out the story again and retake the test. This time, everyone was instructed to try to answer accurately. The results revealed that, while the truth-tellers did respond more accurately than the fake amnesiacs, the fake amnesiacs didn't do any worse than the students who weren't tested at all. The results were the same for a second story, which involved giving nuts to a person with allergies, resulting in their death. I say the difference between the fake amnesiacs and the truth-tellers is probably completely due to the fact that the truth-tellers had a chance to practice the accurate story.

"In other words, pretending to have amnesia doesn't hurt your memory, but rehearsing the correct answers improves it. Mr. Slater predictably would have a testing record consistent with a recall of the murder and, in my opinion, he is trying to hide what he remembers from the jury. He not only knows what he did, but he knew at the time, and the drug Serenity had nothing to do with it."

Riley jumped to his feet. "Objection. Calls for speculation."

The judge sluggishly sat forward. "Objection overruled. Please continue."

Loukas fought to stay awake. And he nearly laughed aloud at Olmstead. He couldn't help it. The man was an idiot He looked over at the other jurors. Most of them also appeared to be struggling to stay awake. What a bunch of bullshit!

Feeney looked at the jury. She looked pleased with herself. "I have no more questions. Thank you Dr. Olmstead."

"Your witness, counsel," Flick intoned.

I wondered if it was just me, or if anybody else had the slightest idea what the hell Olmstead was talking about. I looked at the jury. All of them appeared half-asleep. Except for Loukas. He had a silly grin on his face. I stood and looked at Olmstead for a moment. "Doctor, have you ever tested the drug Serenity in any of your experiments?"

"No."

"Have you examined any of the numerous case reports received by the Upright Company describing acts of violence and suicide by people taking Serenity?"

"No."

"Is it important when conducting research on the amnesia effects of a given drug to understand the history and experience of the drug?"

"Yes, of course."

"Yet, it is my understanding that you have not done any such research with Serenity. Is that correct?"

"I have spoken to several Upright scientists about the drug, and they have assured me that there have been no problems with Serenity. In my opinion, my inquiry was sufficient to provide me with the information I needed to formulate my opinions about Mr. Slater."

"Move to strike the answer as unresponsive. Hearsay, pure and simple."

I knew that Judge Flick would probably allow the answer, but I had a reason for placing the objection. I wanted to lay a foundation to strike the man's testimony based upon mere conjecture. I wanted the jury to realize that an opinion reached by talking to employees of a drug company was nothing but conjecture.

Flick didn't look up. "Objection overruled. Continue, Counsel."

"So, the answer to my question about whether or not you have done any research with Serenity is that you have not done such research. Is that correct?"

"That is correct, Mr. Riley."

"Can you identify those Upright employees you spoke with?"

"Yes. Let me check my notes." He looked down at a piece of paper in front of him.

"I spoke with Cyrus Messner and a Mister Hagstrom. I don't recall his first name at the moment."

"Did you speak with Dr. Kenneth Smythe?"

"No. His name did come up in my conversations with the other two men, but I did not speak with him personally."

"Are either of the two men you spoke with trained scientists?"

"These men were employed by Upright to develop the drug Serenity, so I would assume they had some scientific background."

"So, when you said earlier that you spoke to scientists at Upright, it was a guess on your part that they were scientists? Is that correct?"

"Yes, I assumed they were scientists."

"If it turns out that Messner and Hagstrom are not scientists, do you agree that your earlier statement that you relied on statements of Upright scientists to form your opinion would be wrong?"

"Why would a drug company have someone not scientifically trained responsible for the development of a drug?"

"That's a good question, Dr. Olmstead. Perhaps you can ask Mr. Hempstead that question after you finish your testimony."

Hempstead stood. "Objection, Your Honor. That was not a question. Mr. Riley can't have a conversation with the witness without a question and answer format."

Flick hesitated. He didn't understand what Hempstead was talking about. "Objection sustained. Proceed with a question and answer format, Mr. Riley."

"Did you speak with any trained scientists at Upright in forming your opinions about Serenity?"

"I thought I answered that. I spoke only with Mr. Messner and Mr. Hagstrom."

"Let me see if I understand the basis for your opinions correctly. You assumed that these two men employed by Upright had sufficient scientific training to develop Serenity and based on that assumption you rely on what they told you about the safety of the drug in forming the conclusions and opinions you have given today. Have I got that right?"

"Well I wouldn't quite put it that way."

"Let me ask it a different way. Do you agree that you have relied in part on what these men told you about Serenity in forming your opinions?"

"As I said earlier, my inquiry was sufficient to provide me with the information I needed to formulate my opinions about Mr. Slater."

"And, just to clarify what you mean, when you say 'my inquiry,' you are talking about conversations with Mr. Messner and Mr. Hagstrom, who you 'think' are trained scientists. Is that correct?"

"Yes, that is correct."

"Did you specifically review any written documents provided to you by Upright in formulating your opinion?

"No. I previously testified that I had not seen anything."

"What was the nature of your conversations with either Mr. Messner or Mr. Hagstrom about Dr Kenneth Smythe?"

"I was informed that initially Dr. Smythe was in charge of the Serenity product, but he suffered an unfortunate mental breakdown and was removed from responsibility for the product."

I looked at Gary Newton. We had to track Smythe down and talk to him--protective order or not.

"Doctor, let me ask you this. Am I correct in assuming that both Mr. Messner and Mr. Hagstrom told you there were no problems specifically as they related to acts of violence or suicides in persons taking Serenity?"

"Yes, that's correct. I believe that I had previously stated that."

"Did either of these gentlemen tell you about any specific studies that had been conducted by Upright on the drug?"

"No. It wasn't necessary, in my opinion. Upright has the reputation of being one of the greatest pharmaceutical companies in the world, and I feel I am entitled to take information given to me by employees of that company at face value."

I looked at the Judge Flick. "Your Honor, I object to the answer given by the witness, and I would ask you to instruct the jury to disregard it."

Flick sneered at me. "Objection overruled. Please continue, Mr. Riley."

I returned my attention to the witness. "Have you reviewed the study conducted at Jackson Prison by Upright, or did you discus that study with either of the two men you mentioned?"

"No. We discussed no study in particular. It wasn't necessary for the reasons I have previously stated."

"Did you review or discuss the animal studies conducted on Serenity by Upright?"

Feeney stood and shouted, "Objection! Mr. Riley is now badgering the witness. Dr. Olmstead has testified already that he did not review or discuss any particular studies in formulating his opinion."

Flick glared at me. "I agree. Move on to something new."

I checked my notes. "If animal or human studies conducted by Upright were to show that a certain percentage of those exposed to the drug exhibited violent tendencies, would that be an important piece of information to you in formulating your opinion?"

"No. I thought I had already testified that there was no such information available to me and, in any event, such information would not be necessary for my opinion. My own research carries much more weight, in my view."

"So I understand what you are saying. If the Upright company as a result of their own testing and research knew any information about the dangerous potential of Serenity causing violent tendencies, it would have no bearing at all on your opinion about Mr. Slater. Is that a correct summary of the basis for your opinion?"

"Yes, it is. I think you have stated it very well, Mr. Riley." Olmstead looked at the jury and preened.

I was the one who should be preening. I tried hard to keep a straight face. "And, from what I understand of your opinion, you did not personally administer any of your testing to Mr. Slater, nor in fact request to do so, and you think he is faking his amnesia based on test results of others who took your test. Have I stated that correctly?"

"Yes."

"You would agree that it may have been more helpful in presenting your testimony and opinion to actually test Mr. Slater and present your test results of Mr. Slater to this jury?"

"Yes, anytime there is more information, it is always helpful."

"And, once again, you did not test Mr. Slater, or even ask to test him. Is that correct?"

"Yes, that is correct."

"I have no more questions of this witness."

Feeney huddled with Hempstead and Olmstead before he left the stand. She walked back to the podium.

"Your Honor, we have no more questions for this witness. May he step down?"

Flick nodded, and Olmstead stepped off the witness stand.

Quite frankly, I was surprised. Olmstead's testimony was meager in the extreme, but evidently Feeney thought she had presented enough to get a conviction of Slater. I now knew the reason Hempstead allowed Feeney to present the witness. He would have been embarrassed to do so.

I stood. "Your Honor, at this time I have a motion to take up out of the presence of the jury."

Flick nodded to the bailiff, who escorted the jury out of the room. I stepped to the podium when the door to the jury room closed.

"Your Honor, at this time I move that the testimony of Dr. Olmstead be stricken from the record on the basis that he has not presented a sufficient scientific basis for the rendering of an opinion. He has admitted that he did not request testing on Mr. Slater, nor did he do any such testing on Mr. Slater--that such testing results would have been helpful in presenting his opinions, that he reviewed no documents from Upright Labs on the safety of Serenity, that if the drug did have dangerous tendencies as evidenced in Upright's animal and human research it would not affect his opinion, and that his opinions as to Serenity's safety were based on hearsay conversations with two non-scientist employees of Upright. Finally, there is Dr. Olmstead's research that he vividly presented in detail. I must admit that I found that it was fascinating to hear about college students faking amnesia in regard to chicken bones, but I have a hard time grasping how it could seriously be of any consideration or relevance to the issues in this trial. I might add that I am truly sorry about Ollie the dog's death, but I also fail to perceive what that story has to do with the charges brought against Mr. Slater. It is well established that experts who testify about scientific matters must have a scientific basis for their opinions. This condition has not been satisfied with the presentation of Dr. Olmstead's testimony, and I request that his testimony be stricken and the jury so informed."

Feeney was obviously flustered. "Your Honor, can we have the lunch hour to formulate our response to Mr. Riley? This was totally unexpected."

Flick nodded. "We will recess until after lunch, and then I'll hear your response, Ms. Feeney."

After lunch, Feeney stood. "Your Honor, can we approach the bench?"

To be frank, I hadn't counted on the ineptness of the assistant prosecutor. Her dismal performance so far was a plus for Slater. I looked around the courtroom.

Hempstead sat at the prosecution table and stared straight ahead. I was right about him insofar as Olmstead. I knew why he hadn't done anything in this trial yet other than his one objection during my cross-examination of Olmstead.

The judge nodded. Feeney looked around at Hempstead and smiled. "Ms Feeney, I have thought about Mr. Riley's motion to strike Dr. Olmstead over the lunch hour. I don't think you need to present any argument. I am going to deny his motion. Are you prepared to move on?"

"Your Honor, the prosecution rests."

I thought for sure that there would be someone better than Olmstead waiting in the wings to testify for the prosecution. I know that Hempstead had a boatload of experts in the civil litigation, and I expected to see one or two of them here. Was I missing something here?

Flick nodded. "Very well. Mr. Riley, are you prepared to start your case?"

I stood, "Yes, your honor." The prosecution resting without offering any real expert testimony about Serenity surprised me. But, even more, I was surprised that Hempstead had done nothing in the trial so far. There must be some reason for letting Feeney present the prosecution case on her own.

"Bring in the jury." Flick nodded toward the bailiff.

CHAPTER 58

I started Slater's defense by standing up and giving my opening statement, which I had reserved until the end of the prosecution's case. I planned to say what I had to say in about five minutes. My goal was to keep is short and simple. I would tell the jury that my client had, in fact, taken the life of his wife. I knew it was unusual for a lawyer to admit anything against the interests of his client, but in this case I had no choice. In delivering my short speech to the jury, I needed to make eye contact with each one of them and stand a respectful distance away from the jury box to avoid having the jury feel I was invading their space. I would use Slater's first name to humanize him with the jury.

I spoke carefully.

"Ladies and gentlemen. This case, in every sense of the word, is a real tragedy. It is now Jay's turn to present his case and place this tragedy into the proper perspective. The proofs will demonstrate that he and his wife were having marital difficulties. Jay was not an angel in this marriage. He did some things of which he was not proud. The marital discord was causing him to lose sleep and he began to suffer from insomnia such that he could not function adequately on a day-to-day basis. He sought help from his doctor who prescribed a new drug, Serenity, which had been on the market for a few short months. You have already heard testimony from Jay's doctor about why he prescribed Serenity. Serenity was supposed to help Jay get some much-needed sleep and it probably did help him for the short period of time he took the drug. But Jay's use of Serenity set the stage for this tragedy. The proofs will show that even before Serenity was placed on the market, during the pre-marketing testing period, both in animals and human beings, the drug caused violent and aggressive behavior in those on the drug for a few short weeks. Test animals taking the drug were killing littermates. Before the drug was placed on the market, some prisoners being tested at Jackson prison committed suicide and, in one particularly disturbing case, a prisoner murdered a prison guard after being on the drug, like Jay, for just a few short weeks. Both before and after the marketing of this drug, users of the drug who suffered these aggressive and violent outbursts also suffered at the same time from complete amnesia of the event. This is a phenomenon called anterograde amnesia. Persons who killed loved ones, or attempted to kill themselves, had no memory whatsoever of the time period surrounding the incidents. Please note that during the prosecution's case, you heard none of this information. The proofs will demonstrate that the company who sought to bring this drug on the market and sell it to thousands upon thousands of our fellow Americans, knew about these terrible reactions but withheld this dangerous information from the Food and Drug Administration. It is fair to suggest that the drug would never have been allowed on the market if the company had been honest about the dangers it knew to exist. Countries around the world have banned the use of Serenity for the same reason; it is a dangerous drug. Jay was prescribed Serenity four months after the drug was placed on the market. By that time, the company selling this drug had already received additional numerous reports of suicides and killings of loved ones and never attempted to bring this terrible information about the drug to prescribing physicians throughout this country. Three weeks to the day he began taking this terrible drug, Jay killed his wife.

"The real culprit in this courtroom is the drug Serenity. In the truest sense of the word, Jay, like his wife, is an unfortunate and tragic victim of this drug. The charges filed against Jay require the proof of a conscious intent, to commit murder. Because of the impact of this terrible drug, Serenity, Jay was incapable of forming such an intent necessary to kill his wife. And, like others before him, he has no memory of the event. At the conclusion of this case, I will be asking you to render a verdict of not guilty on Jay's behalf, not because he did not perform the physical act of taking his wife's life, but because he was incapable of forming the required intent to do so. The court will instruct you at the end of the trial that intent is a necessary part of the alleged crime. The proofs will demonstrate that, due to Serenity, Jay was incapable of forming such an intent."

As I concluded my statement I stood for a moment and assessed whether my words had any impact on the jury. They had given me their full attention and they were still maintaining eye contact with me. I was satisfied. Now I had to set about proving what I just told them.

My first witness was Ralph Schneidermann, the psychiatrist. He loved the courtroom, and he loved testifying. The truth be known, I also loved when he was an expert witness in my trials. He understood his role in a courtroom, and he almost always got the job done right. He had the gift of gab. He was charming, good-looking, and he could work a jury until they were eating out of his hand, so to speak. He strode confidently to the witness stand, raised his hand, and swore to tell the truth. During his witness prep, he'd offered me a variety of theories about why Serenity was the culprit in Slater's case.

"Ralph, I don't need theories. The judge won't allow them. I need good, sound opinions based on the facts."

"I'll try. I'll do the best I can."

As he sat down in the witness chair, I was still unsure about the direction his testimony might take. "Good morning, Doctor Schneidermann."

"And good morning to you as well, Mr. Riley."

We went quickly through his credentials, and I offered his curriculum vitae as an exhibit. It was admitted into evidence.

"At my request, did you examine Jay?"

"Yes, I did."

"Could you describe how you conducted your examination of Jay and what your findings were?"

"Yes. I conducted three separate, lengthy interviews with Mister Slater over a period of four months. The first exam was conducted on May 3, 2008--four days after his wife's death. The second interview was one month later, and the third was four months after the death of

252

his wife. The feature unique to all three of these interviews was Mister Slater's total inability to recall any details concerning her death."

Schneidermann looked at the jury. They were paying rapt attention. "At the time of the first interview, I found Mister Slater to be confused and disoriented. For example, when I asked him his name he said, 'They tell me my name is Jay Slater.' He stared vacantly at me when I asked him questions and could not give me the date or the time of day. This disorientation in time, place and person is characteristic of a person suffering brain injury for a number of reasons, including drug toxicity. At the time of the second and third interviews, he was fully oriented to time, place and person, meaning that his disorientation at the first interview was temporary and associated with some type of insult to the brain in that time period. Because of his disorientation, I was unable to conduct an adequate history at the first visit, but I did have information that he had been taking a drug known as Serenity for about three weeks prior to the death of his wife. The condition that I observed in him is called anterograde amnesia."

"Anterograde amnesia?" I asked.

"Yes. Anterorgrade. This means that the person can remember events in the past, but not in the specific time frame. On his second and third interviews, Mister Slater demonstrated adequate memory for past events in his life other than the time of the death of his wife."

"Do you have an opinion as to the cause of Jay's anterograde amnesia?"

"This disorder is usually caused in one of a few ways: One type is caused by a class of drugs known as benzodiazepines. Another type of cause is a traumatic brain injury in which there is usually damage to the structure in the brain known as the hippocampus. It can also be caused by shock or an emotional disorder. Illness, though rarely, can also cause anterograde amnesia if it causes encephalitis, which is inflammation of brain tissue. Other than the benzodiazepines, the memory loss is usually episodic or continuous. With that class of drugs, the type of loss is limited to the period of time that the drug is in the person's body. Serenity is a benzodiazepine and, because of Mister

Slater's history of taking the drug, I concluded that Serenity was the cause of his anterograde amnesia."

We had the first part of the problem covered. The next part was going to be more difficult. I framed my next question carefully. "Doctor Schneidermann, the proofs in this trial so far have shown that Jay was involved in the death of his wife. Do you have an opinion as to whether or not Serenity played a role in causing that tragedy to occur?"

"Yes, I do have an opinion. My opinion is that the drug Serenity taken by Mister Slater caused him to perform the tragic actions which resulted in the death of his wife."

Now the difficult part. "What is the basis for your opinion that Serenity caused Mister Slater's actions resulting in the death of his wife?"

"My opinion is based on my background, education and training as a psychiatrist, my familiarity with benzodiazepines, the class of compounds to which Serenity belongs, and the well-recognized relationship between use of these drugs, particularly Serenity, and acts of violence. The United States is the only country in the civilized world that continues to allow Serenity to be marketed because of its propensity to cause users of the drug to commit violent acts against themselves or others."

"Did Jay murder his wife?"

"No. Under the definition of murder, it would be necessary for him to intend to kill his wife. Mister Slater, under the influence of Serenity, could not form an intent to kill his wife. His wife, Sylvia, was an unfortunate victim of the reaction to the drug, which caused Mister Slater to perform this tragic act.

I was satisfied. His well-rehearsed, careful use of language had gone before the jury better than I planned. We had avoided the word "murder" to describe what Slater had done to his wife. We had agreed to his use of Slater's wife's name. Calling her by her first name was a nice touch, I thought. "Are the opinions that you have rendered made with reasonable medical certainty?"

254

"Yes.

"Thank you, Doctor. I have no more questions." I returned to my chair and sat down.

Flick looked at Hempstead. "Cross-examination, Counsel?"

Lester Hempstead, to no surprise, stood to conduct the cross-examination. He approached Schneidermann. "Good morning, Doctor."

"Good morning."

"You are being paid for your testimony today. Isn't that correct?"

"No, sir."

"You're working for free?"

"No. You asked me if I was being paid for my testimony. I'm being paid for my time. Not my testimony." Score one for Schneidermann.

Hempstead smirked. "Let me ask the same question a different way then. How much have you been paid to date for the time you've spent in this case?"

"That's complicated."

"Complicated? How could it possibly be complicated?"

"It's complicated by the fact that Mister Riley has retained my services in other Serenity litigation as well, and I am not able to tell you about those other matters because the judge, as I understand it, will not permit discussion in this case about those matters. And, to answer your question then, much of the time I have spent involves research and evaluation of Serenity common to all these matters." Score two for Schneidermann.

Hempstead was pissed. He'd fought hard to keep any mention of other Serenity cases out of this trial, and his own questions and Schneidermann's tart answers had brought them in. I could almost hear the wheels spinning in his mind. He wanted to ask the judge to censure Schneidermann in front of the jury for mentioning other Serenity cases, but it was his own questioning that brought the topic into play. The judge would overrule him and tell him exactly that. If I were going to guess, I would say that he was going to drop the topic of compensation and go on to other matters. I was wrong.

Hempstead wouldn't let it go. "Tell the jury how much you've charged Mister Riley for the time spent on Serenity matters?"

I was on my feet. "Your Honor, I object. As I understand the pretrial ruling of the court, this question is improper. Just because Mr. Hempstead has already breached the court's order by his questions doesn't mean that he can continue doing so." The minute the words were out of my mouth I realized that I should not have made the objection. I wanted to get in evidence about other Serenity cases. I wanted the jury to hear as much as possible about what Serenity was doing to others.

Flick looked at Hempstead. "What about that?"

"Your Honor, this should be taken up out of the presence of the jury. May we approach the bench?"

The lawyers for both sides moved to the sidebar. Hempstead continued, "Judge, Mr. Riley has set me up by priming his witness to introduce the topic of other cases like he did."

Flick looked at me.

I shrugged my shoulders. "Judge, I wasn't the one who asked the questions that opened the door. Mr. Hempstead knows full well that, in the Scruggs case, the doctor is a designated expert witness and, in his deposition in that case, he answered the same questions that Mr. Hempstead asked here in the same way."

Gary Newton handed me the copy of Schneidermann's deposition, and I turned to the page where his answers appeared. I read them to Judge Flick. They were identical to the answers given by Schneidermann today in court. "I think it is reasonable to conclude that the very issue that Mister Hempstead fought so hard to exclude has now been opened by him."

I could also read Flick's mind. His brain cells were jumping through hoops to try to save Hempstead's sorry ass. To my surprise, he agreed with me, but he didn't realize it. His gut instinct was to rule against me in any way that he could. Flick looked at Hempstead.

"You have opened the door, Counsel. I will overrule the objection."

The jury filed back into the courtroom, and Hempstead resumed his questioning. "The question is, doctor, how much time have you spent on all Serenity-related matters?"

"So you want me to answer a different question than you asked before?"

Flick interrupted. "Doctor, answer the question."

Schneidermann flashed a quick smile at the jury. Most of them smiled back. They were enjoying the battle of wits between Schneidermann and Hempstead. "I have spent thirty-seven hours on all Serenity-related matters."

"How much money have you received from Mr. Riley for the time you have spent?"

"To date, I have received twenty-five thousand dollars."

Hempstead made a big show of going back to his table, picking up a calculator and returning to the podium. "Let me see." He punched in the numbers. "Let's do the math. Twenty-five thousand dollars for thirty-seven hours work comes to . . .six hundred and seventy-six dollars per hour." Hempstead enunciated the amount as if it was all the money in the world. "Is that what you charge for your time, Doctor? Six hundred and seventy-six dollars per hour?"

"No sir, it's not. If I may explain?"

"Your lawyer will give you the opportunity to explain it when he gets to ask questions."

I was on my feet again. "Your Honor. First, I object to the characterization by Mister Hempstead that I am Doctor Schneidermann's lawyer. That is improper, and Mister Hempstead knows it. Second, the doctor would like to explain his answer, and he should be given the opportunity to do so at this time."

Flick surprised me again. "I agree. Explain your answer, doctor."

"Shortly before Mister Riley contacted me on Mister Slater's matter, I received a phone call from a lawyer representing Upright. That lawyer was from Mr. Hempstead's law firm. He offered me twenty-five thousand dollars as a retainer if I would agree to serve as a consultant to Upright and his law firm on Serenity-related matters. When Mr. Riley contacted me, I told him about the proposed offer from Upright, and I also told him that I would work for his clients but would need a twenty-five thousand dollar retainer. My usual fee for rendering treatment to my patients is two hundred dollars. If I participate in litigation-related activities, it takes me away from my practice. The fee I charge represents time away from my practice. My agreement with Mr. Riley is that the twenty-five thousand dollars will be used to compensate me on my hourly fee basis. If I have done my math correctly--I don't have a calculator like Mr. Hempstead--my current charge to Mr. Slater's case, as well as the other cases, is $7400." He sat back and smiled at the jury. Most of the jurors smiled back. They liked the calculator comment. Score three for Schneidermann. None for Hempstead.

Hempstead regrouped. "Let's move on, doctor. How long have you worked with Mr. Riley in a professional capacity?"

"In this case, or in general?"

"In general."

"I think it's about eight years now."

"How many times have you testified in court for clients of Mr. Riley's?"

"Five. This is the sixth."

"How many times have you consulted with Mr. Riley on individual cases, whether or not it resulted in you giving trial testimony?"

"I checked my records this morning because I thought you might ask. I have consulted with Mr. Riley on a total of sixteen cases over the eight years I've known him."

"And how much have you earned in hourly fees in all the cases that you have worked on for Mr. Riley?"

"Always two hundred dollars per hour."

"I mean the total amount."

"I don't have that figure. I could call my secretary over lunchtime and get it for you, if you want."

Flick was getting impatient. "Let's get on with it, Mr. Hempstead."

"Doctor, have you ever treated a patient with anterograde amnesia?"

"No. Thank goodness, it's a rare occurrence."

"Have you ever done hands-on research on anterograde amnesia?"

"I have not personally done any hands-on research, but I have read every article in the peer review medical literature on the subject of Serenity and anterograde amnesia. I spent a total of twenty-two hours doing that."

Hempstead was angry. "Your Honor, I request that you instruct the witness to respond only to my questions and not make statements outside the scope of the questioning."

Flick looked at Hempstead. "I was wondering when you were going to object to that." He leaned toward the witness. "Doctor, just answer the question that is asked of you. Don't make speeches or gratuitous comments that don't pertain to the question."

"Was I doing that? I consider reading medical and scientific articles research, which is what Mr. Hempstead asked me about. I'm sorry, Your Honor. I'll try to do better." Schneidermann raised his eyes at the jury and smiled. Again, most of them smiled back.

I hoped that Schneidermann didn't try to push back too hard. So far, he controlled the cross-examination.

Hempstead continued. "You testified that you interviewed Mister Slater three times. Where did these interviews take place?"

"At the Wayne County jail. There is an interview room on the third floor."

"Was anybody other than you and Mr. Slater present at these interviews?"

"No. Wait. I take that back. There was a guard inside the room during the first interview."

"Why was that?"

Schneidermann thought for a moment. "Mr. Slater was like a zombie at that time. He was in jail because his wife was dead. I requested that the guard stay in the room because I was uncertain whether Mr. Slater was still toxic from Serenity."

Four for Schneidermann. So far, I thought, it was four to nothing. This was going a lot better than I expected.

Hempstead hesitated. The cross-examination had been a disaster. He appeared distracted, and I wondered why. I had been up against him any number of times, and he was a worthwhile opponent. I'd seen him take apart a number of fine experts because he was always well prepared. He just didn't have it today.

"I have one final question, Dr. Schneidermann. The testing of Mr. Slater's blood at the time he was admitted to Detroit Receiving Hospital indicated that the Serenity level was much higher than one would expect from a single dose. Can you say, with any kind of certainty, that the last dose of Serenity Mr. Slater had before his admission to the hospital was taken before he killed his wife?"

Schneidermann sat for a moment. "No. I can't say for certain."

"That completes my cross-examination, Your Honor."

I checked my notes. Except possibly for the last question, Hempstead hadn't touched Schneidermann or his opinions. No reason to press my luck. "I have no questions on redirect. May the witness be excused?"

Schneidermann stepped down after sharing one last smile with the jury. The only one who didn't smile was Dimitrios Loukas. He was too busy checking out Linda's legs.

Flick recessed trial until the afternoon.

CHAPTER 59

The afternoon session started promptly at one o'clock. When the jurors were seated, Flick nodded in my direction. "Call your next witness, Mr. Riley."

"Your Honor, the defense calls Jay Slater."

I knew I was taking a chance putting Slater on the stand. He had the constitutional right to remain silent. The prosecutor had the burden of proof and, if Slater chose not to testify, the judge would tell the jury the fact he had not given testimony couldn't be used against him. In most criminal cases, defense attorneys never put defendants on the stand. It was too risky. Too much could go wrong, and if a defendant had a history of bad behavior other than the crime for which he was being charged, the prosecutor could ask questions to bring this history out in front of the jury. This case was different. I didn't see much choice for Slater. He needed to stand up and tell the jury he didn't remember killing his wife. There was no other way to get that crucial fact into evidence. Slater had no criminal history--had never received so much as a traffic ticket. But he would be subject to cross-examination by the prosecutor, and it was a risk I had to take. I had talked to Ralph Musilli, the self-designated criminal expert attorney, about this, and he agreed with me. Despite his promises of assistance on Slater's case, this was Musilli's only contribution.

I stood at my seat and asked my questions. "Would you please state your name, for the record?"

"Jay Slater."

"Jay, you were married to Sylvia Slater for how many years?"

"Six years. Sylvia and I got married on January 15, 2002."

"Did you and Sylvia have any children?"

"No. She couldn't have children. She had a bad infection when she was a teenager and had to have surgery. The surgery made it impossible for her to have a baby."

So far, so good. Slater was speaking softly, but clearly. He made good eye contact with the jurors.

"Jay, the prosecutor has mentioned that you and your wife were having difficulties in your marriage. Did the two of you talk about divorce?"

"Yes we did. We decided that before we went ahead and did something like that, we would try to see if we could patch up our marriage. We decided to start marriage counseling and had already made an appointment with a counselor. We made the appointment the week before her death."

"Jay, there have been a number of references during this trial to a drug called Serenity. Did there come a time when you were prescribed that drug?"

"Yes. I was having trouble sleeping, and my doctor prescribed that drug for me about three weeks before I killed my wife."

"We will talk about that in a few moments, but first tell me whether or not you took the Serenity the way the doctor prescribed it for you?"

"Yes, I did. I took one every night at bedtime. As I said, it was supposed to help me sleep."

"Did the drug help you sleep?"

"Yes, it did. It seemed to help a lot."

"Who prescribed the drug for you?"

"My doctor. Doctor Ralph Greene. He testified earlier. He told me it was a new drug on the market and was better than the other drugs that were supposed to help people who couldn't sleep."

"Did you know about this drug Serenity before you went to Dr. Greene?"

"No."

"Jay, the evidence in this case so far indicates that you were the person who killed your wife on April 29, 2008. Is it true that you did kill your wife on that date?"

"I have no reason to doubt the evidence, but if I did I do not remember it."

Good answer. We had worked hard to get him to answer that question exactly as he did. "What is the first thing you do remember after the death of your wife?"

"I remember people talking to me while I was in jail. You were one of them. You told me that you were my lawyer. I was surprised. I wondered why I needed a lawyer."

"When did you first learn that your wife was dead?"

"You told me on that first day we met. I was shocked."

I paused for a moment. This was as good as it was going to be, so I decided to quit.

"Your Honor, that completes my questions for Mr. Slater."

Feeney stood and stared at Slater. I could swear she was licking her chops as she approached him. Slater wiped his mouth and put his hands on the edge of the witness stand and studied them. He was determined to not let her see how nervous he was. I wondered, once again, why she was doing the questioning. What was the deal with Hempstead?

"Mr. Slater, does the telephone number 313-590-3537 sound familiar to you?"

"Yes."

"That it is your cell phone number. Isn't it?"

Slater nodded.

Feeney spoke sharply. "You'll have to answer. Yes or no."

"Yes." He nodded again.

"Did you know Deborah Anton?"

I jumped to my feet. "I object, Your Honor. This is beyond the scope of direct examination." I sure as hell didn't want the jury to hear about all of Slater's women again.

Flick gave me his sarcastic grin. "I'll give some leeway to Ms. Feeney. Answer the question, Mr. Slater."

Slater shook his head. "Yes. She is a friend. She testified about that."

Feeney stared at him. Slater studied his fingernails.

"Let me try it this way. Do you know that Deborah has 586-778-8225 for a telephone number?"

On my feet again. I couldn't let this get out of hand. "Objection. Beyond the scope of direct examination."

"Denied. Answer the question."

Slater nodded.

"Please answer yes or no."

"Yes."

Feeney took a moment and checked her notes. "That number sounds familiar?"

I stood. "Objection, Your Honor. Asked and answered."

"Sustained. Move on, Counsel." The judge looked bored, Slater thought.

"Let me try another number. Do you know anybody at the phone number 248-540-6020?"

On my feet again. "Objection, Your Honor. Is Counsel going to go through the entire Detroit area telephone book? I object on the basis that it is beyond the scope of direct examination and is irrelevant.

Flick responded, "Denied. Answer the question."

Jay answered. "It doesn't sound familiar."

"Did you know Alison McKechnie, who testified earlier?"

Judge Flick interrupted. "Counsel, is there a point to all of this? If there is, please make it and get on with your cross-examination."

Feeney looked at the judge and reddened. "Yes, there is a point to my questions, judge. If I can have some leeway on this line of questioning, it would be appreciated. It won't take much time."

"Continue, but please move this along."

Feeney looked at her notes. "Do you know anybody who has the cell phone number 586-472-3120?"

"No." Slater was certain he didn't know anyone with that number. He suppressed a grin because Feeney forgot about the McKechnie question. His glee was short-lived.

"Let me back up a moment. Does the name Alison McKechnie sound familiar?"

I jumped to my feet again. "Objection. What relevance does the fact that a name might sound familiar have?"

The court nodded. "Agreed. Objection sustained. Move on, please."

Feeney checked her notes. "Do you know Alison McKechnie?"

Slater leaned forward and then looked sideways at the judge. "Your Honor, I didn't hear her question."

"Please keep your voice up, Counsel."

Feeney nearly shouted the question. "Alison McKechnie. Do you know anyone by that name?"

Slater shrugged his shoulders as I stood. "Objection, Your Honor. Mr. Slater has answered the question."

Flick nodded. "Agreed, Counsel. Please move on."

Feeney hesitated. Looked at her notes again. "Do you know anyone who has the phone number 586-472-3120?"

I was getting angry. "Your Honor, this question has been asked and answered."

The judge glared at Feeney. "Counsel, I've heard just about enough. If you have any questions that pertain to this matter, please ask them. If not, stop wasting the court's time."

Slater watched Feeney. I thought she was going to cry. She shuffled her notes. "That completes my cross-examination." She looked up at the judge. "Reserve the right to re-cross the witness."

The judge nodded toward me. "Any re-direct examination, Mr. Riley?"

I stood and looked at Slater. "Jay, have any of the questions asked by Ms. Feeney caused you to want to change any of the testimony you have given here today?"

Slater shook his head. "No."

I looked at the court. "I have no further questions. May the witness stand down?"

Feeney stood. "Subject to recall."

I pressed the advantage. "If the prosecutor is trying to hide something, let her bring it out now. She does not have the right to recall Mr. Slater on her own whim. This is a trial subject to certain rules, and those rules require timely asking of questions during her cross-examination. She can't wait until she feels like asking them. Her cross-examination is over. There is no basis for recalling Mr. Slater."

"I agree with Mr. Riley. Counsel, you have completed your cross-examination. Your only opportunity to conduct further questioning of Mr. Slater will be if Mr. Riley recalls him as a witness."

Slater took a deep breath and stepped down from the witness stand. "Bitch," he whispered as he sat down next to me. Feeney hadn't asked Slater about the conversation that McKechnie had testified to--the discussion of the sleeping pill and killing of wives. Slater told me that he didn't remember any such conversation, but if I were the attorney on the other side, I'd want the jury to hear about that conversation again. Just to plant the seed that the murder was planned with knowledge that the drug could cause a murder to be committed. But I wasn't on the other side and, as far as I was concerned, the less they heard about that claimed discussion, the better for Slater.

Flick addressed the jury. "We'll break for the day. I'll see you tomorrow morning. Please be on time."

I took a deep breath. I'd taken a big chance putting Slater on the stand. Feeney's dismal performance was a big plus for him.

CHAPTER 60

At the end of the day, Gary, Linda and I decided to make a detour on our way back to the office. We walked to our favorite watering hole and ordered drinks.

"Juror number eleven likes my legs." Linda flashed a smile.

I looked at her, swept my eyes down at her legs, and then laughed. "Everyone in the courtroom likes your legs. Why would he be any different?

Linda smiled. "I think that's why he had his seat changed."

Gary grinned. "That's what I think."

I leaned forward so that I could hear Linda better. The background noise in the Brasserie, the bar just across the street from the courthouse, was getting noisier by the minute as happy hour progressed. I told her what I knew about the move. "The bailiff said Loukas was allergic to perfume and number seven, the Henson lady, had doused herself in it. Hell, I could smell her from our table. Where does she get that crap?"

"That may have been what he told the judge, but I know he changed seats because of my legs." She sipped her drink and made a face. "This is pretty strong."

I grinned at her. "Well, your assignment then, for the rest of the trial, is to keep him interested. Maybe you could do the Sharon Stone thing. What was the name of that movie?"

"Basic Instinct. Forget it. I can't even go to bed without wearing underwear."

"That's what you can do. Flash him every time Hempstead stands up to talk. Loukas's a strong person. I wouldn't be surprised if he turns out to be the foreman. Did you see him smile when Feeney was questioning the prostitute? Your drink too strong?"

"Yes, it is." She nodded.

CHAPTER 61

The next morning, I looked forward to the testimony of my next witness. Slater needed the help. I rose and addressed the court.

"The defense calls Dr. Sam Giovanni."

Giovanni was an expert in toxicology, and I'd hired him to provide testimony for my clients on a number of occasions in the past. He was a good man and had a distinguished scientific background. He had been a professor of medicine at the Wayne State University School of Medicine for thirty years and had written more than one hundred research articles about the toxicity of various drugs. His work was published in numerous scientific journals. He had received many awards and honors for his professional activities. After going through his credentials, I got right to the point.

"Dr. Giovanni, do you have an opinion as to whether or not the drug Serenity played a role in causing the death of Rosalind Slater at the hands of her husband?"

Giovanni looked at the jury as he spoke. "What we have in this case is a clear example of what the drug can do. This man takes Serenity for three weeks, and the drug reaches toxic levels in his bloodstream that, in turn, creates a condition in him called anterograde amnesia. This is the medical term for what happened to Mr. Slater. He looks normal and acts normal, except that he goes home and kills his wife. He has no memory of doing so. Without this potent drug in his system, it is my opinion that he would not have killed his wife. So the answer to your question is yes, the drug definitely caused the death of Mrs. Slater."

I glanced over at the jury. There were listening carefully. So far so good.

"What is the basis for your opinion that Serenity caused Mr. Slater to kill his wife?"

Giovanni sat back. "First, let me say this. There are no epidemiological studies that have been done to absolutely prove that the drug causes this type of effect. The reason is that it would be unethical to conduct such studies. Medicine and science simply do not permit performing studies when the potential outcome involves the possibility of death in human experiments. For example, we can study drugs that lower blood pressure or blood sugar because the end results are simple measurements. If the question that must be answered is, 'Did the drug lower blood pressure?' simply measuring the blood pressure will tell us the answer. The same as to blood sugar. One can measure blood sugar. When the issue becomes whether or not a drug is capable of causing a horrendous reaction, such as experienced by Mr. Slater, it would be unethical and immoral to conduct such a study. Death is not like low blood pressure...."

I cut Giovanni off. He was wandering. "So, Dr. Giovanni, what kind of information do you use to make cause and effect decisions when it would be unethical to conduct a formal epidemiology study?"

Giovanni glared at me. He didn't like to be interrupted. "Epidemiological."

"What?"

"You said epidemiology study. That's not the correct word. You should say epidemiological study."

I looked at the jury. They enjoyed watching Giovanni scold me. Whatever it takes. "Let me correct myself. What kind of information do you use to arrive at a scientific conclusion about the harm a drug can cause when formal epidemiological studies cannot be done for ethical reasons?"

He looked over at the jury and winked. "You see, you can teach an old dog new tricks." The jury laughed. They liked this guy. All well and good. "But let me get back to your question. Instead of formal epidemiological studies, we look at animal studies. We look at what experiences have been seen and reported by doctors, not only with Serenity, but also with other drugs in the same pharmacologic category. We look at the chemical structure of the drug. We look at the dosage of the drug. We look at what the medical literature says about the drug. A responsible scientist gathers all of the information one can find and makes conclusions based on that information."

"Let me repeat the question I asked a few minutes ago. What is the basis for your opinion that the drug Serenity caused Mr. Slater to kill his wife?"

Giovanni glared at me again. He removed his glasses and cleaned them with a handkerchief he'd removed from his pocket. He placed the glasses back on his nose. "As I mentioned, my opinion is based on indirect evidence--animal studies and case reports. Plus, similar reactions seen with other drugs in the same pharmacologic category as Serenity, except not with the same order of magnitude."

"Will you describe the specific evidence you have relied on in forming your opinion in this case?"

"There have been a substantial number of case reports from many physicians throughout the country--throughout the world--of patients committing violent destructive acts against themselves or loved ones after taking doses of Serenity resulting in toxic levels after two to three weeks of taking the drug. These reports are so numerous worldwide that Great Britain, Canada, Holland, France, Spain, and many other countries have banned use of the drug. In fact, the only country in the world that permits this drug to be marketed is the United States in a dose much lower than was taken by Mr. Slater.

"As to animal studies, the manufacturer performed some simple studies that showed nearly identical outcomes to the human experience--rage reactions resulting in self-destructive behaviors or attacks on other animals in the same cages. These were dose-dependent reactions. The higher the dose, the greater the number and extent of the reaction."

I looked at the jury. They were listening attentively. It was time to pop the big question. "In your opinion, did Mr. Slater intentionally murder his wife?"

Giovanni took his time in responding. I liked the dramatic moment it created. "It is my opinion that, due to the toxic effects of the drug, Serenity, Mr. Slater did not possess the ability to intentionally perform the act of murder on his wife. He may have killed her, but he did not murder her. May I elaborate?"

I nodded. "Please do so."

"The act of murder requires two things. First, it requires the death of a person at the hands of another. The second is a specific intent to take the life of that person. Without that specific intent, you cannot have the act of murder. Mr. Slater, while under the toxic effects of Serenity, was incapable of forming the specific intent to murder his wife."

I paused to let the jury ponder Giovanni's statement, and then continued, "What is the basis for your opinion that Jay did not intentionally kill his wife?"

He looked perturbed. "I thought I just answered that. But let me repeat myself. Many case reports, animal studies, the sum of the available experience worldwide with Serenity." Giovanni leaned toward the jury. "Have I made myself clear?" The jury tittered and laughed.

"Yes, and thank you very much. The witness is with the prosecution. That is all the questions I have for now."

The judge nodded toward the prosecutor. "Your witness."

Hempstead stood and looked at Giovanni. "Dr. Giovanni, you have testified several hundreds of times in court trials, is that correct?"

Giovanni looked at the jury and grinned briefly. "Yes, that's true. I have appeared in court a substantial number of times as an expert witness . . . even on behalf of some of your clients." Several of the jurors grinned back.

Hempstead scowled. "I didn't ask you that."

Giovanni shrugged. "I thought you were trying to make the point that I'm a highly qualified expert."

The judge almost shouted. "The two of you stop arguing. Proceed on a question and answer basis." All the jurors were smiling now.

Score one for Giovanni, I thought. How could Hempstead have walked into that one? Hempstead was too experienced to show his embarrassment, but I knew the man. Someone back at his office would pay for the mistake of failing to remind him that Giovanni had testified for another lawyer in his office several years ago. I remembered that case. Giovanni testified against my client, and he kicked my butt. Giovanni was good. He knew how to work a jury. I contacted him on another case after that experience, and we had been friends ever since. I was surprised that Hempstead didn't know this.

Hempstead continued. "Let's talk about animal testing. Isn't it true that animal testing for toxicity of a drug is generally conducted at doses many times greater than a human being may receive?"

"In general, that's true. Yes, sir."

"No human being would ever take ten, fifteen, or one hundred times the recommended dose of a drug, is that correct?"

"Yes, if I may explain . . ."

"Not only would a person not take ten, fifteen, or one hundred times a recommended dose, it would probably kill that person if that happened, is that correct?"

"Yes. I'd like to explain."

"And isn't it true that, in all of the Serenity animal studies, not one animal received less than ten times the recommended daily human dose?"

"That's right. If I may explain . . ."

"And it is those animal studies that form, at least in part, the basis for your opinion that Mrs. Slater's murder was caused by Serenity. Isn't that correct?"

"First of all, there's no maybe about it."

"Move to strike as non-responsive."

Flick lashed out. "Just answer the question. The jury is instructed to disregard the witness's last comment."

"The questions is, doctor, isn't it true that these animal studies form part of the basis for your opinion that the drug may have caused harm?"

"Yes."

Giovanni sat silently and adjusted himself to face the jury squarely. "If I may be permitted to explain."

"Do you know any responsible scientist in the world who would say that an animal test using 10, 20, or 50 times the human dose of a drug could be unequivocally used to conclude, by itself, that the drug was capable of causing the same effect in a human being?"

"By itself? No. And I don't believe I testified to that."

"Move to strike the response as unresponsive."

Flick glared at Giovanni. "Objection sustained, and the jury is instructed to disregard the last answer. Now, doctor, if you would be good enough to follow the rules of this court and answer the question Mr. Hempstead has asked you."

Giovanni smiled at Flick. "I should answer the question even if it is misrepresenting what I have said earlier?"

Flick's face reddened. I looked over at the jury. They loved this battle of wits. Flick snapped. "Just answer the question."

"No."

"You refuse to answer the question?" Flick was livid.

"I am answering the question. That is my answer. If, in theory, a scientist would use animal data and nothing else, it would not be appropriate to conclude unequivocally that the drug caused the same effect in humans."

Hempstead interjected. "Doctor, yes or no? Would any reasonable scientist use animal data alone to unequivocally state that a drug caused a problem in human beings?"

Giovanni looked at the jury and shrugged. "I thought I just answered that. No."

Hempstead continued. "Are animal studies crucial to a determination of whether or not a drug causes harm in a human being?"

Giovanni pondered the question. "Do you mean can a drug be shown to cause harm in humans without the benefit of having animal studies?"

"Yes. That is exactly what I mean."

"Yes. In that sense, animal studies may not be crucial to such a determination."

"Let's switch topics. You mentioned case reports."

"Yes, I did."

"Case reports are anecdotal reports from doctors reporting individual potential associations between usage of a drug and some type of adverse effect. Is that correct?"

"Yes. If I may explain..."

"Case reports are not epidemiological studies. Correct?"

"Yes, they are not epidemiological studies."

"I mentioned the word 'association.' Would you agree that the fact that most people who develop cancer of the breast also wear dresses be an example of an association between breast cancer and the wearing of a dress?"

"Yes, I would agree that such a description is an association."

"Would you also agree that dresses do not cause breast cancer?"

"I don't think you need an expert to tell you the answer to that question."

Flick interrupted. "Doctor Giovanni, just answer the question."

"No. Dresses do not cause breast cancer."

"No more questions, Your Honor." Hempstead turned around and strode back to the defense table. Looked at Flick. "That completes my cross-examination. I have a motion."

Flick nodded, and Hempstead continued, "At this time, I move to strike the testimony of Dr. Giovanni on the issue of whether or not Serenity caused the murder of Mrs. Slater. Dr. Giovanni's own testimony acknowledges that animal studies are not crucial in the question of whether a drug causes harm in a human being. If the animal studies are not crucial to a determination, it follows logically that no conclusion about the relationship between human use and harm can properly be drawn from such studies. The same reasoning applies to case reports. If such reports are merely anecdotal and examples of associations between drug use and harm, but do not constitute epidemiological studies, they must not be permitted to be used to determine that Serenity was a possible cause of Mrs. Slater's death. The whole is equal to the sum of its parts. Here we have two parts, neither of which alone can constitute proof of potential harm. Because both of the parts are deficient, it logically follows that the whole is deficient. You can't take two bad apples and put them together and say you have good apples. Science doesn't work that way. "

Flick glanced at me. I stood slowly, formulating an appropriate response.

"Do you have a response, Counsel?"

"I certainly do, Your Honor. If I may be permitted to ask the witness several questions as a follow up on redirect?"

Flick leaned forward. Looked at me over the top of his bifocals. "Counsel, you know the rules. You had the obligation to properly qualify your witness. After you tendered the witness, the other side has the right to challenge your offer. We now have a record from both sides. No further testimony is necessary. Do you have anything else before I make my ruling?"

I opened my mouth, started to speak, and hesitated. "If I might have a moment to review my notes." I glanced down at my notebook. I didn't think that Hempstead's challenge to someone of Giovanni's stature would be taken seriously. I tried to think while I pretended to read my doodling on the notepad. What the hell was I going to say to Flick, who had obviously made up his mind? I looked over at Newton who had written a note. He shoved the notepad in my direction.

I read Gary's printed statement aloud to Flick. "Judge. Dr. Giovanni has an opinion that Serenity caused the death of Mrs. Slater. The basis for his opinion does include Upright's animal studies and the case reports received with regard to this drug. If he would be permitted to clarify the essence of the basis for his testimony, he could clear up the possible confusion the court is having with this issue . . . ."

"Stop, Counsel. You know better than to argue your case in front of the jury." Flick nodded at the bailiff. "Take them to the jury room. We'll continue this in their absence."

"All rise," the bailiff intoned, and the jury slowly filed out.

Flick leered at me. "I'm surprised that you would resort to making statements like that in front of the jury."

What was this all about? I looked around the courtroom and tried to put the pieces of the puzzle together. So much had happened in this case that didn't make sense. What was it? The judge, in a way that made me look incompetent in front of the jury, criticized everything I did at trial. Things had gone wrong from the very first moment. The judge was accusing me of doing something improper. The dog and pony show Hempstead and the judge had just put on in front of the jury was having an effect on the jurors. They wouldn't look me in the eyes anymore as they filed out of the courtroom. In thirty years of trial practice, I'd never been double-teamed like this by defense counsel and the trial judge.

"I'm waiting for a response, Counsel."

"The record should reflect that you permitted Mr. Hempstead to make his motion and present his argument in the presence of the jury. I do not understand why you would scold me in front of the jury for responding in the same way. You have also permitted the testimony of the prosecution's only witness, Dr. Olmstead, which was based on hearsay and conjecture supplemented by the statements of non-scientists at Upright regarding the safety of the drug. I would respectfully request that the court apply the same standard to the instant motion as it did to the prosecution's witness."

Flick glared at me. "Do you have anything of substance? If you don't, I am prepared to make my ruling."

Flick grinned his feral grin. I couldn't stop now.

"Yes, I do have some more, Your Honor. First, the statements I just made are statements of substance. Second, Dr. Giovanni is a man and scientist of impeccable reputation and knowledge as both Mr. Hempstead and I have found out over the years. To properly analyze this motion, I urge you to compare the essence of this expert's opinion with that of Doctor Olmstead. Doctor Giovanni personally examined the records in this case as well as the records of Upright in the research and development of Serenity. He has looked at the animal tests and the case reports received by Upright. He has done more than talk to two non-scientists at that company. As you may recall, Dr. Olmstead did not examine any documents whatsoever. Dr. Giovanni has clearly assisted the jury in their need to discern the effects of Serenity on Mr. Slater. I respectfully request that the motion be denied. To compare what Olmstead presented as the basis for his testimony, with Dr. Giovanni tells the court all it needs to know in denying the motion.

Flick looked around. His face turned red. He was pissed at my implicit suggestion of his bias, but I was right. He was also flustered. It was the first time in all of my encounters with the man that he seemed unsure of himself. He stood.

"I am taking this motion under advisement. We will resume tomorrow morning at nine o'clock, and I will present my decision at that time. Bailiff, send the jury home." He walked quickly out of the courtroom.

We scrambled that night to put the rest of the case in order. I feared the worst--that Giovanni would be stricken as a witness. If that happened, Slater was in real trouble.

CHAPTER 62

Out of an abundance of caution, I arrived in court the next morning with some additional arguments about Giovanni's testimony. When the judge took the bench, I asked to be heard. He nodded.

"I would like to make a record out of the presence of the jury as to Dr. Giovanni's testimony in response to the motion. It is my position that, in order to evaluate the legitimacy of this motion, you must understand the essence of Doctor Giovanni's opinions, as well as his reasoning underlying those opinions."

"Counsel, you obviously weren't listening to me yesterday. It is your job to properly qualify a witness in order for that witness to render an opinion. It is Mr. Hempstead's job to point out to the court any inconsistency that may or may not invalidate that opinion. Just because someone is called doctor does not automatically entitle him or her to walk into my courtroom and offer an opinion on anything that they think is important. A witness must have a proper basis upon which to render an opinion. If you have nothing further to say, I am ready to rule."

"Judge, I do have something further to say."

"No matter. Nothing you could say would change my mind."

I stood there, dumbfounded. I was at a loss for words and I felt the icicle form in my chest. I held my breath, waited for the stab of pain to disappear. What the hell was going on? The judge was dead wrong. I should be allowed to make a separate record so that the appellate court would have a complete record to determine whether or not Giovanni should have been permitted to testify. I was used to judges making wrong decisions. They made wrong decisions all the time. But this guy was different. He was not only dead wrong, but he was shutting down the mechanism for reversing his decision. I was being prevented from demonstrating to an appellate court the error of the trial judge. The right of appeal was how the system worked. That's what made it fair. Anything less than that turned the system into a kangaroo court.

Flick continued, "Dr. Giovanni will not be permitted to testify on the issue of cause. He has indicated that animal studies are not crucial to a cause determination, but curiously, he appears to try to rely on animal studies in giving his opinion in this case. How Dr. Giovanni arrives at this opinion with information that he concedes is not crucial baffles me. The same reasoning applies to his position on case reports. It stretches the limits of the court's imagination and, I might add, patience, to have wasted so much time in dealing with a witness who does not have a proper scientific basis for rendering an opinion. Your motion is granted, Mr. Hempstead." Flick looked at the bailiff. "Bring the jury back in."

I couldn't let it go that easily. "Your honor, I formally move for a mistrial at this time. I do so on two bases; first, the court has erred in striking Dr Giovanni's testimony. He is an esteemed scientist whose opinions are the result of his education, training and experience as well as review of the materials in evidence in this matter. Second, the court has improperly refused to allow me to clarify any confusion it may have with respect to Dr. Giovanni's opinions, and respectfully, it is abundantly obvious from the record that the court is confused with respect to these opinions."

Flick reddened. He was angry with me and I was happy that he was angry. Finally, he spoke. "Sit down, Mr. Riley. I have ruled. Your motion for mistrial is denied." He gestured to the bailiff to bring the jury back.

After the jury returned, to the courtroom Flick gave his little speech.

"Members of the jury, the testimony of Dr. Giovanni is stricken from the record. You are hereby instructed that you are to completely disregard his testimony." Flick looked at the jury. "I have a meeting with other judges to attend this morning. We are going to adjourn until this afternoon. Be back here by one o'clock." He gave me a sarcastic grin as he stood and left the courtroom.

More than ever, I needed Alex Hartley and Jan Emrich. Without them, Slater was going to spend the rest of his life in prison. With them, the odds were better, but I thought it was still a tossup on what the jury would do. When I got back to the office, I called both of them just to stay in touch. I wanted, needed both of them on board. I explained the situation to Emrich and she thought she might know someone else who would make a good witness.

"There is a Doctor Vogelgang in Europe who was a leader in getting the drug removed from the European marketplace. Should I contact him and see if he would get involved?"

"No harm in trying." I thought it was unlikely that Flick would permit me to add another witness in the middle of trial, but it would be worth a shot if it worked out.

Emrich called Vogelgang and explained what was on her mind.

"I'm the FDA monitor for Serenity in the United States. As you know there are serious problems with the drug, but it seems as though here no one is interested in looking too deeply into the problem. Personally, I think the drug should be removed from the market. If not that, a warning on the labeling is necessary to warn physicians who are prescribing around the country like it's peppermint candy."

"I agree with you that if the drug is not taken off the market, there should be a stern warning attached and strict limitations on the uses of the drug."

Emrich found Vogelgang's foreign accent charming. His pronunciation was clear and incisive.

"I've exhausted all avenues but one. There is an extremely important law case pending in Detroit, Michigan and I have agreed to appear as an expert witness in that case. My reason in calling you is to ask if you also would be willing to appear as an expert witness in this matter."

There was an awkward period of silence on the other end of the phone.

Emrich said cautiously, "Are you still there?"

Vogelgang spoke. "I have read about the American system of justice. The lawsuits, lawyers and so on. In my opinion it is abhorrent for an uneducated jury of laypersons to have the responsibility of deciding matters of science. I would not want to involve myself in such matters." He paused, "So thank you very much for asking, but my answer is no."

CHAPTER 63

One of the names Emrich gave me was that of Myra Huggins. She was Cyrus Messner's executive secretary at Upright. Emrich had outlined for me why she would be an important witness. I subpoenaed her to testify, and Hempstead agreed to produce her on Wednesday morning.

Huggins thought she was supposed to testify on Tuesday. She arrived at the courthouse on Tuesday morning and waited outside the courtroom in the hallway as she had been instructed.

At the morning break, she went inside and approached Hempstead, the lawyer she met with last week. "I'm Myra Huggins."

He looked at her, surprise on his face. "I thought I told you to be here Wednesday. Tomorrow."

"You said Tuesday It's no problem. I can come back tomorrow." She turned to leave.

"Wait a second. Are you staying some place locally tonight? Do you have a number where I can reach you if necessary?"

"I'm driving back to Tecumseh. I'll be home tonight. I'll give you my phone number."

She looked around the courtroom while he wrote her number down. Looked at all the lawyers sitting there, waiting for the judge. She was halfway down the aisle toward the door when it hit her. Stunned, she turned around to make sure she wasn't imagining things. She knew the woman sitting at the table alongside the lawyer for the other side. It was Linda Hurley. Myra never forgot a face. What was she doing here? Why was she sitting at the wrong table? Something wasn't right. She wondered if the lawyers knew that she used to work for Upright.

CHAPTER 64

The trial was moving along now. It was getting interesting. Riley was a good lawyer. Loukas felt better as the days progressed. Life was good. A good night's sleep--make that a great night's sleep--and now the paralegal babe was sitting there, skirt at mid-thigh, flashing him a bright smile. He never realized that skirts could be that short. She had a nice pair of legs. She obviously liked to show them off and she liked him. He wondered if it was proper for a juror to take her out for a drink. The judge had warned them about talking to the parties or lawyers, but he didn't say anything about legal assistants.

She glanced over again, like she could read his mind. Flashed that smile. It was getting hot in this courtroom. Reluctantly, he turned his attention back to the witness, who was droning on and on about something.

He tried to listen but his mind wandered. Taking two of those pills each day was working, he thought. He was sleeping well. His asshole brother-in-law was minding the store and Loukas nearly laughed aloud as he realized the entire morning had gone by without thinking about the store. During lunchtime, he didn't bother calling to see if everything was all right.

Geez, this witness was boring. The sleep expert. Riley was right. He was the sleep expert. This guy could put anyone to sleep. The witness spoke in a low monotone. Loukas looked back at Linda. Watched as she shifted in her seat. She re-crossed her legs. He enjoyed the show.

🖊 🖊 🖊

This guy, Professor Myron Clackner, was supposed to be the sleep expert, but I hadn't counted on him putting everyone in the courtroom to sleep. I looked down at my notes. Glanced at the jury and then the judge. A kind of stupor had set in--a vague sensation of time coming to a halt. The only juror who wasn't falling asleep was Loukas, and I knew why. No way was this Clackner as interesting as Linda's legs. My mistake was putting this guy on the stand after lunch when everyone was sleepy. I checked my notes again. I would take him off the stand right now, but I needed to buy some time while various issues with Hartley and Emrich were worked out. Clackner was droning on and on about a question that I had asked. He had talked for so long, I nearly forgot what the question was.

I interrupted him in the middle of a sentence. "Doctor, have you formed an opinion as to whether or not the sleep patterns caused by the drug product Serenity differ in any significant way from normal sleep patterns?"

The man glared back at me. He was pissed. "I was coming to that. Would you like me to continue what I was saying?"

Hempstead was on his feet. "Your Honor, Mr. Riley can't interrupt his own witness."

The judge was slow to respond. It took him a moment to get oriented. I wasn't going to let this get out of hand.

"Your Honor, in the interest of saving some time, I merely asked the witness a new question so that these matters would be clarified for the jury."

The judge looked at Hempstead. "What's wrong with that, Counsel?"

Hempstead simply shrugged his shoulders and sat down. The judge looked at me.

"You may proceed."

I smiled at the jury. This exchange with Hempstead had been the most exciting part of the afternoon. I felt it, and the jury felt it too. "Doctor, have your formed an opinion as to whether or not the sleep patterns caused by the drug product Serenity differ in any significant way from normal sleep patterns?"

"Yes." Professor Clackner was still upset at the interruption of his speech. "I've been wondering when you were going to ask that question." He smiled back at me and continued, "The reticular activating system, RAS, is a specific area of the brain. It is believed that there are two naturally occurring chemicals in the RAS. One of these chemicals, serotonin, puts us to sleep. The other chemical, acetylcholine, wakes us up. These two chemicals are present normally in the RAS in a cyclical fashion. While we are awake, a certain group of cells in this area of the brain produces serotonin until the level of serotonin gets high enough to make us sleep. While we are sleeping, a different group of cells makes acetylcholine until the level of that chemical gets high enough to cause us to wake up. Then, the process repeats itself--day after day--from birth until death."

Clackner stopped, looked at the jury, and wiped his hands on his jacket. "Please understand that this is a very simplified explanation of the complex nature of sleep. I would hardly expect any one of you to understand."

I shuddered. I hated it when an expert witness talked down to jurors like they were idiots. Clackner continued. "If these chemicals are disrupted, it is obvious that sleep patterns may be disrupted, as well. For example, during periods of intense stress, the brain makes an abundance of serotonin that is used by other parts of the brain. If the stress goes on too long, the cells in the brain that produce serotonin become exhausted, and they cannot continue to produce enough of this chemical to meet the brain's demands. When this happens, sleep is interrupted."

Clackner paused again. Looked over at the jury. I followed his gaze. They could hardly keep their eyes open. I had to do something to put some life into this guy's presentation. "Let me interrupt again, doctor." I raised my voice, and several jurors shifted to more attentive postures. "Are you saying that sleep disorders are caused by a chemical imbalance in the brain?"

Clackner glared back at me like I was the village idiot. "Yes," he said. I glanced again at the jury. I didn't know what was worse. Having the jury sleep through this testimony or being awake enough to see what an asshole this guy was. I bit my lip to keep myself from saying something I might regret.

I decided to cut his testimony short. "Doctor, do you have an opinion as to the role Serenity played in the death at Mrs. Slater?'

Clackner stared at me. He knew I jumped way ahead of him in this planned testimony. He hesitated. "Yes, I think Mr. Slater's use of Serenity caused his wife's death because the drug caused a toxic chemical imbalance in his brain. As a result of this toxic effect, he committed an act about which he has no memory. This is called anterograde amnesia. The bizarre nature of the violent act coupled with this form of amnesia is a classic indication of a toxic drug reaction for a drug in this category. Other drugs in the same category of compounds such as Valium, Xanax and Halcion are well known to cause these types of reactions."

"Thanks, Dr. Clackner. I have no more questions."

Judge Flick nodded toward Hempstead. "Your witness, counsel."

Hempstead rose slowly. My guess was that he had concluded that Clackner confused everyone with his testimony. Although Clackner had recited the magic words of causation for me, I figured that Hempstead would count on the jury pretty much disregarding what the witness had said. Hempstead would ask few, if any, questions.

He started, "Doctor, I note that you did not use case reports or animals studies to help you form your opinion about Serenity in this matter, did you?"

"No sir, I didn't. No need."

"Thanks, Doctor. That's the only question I have for you."

My initial thought was to refrain from any additional questions, but I was intrigued by the point Hempstead made. Although Judge Flick had ruled repeatedly that case reports and animal testing could not be used in this case to prove cause and effect, I hadn't given up the idea that they would be useful for a scientist in assessing the potential for harm. The question Hempstead posed together with Clackner's answer, if left unchallenged, would support Flick's rulings during appeal, if there was one. The problem was that I didn't know what Clackner would say if I pursued the subject. We hadn't talked about it and the cardinal rule for a lawyer was not to ask a question if the answer was unknown. I weighed the pros and cons in my mind as I stood. I had to take the risk. I took a deep breath.

"Doctor Clackner, with respect to Mr. Hempstead's question about animal testing and case reports, is the reason that you didn't rely on them in your testimony because you confined yourself strictly to the known pharmacological effects of Serenity and drugs like it in formulating your opinion?"

"Yes, by no means should my answer imply that animal testing and case reports are not important factors to consider. They are very useful."

"Thanks again for your time." I looked at Flick. "That's all I have."

Flick looked over at Hempstead. "Anything further?"

Hempstead shook his head. "No, your honor."

I expelled my breath. I took a big chance. It worked out just fine.

CHAPTER 65

I slept poorly the night after Clackner's testimony. Coming up was a big day--the biggest of the trial, as far as I was concerned. The "make or break" day. After reviewing the documents and speaking last evening with Emrich, I knew what I wanted from the upcoming witnesses. If things went as planned, it could mean Slater's freedom. As an old trial lawyer, however, I knew that things never really happened in a courtroom according to plan. I tossed and turned all night, and just as soon as I felt I had settled down, the phone rang. I answered the phone halfway through its first ring.

"Bobby? Hope I didn't wake you. I know you get up early. Wanted to reach you early."

I checked my watch--a little past five o'clock.

"No problem, Linda. I've been up for awhile. What's up?"

"I've got this splitting headache. Can't make it to court today. I'm terribly sorry."

I grunted. I understood why people missed work. But a headache? During trial?

Linda continued. "It started last night. I knew it'd be bad this morning, so I went to the office and got everything for today all set up, ready to go. I'm really sorry, Bobby."

"Just get some rest . . . and get better," I mumbled. "I better get going. Get down to the office. Check things out."

I bit my tongue. I felt like saying something nasty. Something I might regret. I fought the temptation.

When I got to the office an hour later, I was pleasantly surprised. Linda had been there and everything was ready for the three witnesses. All in order. I breathed a sigh of relief. One less thing to worry about.

Myra Huggins was the first witness of the day. I had subpoenaed her because Emrich told me how important she was to the case. Unless she was prepared to lie, her testimony would break the case wide open. After she was sworn, I approached the podium with my notes and neatly arranged stack of exhibits. The judge nodded at me to proceed.

"Good morning. Would you state your full name?"

"Myra Huggins."

"You are an employee of the Upright Corporation. Is that correct?" I looked at my typed notes. There were a couple of specific exhibits that were to be introduced through this witness. "Yes. That's correct."

"Would you describe your job responsibilities at Upright?"

"Yes. I am the secretary and administrative assistant for Mister Cyrus Messner, who is the director of the research department at Upright." The judge smiled at the jury. Scowled at me. "Proceed, Counsel."

I walked over to the witness stand. "Ms. Huggins. I ask you to identify Exhibit 245 for the record, please." The exhibit was the draft of the report that Emrich had obtained from the doctor who conducted the research at Jackson Prison.

Huggins froze as she looked at the document. A look of terror. She looked helplessly up at the judge and over at the defense table. She started to speak, stopped, swallowed, and tried again. "This is a rough draft of a report. The final report was called the Jackson Prison Report. This is the first rough draft of that report."

Hempstead was on his feet. "Your Honor. Objection. The only draft of the Jackson Prison Report that was provided to Mr. Riley was Exhibit 244, the final draft. We know nothing about a first rough draft."

"Gentlemen. Approach the bench." The judge gave the jury an exasperated shrug of his shoulders.

"Is Mr. Hempstead right, Counsel?"

"No. He's not, Your Honor. It's true that he did not give it to us, but we obtained it from the FDA through a Freedom of Information request." I was stretching the truth a bit. I had made a formal request to the FDA several months ago, but there'd been no response yet. Because Emrich was a FDA employee, I was technically correct in my statement.

Hempstead raised his voice a notch higher. "There's no proof that this document is authentic. No proof that it came from the FDA."

"Judge. That's exactly why I've asked the question of Ms. Huggins. It's a draft that she prepared. She's the person who can authenticate the document."

The judge stared hard at me. I maintained eye contact. Didn't want the bastard to think he could push me around. "Objection overruled. I'll allow the question."

I walked back to my table and picked the exhibit up. I turned and looked at the witness. "Do you have the question in mind?"

"Yes. As I said, this is the rough draft of the Jackson Prison Report."

"Are you the person who prepared this document?"

"Yes. I typed this document from the handwritten notes provided by the prison doctor and nurse."

I took a deep breath. Here we go. "Ms. Huggins. Were you given any instructions by any of your supervisors at Upright as to what you should do with this rough draft?" I held the exhibit in the air. I noticed that the jury was watching Huggins carefully.

"Yes. I was told to destroy the document."

A buzz swept through the courtroom. The judge picked up his gavel and pounded twice. "I will not have any disruptions in my courtroom. I'll throw everybody out if this happens again."

The room was instantly quiet.

Huggins squirmed, and her eyes darted back and forth between Hempstead and me.

"Why didn't you destroy the document?"

She fidgeted, and then looked at me. "I don't throw away anything. It's always helpful to be able to go back and figure out what happened if a question comes up."

"How do you know that this is the document you prepared?"

"There are two ways. First, my initials, m.h.--small m, small h-- appear on the lower left of the page. This means that I typed it. Second, I remember typing this. I thought it was unusual for them to ask me to destroy it, so I made a copy."

"You mentioned preparing this document from handwritten notes. Where are those notes, if you know?"

"I put them back in the file after I finished typing up the report. I returned the file, together with the typed report, to Mr. Messner."

"Mr. Messner? That's Cyrus Messner, head of the research department?"

"Yes."

"Your boss?"

"Yes."

"Mr. Messner is the one who told you to destroy this document?" I held the exhibit in front of her and turned so that the jury could see.

"Objection, Your Honor. There's no testimony as to who told her."

The judge looked curiously at Hempstead. "Overruled."

I hadn't taken my eyes off Huggins. "Do you remember the question before the interruption?"

"Objection, Your Honor." Hempstead jumped to his feet again. "I made a valid objection. I object to Mr. Riley's characterization."

The judge glowered at me. "I agree. If you do that one more time, Counsel, I'm going to cite you for contempt. Is that clear?"

I nodded and turned back to the witness stand. "Ms. Huggins, let me rephrase the question. Who told you to destroy this document?" I held it high in the air, over my head between two fingers, and looked at it while I waited for her response.

Her response was barely louder than a whisper. "Mr. Cyrus Messner."

"I'm sorry, Ms. Huggins. But I didn't hear you."

A little louder. More forcefully. "Mr. Cyrus Messner."

The entire jury, I noted, sat up straighter.

"Let's look at Exhibit 254--the final draft." I walked up to the witness stand and handed the document to the witness. "Did you prepare this document?"

"No, I didn't."

"How do you know?"

She held the piece of paper up and pointed at the lower left-hand corner.

"Linda Hurley prepared this. Her initials are in the corner there, l.h.--small l, small h."

"Who does she work for?"

Huggins sat, frozen. She appeared even more nervous than she'd been.

"She . . . she's not at Upright any longer. She is—was--Mr. Messner's research assistant."

A thought flashed through my mind. I couldn't quite put it together.

"Thank you, Ms. Huggins. I have no more questions."

Huggins looked relieved. Started to stand. The judge leaned toward her. "Stay seated. Mr. Hempstead has the right to ask you some questions."

Huggins appeared to shrink as I watched Hempstead approach her. Based on my past experiences with him, he was fond of beating up on vulnerable witnesses, and Huggins was a sitting duck. Hempstead gave her an artificial smile as the small woman pressed herself against the back of her chair.

"Miss Huggins. How long have you worked for Cyrus Messner?"

"Fourteen years."

Hempstead replaced his smile with a scowl and shook his head slowly while he looked first at Huggins and then the jury. "And you consider yourself to be a loyal person?"

Huggins nodded.

Hempstead took his time. Took another step toward her. "Was that a yes?"

"Yes."

"I can't hear you." Another step forward.

She looked up. "Yes."

"In addition to working for Mr. Messner for fourteen years, you have been an employee of Upright for nearly twenty years. Is that correct?"

She looked down again. She was wringing her hands. "Yes."

"Louder, please. No one can hear you."

"Yes."

I thought she was going to start crying. Hempstead raised his voice. "You have no scientific training. Isn't that true?"

"Yes."

"While you did graduate from high school, you have never attended college. Isn't that correct?"

"Yes."

"Not for one day, correct?"

"Yes."

"While you were in high school, the closest you came to a science course was freshman biology. Is that correct?"

"Yes."

Hempstead had a way, I thought, of making questions sounds like directives.

"You received a C in that freshman high school biology class. Did you not?"

"Yes."

"That class is the sum and total of your entire training in science?"

"Yes."

"In the fourteen years you have worked for Mr. Messner, has he ever requested your advice or opinion on matters of a scientific nature?"

"No."

"Not once?"

"No."

Hempstead lowered his voice and took another step toward her. "Let me ask you this. Has any person ever asked you for your scientific opinion or advice on any project during your nearly twenty years of employment at Upright?"

I jumped to my feet. "Objection. This witness has been brought into this courtroom to testify in a very limited area. It has never been suggested or implied that she is an expert in any field of science. With respect to Ms. Huggins, she is a person whose responsibility only involves the preparation and keeping of scientific information in an accurate fashion."

Flick glared at me. I was surprised. I would have thought that, by now, he would have understood what was going on in his courtroom.

"Approach the bench, Counsel."

Hempstead and I walked to the sidebar.

Flick scowled. "Do you have a legitimate objection, or are you just trying to interrupt Mr. Hempstead?"

I thought carefully before I spoke. "Judge, my objection is proper. This is a witness with no scientific training. None whatsoever. However, I have not presented her testimony as an expert witness in any field of science. She is a fact witness only to the extent that she had been ordered by Cyrus Messner to destroy a document and retype it as though the original never existed. That is the extent of her testimony. It doesn't matter whether she has a scientific background or not."

Flick snapped. "I am going to overrule your objection. The next time you make a speech as part of an objection obviously intended to coach a witness, you are going to spend the night in jail. Do I make myself clear?"

I stared at the judge, and he stared back at me. Flick was the first to break eye contact. He muttered, "Don't push me. I mean it." He waved the two of us back to our respective tables. Instead of moving away, I stood there, frozen. I could feel my mouth go dry. I couldn't believe what I was hearing. I felt like throwing up. What was happening here was not right. It didn't meet any notion of fairness. I couldn't believe that this judge would do this, particularly when the court reporter was sitting there taking down every word that was spoken. I was getting sick and tired of the judge's threats. Sick and tired of his favoritism towards Hempstead.

"I said, 'return to your seat, counsel.'"

I walked slowly back to my table, and Hempstead resumed his questioning. "You are not an expert in pharmacy, are you?"

"No."

"You are not an expert in any area of science, are you?"

"I thought I already answered that. No I am not, and I don't claim to be."

Huggins had just about had it with Hempstead. After she answered the question, she sat up and squared her shoulders. Hempstead just stood there mulling over his next question. I knew what Hempstead was thinking. He too had noted the subtle shift in Huggins's posture. I knew what he wanted to ask her, and I also knew that he, being the trial lawyer that he was, wouldn't ask it.

Hempstead looked at Flick. "That completes my cross-examination, Your Honor. I have a motion that I'd like to take up out of the jury's presence."

Flick gestured to the bailiff, and the jury filed out of the courtroom.

Hempstead waited until he saw the jury room door close. "Judge, I move to strike Miss Huggins's testimony. By her own admission, she is absolutely unqualified to render any type of factual or expert opinion as to what should have been done scientifically in this case. The fact is that she is a mere typist, and whatever she says about what should or should not have been done is immaterial, irrelevant, and highly prejudicial to my client. To allow a high school graduate with a ninth grade biology course to come in here and tell a jury what a modern, sophisticated pharmaceutical company should be doing is ludicrous."

Flick gestured at me to respond. "First, as a preliminary matter, I have not been given the opportunity for re-direct examination. Having said that, Mr. Hempstead has done a good job of misstating the issue. The witness has told us about one thing, one fact. She was ordered by her boss to destroy the initial draft of the first study conducted on human beings to evaluate the safety of Serenity. She testified that she was instructed to substitute a sanitized version in its place and throw away the original. This has nothing to do with science. It has to do with the basic notion of morality in our society. Even children know the difference between right and wrong."

Flick interrupted. "I'm prepared to rule. Do you have anything else, Mr. Riley?"

"Yes, I do."

Flick waved his arm. "I've heard enough. This witness's testimony will be stricken, and the jury instructed to disregard it. The court fails to see how the testimony of this witness is relevant, in any respect, on the issue of whether or not Mr. Slater murdered his wife. Because her testimony is not relevant, it has no probative value, and its use will not be permitted in this matter.

I felt like I'd been slapped in the face. "That's outrageous!"

"Mr. Riley, be quiet. That little outburst just cost you one thousand dollars. Anything more out of your mouth like that, and you will be spending the night in jail. You do not talk to the court in this manner."

I glared at the judge. The icicle eating away at my chest reminded me that I needed to relax, close my eyes, and let the pain melt away. I took a deep breath and looked at Flick.

"Judge, I would like to have the record reflect that this is not the first time in this trial you have threatened me with contempt, jail and fines. I have been trying lawsuits for more than thirty years and have not had a threat one other time in my career like you are making to me on a daily basis. I will also say for the record that as an officer of the court, I take my obligation to represent Mr. Slater with zeal very seriously. I am prepared to do whatever the court orders so long as my objection to the court's ruling is duly noted. At this time, Your Honor, I move that the trial be stayed until I can take your latest ruling to the court of appeals."

"Denied."

Flick looked at Hempstead and then back at me. "Do you have anything else? If not, we'll break for the day."

The sharpness of the icicle sliced through my chest. I took a deep breath. "Judge, in all fairness, I should be permitted to complete my record by asking this witness some additional questions on re-direct examination. With due respect, I think your ruling is reversible on appeal, and I implore you to allow me to finish what Mr. Hempstead has started." I forced myself to take another deep breath.

Flick sat up straight and smiled his feral grin. He obviously wasn't used to lawyers talking to him like this. Well, kiss my ass. If Huggins's testimony is thrown out, I might as well pack my bags and go back to the office now. That was the trouble with judges. They thought they were infallible. Flick was a pompous asshole and thought he was God.

Flick hesitated. He knows, I thought, that striking a witness even before the testimony of the witness was completed is grounds for reversal. "I'll permit some re-direct." He looked at his bailiff. "Bring the jury back."

I thought hard. The rule of thumb, the First Commandment of trial practice, was never ask a question when you didn't know the answer. I had to gamble. I had no choice. If I was reading Huggins right, she would do the right thing. I stood slowly and composed the question in my mind before I spoke. "Why didn't you destroy the first draft the of the Jackson Prison study when you were ordered to do so by Mr. Messner?"

Hempstead yelled, "Objection! Beyond the scope of cross-examination."

Flick leaned forward. "Sustained." He turned and looked at the jury. "Sometimes lawyers don't do things right. Counsel neglected to ask the right questions during his direct examination. The rules require me to restrict him from improperly asking those questions now." He looked at me and nodded for me to continue.

I felt my ears turn red. I was angry. I took a step toward the witness. "Are you a loyal person?"

"Yes."

"If Mr. Messner told you to jump off a bridge, would you consider it to be disloyal if you disobeyed him?"

"No, I wouldn't. I know the difference between right and wrong. I don't have to be a scientist to know that."

Bingo, I thought. "Even though you're not a scientist, you knew it was wrong to destroy the first draft of the Jackson study?

"Objection." Hempstead sounded like a raging bull.

"Yes."

Flick glared at Huggins. "You will not answer when there is an objection pending. Do you understand me?"

Huggins cowered against the back of her chair.

Flick addressed the jury. "I am sustaining the objection and excusing the witness. You are to disregard the last question and answer. Strike it from your minds as if it never existed. We're breaking for the weekend. I will see you at nine o'clock Monday morning."

I was actually relived as I left the courtroom. In my judgment, Flick's ruling had now gone beyond reason and I would have no difficulty reversing him on appeal. It was a win-win situation. If Slater was acquitted by the jury he would win. Even if he was found guilty he would win a second opportunity to plead his case.

CHAPTER 66

The first thing I did when I got back to the office was to place a call to Hartley. It was a rough day. As I dialed the phone, I noticed my hands were still shaking. He wasn't in, so I left a message for him to return the call. The little stab of pain. There it was again. A stab of pain, more like the sudden touch of an icicle probing deep in my chest. When it occurred, I savored its vanishing. The pain would melt as quickly as it had appeared. It was happening more frequently of late and was greater in intensity--lasting longer. Unrelated to anything, except maybe my smoking. I looked at the lit cigarette in my hand, took one last deep drag, and stubbed it out in the ashtray. I hadn't mentioned this nuance in my life to anybody--not anybody. I knew what would happen if I did. Advice to stop smoking. See a doctor. Get a checkup. All that crap. Who had time for such things?

"You all right?" I looked up. Linda was standing right in front of me on the other side of the desk. I hadn't seen her come into the office.

"Just thinking."

"You sure you're all right? You're as pale as a ghost."

"I'm fine." I gave her a look meant to end the discussion.

She looked worried. "You don't look fine. When was the last time you saw a doctor?"

"I said I'm fine. Drop it." I waved my hand--waved away the topic of discussion.

"I can make an appointment for you."

"I don't need a mother. Let's get busy. What have you got?" I sat up straighter, sucked in my gut.

"You're not going to do your clients much good if you drop dead of a heart attack."

Jesus Christ. Where did that come from? She was staring me down, ooking directly at me with those cobalt blue eyes of hers. I felt a trickle of perspiration under my arms.

What the hell are you talking about?"

She kept her eyes on me while she sat down. "Bobby. I'm not trying to be a pain in the ass. People our age--they run into health problems. It goes with life. I can say this to you. We go back. You need to see a doctor. I can tell. I can't tell you what's going on with you, but you need to see a doctor."

"What I need is a drink." I grinned. Tried the wave of the hand again. Maybe it would work this time.

"You're not listening to a word I'm saying."

"Now you are being a pain in the ass. You think I've got time to see a doctor? I'm in the middle of trial."

"You have me worried."

I forced a smile. "Never give up the ship. The bigger they are, the harder they fall. It takes two to tango. When the going gets tough, the tough gets going. Pick a cliché. One of them must fit."

She laughed. "I can remember you saying those very same things back in high school."

"Can't teach an old dog new tricks."

"I think I better leave before you get completely out of control." She flashed a smile and turned away.

"Just a second," I murmured. "I thought you were sick. Why are you here at work?"

She stopped and turned around. "I felt better after I'd been up for awhile."

Linda left my office. After a moment, Mary stood in the doorway. I looked up. . "May I have just a word?"

"Sure." I gestured to the chair. Mary remained standing.

"What do you think about Linda?"

"I don't understand. What do you mean?"

"I mean exactly what I'm asking. What do you think about Linda?"

"She's a nice girl." Good-looking too, I thought. Better not say that.

"Good worker too. Why do you ask?"

"Bob." She looked around and lowered her voice. "We need to talk – now. I'll be right back. There's something you need to see."

CHAPTER 67

Messner sat at his desk and looked at the Whale. "The stupid bitch called me direct from her office. They know what's going on."

Hagstrom raised an eyebrow. "How do you know?"

"Two minutes after she called me, another call comes in from the same number. Different voice. Tried to pass it off as a wrong number."

"No question about it?"

"None. None whatsoever." Messner eyed the Whale.

"What are you going to do?"

"I've got a plan in mind." Messner spent the next fifteen minutes spelling it out.

When he finished, he sat back, and the Whale smiled. "That's the oldest trick in the book."

I said, "That has to be one of the oldest tricks in the book." I directed a half-smile at Mary. I couldn't believe what I was hearing. I didn't want to believe it.

Mary replied, "It may be the oldest trick in the book, but it also answers a lot of questions about what's been happening around here."

The icicle melted in my chest and I rubbed my left arm, tried to stop the numbness before it began.

"What made you do this?" I gestured at the piece of paper on my desk.

"I can't even tell you what. Just a feeling." Mary shrugged her shoulders.

I glanced again at the paper. Mary had printed out today's office phone record for me. It was unmistakable. Five calls had been placed from an office phone directly to Upright. Another four calls were to a similar number in the same area code.

"You're sure this is Messner's number? Tell me again."

"No question about it. I called it myself. Played dumb, like it was the wrong number. His secretary told me it was his direct line."

"How do we know that it was Linda who made these calls?"

Mary glared at me. "Who else would it be? Bob, I know she's an old friend, but you've got to deal with this before she does any more damage."

I breathed deeply. Felt the icicle. I closed my eyes. Waited until it melted. Maybe I should see a doctor

"You all right? You look grey."

I rubbed my arm again. The numbness subsided. "I'm fine. My arm has been bothering me lately. I'm not a spring chicken anymore." I attempted a grin. It felt more like a grimace.

"Bob, you need to throw her ass out as fast as you can."

"I hear you. Let me sleep on it. One day won't make a difference. Let's wrap up here. Call it a day."

I locked the door of the office after turning out the lights and walked Mary to her car. I stood and watched as she drove away, and then I drove slowly home.

Not much to eat in the house, so I had a liquid dinner--a half-bottle of bourbon. I wouldn't be in court tomorrow so I could drink to my heart's content. Or should I say discontent?

I fell asleep in front of the TV. Around midnight, I got up and went to bed after having my last cigarette of the night at bedside.

Betrayal. That was the word that spun around in my mind as I tried to sleep. That was it. Betrayal. Pure and simple.

I sat up on the edge of the bed, shook the last cigarette out of the pack, and threw the crumpled container on the floor. I searched for my lighter and finally turned the light on to find it. Big surprise. It was sitting right where I left it. I lit a cigarette, took a deep drag, and squinted. The bright light hurt my eyes. The bedside clock said two o'clock.

I looked at the other side of the king-sized bed. The empty side. A wave of anguish swept over me as the extent of my loneliness engulfed me. Was there anybody I could talk with about this--how I felt? I grunted. Until today, Linda was on the list as someone who might listen. I looked over at the other side of the bed again and felt a lump in my throat. I stood, walked into the kitchen, and poured a generous portion of bourbon into a drinking glass, tossed it off in several large swallows. I sat down at the kitchen table and placed my head in my hands. Old friend Linda, why did you do this to me?

I thought for a while. I knew exactly what I needed to do--what I had to do. Mary was right. I returned to bed and tossed and turned the rest of the night.

While shaving the next morning, I looked in the mirror. Ten years older than yesterday. Mary was right. I had to keep reminding myself. This had to be done. There was no way around this nasty turn of events. I picked up the phone and called Linda at home. I asked her to meet me at the office this morning even though it was Saturday.

CHAPTER 68

Two o'clock in the morning, and Linda was still wide-awake. She tried to close her eyes and turn off her thinking, but it didn't help. She'd heated a cup of tea around midnight, but that didn't help. Whose idea was this? Linda grimaced when she thought about the mess she was in. She felt dirty. She felt used. But whose fault was it? She had no one to blame but herself.

At first, it sounded exciting and glamorous. She would have done anything--literally anything--to help Messner. Anything that brought him pleasure also brought her pleasure. That was just the way she was. Messner had helped her get up the emotional strength to leave her husband. That was a good thing. She needed the extra support he'd given her, emotionally and physically--not to mention financially. When he had first suggested the plan, it sounded exciting. She thought back to the first conversation about the topic.

"Why so glum? With Serenity sales like they are, you should be riding high." Linda put her hand on his leg, moved closer to him.

Messner was driving. They were on the way to the motel. He looked over at her.

"It's the fucking lawyers. They're driving me crazy with all the lawsuits."

"It can't be that bad." She gently rubbed up and down his thigh.

"Mmm. That feels good. Don't stop. It is that bad. The biggest pain in the ass of all is this Riley character."

"Who's that?"

"Lawyer named Riley. Bob Riley. From Detroit. Son of a bitch was the first to file, and I hear that he is lining up new clients every day. Fucking ambulance chaser."

"I went to high school with a Bob Riley in Detroit. He's a lawyer. I wonder if he's the same one."

"There are a dozen lawyers named Riley in every fucking city in the country."

"I can check and see if it's him. If it is, I'll call him and tell him how nice you are and to stop suing us."

"Fat chance."

"No. I'm serious. We dated back in high school and college. I'll tell him about you, and you can meet with him and show him how good the drug is. There must be a big mistake someplace because Serenity is such a good drug. I'm sure he would appreciate it. He's a nice guy. Of course, that depends on if he's the right Riley. Oops. There's somebody else paying attention."

Her hand had slid up his thigh to his groin, and he was fully erect. She unzipped his pants and put her hand inside.

"You should pull over someplace so that I can teach this naughty boy some manners."

"We're almost there. I can't wait."

Two months later, Linda's divorce was final.

"I feel free, like a new person." She hugged Messner.

"That asshole wasn't good enough for you."

"It's over now. I can start to live."

Messner sat up in bed. "Remember that Riley lawyer we talked about? The one from Detroit? You said you went to high school with him?"

"I remember. I didn't say it was him for sure. Just that I went to school with a Bob Riley who became a lawyer."

I checked him out. He graduated the same year you did from Denby High School. He is the same guy. You used to work for a law firm, didn't you?"

"You know I did. Just before I came to work with Upright."

"What would you think of taking a sabbatical and going into the legal field again?"

She pursed her lips, brought the covers up to her chin, and changed positions. The transition in her thinking had been gradual the past few months; from thinking of herself as the potential Mrs. Messner to someone now realized what he was--a total asshole who would step on his mother to get ahead. Now she was stuck somewhere between the proverbial rock and the hard place. Riley didn't know about her yet--what she was and what she had done. It was just a matter of time until he did. What could she do to extricate herself from this situation? As a young child, she had known the difference between right and wrong. The older she got, the more complicated things seemed to get. Mistake number one had been the affair with Messner. Now that seemed to pale in significance to what she'd done. It seemed right at the time to follow his suggestion to get Riley to hire her. What seemed so right then now seemed so stupid. It had taken her a while to realize that Messner was using her.

When she started working for Riley, she believed that lawsuits and lawyers were the scourge of society. Working side by side with Riley and Gary Newton the past few months had awakened her to the true nature of the battle. It was David against Goliath--a struggle of right against might.

When she thought about what she had done--the role she had played in screwing up Riley's case--she shivered. Was there anything she could possibly do to make it right? She shivered again when she thought about Messner. She had been emotionally vulnerable, and he was charming. Swept her right off her feet and into what seemed now like a hundred different hotel rooms. She had to do something. She looked at the clock at her bedside. Time to get up. Had she slept? When Bob called and asked her to come to the office, she'd forced herself to sound cheerful on the phone, like nothing happened. She dragged herself out of bed and dressed carefully.

CHAPTER 69

Saturday was always my favorite day of the week because it was the day I could get things done. The office was closed, the phones didn't ring, and I had private time to sit at my desk and think--gather my thoughts. Saturdays were particularly important when I was in trial because it gave me the only opportunity to plan for the coming week and catch up on the past week. Get all my ducks in order, so to speak.

This Saturday was going to be different. When I'd called Linda from home, she sounded chipper as usual.

"Linda, I'd like you to come into the office this morning. I have a few items I need to go over. Can you be there by ten o'clock?"

"Sure thing. I'll be there."

She didn't have a clue, I thought.

On the drive to the office, I thought about how to go about this. I should have a witness, so I called Gary from my cell phone and asked him to be there as well.

We were sitting in my office when Linda walked in.

"Have a seat." I gestured to the chair next to Gary's in the front of my desk.

She sat down, and the smile on her face was gone. "Is there something wrong?"

I looked hard at her. Was she really going to try to bluff her way through this?

"Why don't you tell us?" I tossed the phone bill across the desk toward her. "Take a look at that before you answer."

She didn't look at the phone bill. "I know what that is. I don't need to see it."

Mary was right. I have never hit a woman in my life. But I felt like slapping Linda's face. I felt like hurting her.

"Tell us about these calls. Why were they made? We made a call yesterday to the law firm you told me you worked for. They never heard of you. You lied to me. All the things you said over the past few months have been lies."

"Bobby, I can't tell you how badly I feel."

"I need to have you tell your story to the judge. But first, I really have only one question. Why would you do this?"

"I . . . don't think I can do that. Why don't we keep this between just us? I can tell you some things that will help." Her eyes teared up.

I stood and went to the window. Looked down at the street. I walked to my desk and sipped a glass of water, shifted my weight from one leg to the other.

"I can't do that. I won't do that. Two wrongs don't make a right." I looked directly at her. She seemed to shrink before my eyes.

Linda spoke quietly. "They've deliberately withheld stuff from you. Stuff you can use . . ."

"Stop. I don't want to hear this." I put my hands over my ears. Kept them there until she stopped talking. When I took them away, she started again.

"Dr. Smythe. Dr. Ken Smythe . . ."

"Dammit, Linda. Just shut up. I want you to leave now. Just stop talking, and leave the office. Don't come back."

She didn't understand. She kept talking. I stopped listening. I really didn't expect her to fathom the harm she had done. Deception was destructive. The closer you were to the one being deceived, the greater the pain the deception causes. It was her burden to live with what she had done. Gary and I needed to talk. I had to try to understand what was happening. The harm was done. There was no way to undo it, but I had to try.

She stood and pleaded with me. "I'll write out everything you need to know . . ."

"Enough. Not another word." I walked to the door, opened it, and gestured for her to leave. She flinched as she walked by my outstretched arm. I watched her until she left the building, locked the front door behind her, and took the bottle of bourbon from the storage room back to my office. I took two cups and poured a generous amount in each for Gary and me. I took a deep swallow and waited for the welcome burning sensation. I pounded my fist on the desktop.

Gary sat quietly and sipped his drink. "What are you going to do?"

Damned if I know. I've just got to think this through. "What are your thoughts?"

"You've got to let the judge know, and you can't wait. I think you should call him now."

I checked my telephone directory and called Flick's courtroom. No answer. A recorded message suggested calling back or leaving a brief message. I hung up and called the main number at the switchboard of the courthouse. I explained to the person who answered that I needed to reach Flick immediately. He said Flick was out of town and couldn't be reached until Monday morning.

"Who is the judge on call?" There was always a judge on call during the weekend for matters that couldn't wait for normal weekday business hours.

"Judge Pendergast. Can I put you through to his office?"

"Yes." This was the only positive thing that had happened so far this morning. Pendergast was a good friend. We had worked in the same law firm as young lawyers and had shared many good times during that time period. He was appointed to the bench shortly after I left the firm to start my own and had been re-elected several times. I tried several lawsuits in his courtroom, and he never let the friendship get in the way of being fair and impartial, a characteristic for which

I admired him greatly. All I wanted as a trial lawyer was a fair and balanced playing field, and that is what Pendergast was known for.

I asked his clerk if I could see him right away. She left the phone for a minute and came back to tell me that the judge could see me in an hour. Gary wanted to go with me to back up my story if it was necessary.

Pendergast ushered us into his chambers and sat down behind his desk.

"Bob, it's great to see you. I miss the old days. What can I do for you that requires so much urgency?"

"Bill, I am in a real dilemma."

I went on to tell the complete story. When I finished, he whistled through his teeth.

"You are right. This is a dilemma. You've known her since high school?"

"Yes. We actually dated for a couple of months the first year of college."

"Now the question is, how can this be handled without screwing up your trial and ruining your reputation? Get her in to talk to me right now."

"I'll try. She was pretty upset when she left the office. She was terrified about having to potentially tell Flick about this because she has seen him in action during the trial."

"Any reason why she might try to lie her way out of this--blame it on you?"

"It would be my guess right now that Linda will tell the truth. On the other hand, if they have some hold on her, she might try to lie her way out of it."

I looked at Gary, who had sat quietly throughout the entire exchange with the judge. He nodded. "She was pretty upset. But I think she'll do the right thing."

Pendergast looked at me. "Bob, we have always been straight with each other. I believe you about this deal. Even if Flick knows you did nothing wrong, we both know that Flick can be a real asshole, and if he wants to nail your ass on this, he will. I know he doesn't like you. In the past, he's mentioned that he thinks you're responsible for his father's death. From what I hear, he's been pretty rough on you during this trial. Get her on the phone right now. If she hesitates about coming down to see me, I'll get on the phone and lay out the options for her. Maybe the fear of sitting in a jail cell will give her religion."

Me responsible for his father's death? I never heard such a thing. Flick's father had committed suicide during my DES trial, but at the time no one had the slightest idea why. Why in the hell would Flick blame me for it? I forced myself back to the present. I had Linda's number on my cell phone.

"Linda, this is Bob. I'm sitting in the chambers of Judge William Pendergast, and I've told him the situation. He wants you to come down here right now so you can talk to him."

"I don't think I can do that."

"Linda, I don't think you realize how serious this is."

"I'm scared."

"I know you're scared. But that's not important right now. What is important is that Mr. Slater has been in jail for a long time waiting for his day in court. Judge Flick could declare a mistrial, and that would mean that Slater would have to spend a lot more time in jail before his case could be heard. Then, there's me. You know the way that Judge Flick is treating me, and if he thinks I am responsible for hiring you away from Upright to get inside information, he'll throw the book at me. If I were a judge I would do the same thing if I thought a lawyer pulled a stunt like this. You need to set the record straight. For Mr. Slater, for me . . . and for you."

"Oh Bobby, I'm so sorry, but I just can't."

I nodded at Pendergast. It was time for him to take over. He took the phone from me.

"Ms. Easterbrook, this is Judge Pendergast. Mr. Riley and his colleague, Gary Newton, are sitting in my chambers with me right now. Mr. Riley has filled me in, and I have listened to his side of this phone conversation. I need to hear your side, and I need to hear it while you are sitting in front of me. Without trying to upset you any further, we can do this one of two ways--either you come down voluntarily right now, or I will order a deputy to come out and get you. It's your choice. One or the other, but you must come down here so that I can hear your side of the story."

"I . . . I'll come down."

Gary and I waited for Linda in the judge's waiting room, while the judge busied himself in his chambers. She walked in nearly an hour and a half later and was accompanied by a distinguished looking gentleman in a dark business suit and red tie.

She introduced us. "Bob, this is my lawyer, Howard Barnett. I thought I should have a lawyer present."

Barnett and I shook hands. He was vaguely familiar, but I couldn't place him.

We told the judge's secretary we were ready to see him. She ushered us into his chambers, and I made the introductions.

We sat at the judge's conference table--Gary and I on one side, Linda and her lawyer on the other, and the Pendergast at the head.

Barnett spoke first. "Before we start, Your Honor, I have discussed this situation with my client, and I am reluctant to let her speak if, in doing so, the possibility of incriminating herself exists."

The judge thought for a moment. "I can see your point. Let me suggest a way around it. I'm really interested in the answer to only one question. Did Mr. Riley know that your client was employed by Upright at the time he hired her to work in his office?"

Linda and Barnett looked at each other. He waited a moment and shook his head.

"I can't permit her to answer that question. I might add that how would she know what Mr. Riley knew at the time he hired her?"

I felt a sinking sensation deep in my chest. What in the hell was going on? Who was this guy? Did Linda have a change of heart?

Pendergast wasn't going to give up. "Let me ask it another way. Did she tell Mr. Riley that she was employed by Upright at the time he offered her a job?"

Barnett held up his hand to warn Linda to keep quiet. "Judge, could I meet privately with my client for a minute?"

"By all means. You can either use the courtroom or the jury room next door."

Barnett and Linda went into the courtroom.

When they left the room, I looked at Pendergast. "I have a bad feeling about this. I don't think she's going to be much help to me if she refuses to talk."

"I think you're right. I can give her a grant of immunity, but Flick would have a shit-fit if I did. I'll think about that. I may do it, anyway. I'd like to have this resolved for you before Flick gets here on Monday. If I don't, your ass is grass."

"I can't tell you how much I appreciate your concern."

Barnett and Linda came back into the room. When they were settled, Barnett spoke, "On my advice, my client will not answer that question unless you can do something to relieve her of any possible criminal sanctions."

Pendergast stood. "I'm going to have my secretary find an assistant prosecutor. There's always one in the building."

Ten minutes later, a young man who looked young enough to be my grandson walked into the room. "How can I help you, Judge?

An hour later, Linda had a written guarantee of immunity. All that was necessary now was for Pendergast to hear her story.

We gathered in the conference room again. The assistant district attorney was also present. Linda talked for an hour. I had the full story now. It was worse than I thought. My high school friend--my old girlfriend--had told Upright everything I was doing on the Serenity cases. Everything. Down to the finest detail. As I walked away from the courthouse, I thought about it. What would have happened if Flick wasn't away for the weekend? My career would have been over.

CHAPTER 70

I had the rest of the weekend to think about how to handle Flick with this Linda situation. I sat at my desk with my head in my hands and tried to think. I struggled to deal with my anger. It took me awhile to think rationally. The damage that Linda's deception had inflicted was obvious. I fancied myself a good judge of character. I had been sucked into the vortex of Linda's deception. If Linda was being truthful now, she had come to work for me specifically to destroy my efforts against Upright. Then she had a change of heart and wanted to help --a day late and a dollar short. I smiled ruefully. Trouble was, there was the simple matter of ethics. Now that Linda had come clean, there was a whole lot of explaining to do. I knew that Flick would naturally assume I was in the wrong.

Now that Linda was protected, it would serve Slater's interests if I came on strong.

Gary and I worked all day Sunday on a draft brief laying out both the facts and the applicable law. By late Sunday we were done with the brief, and I was satisfied that we were in good shape on the coming argument. Mary came into the office and typed the final draft of the brief, and we all went home at midnight.

CHAPTER 71

Monday morning, I was surprised that the defense team was in place when I got to the courtroom. The bailiff came over to my table. "Mr. Riley, the judge wants to see you in chambers." No good morning greeting. No usual smile.

Gary and I started to walk toward the door of Flick's chambers. The bailiff put up his hand like a cop directing traffic. "He wants to see you alone, Mr. Riley. Just you. He's waiting. Go right in."

Gary and I looked at each other. I shrugged my shoulders and entered Flick's chambers. He was sitting behind his desk in his shirtsleeves. In front of his desk, his black robe was tossed across one of the two chairs. He gestured with a pointed finger that I should sit in the other.

"You have an employee named Linda Easterbrook?"

"Yes, Your Honor. As a matter of fact, I have filed a brief this morning with respect to that so-called employee. She was placed in my office by the defendant as a spy to provide them information about my case preparation."

Flick studied me over the top of his bifocals. "Counsel, you and I are like oil and water. You have an attitude that you can do anything you want in my courtroom, and I am sick and tired of your shenanigans. I remember my father telling me the same thing about you when I was a youngster. Now, let me tell you this in no uncertain terms. Mr. Hempstead has filed a motion claiming that you hired a secretary from Upright's research department to help you prepare your case. I am not surprised that you would stoop so low. You give all lawyers a bad name. I think your conduct is reprehensible. I wanted to bring you into my chambers just to tell you personally that, unless you have a magic rabbit in your hat, I am going to fuck you over so bad that you'll wish you never become a lawyer or set a foot in a courtroom. You're fucked."

I was glad I was sitting down. I steeled myself for what I had to do. Flick glared at me through those flinty eyes, feral grin on his face, waiting for me to genuflect or something. I took a deep breath. Here goes.

I looked back at him. "What Hempstead says is complete and utter bullshit."

The judge never took his eyes off me. He stood. "We'll see about that." He took his robe from the chair next to me and started to put it on. "Unless you can find that rabbit, you are dog meat. I can't tell you how much I am going to enjoy this. Now get the hell out of here."

Not exactly the kind of meeting a lawyer wanted to have with a judge. I stood and walked to the doorway. Turned back and looked at Flick. "Thanks for listening to my side of the story."

I walked out. My hands were shaking, my vision was blurry. The cold icicle pierced my chest. I stopped halfway back to the courtroom to catch my breath and waited until the pain subsided. Gary was sitting at our table in the courtroom. I bent over and whispered in his ear. "We are going to need Pendergast right away. Go get him." Newton nodded and left the courtroom.

Two minutes later, Flick was on the bench. He looked around the room and waited until everyone was settled. "I have before me a motion. We will not speak of the subject matter of this motion in an open courtroom, but I can assure you that I intend to get to the bottom of the accusations that have been made. An issue that has been raised is whether I should grant a mistrial. I am not convinced at the moment that a mistrial is warranted and will deny that motion. Now, gentlemen, if you would approach the bench for a moment?"

He gestured toward Hempstead and me. When we were standing in front of him, he leaned forward and whispered, "I want Linda

Easterbrook in my chambers at noon today. It seems that one or the other of you ought to be able to produce her."

I looked at Hempstead, who had a smug look on his face. Hempstead spoke, "Your Honor, I assume that, because she is Mr. Riley's employee, he will produce her for you."

Both men looked at me.

"Your Honor, I have severed any contact with Ms. Easterbrook. Could the court issue a subpoena? I will have it served."

Flick nodded. "Another thing. Given the sensitive nature of the subject matter, I will hear arguments and whatever testimony is necessary in my chambers so this does not become a three-ring circus."

I thought for a moment. "Your Honor, I object to making this a closed hearing. The public, including the press, have the right to hear this in open court."

Flick shot me that feral grin. I was learning to despise it. It may have been my imagination, but its appearance seemed to be always directed at me. "Mr. Riley. I am surprised. You should be the last person to want this heard in open court."

I couldn't help myself. The words were out of my mouth before I knew it. "Your Honor, based on our meeting between just the two of us in your chambers this morning, I think I stand a better chance of a fair hearing held out in the open. While I won't repeat verbatim what you said to me in chambers, it is clear to me that you accept Mr. Hempstead's position as gospel without any effort to hear my side of the story. I would like that story to be told in public."

Flick's face reddened. "Very well. Have it your way. It's your funeral." Flick looked at the court reporter who was transcribing the conversation. "Strike that last comment from the record." She nodded.

I nearly shouted. "Your Honor, I object to the striking of that comment. I think the record should reflect everything that is happening in this courtroom including comments from your Honor that indicate a bias in favor of one of the parties. I also want, at this time, to make a statement about the conversation that took place between us in your chambers a few minutes ago so that whatever tribunal may hear this matter can decide whether or not the proceedings were conducted fairly and impartially. In that meeting, you indicated quite clearly to me that you had a personal vendetta against me based upon what your father told you about me when you were a child and that you were going to accept Mr. Hempstead's version of events without even considering or hearing my version. I would like to make one inquiry of the court before we go any further. Has the court read my brief and motion? Does the court even know that I filed a motion and brief in support of the motion this morning?"

I looked at Hempstead, and he was no longer smiling. Flick's mouth was open, and he was visibly angry.

Gary Newton walked into the courtroom and came to my side. He whispered, "Judge Pendergast is in the hallway. Should I bring him in?"

I looked at Flick. Thought about his magic rabbit statement. "Your Honor, I have a witness outside the courtroom right now. I request that the court hear this witness before we go any further."

Flick said, "I think I have heard quite enough from you, Mr. Riley. I am prepared to rule."

"Your Honor, my witness is Judge Pendergast." I gestured to Gary to bring the judge in.

All eyes in the courtroom turned to watch Judge Pendergast as he walked in and sat down in the first row of seating.

Flick spoke, "Judge Pendergast, good morning. To what do we owe the pleasure?"

Pendergast stood. "I understand there is an issue about Linda Easterbrook. I was the weekend assignment judge and, in your absence, I had the opportunity to take her testimony on the motion Mr. Riley brings before you this morning. Mr. Riley has requested that I appear personally before you to describe what I discovered."

Flick looked like someone slapped his face. He was speechless. I decided to bridge the gap. "Your Honor, may I put Judge Pendergast on the witness stand and have him testify about his findings?"

Hempstead jumped to his feet. "Your Honor, this is highly irregular. With all due respect to Judge Pendergast, there is no precedent in American law for one judge to walk into the courtroom of another judge and give sworn testimony about the second judge's case. As I understand it, Judge Pendergast's findings are summarized in the brief filed by Mr. Riley. There is no need to buttress his findings by having him testify."

Flick spoke quietly. "I'll listen to what Judge Pendergast has to say."

Pendergast's testimony took an hour. Hempstead elected to not cross-examine him. Flick asked no questions. After Pendergast left the courtroom, Flick said, "I'll meet with all counsel in my chambers . . . now."

As we all settled ourselves in the various chairs in Flick's chambers, he cleared his throat, asked if the court reporter was ready. She nodded.

"Given the circumstances, I see no need to question Linda Easterbrook any further. Judge Pendergast has described quite thoroughly what she said under oath. Let me ask you, Mr. Hempstead. Did you know that Easterbrook was in Mr. Riley's office as a spy for Upright?"

"I was as surprised to hear about this as you were, Judge."

"I am glad to hear that. The question that I am now faced with is how much damage was done to Mr. Riley's client because of Easterbrook's spying. What do you have to say about that, Mr. Riley?"

"It would be difficult for me to say. The net impact on Mr. Slater's case is unknown, but I think it would be fair to say that it would not be favorable. I would need some time to put together a list."

"I'd like to put this incident to rest and get on with the trial. Any objections?" Flick looked at both Hempstead and me for a response. Hempstead shook his head.

I couldn't let this drop so easily. "Judge, it's important to hold those responsible for this travesty accountable for their actions. Cyrus Messner from Upright played a major role in perpetrating this fraud on the court. As the court is aware, Mr. Slater's case is not the only one I have involving Serenity. The extent to which Upright is privy to my work product is very much a concern for me in those cases, as well. Rather than 'putting this nasty incident to rest,' as you suggest, Mr. Messner and Upright should be censured publicly and the jury be told specifically about what has been done. They need to be told that Messner's acts were criminal and violated federal law. I would be pleased to submit a proposed jury instruction to you on the issue. Upright's and Messner's conduct has become a big part of the facts in this trial that the jury should be permitted to evaluate. I would also request that the transcript of Linda Easterbrook's statement to Judge Pendergast be turned over to the prosecutor for an evaluation of the criminal culpability of Messner. Additionally, I would like to recall Ms Huggins as a witness and have the court reconsider its prior rulings as to the admissibility of her testimony in light of the fact that we now know that Upright will do whatever it can do, illegal or not, to attempt to make its drug appear safe. As the court may recall, it struck Huggins's testimony even though that testimony described other criminal conduct of Messner. All of this information should be made part of the jury's consideration."

Flick thought for a moment. "The only issue in Mr. Slater's case that involves Serenity is whether or not the drug made him kill his wife. I fail to see what probative value Mister Messner's conduct has in helping the jury make that decision. The drug could have been whipped up by a bunch of high school seniors in a chemistry class, but if it didn't cause Slater to kill his wife, what possible relevance to how the drug was made is there? Now that I think about it, I'm placing a gag order on any discussion about Linda Easterbrook. If word gets out, if this goes public, the courtroom will be swarming with curiosity seekers and reporters. I will not let this trial turn into a three-ring circus."

This guy just didn't get it. I was astounded by Flick's stupidity. I had to respond in a way that didn't offend him, but it was going to be difficult. "Your Honor, with all due respect, this 'incident,' as you call it is vital information in Mr. Slater's case because exactly the kind of conduct he is being accused of was happening in other situations which Upright and Messner fraudulently attempted to hide. In other words, the history of this drug includes a pattern of harm identical to the harm at issue here. For example, in the Jackson Prison study, there were three prisoners who had reactions to the drug similar to Mr. Slater. The criminal conduct of Messner and Upright in falsifying the data submitted to the Food and Drug Administration is the only reason the drug is on the market. The jury is entitled to know that information."

Flick stood. "Let's recess until after lunch. I'll take your suggestions under advisement, Counsel. Until then, there is a gag order on all matters relating to Easterbrook."

I was upset by Flick's response to the Linda issue. Given how he treated me in his chambers, there was no doubt in my mind that he would have punished me however he could if I had been in the wrong. Once he knew that Upright was the culprit, Flick's reaction was mild in comparison. He should throw the damn book at Messner and cite him and Upright for contempt. Instead, he was bending over backwards to ensure that the jury and the public never found out. I should be allowed to recall Huggins to set the record straight. There was no doubt that Flick intended to gut my case. He was way out of line in protecting Upright with his frigging gag order.

My options seemed hopeless. I had the rest of the day to come up with something. I needed to regroup. I needed Alex Hartley to come in and tell the jury what this case was all about. Emrich would probably be a better choice than Hartley. I thought about her status as a federal employee. What kind of hoops would I have to jump through to get permission to call her in this case? I thought about Smythe, too. Flick's previous order prevented me from contacting him or his wife, but I could subpoena him. Shake that tree. See what falls out. When I got back to my office, I called Hartley and filled him in on the details. He told me that he and Emrich would both appear as witnesses. He reported on Emrich's unsuccessful attempt to bring Vogelgang on board. Hartley said that he and Emrich would meet with me later that afternoon in my office.

CHAPTER 72

I went back to the courtroom at one o'clock, but no judge and no Lester Hempstead. Ten minutes later, Flick's secretary came into the courtroom and told me the judge wanted to see me in chambers. I walked into his chambers and was surprised to see Hempstead already there. Flick had a look on his face. It looked like a smile, but I doubted it. "Sit down."

I sat in the remaining chair.

"I am putting the Easterbrook issue on hold. Mister Hempstead would like to meet with you privately, and I have no objection to that. We will adjourn the trial until tomorrow morning. I will see you then."

I went back into the courtroom and packed my materials away. One of Hempstead's associates came over to my table and handed me a folded note. "Meet me at Scott Fountain at two o'clock." It was signed by Hempstead.

Why would he want to meet there? What was so secret that we had to meet in a location away from the courthouse or our offices? Scott Fountain was a landmark on Belle Isle, a small island in the middle of the Detroit River about three miles from downtown Detroit and the courthouse.

The fountain was built on Belle Isle with funds left to the city of Detroit by millionaire James Scott in 1910. The bequest was conditional--to receive the funds, the city also had to erect a life-size statue of Scott. This condition outraged the respectable citizens of Detroit. According to an old newspaper article, Scott was a "playboy who played elaborate practical jokes, feuded with his neighbors, told dirty jokes, drank, gambled, and probably consorted with loose women." To put it bluntly, it was a strange place to meet.

I sat on a bench adjoining the fountain and faced the direction I thought Hempstead would approach. The air was fresh as the sun shone brightly in a cloudless sky. Pigeons strutted around me waiting for handouts. Visitors liked to feed the pigeons, and there was a small stand nearby where one could purchase a small bag of seed for that purpose. I closed my eyes and basked in the feel of a breeze on my cheek, the sun on my face, and the rumble of city traffic in the distance. Birds were singing. It felt good to be outside. I wondered what Hempstead had in mind.

He approached me at a slow, deliberate pace. Before he reached me, he stopped and lit a cigarette. We both wore our trial garb, but his red bow tie looked a bit ridiculous in this park setting. He sat down next to me without saying a word. We watched the pigeons for a while. He finally broke the silence. "I want to make a deal."

"A deal?"

He nodded. "Yes. A deal."

I assumed he wanted to talk about Easterbrook.

"She told me everything. " Hempstead turned toward me and took a deep drag on his cigarette. "We met in my office during lunch. I had to hear it for myself. Everything she told Pendergast is true." He grimaced. "I want to apologize. I want you to know that I had nothing to do with Easterbrook. The first I heard about it was when I read your motion. We've had a lot of battles over the years, but there's never been a question in my mind about your personal integrity. Never. It is important to me that you know that." He hesitated, "It's also very important to me that I come through this matter with my integrity intact. We've never been friends, but what I want to preserve is something far deeper than that. Mutual respect." A grin broke out on his face and he reached over and offered me his hand.

We shook hands. I said, "Lester, I feel the same way."

Hempstead held my hand in his firm grasp. "But that's not why we're here."

I extracted my hand from his. "Then why are we here? "

Hempstead hesitated again. His frequent pauses created a sensation of time slowing down. "I've got another note for you." He reached into his jacket and pulled out a folded piece of paper. Handed it to me. "Look at it, and I'll explain what it means."

I unfolded the note, and there was a number written on it. A very large number--with a lot of zeroes, with a dollar sign in front of the number. I looked at him for an explanation. Hempstead nodded toward the note. "The people I work for in this case want the Serenity civil litigation to go away--all of it. That's the number on the table to make it happen."

Holy shit, I thought. "You're offering me that much money on my civil cases?"

"No. That's the amount that's offered for all the pending civil cases in the country."

"Why are you telling me this? I don't represent all the civil cases in the country."

Hempstead looked at me. I looked back at him. Was this a joke?

"We want you to call a meeting of all the lawyers in the country handling cases involving Serenity. We want you to make your best effort to get them to agree to settle all of the cases. Take your time and do the math on the figure on that piece of paper. It averages out to two million a case. There are seventy-six cases out there, including Scruggs and the rest of yours. We will pay you an additional million-dollar fee just for putting the deal together."

There's got to be a catch to this. "What's the catch?"

"Several things. All of the lawyers in current cases must agree. No deal if they don't. Every case will be subject to a protective order. No talking about it. Period. These cases will just disappear from court dockets around the country." He added, "Flick will coordinate the settlement to give it judicial approval."

This conversation was mind-boggling. The last few days apparently touched a sensitive nerve at Upright. Until this moment, I hadn't given any thought to settling Scruggs. My efforts had been focused on Slater the last few weeks. Settlement talks were rarely on the agenda in civil suits involving the drug industry. Such talks only occurred after forcing a plaintiff into a long costly trial. In my experience, the decision to settle usually waited until the beginning of jury deliberations and was dependent on a trial lawyer or psychologist's assessment of the likelihood of a large verdict. It was difficult for my mind to change gears from trial mode and think settlement. A trial required a war mentality, whereas settlement required compromise; two mindsets totally dissimilar.

I thought about the role Hempstead was suggesting for me in settling all the cases. I had been involved in situations involving multiple cases in the past. Getting agreement from every lawyer who represented a client would be difficult, if not impossible. The lawyers with the worst cases always thought their individual case was the best. And they practiced a negotiating strategy resembling blackmail knowing that a group settlement might fall apart if their unreasonable demands were not met. I could envision that happening in this litigation, although any lawyer should be ecstatic walking away with a two-million-dollar settlement for a client in Serenity litigation. The amount being offered was truly staggering. Yet, to some lawyers, there may be no dollar amount that would ever be enough. Upright's offer of two million in each case would result in lawyers who would think they could try the case.

"What if some lawyers hold out?"

"We've got to have one hundred percent participation, or no deal. Knowing Flick, he'll hammer any lawyer that won't go along."

My mind was working fast now. "What about future cases?"

"We've thought of that. If, and when, any new case is filed, you would approach the lawyer involved and reach a settlement agreement. We have a contingency fund available for that purpose. All under the cloak of secrecy, of course. And, of course, you will receive a handsome fee for each negotiated settlement."

I was curious about something. "What if I just walk away now and turn it down or tell the press about this offer?"

"My suggestion is don't even think about it. You're not Flick's favorite person. Take a wild guess as to how he would react."

"You're suggesting I have no choice."

"Not much of a choice. It's an either or situation. Accept or reject. I know what I'd do. Easy decision."

"I've got to speak with my clients." I thought of something else. "I assume that Slater will be part of this settlement."

"A lot of good that will do him. From my reading of the jury, he's going bye -bye."

"And if he isn't convicted, if he walks away, I plan on filing suit on his behalf. You'll have to set aside two million for him. . . .as a contingency."

Hempstead stared at me for a moment like I was crazy.

He didn't know that Hartley and Emrich were sitting in my office getting ready for their appearances in court tomorrow. And that I was going to see Ken Smythe later tonight.

"I'll bring it up with my client. I'll assume they'll go along with it if he's acquitted."

"But that brings to mind another question. What about the other criminal cases in the country asserting a Serenity defense?"

"That's our concern. Not yours. If we go ahead with this, if you give the green light on settlement, we will move quickly."

"I'll speak to the Scruggs's daughter and the rest of my clients right away."

"Call them right away. You've got the rest of the afternoon. We'd like to hear as soon as possible. If Flick thinks that we're moving in a settlement direction on the civil cases, he'll be easier on you."

I left the island in a daze. It was a lot to think about in the middle of trial. It was difficult to think about settlement when I was locked in a take-no-prisoners battle.

CHAPTER 73

Emrich and Hartley were sitting side-by-side in the conference room when I got back to the office. They looked pretty cozy.

Gary Newton took me aside. "They're acting like a couple of love birds."

I thought that was a good thing--made it more likely that they would agree on key points of testimony. But Newton was right. I could damn near smell the pheromones in the room when I entered. Gary and I shared an amused look.

Hartley smiled at me. "We've gone through these materials and read the trial transcript of the witnesses. What do you need us for? Everything that needed to be said has been said." Emrich nodded in agreement.

I sat down across the table from them. "Strength in numbers. It's helpful to hear similar testimony from more than one expert. It lends credence when scientists agree on a topic, particularly when the topic is novel or controversial. Plus, the judge has tossed out some testimony that should have stayed in."

Looking at the two of them, I doubted they had read much of anything before my arrival. They were mooning over each other. Maybe it wasn't such a good idea to prepare them at the same time. I could say one thing. They sure as hell made an attractive couple. "Let's get started."

The next four hours went by quickly. I was impressed with their grasp of the facts and the way each of them stated their respective take on the dangers of Serenity. Any reservations I had when I walked into the room were long gone by the time we were done. Because of my commitment to Smythe, I begged off going to dinner. I could tell that they were heartbroken, but off they went.

Before I headed out to meet Smythe, I had the business of the settlement to handle. Janet Murley, the Scruggs's daughter, was waiting in the reception area. I ushered her into my office and sat behind my desk. "How's your mom doing?"

"Not well. I had to put her in a nursing home last month. She hasn't recovered well from being shot and losing Dad."

"I'll make sure I stop and visit her once this trial is over. But first, I've got some good news."

"That's surprising. I've been reading the papers about your trial. Doesn't sound like things are going too well."

"Upright has made you an offer of settlement."

"You're kidding."

"No. I'm not. There are a lot of conditions attached, and I think it's unlikely to happen. But it is my obligation to tell you and allow you to participate in the decision as to what we should do."

After I related the details to her, she asked a very smart question. "Why can't we just do this in our own case? Why do we have to involve anybody else?"

"According to their lawyer, they want the litigation to go away. I'm light years ahead of other lawyers handling these cases, and they believe that your case may be the pivotal case that will bring them down.

"I won't agree with any offer unless they agree to remove the drug from the market." She was no dummy. If I lost a loved one to the drug, I would want the same thing.

"Quite frankly, that's not going to happen. It is not the function of a civil suit to make it happen. Your lawsuit is about money. The question is 'how much money will appropriately compensate you for your loss?' That's it. If I were to go back to them with a demand to take the drug off the market, the deal would be off. I agree with you. I think the drug should be off the market, but that's not my decision or yours."

I related the terms of the offer in detail. She was receptive. Two million dollars was a lot of money. Her father was dead, and her mother was dying. She was single, a very attractive person, and making thirty-two thousand dollars a year as a bank teller. That kind of money would change her life. She pondered the deal for a moment. She stood and gave me a nice hug. "Make it happen."

I spoke with my other clients by phone and received immediate approval from each of them. It boggled my mind. Two million bucks for each Serenity case in the office.

I still had a few minutes before I needed to leave for my meeting with Smythe. I spent the time talking with Gary. We were excited about the settlement offer and about tomorrow. As I drove to Ann Arbor, I wondered how tomorrow could possibly be more exciting than today. What a day, and the best was yet to come! If I was right, my meeting with Ken Smythe would be the icing on the cake.

CHAPTER 74

I don't believe in love at first sight, but I considered changing my mind when Anne Smythe answered the front door and ushered me into the living room. I stammered when she asked if I would like something to drink. "Ken is upstairs putting the kids to bed. He'll be down in just a minute." I was at a loss for words, so I just shook my head. She was a beauty, and I couldn't stop staring. It wasn't anything that she did or said. It was just her. I managed a question. "How many children do you have?"

"Two. Six and seven years old."

I felt like a fourteen-year-old boy talking to a girl for the first time. This woman mesmerized me. My reverie was interrupted when her husband walked into the room.

"Hi. I'm Ken Smythe." I was relieved to see him.

I stood, and we shook hands. "I'm Bob Riley."

"I'll make some coffee --unless you'd like a beer?" She stood at the doorway to the kitchen and looked at me. Be still, my beating heart.

"A beer would be nice," Smythe said.

"Me too."

She came back with a glass of beer in each hand. "I'll leave you two alone now."

Smythe and I sat knee to knee. I was on the couch, and he sat in the chair. He set a package of materials on the coffee table in front of us. I resisted commenting on his beautiful wife. I felt stupid for thinking about her.

Smythe looked at me. "Where would you like to begin?"

I gathered my thoughts. "Let me ask you first. Are you willing to come into court and testify on behalf of my client?"

"That depends. Truthfully, I'd rather not. I spoke with Jan Emrich earlier today, and I would suspect that she'd be able to give you whatever you need. She and I are on the same page."

I knew that already. Emrich had said the same when she told me that she'd rather not testify and that Smythe would be a better witness. She told me the same thing about Hartley. Hartley told me the same thing about her. Emrich relented after having spent the day with Hartley and now seemed eager to help. But I wanted Smythe in court too. An employee of Upright. A stand-up guy. A credible witness didn't come any better than him.

"Let's talk and see where we end up. Just keep an open mind on the subject. Is that all right?"

"Fine with me."

I reached into my briefcase and pulled out the subpoena. I handed it to him.

"Here. Consider yourself served. If I do have to call you as a witness, you can say you had no choice."

We spent the next three hours going over the history of Serenity and his involvement. I was impressed with the guy. He would make a superb witness. I told him so. "You would be the icing on the cake,"

"You asked me to keep an open mind, and I will. I ask the same of you. If I come to court and testify, it'll mean the end of my career at Upright. It will jeopardize my employability in the drug industry. I'll be a pariah. Nobody will hire me. I need to trust you to keep that from happening unless it's absolutely necessary."

I nodded. I understood his dilemma. To sacrifice Smythe for Slater's benefit was not a tradeoff that made me comfortable. I promised I would do whatever I could to keep him from testifying.

The meeting was productive, however. Smythe had given me some additional documents about the dangers of Serenity. At the end of the evening, my heart rate went up when his wife came back into the room to say goodbye. She was really something.

What a night. What a day. Even with everything else that had happened, it was Anne Smythe that I couldn't stop thinking about. As I drove home, I laughed to myself when I had a thought. Rather than her husband, Anne Smythe was the icing on the cake.

Anne snuggled up to Ken in bed. "What did Riley say when you told him about being hospitalized?"

"He didn't ask, and I didn't bring it up."

She hugged him. "Just as well. He probably wouldn't want you as a witness if he knew. He wouldn't understand."

He reached over and turned out the light. "I hope he never finds out."

CHAPTER 75

Next morning, when we arrived at court, Flick wanted to meet in chambers. He wanted an update on the settlement status.

"I spoke with my clients last night, and they all have given me authorization to settle." I think Flick almost smiled when he heard the news.

He said, "I'll tell you what. I've given a lot of thought to the global settlement that Upright proposes. We're going to take the rest of the week off from trial and get the process moving." He looked at me. "Riley, you make calls to the other lawyers today. Get them here Saturday, noon, in my courtroom. Tell them they need to be able to reach their clients by phone or bring them with them. Hempstead, you keep your client in line. I don't want Upright backing out of this or playing games. We can wrap this up by the end of the day on Saturday."

I nearly fell out of my chair when he smiled at me. A full-blown smile. At me, my new best friend.

We went back into the courtroom, and Flick spoke to the jury. "A matter has come up of the utmost urgency. As a result, you are excused until next Monday. You are free for the rest of the week. Enjoy the time off. Remember my admonition to not talk about, listen to, or read reports about this case on TV, radio, or the newspapers. I'll see you all Monday."

Flick left the courtroom. The jury filed out. Juror Loukas looked over and gave me an angry look. He's probably wondering what happened to Linda. Going through leg withdrawal. I smiled at my joke. I tried it on Gary. " Loukas's going through leg withdrawal."

Gary just looked at me. He didn't get it. He shrugged. And said, "Something is the matter with him. I'm worried about him. I had him down as a solid supporter of our case. Something's happened. I think we've lost him."

Gary and I walked back to the office and broke the news about the delay to Hartley and Emrich. They both grinned. To say they weren't disappointed about having until next Monday to spend time with each other would be putting it mildly. When they left, I brought Mary into my office. Hempstead had given me a list of the lawyers in the country with pending Serenity cases, and I asked her to arrange a conference call. There were a total of seventy-six cases in all. I was optimistic. Once these lawyers heard the numbers, I thought they'd fall in line. It was too good to be true. Twenty minutes later, Mary buzzed me, "Everybody's on the line. You're good to go."

I picked up the phone and started talking. To say that everything went like clockwork would be an over-simplification, but it'd be a good description. By nine o'clock the next evening, I'd received fax confirmations from the thirty-two lawyers on all the cases authorizing me to settle. It was a strange day, I thought, as it was coming to an end. I couldn't get my mind off Anne Smythe. This is so stupid. She is another man's wife. She is at least thirty years younger than me, young enough to be my daughter. Yikes, maybe young enough to be my granddaughter. She wouldn't give me the time of day if I asked. I was not one to obsess over things, but I was obsessed with her. I replayed meeting her over and over in my mind. I constructed a few fantasies that will be unmentioned. Had she felt the same jolt of electricity?

I called Hempstead the next morning and told him about the agreements. In a conference call, we told Flick the Saturday conference was unnecessary. He was elated. Judicial procedures allowed for transferring all the settled cases to his docket, which meant that he would get credit for disposing of them. Judges around the country, for the most part, had one thing in mind when it came to trial dockets. Get the damn cases off the books. He'd be a hero in the eyes of his peers.

I forced myself to stop thinking about Anne Smythe. I had no choice. I had to get my focus back on Slater. By and large, Flick had gutted my case. My big guns, Clackner and Giovanni, had not been permitted to give opinions on the big issue of Slater's defense--the role of Serenity in causing his wife's death. Schneidermann had given his opinion on the issue, but he was a clinician and not a scientist. The jury might discount his opinion. I needed to bolster the causation proofs, and Emrich and Hartley were the persons who could do it best. The same with Smythe.

I thought about Smythe. Did I really need him to testify, or could I do just as well without him? With the change in Flick's attitude, maybe I didn't need him. Flick had to give me a little leeway now that we were best of friends.

CHAPTER 76

When the trial resumed the following Monday, I started by calling
Emrich to the stand. "Would you state your name?"

"Doctor Janice Emrich."

"Would you tell the jury about your educational background?"

Jan spent a few minutes telling the jury about obtaining a doctorate
degree in pharmacology after graduating from Princeton.

"Are you familiar with the drug Serenity?"

"Yes, I am."

"How do you happen to be familiar with that drug?"

"For the past eight years, I worked as a principle investigator
at the Food and Drug Administration in Rockville, Maryland.
My assignments in that position included the review of new drug
applications submitted by drug manufacturers for the purpose of
obtaining approval for the marketing of the drugs. Without such
approval, a manufacturer cannot legally market a drug in the United
States. I became familiar with Serenity in that capacity because I
was designated as chief investigator of the drug. I was responsible for
reviewing and evaluating the new drug application of Serenity for the
purpose of recommending or rejecting its approval."

"You say you 'worked' at the FDA. That implies that you are no
longer working there. Is that correct?"

"Yes, that is correct."

"Would you tell the jury why you are no longer at the FDA?"

"Yes. We approved serenity in January 2008. Within three or four months, a number of case reports came into me at the agency that suggested that something was seriously dangerous about the drug. I commenced an investigation and discovered that the manufacturer had submitted fraudulently conducted studies in order to get approval of the drug. I made the recommendation to my superiors at the agency that the permission to market Serenity be withdrawn, but my request was denied. I was removed from my position and essentially given a job as a secretary in an obscure division of the agency dealing with livestock. It was the agency's equivalent of being shipped to Siberia for my not going along with the program, so to speak."

At this point, I was puzzled by the lack of resistance to her testimony from Hempstead. His silence was letting me get away with murder. Let me rephrase that. His silence was allowing me to bring much needed evidence in front of the jury. I decided to push the envelope on the issue of case reports. "You mentioned case reports. What are they?"

"When a drug is on the market, a person may suffer a serious side effect or reaction from the drug. If a physician recognizes the problem as having a connection with the drug, he or she can report the observation and connection to the FDA. Before a drug is initially marketed, the number of people exposed to the drug is too small to detect potential problems that may be serious but don't occur with a high frequency. The system of adverse case reporting serves, in this regard, as an early warning system for potential problems when the drug begins to be widely used after marketing. It is sometimes the only way that serious problems can be detected. It is invaluable in determining whether a drug is causing a problem. Case reports stand out like a red flag that tell us something is wrong with the drug. While one or two such reports may be only a suggestion of a potential problem, multiple similar reports indicate a real connection between the drug and the harm being reported. In other words, if a pattern of events is reported it is likely that there is a causal connection."

"What pattern of case reporting did Serenity show after marketing?"

Hempstead jumped to his feet. "Your Honor, you have ruled previously that the subject matter of case reports is inadmissible. I object to the question on the basis that it seeks a response which is inadmissible and irrelevant."

Flick looked at both of us. "Approach the bench." He glared at me when we reached the sidebar. Apparently things were back to normal. "What are you doing? I ruled case reports inadmissible in this case. Why are you bringing them up again?"

"With respect, Your Honor, I think Doctor Emrich is the one unique person who can demonstrate why case reports are important, if not vital, in evaluating a cause and effect relationship between a drug and a harmful action of that drug. As Doctor Emrich has already testified, sometimes the only way a serious problem can be discovered is via case reports. Also, my question did not deal with the concept of an individual case report, but a pattern of case reporting. As Dr. Emrich has just testified, it is the pattern of multiple reports that is important, not the individual case report."

"I don't agree. You have deliberately violated my prior rulings on this issue."

He waved us away and then turned to the jury. "Mr. Hempstead's objection is sustained. Case reports are not to be considered as evidence of a harmful effect. You are instructed to disregard the testimony of the witness concerning adverse case reporting." He looked at me. "Move on, Counsel." What a short honeymoon that was. My new best friend had abandoned me.

I had a backup plan. Emrich, Hartley and I had discussed the likelihood that case reports would not be permitted. We worked several hours last night on the alternative. "Doctor Emrich, are you familiar with the pharmacological properties of Serenity?"

"Yes, I am. It is in the category of compounds known as benzodiazepines. Drugs in the class are used to reduce anxiety, promote sleep, reduce jet lag and to take care of a variety of other problems. Serenity is the most recent addition to that group of drugs."

"Are there any differences between benzodiazepines, in general, and Serenity, in particular?"

"Yes, there are substantial differences. Would you like me to elaborate?"

I looked over at the jury to see how well they were following her testimony. All, except Loukas, were paying attention. Loukas sat there staring at the wall, arms folded. Was he still pissed because Linda wasn't showing up? If he only knew the reason why.

"Yes, please do so."

"Serenity is more potent than any of the other drugs in this category by at least twenty times. For example, if Drug X controls symptoms at a level of 20 milligrams per dose, it would be expected that Serenity might have the same effect at one milligram per dose. In the field of pharmacology, there is a concept known as the margin of safety. With any given drug, there is an effective dose relative to a higher dose, which produces side effects. In some drugs, the effective dose is a small percentage of the dose producing side effects. In the benzodiazepines as a class, the effective dose is generally one-fifth of the dosage that will cause problems. Serenity is unique in that its effective dose is less than one half of the dangerous level of the drug in users. The margin of safety is less than fifty-percent--not eighty or ninety percent like most drugs."

"What does this mean in practical terms?"

"If a person taking one Serenity a day accidentally takes a second tablet on a given day, that person has taken a toxic dose of the drug, and adverse effects will likely be seen. If a person is taking a different benzodiazepine, taking a double dose inadvertently does not move the dosage into the toxic range. That is to say, the margin of safety is much greater than that of Serenity. The threshold of safety is breached too easily in Serenity."

Here we go again. I had to keep trying. "Are there scientific studies done with Serenity that show the kinds of dangers caused?"

"Yes, the manufacturer of Serenity conducted a study which clearly indicates the risks and harm caused by the drug."

"Can you tell the court and jury about that study, please?"

"Objection, Your Honor. May we approach the bench?" Things had gone so smoothly I thought Hempstead had gone to sleep. Flick nodded, and we gathered at the sidebar.

"Your Honor, you have already ruled that testimony pertaining to this study is inadmissible. Counsel is seeking to circumvent the prior ruling of the court."

Flick looked at me. "What about it, Counsel?"

"Your Honor did rule that an earlier non-scientist witness, Myra Huggins, was not permitted to testify about this study even though she was the person who typed both the preliminary and final drafts. As I recall, the ruling was that she could not testify about the study because she was not a scientist. With Doctor Emrich, a scientist whose job at the FDA was to evaluate the safety of the drug, I am seeking to establish that the study conducted by Upright scientifically demonstrates a causal connection between taking Serenity and violent behaviors in users."

"What problem do you have with that, Mr. Hempstead?"

"Your Honor has already ruled on this. We can't keep going back and letting Mr. Riley try to change your mind. Your prior ruling is the law of the case."

Flick thought for a moment. "I agree. Move on to another topic, Mr. Riley."

Flick turned to the jury as we returned to our seats. "The objection is sustained. You are to disregard any testimony with regard to the study performed by the manufacturer as a basis for assessing causation."

I bit my lip to prevent my attacking Flick verbally in front of the jury. This latest ruling was no surprise, but in terms of sheer stupidity and bias on his part, it was clear that Flick was nothing other than Hempstead's puppet. He would do or say whatever Hempstead wanted to hurt my case. Nothing had changed since I busted my ass to put the settlement together to make the judge look good.

I forged on. "Doctor Emrich, do you have an opinion as to whether or not the Serenity ingested by Jay Slater for the three-week period prior to the death of his wife caused, or contributed, to the death?"

"Yes, I do."

"What is your opinion?"

"My opinion is that there is no question but that Serenity caused Mr. Slater to take the life of his wife."

"Is your opinion based on reasonable scientific probability?"

"Yes."

"That completes my questioning. Thank you, Doctor Emrich."

Hempstead stood quickly and approached her.

"You use the title doctor, but you really don't treat people, do you?"

"No, I don't. As you well know, there are different kinds of doctors. I am a doctor of pharmacology. People who deal with me professionally call me Doctor. Because I am here testifying in a professional capacity, I am using the designation."

"But the question I asked is whether or not you treat people."

"And my answer to that was no. Apparently you weren't listening."

She had spunk. I liked that. Go, girl. I looked at the jury. They liked her response too.

"You indicated that you have been removed from your responsibility for Serenity by your superiors. Is that right?"

"Yes, that's right, and I mentioned the reason for my removal."

Hempstead looked at Flick. "Your Honor, can I get a little help here? The witness does not seem to understand that her obligation is to just answer my questions."

"I agree. Ms. Emrich, please answer the questions that Mr. Hempstead is asking. If anything needs clarification, Mr. Riley is certain to bring it up with you when he has his next chance."

"Thank you, Mr. Flick."

The courtroom went silent. Oh shit, I thought.

"What did you call me?"

"You called me Ms. Emrich. Because you did, I thought you preferred informality in the courtroom."

Flick ground his teeth. He turned red. The jury was loving this exchange. Flick swallowed. "You're right, Doctor Emrich. I apologize."

She smiled at him and then at the jury. "Apology accepted, Your Honor. And please accept mine in return."

This was not a woman to be pushed around.

"Let's move on." Flick gestured impatiently at Hempstead.

Before Hempstead could respond, Flick interjected, "Excuse me. Doctor Emrich, you are to answer the question that is asked. You are not to go beyond the answer to the question. Do I make myself clear?"

"Yes, Your Honor."

Flick nodded at Hempstead who asked, "Was it Morton Levitt who transferred you to another department in the FDA? Who removed you from your responsibility for Serenity?"

"That's two questions. Which one do you want me to answer?"

Flick was getting antsy. He growled at Hempstead. "Mr. Hempstead, don't complain about her answers if you are going to ask two questions at once. Now ask a proper question." I heard a couple of quiet chuckles from the jury box. I looked over, but couldn't tell who it was.

Hempstead's face turned red. "Was it Morton Levitt who transferred you to another department?"

Emrich smiled sweetly at the jury. "Yes. Mister Levitt arranged for me to be transferred to another department to keep me quiet about Serenity." The jury knew what she was doing. They were enjoying the dialogue, all except for Mister Loukas. He sat with his arms folded across his chest.

Flick leaned toward Emrich. "Doctor, this is the last time I'm warning you about your answers. Do you understand?"

"Perfectly, Your Honor."

"Proceed, Counsel." He nodded at Hempstead. Emrich looked over at me. I signaled for her to tone it down. The line was always thin. Juries loved an underdog. It was dicey when the underdog crossed the line. Emrich may have already breached the rapport she'd had with the jury. Maybe yes, maybe no, but she was close to the line. She needed to play fair with Hempstead, and to this point in her testimony, she hadn't.

Hempstead resumed his questions. "As I understand it, you quit your job at the FDA. Is that right?"

"Yes, sir. I did."

I put an asterisk in my notes beside this question and answer. When my turn came to ask some more questions, she needed to tell the jury why she quit.

"Who have you talked to about your testimony here today?"

"Mr. Riley, Dr. Alex Hartley, and Dr. Gary Newton."

"Doctor Newton? Who's that?"

"Doctor Gary Newton is the lawyer sitting next to Mister Riley." She pointed at Gary. "He's Mr. Riley's associate. He's a doctor and a lawyer. That's why I call him Doctor Newton. Out of professional courtesy."

She was close to the line again. I couldn't help but smile. Gutsy lady. Hempstead stepped back to his table and conferred with his colleagues. He looked up at Judge Flick. "I have no more questions."

I stood. "I have a few follow-up questions. This man, Mister Morton Levitt, who removed you from your position as chief Serenity investigator, is not a trained scientist. Is that correct?"

"Yes, that's correct."

"Do you know about Mr. Levitt's educational background?"

"I know that he went to college and that he flunked out of medical school in the first year."

I had one final question. "Doctor Emrich, you testified that you quit the FDA. Why did you do that?"

"Yes, I did quit. My professional responsibilities in approving and monitoring the safety of Serenity were a duty I owed to the people of the United States. Once I became aware of what the manufacturer did in order to obtain approval of the drug, I intensified my efforts to investigate the safety of the drug. Other countries all over the world were banning Serenity because of the negative effects which were reported. I found myself wondering what I had missed in evaluating the new drug application. I studied the application in detail and came here to Michigan, to Ann Arbor, to interview key persons who were involved in the research. Once I concluded my investigation, I took my findings to Mister Levitt, who laughed at me and chided me for, as he put it, 'trying to bite the hand that fed me.' When he did nothing with my report, I went to the legal division of our agency. The lawyers in the agency agreed with me that Serenity was an appropriate subject for investigation by the U.S. Department of Justice. Shortly thereafter, I left the agency. I do not know what the current status of the investigation is."

"Thank you, Doctor Emrich. That's all I have."

As she stepped down from the witness stand and left the courtroom, I wondered if her abrasive style had damaged her credibility with the jury.

I monitored the jury as best I could during her testimony, and the reactions appeared to be favorable. Gary gave me a thumbs-up as I sat down. The one exception appeared to be Loukas. He sat stone-faced throughout her testimony, arms folded across his chest. He didn't look at Emrich while she was on the stand, and he avoided eye contact with me, as well. Then again, he wasn't looking at Hempstead or the judge either. I wished that there were another pair of legs in the office that I could bring in to win him back. Damn Linda. She'd fucked me in more ways than one, and not one felt any good.

"Any more witnesses, Mr. Riley?"

"Yes, Your Honor. He's waiting in the hallway. Let me get him."

Hartley was sitting on a bench just outside the courtroom with his arm around Emrich. She was crying, and he was speaking quietly to her. He looked up. "What happened in there?"

"She did fine. Wonderful, in fact."

"That's not what she said. She said the judge constantly scolded her because he didn't like her answers."

"We can't talk about this now. They're waiting on us."

Hartley squeezed Emrich's shoulder and stood. "Let's go. I'm mad as hell."

CHAPTER 77

Loukas' thoughts wandered all over. He knew he should have told the judge he was taking Serenity, but he told Flick he wasn't on any medications when he was asked at the beginning of the trial. His doctor started him on Serenity a couple of days before the trial started. If he told the judge then, he knew what would have happened. He'd be right back at the grocery store, and he wasn't ready to go back. Now, he didn't know if he ever wanted to go back.

He looked over at Slater. The son-of-a-bitch says Serenity made him do it. What a bunch of bullshit. All this talk about studies and dosages pissed him off. He was taking the drug, and he felt fine. More than fine. It was the best he'd felt in a long time. That asshole Riley caught him looking at his precious fucking assistant one too many times, and now she was gone. The lawyer was jealous as hell because she had taken a shine to Loukas—she was coming on to him all the time, smiling at him like she did. When he looked at her, she smiled back. He'd been ready to ask her out. The next day, she was gone. Just like that. The old guy, Riley, must have figured it out somehow. He stopped listening to Emrich who was prattling along about something or other. She pissed him off. She wanted to take Serenity off the market. He didn't want that to happen. He liked the drug--liked the feeling it gave him.

He'd been dead inside so long, he thought. He couldn't remember the last time he felt as good as he did right now. Serenity made him feel good.

He looked around the courtroom. He noticed a woman sitting in the second row of seats behind Riley. She was something to look at. He pretended to listen to the testimony, but watched the woman out of the corner of his eye. Her attention was focused on Riley and Emrich. He thought about how he could get her attention, to get her to look over at him. Maybe she was deliberately ignoring him. Maybe Riley told her to ignore him. Old bastard! Loukas shifted in his chair. He moved his hand to see if that would gain her attention. She didn't respond. She didn't know he existed.

Loukas looked at Emrich as she stepped down from the witness stand. She wanted to take Serenity off the market. Fucking bitch. Riley walked Emrich out of the courtroom, and Loukas turned his attention to the woman in the second row. She was sitting by herself, not looking around. He moved again--tried to attract her attention. She didn't notice. She didn't want to notice him. He knew Riley had told her to keep his eyes off him. Old guy like that, telling her what to do. It wasn't right.

Riley came back into the courtroom with a guy wearing a sports coat. No tie.

"The defendant calls Doctor Alex Hartley."

Loukas looked over at the woman in the second row again. Felt himself get hard.

CHAPTER 78

I came back in the courtroom with Hartley and announced him as a witness. While he was being sworn in, I turned around and scanned the courtroom. I nearly moaned aloud when I saw Anne Smythe sitting there in the second row behind my table. She smiled, and I nodded. I turned to Hartley. What was she doing here? I opened my mouth to begin my questioning and garbled the first few words. My tongue felt like it was tied in knots. I stopped and swallowed, cleared my throat, and started over. "Would you state your name for the record?"

"My name is Alex Hartley, M.D."

"What do you do for a living?"

"I practice internal medicine and toxicology at Detroit Receiving Hospital. I have a specialty interest in pharmacology and adverse drug reactions, and I treat referred patients from other physicians for that purpose quite frequently. I am board certified in internal medicine and toxicology. Because of my interest in drug toxicity I went back to school after completing my medical training and obtained a doctorate degree--a Ph.D.--in pharmacology."

"What is pharmacology?"

"The study of drugs."

"Have you testified under oath before?"

"Yes, I testified a long time ago in a case involving another drug. I have managed to avoid coming to court since then. I prefer it that way."

Some of the jurors laughed softly.

"Are you familiar with the drug Serenity?"

"Yes, I am. I have treated a substantial number of patients at Receiving who were suffering from toxic reactions to Serenity."

"Have you treated Jay Slater?" I gestured toward Slater, who was sitting next to Gary at our table.

"Yes, I have."

"Will you tell the court and jury when you first treated Mister Slater and what your findings were at the time?"

"May I look at my notes in his medical record?"

Gary handed Slater's medical records from Receiving to me. "Your Honor, at this time, I move for the admission of Mister Slater's medical records from Detroit Receiving."

Flick looked at Hempstead. "Any objections?"

Hempstead shook his head. "No."

"The records will be admitted."

I walked up and handed the exhibit to Hartley. I took a quick glance at Anne Smythe as I returned to the podium. She smiled. I gave her a quick grin back. I looked over at Loukas. He'd seen the brief exchange and glared at me. What in the hell was going on with him?

Hartley scanned the records. "I first saw Mister Slater on April 29, 2008. My initial contact with him was in the emergency room, where he was being held in police custody. I noted that he was in a stupor and unable to answer my questions. He was covered in blood, and I learned that he had been arrested for allegedly killing his wife with a shovel a few hours earlier. I performed a physical examination on him. Other than his stuporous condition, his pupils were extremely dilated. His various neurologic signs were all within normal limits, but I noted that his reflexes appeared to be sluggish."

"Did you make an initial diagnosis?"

"Yes. My initial diagnosis was 'toxic delirium, etiology unknown.' I couldn't obtain a history from him because of his condition, so my conclusion was tentative at that time."

"Etiology unknown. What does that mean?"

"Etiology is the fancy medical word for 'cause.' What the term means is that, at the time of my initial contact with Mister Slater, I believed he was suffering from a toxic reaction of unknown cause."

"And what is toxic delirium?"

Hartley paused, looked at the jury. "Toxic delirium means that the person is incoherent or mentally incapacitated as a result of exposure to some toxic agent. "

"Did you continue to treat Mister Slater?"

"Yes. Mister Slater stayed at Receiving for three days in police custody. He was transferred to a private room shortly after my initial evaluation in the emergency room. I ordered a TOX screen STAT and made a note in the record to ask the police about any drugs that may have been discovered in the course of their investigation."

"Let me interrupt you for a moment. What is a TOX screen?"

"Blood is taken from a patient and subjected to a sophisticated analysis in the laboratory looking for a wide spectrum of substances that may cause toxic reactions. Six hours after his arrival, I received the report of the TOX screen. Mister Slater had a high level of benzodiazepine in his bloodstream."

"We have had testimony earlier in this case about benzodiazepines. Did you eventually find out if Mister Slater had been taking any drug in that category?"

"Yes, I did. Eight hours after admission, Lieutenant Nowak called me with the information that Mister Slater had a prescription bottle for Serenity in the medicine chest of his home. Doctor Ralph Greene wrote the prescription for Mister Slater on April 8, 2008, for sixty tablets of the drug with two refills. It was written for one tablet daily to be taken at bedtime. The prescription was filled twenty-one days before his admission, and there were thirty-nine tablets remaining in the bottle. I concluded that Mister Slater had taken the drug every day for twenty-one days, as had been prescribed by his doctor."

"Why were the details of the prescription important to you?"

"A lot of the toxic reactions I treat are in people who try to commit suicide by taking an overdose of drugs. It is medically important to know because the level of drugs in the body, and the reasons for that level, dictate how I treat any given patient."

I sneaked a quick glance back at Smythe. She smiled back.

"Were the results from the TOX screen consistent with the daily taking of the drug by Mister Slater?"

"Yes. The dosage prescribed was higher than one would expect, but still within the recommended daily dose of the manufacturer."

"Did this new information cause you to change your diagnosis?"

"Yes, it did. Now that I had an identified source, I changed my diagnosis to 'delirium secondary to acute Serenity toxicity'"

"Have you seen this problem in other users of Serenity?"

Hempstead interrupted. "Objection. Relevance."

Flick appeared annoyed. "Denied. Go ahead, doctor. Answer the question."

"Yes. I've seen and treated patients on a number of occasions with similar reactions to Serenity--before and after Mister Slater."

"Did Mister Slater's mental condition change while he was in the hospital for the first three days?"

"No. He was not responsive throughout that time period. I described him in my notes as obtundent, the fancy medical term for non-responsive."

"Did you continue to treat Mister Slater after his discharge from Receiving?"

"Yes. He was transferred to Wayne County Jail, and I saw him daily for the first two weeks he was there."

"Did his mental status improve during that time?"

"Yes, it did. His thinking gradually cleared over the course of the two weeks. He remembered nothing about what he'd gone through but, other than that, he was able to participate in a normal conversation. He was depressed, of course, when he learned of his wife's death. I avoided any other medications for him because of his reaction to Serenity."

"Do you have an opinion based on reasonable medical certainty whether or not Serenity caused the condition that you observed and treated in Mister Slater?"

"Yes, I do. It is my medical opinion that Mister Slater's condition, toxic delirium, was caused by Serenity."

I waited a moment, glanced quickly back at Smythe. She was looking at me. "Dr. Hartley, what is the basis for your opinion that Serenity caused the toxic delirium present in Mr. Slater during your treatment of him?"

Hartley turned and looked at the jury. "The basis for my opinion is that his medical condition was entirely consistent of a person experiencing a toxic reaction to a drug. He was in a stupor. He didn't know his name. He didn't know where he was. He didn't know the time or date. Doctors refer to this as being disoriented times three. That is, disoriented as to time, place and person. He had been taking Serenity, a drug that is known to cause this kind of reaction in users. Serenity is also a drug in a category of drugs known as benzodiazepines that are well known to cause drug stupor.

"If the evidence indicates that Mister Slater took his wife's life while in the condition you observed, do you have an opinion as to whether or not he was capable of forming the intent to do so?"

"Yes, I do have an opinion, and it is my opinion that Mister Slater was utterly incapable of forming an intent to kill his wife."

"Thank you, Doctor Hartley. That completes my direct examination, Your Honor."

Flick nodded toward Hempstead. "Your witness, Mr. Hempstead."

Hempstead stood and approached Hartley.

"You mentioned that other drug case you were involved in. Isn't it true that Mister Riley was the attorney who hired you in that case?"

Hartley smiled at the jury. "Yes, that's true."

"Regarding the TOX screen taken to determine the presence of drugs in Mr. Slater at the time of his admission, I think you mentioned that the results for Serenity were quote-higher than would be expected – end of quote. Is that correct?"

"Yes, that's correct."

"Now Dr Hartley, isn't it true that the blood level of Serenity found in Mr. Slater's bloodstream was four times higher than what might be expected in a person taking a single daily dose of the drug?"

"Yes, that's true."

"In fact, the level of Serenity present in Mr. Slater was consistent with the taking of four tablets of Serenity all at once. Isn't that true?"

"Yes, that's true."

"And if someone knew that Serenity was implicated in causing the serious side effect we are dealing with in this case, isn't it true that taking a dose four times greater than what is prescribed would increase the likelihood of a toxic response."

Hartley hesitated before speaking. "First of all, the problem we're dealing with here can't be called a side effect. It is a serious adverse reaction due to the use of the drug, and is much more serious than a side effect. An example of a side effect would be experiencing a little bit of nausea or upset stomach following the taking of a drug. The killing of a human being is not a side effect. Having said that, by your question you are implying that Mister Slater deliberately took four tablets at one time before taking his wife's life, and I simply don't believe that it is true. As I indicated, the number of tablets of Serenity missing from Slater's prescription bottle coincided exactly with the number of days he took the drug."

Hempstead turned and looked at the jury before he asked his next question. "You have just told the jury that my last question implied that Mister Slater deliberately took four tablets at one time before killing his wife. Isn't it true, Doctor Hartley, that there is another alternative you have not mentioned and that is whether or not Mister Slater took four tablets at one time after killing his wife?"

Hartley hesitated. "Yes, that's true."

Hempstead stood quietly for a moment. "Thanks, Dr. Hartley. That's all the questions I have."

"Let's recess until after lunch."

As the jury filed out, Loukas looked over at me. He was angry about something. I didn't have a clue as to what was bothering him.

I turned to leave the courtroom. Anne Smythe was standing at the railing that separated the lawyer's tables from the spectator seating area.

"Can I speak to you a minute?" There was a sense of urgency in her voice.

I nodded and told Gary to go back to the office with Hartley. Then I looked at her. "What can I do for you?"

"There are some things you should know. Is there someplace we can talk?" Her smile melted my heart, which was already beating hard. Her closeness had an effect on me hard to describe. But it was real, and it was nice.

"How much time do you need?"

"Only a few minutes."

I was thinking inappropriately. I was thinking motels. She did that to me. Her impact of the other night on me hadn't worn off. In fact, it was intensified.

"We can sit right here. Nobody will bother us. Everyone's going to lunch."

I opened the gate, and she sat down at the table. I sat next to her. "What's on your mind?"

She leaned in close. I smelled her perfume. She put her hand on top of mine. "There's something you should know about my husband. He didn't tell you the other night, but you should know."

"What is it?"

"Kenny was hospitalized in a mental institution recently. While we can't prove it, I think Upright was responsible for putting him there.

If you called him as a witness, they would probably go into that. He's terrified about the possibility."

I thought for a moment. "I am glad that you brought that to my attention. It does make a difference. After this morning's testimony, I don't think I need him anyway. I don't want to hurt your husband. Or you."

I looked directly into her eyes. She looked back. I looked away. I couldn't take it anymore. It was getting warm in here.

"I also wanted to say one other thing." She hesitated. "It was nice meeting you the other night." She leaned closer and kissed my cheek. I could smell alcohol on her breath. That surprised me.

I squeezed her hand. "Thanks so much. I appreciate your bringing your husband's hospitalization to my attention." She stood. Don't do it, I thought. Don't make an idiot out of yourself by saying something that you will regret.

I stood and gave her a little hug. Made sure my body didn't contact hers.

"I enjoyed meeting you too. Please give your husband my regards."

"I won't tell him I came here. This is just between us." She turned and started to walk out of the courtroom. She stopped and looked back at me. "If would be nice to have lunch sometime." That smile again.

She walked out of the courtroom without looking back.

CHAPTER 79

Loukas stood outside the courthouse and lit his cigarette. He wasn't hungry and he had two hours to kill. He was ready for this trial to be over. If he had his way, he would vote to hang that sonofabitch right in the courtroom. It was a nice day. Sunny and warm. He closed his eyes and thought about the woman in the courtroom. The one sitting behind Riley's table, fawning all over the old guy. He opened his eyes. He blinked twice in disbelief. There she was, leaving the courthouse, walking right past him. He dropped his cigarette, mashed it with his foot and followed her.

She walked into a parking garage two blocks away from the courthouse. Loukas stayed back at a distance. He didn't want her to see him. He wanted to see where she was going.

She walked past the garage elevator and took the stairs. He closed the gap between them. She stopped on the fifth floor and went through the door to her car. He watched from the stairwell until she entered the car and fastened her seat belt. He looked around. No one else was on the floor. He moved quickly. He approached the car from the rear, opened the passenger door and jumped into the seat beside her.

"Remember me?"

She struggled to undo the seat belt. "Who are you? Stay away from me."

He reached across and grabbed her by the throat. "Sit still. Stop moving."

"Don't hurt me. Take my purse. I have money."

"I don't want your goddamn purse. I don't want your money. What do you see in that old guy?" He kept his hand loosely on her throat.

"What are you talking about?"

"I'm talking about Riley, that asshole lawyer you watched in the courtroom all morning."

"I remember you. You're a juror. I saw you looking at me."

"Answer me. Are you fucking him? He's just an old man. You need somebody like me to take care of you."

"I don't know what you're talking about. I'm happily married."

"Lying bitch."

Loukas started squeezing her throat. It was easier than he thought. She struggled but was trapped by her seat belt. He increased the pressure. Her eyes rolled back into her head and she stopped moving. Bitch. When she stopped moving, he released his grip. Her head rolled sideways and her tongue protruded from her mouth. She remained still and she looked ridiculous, he thought. He got out of the car and looked around. The floor was full of parked cars, but there was no one else around. He removed her keys from the ignition and opened the trunk. He checked once more to see if they were alone. Then he undid her seat belt, pulled her out of the car and stuffed her in the trunk. He put the car keys in his pocket. He walked back to the courthouse, stood on the steps outside, and lit another cigarette. He wondered when it was that his brother-in-law was going to start running the store. That fucking asshole.

CHAPTER 80

When I got back to my office after my chat with Anne Smythe, the others were eating lunch in the conference room. Gary had ordered a sandwich for me, and I sat down between Hartley and Emrich. Emrich's eyes were red and puffy.

"I know you think you did poorly, but I thought you were great."

Gary spoke. "I think so too."

Emrich looked down at the table in front of her. "I really screwed up. I'm usually not so bitchy, but both the judge and Mister Hempstead got me riled up. They were so condescending."

Hartley reached across me and patted her hand. She looked at him and smiled.

He was beaming. "Gary said you called the judge mister. I would have loved to see that."

I laughed. "It was a great moment. I loved it. The jury did too."

We finished our sandwiches and Gary and I walked back to the courthouse.

"I'm going to rest unless you can think of anything else that needs to be done." I looked at Gary.

"I think we're in fine shape. I can't think of anything else."

When we returned to the courtroom and the jury was in place, I stood. "Your Honor, the defendant rests his case."

Flick smiled. I was keeping track. It was the third time he'd smiled in the past two weeks. He looked at the jury. "We are going to keep on going for the rest of the afternoon. We'll now hear closing arguments.

Each lawyer will have an hour. I expect you'll start your deliberations about four o'clock. You may not reach a verdict today, but at least you'll be able to get yourself organized and elect a foreperson."

I looked over at the jury to see their reaction. They were all smiling. Except Loukas. He appeared to be nervous. He fidgeted. He looked down at his feet and then up at the ceiling. He turned and made a weird face at me.

Flick wanted to move us along. He nodded toward Hempstead. "Proceed with your closing argument, Mr. Hempstead."

Hempstead stood and faced the jury. He walked over and put his hands on the rail of the jury box. Too close, I thought. He was invading the space of the jurors. Several of them shifted in their chairs, uncomfortable at the closeness of the large man with the red bow tie.

"Ladies and Gentlemen. Very shortly you will enter the jury room to begin your deliberations. The facts that you are to decide are simple and straightforward. Did Mister Slater murder his wife in cold blood? I suggest to you that your deliberations will be easy because the proofs quite convincingly show that he bludgeoned his wife repeatedly with the bladed metal end of a shovel until she died a painful death. The act was brutal and merciless. The act was performed with the intention of ending her life. Evidence has shown clearly why this murder was committed.

"The Slaters were headed toward divorce court. The couple had an elegant lifestyle supported by the wealth of Mrs. Slater's trust fund provided by her family. It was a gravy train for Jay Slater. If the divorce went through, his ability to live a fancy lifestyle was going to end. He'd be out on the street. The running around with other women-- the hanging out in bars and nightclubs--would be over. The only way he could salvage the threat to his carefree life was to end his wife's life so that he would inherit her wealth. His plan was well thought out and will succeed only if you allow yourself to be fooled by his lame defense. There was a popular comedian back some time ago that would deliver a gag line for great laughs. He would say, 'The devil made me do it.' The audience would clap and cheer. What Mister Slater offers here is a variation on this theme. 'The drug made me do it,' but there should be no clapping and cheering. It is an outrageous claim designed with one purpose in mind--to escape responsibility for the murder of his wife. The drug is not responsible for Mister Slater's actions. He is responsible. On behalf of Mrs. Slater and the people of the State of Michigan, I ask that you return a verdict of guilty against Jay Slater for the vicious, deliberate and wanton murder of his wife in the first degree."

Hempstead stood still for a moment and let the impact of his words sink in with the jury. He then returned to his seat. It was an impressive performance. Now it was my turn.

Flick turned and nodded toward me. I stood and faced the jury. Waited until all eyes of the jurors were on me. Loukas was looking at the ceiling, his hands fidgeting. I wasn't going to wait for him.

"Members of the jury. On behalf of Mister Slater I want to thank you for your time and attention during this trial. My client, Jay Slater, is in a dilemma because he is in a terrible situation that none of us would ever wish to happen to either our loved ones or ourselves. It is true that he and Mrs. Slater were headed toward the breakup of their marriage. They had not been getting along well, and you heard Mister Slater describe how painful that process was to both of them. Prior to her death, the divorce process was put on hold, and the couple made plans to undergo marriage counseling--a fact that Mr. Hempstead apparently forgot to mention in his argument.

"Due to the marital problems, Mister Slater started having trouble sleeping. His lack of sleep made things worse, so he went to his doctor for help. You heard the testimony of Doctor Greene who told you he prescribed Serenity to help Mister Slater sleep better. You have heard testimony that the Serenity, in fact, did help Mister Slater for a while. His sleep improved, and so did his relationship with his wife. Tragically, however, three weeks to the day he started Serenity, he killed his wife. We do not dispute that fact.

"We have learned from the evidence presented to you about the dangers of Serenity. Countries throughout the world have banned the marketing of the drug because the drug was causing exactly the same kind of reactions suffered by Mister Slater. We heard testimony about two aspects of these reactions--anterograde amnesia and violent acts. Users of Serenity around the world do crazy things to themselves or others, and they don't remember doing it. Mister Slater testified that he had no memory of killing his wife.

"Doctor Alex Hartley, Mister Slater's treating physician at the time, testified about Mister Slater's state of mind within hours of the death of his wife. He was in a stupor--unable to comprehend or remember what he had done or even who he was. Blood tests revealed high levels of Serenity in his body that were sufficient to trigger the toxic state suffered by Mister Slater. Doctor Hartley indicated that he's seen the same problem in other patients exposed to Serenity. The other expert witnesses called on behalf of Mister Slater were Doctors Schneidermann, Clackner, Giovanni and Emrich, who all spoke about the dangers of Serenity. Mister Slater's use of the drug as a sleeping aid resulted in his wife's death.

"Mr. Hempstead's trite little comment about 'the devil made me do it' is totally inappropriate for a serious discussion about the role of Serenity in this tragic death. Serenity's role in this death is not offered as an 'excuse,' but as the reason for Mrs. Slater's death. There has been no evidence submitted by the prosecutor that Mr. Slater was not in a toxic state at the time of his wife's death. The best that the prosecutor has is the conjecture from their expert witness that Serenity must be a safe drug because he talked to two non-scientists who work for Upright, and they told him the drug was safe. In your deliberations I ask that you debate and evaluate the contrast between the foolish statement of the prosecutor's expert with the evidence and testimony presented by the scientists and physician called on behalf of Mister Slater. I respectfully request that you consider all the evidence, together with your own common sense, and render a verdict of not guilty in favor of Mister Slater."

I returned to my seat.

Judge Flick spent twenty minutes instructing the jury on the law that applied to their deliberations. Because of the brevity of our closing arguments, he was ahead of schedule. The jury retired to the jury room to begin their work at twenty minutes past three o'clock.

CHAPTER 81

Anne Smythe awoke with a start. She tried to sit up and her head smashed against something hard. The impact sent pain crashing through her head--a bolt of electricity. Where was she? She opened her eyes. It was pitch dark. She was cold. She was stiff, and her muscles were sore. Her throat hurt. She was thirsty, and it hurt terribly when she tried to swallow. And she had a headache--a sharp, piercing headache that worsened when she moved her head. A trickle of liquid flowed from her forehead.

She was bleeding, she thought. She raised a hand to feel for whatever it was that her head struck. She was enclosed in some kind of metal structure. She moved her hand around and touched what felt like an automobile tire. She reached above her and tried to push the metallic object away, but it didn't move. She was trapped in the trunk of a car, she realized. How did she get here? She started shivering. She struggled to remember what had happened. She was sitting in her car when a man opened the passenger door and entered her car. She couldn't recall what he said, but she remembered him choking her. Then everything had gone dark. She touched her throat with her fingers. It really hurt. She had to get out of here.

She pounded on the roof of the enclosure and yelled. "Help. Help me, please. Is anybody there?"

Nothing. She was stuck in the trunk of a car, and nobody could hear her. She had to do something, and she had to do it quickly. What if the man came back? She felt around the space of the trunk. Nothing. It hurt her hand to pound on the metal. Think. Think. She had to make noise so someone could know she was trapped. She slipped a shoe off her foot and inched it slowly towards her hand so that she could retrieve it. It hurt to move. She finally reached the shoe with her hand and began pounding on the roof with the heel of the shoe. Nothing. No one was there. What time was it? She started pounding on the roof again. She knew he was coming back. She had to get help before he did. She kept pounding. She pounded until her arm tired. She switched arms and pounded some more. She stopped. She thought she heard something. A voice. Someone was out there. Someone was talking to her.

She cried out. "Help me, please help me. I'm trapped in here."

She heard the muffled response. "I'm going to get help. Stay calm."

She closed her eyes and waited. She heard noises again. The rumble of a car motor. Men talking. Suddenly it was light. The bright light hurt her eyes. She squinted.   "Ma'am, let's get you out of there." A police officer bent over her and gently picked her up. "You're bleeding. We'll get you to the hospital right away." She shivered uncontrollably. His partner wrapped a blanket around her.

"Do you think you can walk or stand if I put you down?"

"I'm not sure."

The officer looked at his partner. "You drive. I'll sit in the back with her."

He gently placed her in the back of the police car. They had her at the hospital quickly. She was wheeled into the emergency room after two orderlies placed her on a gurney. She was still shivering. She was so cold.

A doctor came into the space where she was separated from other patients by a curtain. After a quick examination, he pointed to the cut on her head. "I think this will need a couple of sutures. Other than that, I don't detect any real damage. Your throat is bruised, and it will be sore until it heals. The reason you're shivering is because you are in a state of shock. I'll give you something to settle you down. The police would like to talk to you. Are you up to it?"

She nodded. The doctor left, and the two policemen who rescued her from the trunk of the car stepped into the small space.

"Ma'am, do you have any idea why you were in the trunk of that car?"

She nodded. It hurt to speak.

"Can you tell us?"

She nodded again. "I know who it was. What time is it?"

He checked his watch. "Its three-thirty, ma'am."

"I know who did this to me and I can tell you where he is." She remembered Riley's card in her pocket. She retrieved it and handed it to the policeman. "Call Mister Riley. He can tell you where to find him."

CHAPTER 82

The group went into the jury room and started deliberations. The room was small and drab and reeked of sweat.

There were twelve people in the room--twelve jurors. Loukas looked around the room. It seemed like everyone was looking at him. He glared back at those who were more obvious about it.

One of the other jurors spoke. "The first thing we need to do is elect a foreman. Is there anyone who wants to be foreman?

Stella DeHunt raised her hand. "I think I should be foreman. I've taken careful notes, and I have some definite opinions on what we should do."

Gonzales interjected. "I think Mister Loukas ought to be foreman."

Loukas stared at him. Gonzales did understand English. He wanted him to be foreman. What was this all about? He heard other jurors whispering among themselves. He didn't want to be foreman. But he did know what verdict he wanted. Slater was guilty as hell.

"I think we should hang the son-of-a-bitch."

Another juror spoke. "We should wait until a foreman is selected before we start offering our opinions."

A different juror spoke. "I agree. First things first."

Gonzales said. "Let's take a vote. I vote for Mr. Loukas."

Loukas wanted to shout at Gonzales, tell him to go to hell. He looked down at the floor, "I don't want to be foreman." He looked up, "But I also don't want that lady as foreman either." He pointed at DeHunt and she glared back at him.

Another broke the silence. "We're not getting anywhere. Anybody have any ideas or thoughts?"

Loukas started tapping his foot. "We're wasting time. We don't need a foreman. Let's vote. He's guilty as hell."

Rosenberg, juror number one, stood. "We need a foreman first. Then we need to go over the evidence before we make a snap decision like our friend here." He nodded toward Loukas. "Anybody other than Ms. DeHunt who would be interested?"

Gonzales raised his hand. "I nominate you." He gestured toward Rosenberg.

Rosenberg said quietly, "Let's be democratic about this. Let's take a vote."

DeHunt stood. "I think I should have the right to say why I should be foreman before we have a vote."

Loukas glared at her. Who is really interested in what you have to say? "I vote for you." He pointed at Rosenberg.

Gonzales nodded. "Yeah, me too. Everybody in favor of him raise their hands." He gestured toward Rosenberg.

DeHunt stood, "I really would like to speak."

Sit down and shut up, bitch. Loukas raised his hand. Others did as well. Only Rosenberg and DeHunt failed to raise their hands.

Rosenberg looked around the room. "I think the group has decided. I'll take the job. Let's get started. Let's talk about the evidence."

DeHunt sat down and crossed her arms. She stuck out her lower lip and glared at Loukas. Her face reddened.

Rosenberg looked at her. "You mentioned you have some notes. Would you like to comment on the evidence?"

She shook her head.

"Anybody else have anything to say about the evidence?"

Ralph Long, the car salesman raised his hand and spoke. "What bothers me is the dosage level of the drug at the time he killed his wife. I think it proves he intended to kill his wife and he took extra drug after he killed her to make it easy to blame the drug for what he did."

Rosenberg responded. "I agree that is a possibility, but remember that Feeney said she would prove that Slater told a girl friend about reading about the drug, but the girl friend never testified about it. We're not supposed to use statements made by the lawyers unless there is evidence to back it up-."

Loukas looked around the room. He wanted to shout. Why were they wasting time on crap like this? It pissed him off. He was getting angry. He couldn't let this go on much longer. He couldn't risk them letting Slater off the hook if it meant taking the drug off the market. He loved what the drug was doing for him, to him.

"I still think we should take a vote."

Gonzales and several others nodded in agreement. Rosenberg looked at Loukas. "Is there some place special you have to be? Why the rush? We're talking about whether a man should be convicted of murder. We owe him the courtesy of deliberating thoroughly and thoughtfully."

Loukas stood. "All in favor of taking a vote say aye."

There was a chorus of ayes.

"Anybody against taking a vote raise their hands."

Rosenberg and DeHunt raised their hands.

Loukas glared at DeHunt. "You're pissed off just because you're not the foreman."

She shook her head. "You're just trying to railroad this decision. I agree with Mister Rosenburg. We have to be complete in our deliberations."

Loukas scanned the room. "Is there anybody other than miss goody-good two shoes here who thinks the asshole is innocent?"

Rosenberg interrupted. "Hold on. We are going to do this right or I'll tell the judge what is going on. This is not a kangaroo court. We have a serious decision to make and we are going to do it in the right way. And we are going to be civil to each other."

Loukas glared at Rosenberg. Asshole. "On second thought, I think I should be the jury foreman."

Rosenberg stood his ground. "The group elected me and I intend to perform my duty."

Long winked at Loukas. "I agree. I think we should let this guy do his job." He nodded toward Rosenberg. The rest of the jurors murmured their assent. Loukas glared at them all. Assholes.

Rosenberg waited for a moment. "Let's go through the evidence systematically."

The discussion focused on Emrich's testimony for the next fifteen minutes.

One juror said, "Her testimony was believable, but did you hear her call the judge 'mister'?"

Rosenberg interjected, "That is not evidence and, remember, the judge apologized to her for not calling her 'doctor'."

The other juror persisted, "She thinks she's hot stuff. How could she be so arrogant?"

Loukas saw an opportunity. "She wants to take the drug off the market. That's not fair to people who like taking it."

The other jurors turned and stared at him. What was their problem?

Rosenburg spoke softly to him. "We are not being asked to decide whether the drug should be taken off the market. That's a whole different issue which has nothing to do with this case."

How could this guy be so stupid? "You think other people will want to take this drug if we say that it makes people kill?" Loukas spat out the words.

Rosenburg shrugged his shoulders. "You do make a valid point. But I still think we should do the job that we're supposed to do. It's really not our concern whether the drug would be taken off the market or not." Several others nodded.

"Tell you what," Rosenburg continued. "Let's take a vote right now and see where we stand on the guilty issue."

Loukas sneered. "That's what I suggested in the first place."

Rosenburg stood. "Raise your hands if you think Slater is guilty."

Nine of the jurors, including Loukas, raised their hands.

"Who thinks Slater is innocent?"

Two hands went up. Gonzales and Rosenburg.

DeHunt hadn't raised her hand either time.

Rosenburg thought for a moment. "Nine for guilty, two for innocent, one undecided. We need to hear from both sides to understand the reasons for the differences. Any verdict we reach has to be unanimous. Maybe we can resolve our differences by talking it out. Mister Loukas, why don't you explain to the rest of us why you think Slater is guilty?"

All eyes in the room turned toward Loukas.

"I don't think my opinion needs to be explained. I think the asshole is guilty. I think anyone who doesn't think he's guilty is stupid."

Rosenburg's face reddened. "I don't think there's any need to get personal. " He looked around at the rest of the jurors. "Is there anyone else who'd like to take a shot at explaining why you think Slater is guilty?"

Ralph Long raised his hand and stood. "I'll tell you what I think. As I said earlier, I think he took extra drug after he killed his wife to serve as an excuse so that his fancy attorney and highly paid expert witnesses could come into court and blame the drug. That way, the son-of-a-bitch walks away scot-free with millions of dollars in his pocket." Long paused and looked at the other jurors, "Sorry for the language, ladies."

Long continued, "We know he killed her. We know he gets rich if we let him walk away. We know, given the amount of cheating he did on his wife, that we can't believe a word he says. It didn't come out during the trial testimony, but do you all know what 'stress treatment' means? I'll tell you. The woman who testified was a whore, a prostitute. Slater was seeing the prostitute and the barmaid before he killed his wife. She was going to divorce him because she knew what was going on. All the stuff we heard about the drug is a smokescreen. Doesn't mean a damn thing. Slater is guilty . . . guilty as hell."

Long looked around for a moment, then sat down.

Rosenburg stood. "Thanks, Mister Long. Anybody have anything to add to what he said?" No one responded.

"Okay, let me tell you why I think Mister Slater is innocent. First, we know that Serenity is a terrible drug. Other users have killed themselves or their loved ones while taking the drug under the same circumstances as Slater. The prosecutor told us that she would prove that Slater knew that the drug could do these things before he started taking it, but she didn't offer any evidence on this point. The judge told us that we are only to consider evidence and that what the lawyers say is not evidence. We also know that Serenity has been removed from the market in every other country in the world for causing the same thing.

"Next, there is Doctor Emrich. While I agree that she was a little bitchy with the judge, she was by far the best witness we heard. She was the one at the Food and Drug Administration who was responsible for monitoring the safety of the drug. She has her doctor's degree in drugs. She knows a whole lot more about the drug than we do. The same with Doctor Hartley. He was smart. He treated Slater at the time of the killing. I don't think Slater, or anyone else for that matter, would be smart enough to do what Mister Long suggests. Take a drug after the fact to make it appear that the drug caused him to kill his wife. Hartley didn't agree with that theory and I agree with Hartley.

"Next, I want to comment on the judge. It's obvious that he hates attorney Riley. I don't think I've ever seen anyone be so rude to another person in my life. He was mean and nasty and I think he made some rulings against Riley to just make him look bad to us. Its obvious by the negative comments that Mister Long made about Riley that the judge was successful on that point. My opinion of Riley was that he was the best lawyer in the courtroom. He was direct and to the point on every issue. Hempstead, with his red bow tie, and Feeney, with her hysterics, tried to obstruct everything that Riley did. But remember, the prosecutor has the burden of proof. It was up to them to prove that Slater committed murder and the only expert they bring in was that weird Olmstead with his off-the-wall research in what would have been a hilarious skit on Saturday Night Live. I had to struggle to keep from laughing out loud." Rosenburg stopped, looked around. "Am I making sense here? Does anyone want to comment?"

Loukas had an idea. "That's enough talking. Let's take another vote. This time let's make it secret. I'll tear up some paper and make some ballots. We can all write down our vote and I'll count them."

Everyone nodded except Rosenburg. "Agreed, but I think I should do the counting. Either just me or Mister Loukas and me."

The others murmured their assent. Loukas didn't like it. He wanted to do the counting. He thought about what he could do.

He tore several blank pieces paper into small squares and distributed one to each juror. Each juror filled in their response and Rosenburg collected them.

Rosenburg nodded to Loukas. "Let's go to the other end of the table and count."

The two of them sat at one end of the room and the remaining jurors gathered at the other end. Rosenburg put the ballots into a pile on the table between them.

Loukas looked at Rosenburg. "Before we start I need to use the bathroom." Rosenburg said, "Me too. After you."

Loukas stood and went into the small bathroom adjoining the jury room. He closed the door and locked it. He took another blank piece of paper out of his pocket and tore it into squares. Then, he wrote on three of the squares and flushed the rest down the toilet. He put the three squares in his pocket.

When he returned to the jury room, Rosenburg went into the bathroom. Loukas added the three squares to the pile on the table in front of him. Rosenburg came back and the two of them started counting.

"Hold on," Rosenburg said at they finished counting. "There are fifteen ballots here. What did you do?"

"What did I do? What did you do? I count twelve guilty votes."

Their attention was disrupted by a sharp knock on the door. Rosenburg walked over and opened it.

When the two police officers contacted me I was sitting in the courtroom with Slater. One of them showed me the business card I had given to Anne Smythe.

"Are you attorney Riley?"

"Yes."

"Do you know Anne Smythe?"

"Yes."

"There's been an incident between her and one of the jurors. She told us that you would know which one it would be."

"What happened?"

"One of the jurors followed her when she left the courtroom, attacked her in her car, tried to choke her and put her in the trunk of her car."

That could only be Loukas, I thought.

"The jury's deliberating."

"We're here to arrest the guy right now."

"I don't think you can interrupt deliberations."

"It can't wait. We're going to get him right now. Will you identify him for us?"

"I'll do whatever if necessary, but you need to speak with the judge."

The bailiff, an ex-street cop, stood there and listened. "Let's go get him first. Then I'll tell the judge."

We walked to the door of the jury room and the bailiff rapped loudly. He stood back. "I'll go tell the judge."

Rosenburg opened the door. Loukas was standing behind him.

"That's him," I said and pointed toward Loukas.

Both officers stepped forward.

"Sir, step out of the room. You are under arrest for attempted murder. Put your hands behind your back and turn around."

As they left the room, Loukas looked back over his shoulder and smiled.

"We have a verdict. The sonofabitch is guilty. Don't let Rosenburg tell you otherwise."

CHAPTER 83

As soon as I realized what was happening with the jury, I called back to my office and asked a law clerk to research the law on double jeopardy. Within minutes he brought me a copy of a recent appellate decision that I knew would serve my purpose.

Judge Flick called us back into the courtroom.

His face was beet red. He was pissed. I was glad that I wasn't the object of his anger.

"By now, you all know what went on in the jury room. One of the jurors apparently attacked a woman who was in the courtroom earlier. At lunchtime he followed her out of the building to where her car was parked a couple of blocks from here. He attempted to strangle her and put her in the trunk of the car. She was able to attract attention when she regained consciousness. She identified the juror as her assailant after being treated at Receiving Hospital. The police rushed here and my bailiff let them into the jury room without notifying me. There is an issue about whether or not the same juror tampered with ballots from a vote the jury took just before the police arrived." Flick paused, cleared his throat. "Under the circumstances I have no choice but to declare a mistrial. Does anybody have anything to say?"

I stood quickly and gave him the details of the appellate decision. I concluded, "Your Honor, I have a motion. I move that Mister Slater be released immediately. It is well established that double jeopardy attaches to the rights of a defendant in a criminal case after the jury is selected when governmental misconduct causes the mistrial. In the present situation, we have the police barging into the jury room during deliberations and arresting a juror. Inasmuch as this misconduct occurred well after the seating of the jury and was committed by the government, your granting of a mistrial is correct and there can be no finding of guilt on the part of the defendant. He cannot be tried again. I respectfully ask the court to release him now."

Flick looked at me and he was angry. I could tell that the issue of double jeopardy hadn't occurred to him before he granted the mistrial.

"I need to think about this. Court is recessed for now."

Thirty minutes later, he came back on the bench. Flick didn't see any way out of the dilemma. The police had breached the sanctity of the jury room. His bailiff had allowed them to walk in and arrest a juror right in the middle of deliberations. Flick was mad as hell. I felt for the bailiff. However, there was no way to assess the impact of that incident on the remaining jurors.

Flick had no choice. Feeney stood and spoke. "The state objects both to the mistrial and Mr. Riley's assertion that Mr. Slater should go free. It is not clear that double jeopardy attaches. We can look at the law tonight and then argue in the morning. There's no reason to hurry."

I responded, "You have already granted the mistrial. And, as the reason for the mistrial was governmental misconduct, there can be no retrial. So there's plenty of reason to conclude this matter for the defendant. Mister Slater should not be spending one more night in a jail cell because this case is now over. He should be released forthwith."

Flick sat there and looked at me. If he had a choice I knew he'd screw me, but he didn't have a choice. The law was clear. He spoke through a clenched jaw. "I've thought about this. Mr. Riley is right. Double jeopardy does attach to this result and the defendant is hereby ordered to be released forthwith. Mister Slater, you are free to go."

The judge stood abruptly and left the courtroom.

CHAPTER 84

Wednesday, nearly forty-eight hours later, was one of those beautiful spring mornings that one only gets in Michigan. On the third floor of the glass tower, center of the Upright universe, the effect was lost, obliterated by the steady hum of the massive air conditioner, which lent a dreadful, unnatural chill to the air. The carefully drawn blinds of the conference room completed the scenario, wiping out the ability to capture the warm, cozy glow of outside. The conference room was to remain the center of the universe for the entire morning. Messner had seen to that.

All the attendees, save one, knew that the planned meeting was a hoax, starting with the word "consultation." Messner had made sure that the whole lot of them understood why they were there--the purpose of the meeting. They were all present, sitting, watching the target--the thin, bald man sitting opposite Messner at the end of the long conference table. The important end. The further you moved away from the important end, the further down the ladder in terms of prestige, job status, and importance you would have expected things to be. That, however, was not the case with this meeting. The room was filled with the bigwigs of the corporation, right from the CEO to the chief financial officer and a half-dozen silk stocking lawyers filled with their own importance, which was temporarily set aside for this particular meeting. In addition to the reason for the "consultation," everybody in the room understood their respective roles well.

The Whale, Hagstrom, was a brute of a man, a survivor, like Upright itself. Sixty-four years old, a neck wider than his baldhead, a stomach three times larger than his neck. The man's physical appearance was intimidating by its sheer bulk. Add a pair of hooded deep green eyes that glared, unblinking, through oblong steel framed bifocals, and the net effect was that you better get down to business or stay the hell out of his way. He was the only man in the company--the only man Messner had ever met--whose presence usually made him feel uncomfortable.

That was precisely the reason why the Whale was sitting next to Messner--why he was at the meeting with the "consultant." Messner enjoyed the impression the two of them made, sitting side-by-side. He, the elegantly coifed, steel-grey haired senior executive in his Savile Row suit seated next to the slightly disheveled hulk of a man. Brains and brawn. Power--mental and physical.

They both sat and studied their quarry, the consultant. Despite the iciness of the room, the Whale was sweating. A thin sheen of perspiration coated his skull, and Messner sniffed the smell of big man's sweat, akin to the tangy aroma of a locker room. A sign of nervousness in most men, in the Whale, the droplets of sweat rolling off his head and down his face, told you to be careful with this man--this giant. To watch what you said or did.

Messner loved situations like this. The game of human chess. He called the shots. Others made them happen. Everything about this room, this meeting, carefully contrived was intended to be unsettling to the target. The stunning receptionist in the mini-skirt had carefully filled the coffee cups of the dozen people sitting at the table, every pair of eyes in the room on her each time she leaned forward to pour. Messner had glanced at the Whale several times during this routine and nodded. Neither man missed the rapt attention that the target paid to the "skirt," as the routine had been tagged during their planning session.

"Anything else I can do?" She stood at the door, just adjacent to the quarry, after finishing her task. . Messner shook his head, and she turned and left the room, her honey scent filling the air. The target stared hard at the door for several moments, and then smiled at Messner. Messner knew Hagstrom could deal with this prick easily. Anybody that easily distracted by a pretty face was putty in Hagstrom's hands. For a moment, no one talked, each man thinking his own thoughts.

Messner nodded at the Whale--the signal for the fun to begin. Hagstrom looked down at his notes, cleared his throat, and the room went still, punctuated only by the cyclical steady hum of the air conditioner.

"Congressman Roberts, once again, let me welcome you to Upright."

Roberts smiled back. "It's always a pleasure to meet with people in the heartland of America. Sometimes one gets to feel a little isolated with all the activity in Washington."

Hagstrom spoke softly. "I'm sure one does. We've asked you to come here to provide us some direction to a problem we are greatly concerned about. And we also have a favor to ask."

"I appreciate it when somebody gets right to the point. I like that." Roberts smiled at the Whale. Hagstrom peered back through his fleshy eyelids.

"The problem is lawsuits against the drug industry. We are facing a crisis because all of our time and energy is taken in defending against lawsuits. We'd like to give you a short presentation." The Whale nodded to a young man at the other end of the room who dimmed the lights and snapped on a projector sitting on the table. A screen emerged from the ceiling.

The group sat and watched a fifteen-minute presentation on tape. The first half contained excerpts of statements made, or written, by a number of nationally prominent persons about how lawsuits were damaging the economy and stifling corporate incentive. President Bush was seen flat out declaring war against greedy lawyers who would "sue anybody for any reason." The next portion of the tape contained a half-dozen brief segments showing Congressman Roberts defending the right to sue. He was seen at the NAACP national convention mimicking the words of President Bush to the delight of the audience and then driving the point home that the right to sue was guaranteed by the seventh amendment to the U.S. Constitution, a position greeted by a standing ovation.

The screen blacked out, and the Whale nodded at the young man manning the projector, who stood and turned it off. The lights remained dim. Hagstrom looked unsmilingly at the congressman and waited. Messner enjoyed watching the man's discomfiture.

"This is a little unusual. I'm not sure what the point is with this video. I thought I was here to consult with you about an issue related to one of my committee assignments."

The Whale never changed his expression. "Our view is when you enter Congress, you represent the interests of everybody in the United States. As you know, we've contributed more than our fair share to your election campaigns. You didn't hesitate to take our contributions."

"You really do get to the point, don't you?" The congressman smiled nervously at Messner, glanced around the room, and smacked his lips. "This is an area where I don't think I can be of much help to you."

Everybody in the room was quiet, intently staring him down. The Whale turned and nodded to the group. All of the others, except Messner, stood and silently left the room.

Hagstrom forced a smile. Messner knew it was to keep from laughing aloud.

Hagstrom stood. "We've got something else for you to see." He walked to the back of the room and turned the projector on again. The three of them turned their attention to the screen.

The quality of the first few frames was grainy, and the camera was out of focus. It finally settled on the face of a scantily clad young blonde woman. She stared directly into the camera, smiled, waited, and then spoke.

"Hi, Jim. Or perhaps it would be better if I called you Congressman Roberts." She swept her arm around and continued. "As you can see, my husband and I are waiting for you." The camera panned back and forth around the motel room. A young man lying on the bed waved as the camera went by and settled on a full-length shot of the woman's shapely body concealed only by a sheer negligee. In the background, there was a knock on the door. She turned and moved to the door. Congressman Roberts entered and immediately began to undress.

"Stop that. Turn that off."

The Whale reached over and turned the projector off and the screen went blank. He turned the lights up. The congressman was looking grim. He slumped in his chair.

The Whale waited a moment, and then said, "We're in a position here to help you if you help us."

"This is outrageous. Where did you get that?" Messner thought the man was going to cry.

The Whale waited another moment, and then spoke. "This is what we need you to do."

Four days later, Congressman Roberts created a stir at a press conference as he called for Congress to pass legislation to ban lawsuits against the drug industry for any product that had been approved by the FDA.

CHAPTER 85

I went to the doctor the day after the Slater trial ended. I told him about the chest pain, and he sent me right away to the hospital. I underwent all kinds of testing. After the results came in, my doctor told me I'd had a recent heart attack, but there was minimal damage. He sat on the edge of the bed and looked somberly at me.

"Bob. We discovered another problem--more serious than your heart. The chest X-ray picked up several large masses in your lungs. The CAT scan of your abdomen detected multiple similar masses in your liver and one in your right kidney. I've asked an oncologist, a cancer specialist, to evaluate you."

Two days later, my newest doctor, a kid young enough to be my grandson, broke the news. "Mr. Riley. You have an advanced form of malignant melanoma. The malignancy has spread throughout your body. I could treat you aggressively, but it would merely be palliative."

"Let's cut to the chase, doc. How much time do I have?"

He looked straight in my eyes. "Not much, I'm afraid. A couple of weeks. Maybe a month or two. I'm sorry."

After the doctor left my room, I rang the nursing station and asked that I be left alone for a while. I needed to sit quietly and think. If what the doctor said was true, and I had no reason to doubt it, I had a lot to do. I am not afraid of dying. What I am afraid of is how this Serenity affair will turn out without me being around. Slater walks away a free man and a few people in the United States get a substantial settlement for the havoc brought to them by the drug. I sit here in my hospital bed watching Fox News put their spin on Slater. They say he got away with murder. There is no mention of the civil litigation and the huge amount of money that Upright has paid to hide their dirty secrets. On the television, a Congressman is asking for a law preventing lawsuits from being filed against FDA-approved drugs. I can't stand the thought of how this is going to end. I've got to let the world know what this company did. If I don't do something, every juror in the country from now on will be brainwashed into thinking that trials are nothing more than taking from the rich and giving it to the poor. Some victim who was too stupid to take a drug properly. Worse yet is the possibility that our elected representatives might pass a law insulating drug companies from liability for the damages caused by their products. I promised myself that whatever time I had left I was going to spend on telling this story. I got out of bed and put on my street clothes. I walked to the nursing station and signed myself out of the hospital. AMA they called it. Against medical advice. I went home and started writing.

CHAPTER 86

Detroit Free Press

April 22, 2010

The Serenity Whitewash

By Cassie Standard

Reigniting a controversy over the safety of Serenity, the U.S. Food and Drug Administration suggested Friday that the Justice Department investigate whether the Upright Co. hid information that raised safety questions about the controversial sleep aid.

The Agency also admitted its own mistake in not turning over to the Justice Department evidence of errors and omissions in reports of clinical tests of Serenity when Upright was seeking FDA approval.

Friday's report by an FDA task force is the latest in a long-running debate over the safety of what was once the world's most popular sleeping pill.

Over the past three years, at least 100 lawsuits have been filed by users of the drug or their family members, as psychotic episodes, suicides and homicides were blamed on its use. The drug has been banned throughout the world, except for the United States, since 2008 because of these toxic reactions. Upright has settled a substantial number of these lawsuits subject to a protective order, which prevents disclosure of the amounts of these settlements. Local Detroit attorneys Gary Newton and Bob Riley, now deceased, handled the cases against Upright. Newton refused comment on details of the settlement citing the non-disclosure agreement.

A five-month investigation by this writer for the Detroit Free Press in 2008 revealed that Upright had suppressed, minimized, and misrepresented the sometimes-fatal dangers posed by Serenity, which is intended to provide relief from insomnia for most users.

Serenity was first sold in this country in 2008 at recommended dosages of up to half a milligram without limitations on the duration of use. The current dosage is no more than half the original strength for use over seven to ten days.

Most of the psychotic episodes experienced by people using Serenity involved high doses for extended periods. The Free Press's stories spelled out how Upright tried to discredit both consumers and doctors who complained about dangerous side effects. A criminal trial in Michigan against Serenity user Jay Slater charged with the murder of his wife revealed that Upright had omitted roughly a third of the serious reactions suffered by a group of Michigan prison inmates taking Serenity in a clinical study. That omission appears to have raised the largest red flag for the FDA task force.

The agency concluded that the deficiencies in the study of Michigan inmates were not material to the drug's approval. But the task force-- while not accusing Upright of breaking the law--noted that it is a crime to falsify or hide a material fact and said that the errors in the prison study should have been considered material.

The task force concluded that "further inquiry into allegations of criminal misconduct by Upright is most appropriately the subject of consideration by the Department of Justice" and specifically noted the Justice Department's subpoena power. "The Task Force believes that final resolution of the matter will occur only with a Department of Justice assessment and conclusion," the report said.

The report has been forwarded to the U.S. attorney in Ann Arbor, Mich., where Upright is still based after a recent merger with Hydrophonics Inc.

Upright issued a statement standing behind Serenity and repeating its never varying assertion that the drug is safe and effective when used as recommended.

The company spokesman, Cyrus Messner, stated that Upright has "always strived to present accurate information in an honest context to all regulatory authorities. The company has acknowledged that mistakes were made in the past," adding that steps have been taken to improve it's reporting of test results.

When FDA investigator Janice Emrich recommended in 2008 that Upright's alleged "misconduct" be reviewed by the Justice Department, her FDA superiors rejected her efforts and she was removed from her responsibilities for Serenity and reassigned. She subsequently left the FDA after unsuccessfully appealing her reassignment.

The task force did not find evidence of criminal conduct or malfeasance by any FDA employees, but it criticized many of the agency's procedures for self-examination in the wake of the Serenity controversy.

Jay Slater, whose criminal trial first revealed Upright's omissions from the Michigan prison study, was one of the most dramatic examples of a Serenity "victim." The Detroit man killed his wife, Sylvia Slater, by beating her to death after taking high doses of Serenity for several weeks. A psychiatrist testified at trial that Slater was involuntarily intoxicated on Serenity at the time of the death, and Slater's trial ended in a mistrial when a member of the jury, who was also taking Serenity, attempted to murder the wife of an Upright scientist.

One of Serenity's most consistent critics, Dr. Alex Hartley, a prominent pharmacologist from Detroit Receiving Hospital, read the task force summary with a jaundiced eye. Hartley said, "The delay is inexcusable. The good part is they finally admitted making a mistake in not referring this case earlier for criminal prosecution.

WA